TOM
SHARPE

TOM SHARPE

PORTERHOUSE BLUE

BLOTT ON THE LANDSCAPE

Porterhouse Blue first published in Great Britain in 1974
by Martin Secker & Warburg Limited
Blott on the Landscape first published in Great Britain in 1975
by Martin Secker & Warburg Limited

This edition first published in Great Britain in 1987
jointly by

Martin Secker & Warburg Limited
54 Poland Street
London W1

and

Octopus Books Limited
59 Grosvenor Street
London W1

ISBN 0 7064 3062 X

Printed at The Bath Press, Avon

CONTENTS

PORTERHOUSE BLUE

CHAPTER ONE

It was a fine Feast. No one, not even the Praelector who was so old he could remember the Feast of '09, could recall its equal – and Porterhouse is famous for its food. There was Caviar and Soupe à l'Oignon, Turbot au Champagne, Swan stuffed with Widgeon and finally in memory of the Founder, Beefsteak from an ox roasted whole in the great fireplace of the College Hall. Each course had a different wine and each place was laid with five glasses. There was Pouilly Fumé with the fish, champagne with the game and the finest burgundy from the College cellars with the beef. For two hours the silver dishes came, announced by the swish of the doors in the Screens as the waiters scurried to and fro, bowed down by the weight of the food and their sense of occasion. For two hours the members of Porterhouse were lost to the world, immersed in an ancient ritual that spanned the centuries. The clatter of knives and forks, the clink of glasses, the rustle of napkins and the shuffling feet of the College servants dimmed the present. Outside the Hall the winter wind swept through the streets of Cambridge. Inside all was warmth and conviviality. Along the tables a hundred candles ensconced in silver candelabra cast elongated shadows of the crouching waiters across the portraits of past Masters that lined the walls. Severe or genial, scholars or politicians, the portraits had one thing in common: they were all rubicund and plump. Porterhouse's kitchen was long established. Only the new Master differed from his predecessors. Seated at the High Table, Sir Godber Evans picked at his swan with a delicate hesitancy that was in marked contrast to the frank enjoyment of the Fellows. A fixed dyspeptic smile lent a grim animation to Sir Godber's pale features as if his mind found relief from the present discomforts of the flesh in some remote and wholly intellectual joke.

'An evening to remember, Master,' said the Senior Tutor sebaceously.

'Indeed, Senior Tutor, indeed,' murmured the Master, his private joke enhanced by this unsought prediction.

'This swan is excellent,' said the Dean. 'A fine bird and the widgeon gives it a certain *gamin* flavour.'

'So good of Her Majesty to give Her permission for us to have swan,' the Bursar said. 'It's a privilege very rarely granted, you know.'

'Very rare,' the Chaplain agreed.

'Indeed, Chaplain, indeed,' murmured the Master and crossed his knife and fork. 'I think I'll wait for the beefsteak.' He sat back and studied the faces of the Fellows with fresh distaste. They were, he thought once again, an atavistic lot, and never more so than now with their napkins tucked into their collars, an age-old tradition of the College, and their foreheads greasy with perspiration and their mouths interminably full. How little things had changed since his own days as an undergraduate in Porterhouse. Even the College servants were the same, or so it seemed. The same shuffling gait, the adenoidal open mouths and tremulous lower lips, the same servility that had so offended his sense of social justice as a young man. And still offended it. For forty years Sir Godber had marched beneath the banner of social justice, or at least paraded, and if he had achieved anything (some cynics doubted even that) it was due to the fine sensibility that had been developed by the social chasm that yawned between the College servants and the young gentlemen of Porterhouse. His subsequent career in politics had been marked by the highest aspirations and the least effectuality, some said, since Asquith, and he had piloted through Parliament a series of bills whose aim, to assist the low-paid in one way or another, had resulted in that middle-class subsidy known as the development grant. His 'Every Home a Bathroom' campaign had led to the sobriquet Soapy and a knighthood, while his period as Minister of Technological Development had been rewarded by an early retirement and the Mastership of Porterhouse. It was one of the ironies of his appointment that he owed it to the very institution for which he professed most abhorrence, Royal Patronage, and it was perhaps this knowledge that had led him to the decision to end his career as an initiator of social change by a real alteration in the social character and traditions of his old College. That and the awareness that his appointment had met with the adamant opposition of almost all the Fellows. Only the Chaplain had welcomed him, and that was in all likelihood due to his deafness and a mistaken apprehension of Sir Godber's full name. No, he was Master by default even of his own convictions and by the failure of the Fellows to agree among themselves and choose a new Master by election. Nor had the late Master with his dying breath named his successor, thus exercising the prerogative Porterhouse tradition allows; failing these two expedients it had been left to the Prime Minister, himself in the death throes of an administration, to rid himself of a liability by appointing Sir Godber. In Parliamentary circles, if not in academic ones, the appointment had been greeted with relief. 'Something to get your teeth into at last,' one of his Cabinet colleagues had said to the new Master, a reference less to the excellence of the College cuisine than to the intractable conservatism of Porterhouse. In this respect the College is unique. No other Cambridge college can equal Porterhouse in its adherence to the old traditions and to this day Porterhouse men are distinguished [*sic*] by the cut of their coats and hair and by their steadfast allegiance to gowns. 'County come to Town', and 'The Squire to School', the other colleges used to sneer in the good old days, and the gibe has an element of truth about it still. A sturdy self-reliance except in scholarship is the mark of the Porterhouse man, and it is an exceptional year when Porterhouse is not Head of the River. And yet the College is not rich. Unlike nearly all the other colleges, Porterhouse has few assets to fall back on. A few terraces of dilapidated houses, some farms in Radnorshire, a modicum of shares in run-down industries, Porterhouse is poor. Its annual income amounts to less that £50,000 per annum and to this impecuniosity it owes its enduring reputation as the most socially exclusive college in Cambridge. If Porterhouse is poor, its undergraduates are rich. Where other colleges seek academic excellence in their freshmen, Porterhouse more democratically ignores the inequalities of intellect and concentrates upon the evidence of wealth. *Dives In Omnia*, reads the college motto, and the Fellows take it literally when examining the candidates. And in return the College offers social cachet and an enviable diet. True, a few scholarships and exhibitions exist which must be filled by men whose talents do not run to means, but those who last soon acquire the hallmarks of a Porterhouse man.

To the Master the memory of his own days as an undergraduate still had the power to send a shudder through him. A scholar in his day, Sir Godber, then plain G. Evans, had come to Porterhouse from a grammar school in Brierley. The experience had affected him profoundly. From his arrival had dated the sense of social inferiority which more than natural gifts had been the driving force of his ambition and which had spurred him on through failures that would have daunted a more talented man. After Porterhouse, he would remind himself on these occasions, a man has nothing left to fear. And certainly the College had left him socially resilient. To Porterhouse he owed his nerve, the nerve a few years later, while still a Parliamentary Private Secretary to the Minister of Transport, to propose to Mary Lacey, the only daughter of the Liberal Peer, the Earl of Sanderstead: the nerve to repeat the proposal yearly and to accept her annual refusal with a gracelessness that had gradually convinced her of the depth of his feelings. Yes, looking back over his long career Sir Godber could attribute much to Porterhouse and nothing more so than his determination to change once and for all the character of the college that had made him what he was. Looking down the hall at the faces florid in the candlelight and listening to the loud assertions that passed for conversation, he was strengthened in his resolve. The beefsteak and the burgundy came and went, the brandy trifle and the stilton followed, and finally the port decanter made the rounds. Sir Godber observed and abstained. Only when the ritual of wiping one's forehead with a napkin dipped in a silver bowl had been performed did he make his move. Rapping his knife handle on the table for silence, the new Master of Porterhouse rose to his feet.

In the Musicians' Gallery Skullion watched the Feast. Behind him in the darkness the lesser College servants clustered backwardly and gaped at the brilliant scene below them, their pale faces gleaming dankly in the reflected glory of the occasion. As each new dish appeared a muted sigh went up. Their eyes glittered momentarily and glazed again. Only Skullion, the Head Porter, sat surveying the setting with an air of critical propriety. There was no envy in his eyes, only approval at the fitness of the arrangements and the occasional unexpressed rebuke when a waiter spilled the gravy or failed to notice an empty glass waiting to be refilled. It was all as it should be, as it had been since Skullion first came to the College as an under-porter so many years ago. Forty-five Feasts there had been since then and at each Skullion had watched from the Musicians' Gallery just as his ancestors had watched since the college began. 'Skullion eh? That's an interesting name, Skullion,' old Lord Wurford had said when he first stopped by the lodge in 1928 and saw the new porter there. 'A very interesting name. Skullion. A no nonsense damn-my-soul name. There've been skullions at Porterhouse since the Founder. You take that from me, there have. It's in the first accounts. A farthing to the skullion. You be proud of it.' And Skullion had been proud of it as though he had been newly christened by the old Master. Yes those were the days and those were the men. Old Lord Wurford, a no nonsense damn-my-soul master. He'd have enjoyed a feast like this. He wouldn't have sat up there fiddling with his fork and sipping his wine. He'd have spilt it down his front like he always used to and he'd have guzzled that swan like it was a chicken and thrown the bones over his shoulder. But he'd been a gentleman and a rowing man and he'd stuck to the old Boat Club traditions.

'A bone for the eight in front,' they used to shout.

'What eight? There ain't no eight in front.'

'A bone for the fish in front.' And over their shoulders the bones would go and if it was a good evening there was meat on them still and damned glad we was to get it. And it was true too. There was no eight in front in those days. Only the fish. In the darkness of the Musicians' Gallery Skullion smiled at his memories of his youth. All different now. The young gentlemen weren't the same. The spirit had gone out of them since the war. They got grants now. They worked. Who had ever heard of a Porterhouse man working in the old days? They were too busy drinking and racing. How many of this lot took a cab to Newmarket these days and came back five hundred to the bad and didn't turn a hair? The Honourable Mr Newland had in '33. Lived on Q staircase and got himself killed at Boulogne by the Germans. Skullion could remember a score or more like him. Gentlemen they were. No nonsense damn-my-soul gentlemen.

Presently when the main courses were finished and the stilton had made its appearance, the Chef climbed the stairs from the kitchen and took his seat next to Skullion.

'Ah, Chef, a fine Feast. As good as any I can remember,' Skullion told him.

'It's good of you to say so, Mr Skullion,' said the Chef.

'Better than they deserve,' said Skullion.

'Someone has to keep up the old traditions, Mr Skullion.'

'True, Chef, very true,' Skullion nodded. They sat in silence watching the waiters clearing the dishes and the port moving ritually round.

'And what is your opinion of the new Master, Mr Skullion?' the Chef asked.

Skullion raised his eyes to the painted timbers of the ceiling and shook his head sadly.

'A sad day for the College, Chef, a sad day,' he sighed.

'Not a very popular gentlemen?' the Chef hazarded.

'Not a gentlemen,' Skullion pronounced.

'Ah,' said the Chef. Sentence on the new Master had been passed. In the kitchen he would ever be the victim of social obloquy. 'Not a gentleman, eh? And him with his knighthood too.'

Skullion looked at him sternly. 'Gentlemen don't depend on knighthoods, Cheffy. Gentlemen is gentlemen,' Skullion told him, and the Chef, suitably rebuked, nodded. Mr Skullion wasn't somebody you argued with, not about matters of social etiquette, not in Porterhouse. Not if you knew what was good for you. Mr Skullion was a power in the College.

They sat silently mourning the passing of the old Master and the debasement of college life which the coming of a new Master, who was not a gentlemen, brought with it.

'Still,' said Skullion finally, 'it was a fine Feast. I can't remember a better.' He said it half-grudgingly, out of respect for the past, and was about to go downstairs when the Master rapped on the High Table for silence and stood up. In the Musicians' Gallery Skullion and the Chef stared in horror at the spectacle. A speech at the Feast? No. Never. The precedence of five hundred and thirty-two Feasts forbade it.

Sir Godber stared down at the heads turned toward him so incredulously. He was satisfied. The stunned silence, the stares of disbelief, the tension were what he had wanted. And not a single snigger. Sir Godber smiled.

'Fellows of Porterhouse, members of College,' he began with the practised urbanity of a politician, 'as your new Master I feel that this is a suitable occasion to put before you some new thoughts about the role of institutions such as this in the modern world.' Calculated, every insult delicately calculated. Porterhouse an institution, new, modern, role. The words, the clichés defiled the atmosphere. Sir Godber smiled. His sense of grievance was striking home. 'After such a meal' (in the gallery the Chef shied), 'it is surely not inappropriate to consider the future and the changes that must surely be made if we are to play our part in the contemporary world ...'

The platitudes rolled out effortlessly, meaninglessly but with effect. Nobody in the hall listened to the words. Sir Godber could have announced the Second Coming with demur. It was enough that he was there, defying tradition and consciously defiling his trust. Porterhouse could remember nothing to equal this. Not even sacrilege but utter blasphemy. And awed by the spectacle, Porterhouse sat in silence.

'And so let me end with this promise,' Sir Godber wound up his appalling peroration, 'Porterhouse will expand. Porterhouse will become what it once was – a house of learning. Porterhouse will change.' He stopped and for the last time smiled and then, before the tension broke, turned on his heel and swept out into the Combination Room. Behind him with a sudden expiration of breath the Feast broke up. Someone laughed nervously, the short bark of the Porterhouse laugh, and then the benches were pushed back and they flooded out of the hall, their voices flowing out before them into the Court, into the cold night air. It had begun to snow. On the Fellows' lawn Sir Godber Evans increased his pace. He had heard that bark and the sounds of the benches and the nervous energy he had expended had left him weak. He had challenged the College deliberately. He had said what he wanted to say. He had asserted himself. There was nothing they could do now. He had risked the stamping feet and the hisses and they had not come but now, with the snow falling round him on the Fellows' lawn, he was suddenly afraid. He hurried on and closed the door of the Master's Lodge with a sigh of relief.

As the hall emptied and as even the Fellows drifted through the door of the Combination Room, the Chaplain rose to say Grace. Deaf to the world and the blasphemies of Sir Godber, the Chaplain gave thanks. Only Skullion, standing alone in the Musicians' Gallery, heard him and his face was dark with anger.

CHAPTER TWO

In the Combination Room the Fellows digested the Feast dyspeptically. Sitting in their high-backed chairs, each with an occasional table on which stood coffee cups and glasses of brandy, they stared belligerently into the fire. Gusts of wind in the chimney blew eddies of smoke into the room to mingle with the blue cirrus of their cigars. Above their heads grotesque animals pursued in plaster evidently plastered nymphs across a pastoral landscape strangely formal, in which flowers and the College crest, a Bull Rampant, alternated, while from the panelled walls glowered the gross portraits of Thomas Wilkins, Master 1618–39, and Dr Cox, 1702–40. Even the fireplace, itself surrounded by an arabesque of astonishing grapes and well-endowed bananas, suggested excess and added an extra touch of flatulence to the scene. But if the Fellows found difficulty in coming to terms with the contents of their stomachs, the contents of Sir Godber's speech were wholly indigestible.

'Outrageous,' said the Dean, discreetly combining protest with eructation. 'One might have imagined he was addressing an electoral meeting.'

'It was certainly a very inauspicious start,' said the Senior Tutor. 'One would have expected a greater regard for tradition. When all is said and done we are an old college.'

'All may have been said, though I doubt your optimism,' said the Dean, 'but it has certainly not been done. The Master's infatuation with contemporary fashions of opinion may lead him to suppose that we are flattered by his presence. It is an illusion the scourings of party politics too naturally assume. I for one am unimpressed.'

'I must admit that I find his nomination most curious,' said the Praelector. 'One wonders what the Prime Minister had in mind.'

'The Government's majority is not a substantial one,' said the Senior Tutor. 'I should imagine he was ridding himself of a liability. If this evening's lamentable speech was anything to go by, Sir Godber's statements in the Commons must have raised a good many hackles on the back benches. Besides, his record of achievement is not an enviable one.'

'It still seems odd to me,' said the Praelector, 'that we should have been chosen for his retirement.'

'Perhaps his bark is worse than his bite,' said the Bursar hopefully.

'Bite?' shouted the Chaplain. 'But I've only just finished dinner. Not another morsel, thank you all the same.'

'One must assume that it was a case of any port in a storm,' said the Dean.

The Chaplain looked appalled.

'Port?' he screamed. 'After brandy? I can't think what this place is coming to.' He shuddered and promptly fell asleep again.

'I can't think what the Chaplain is coming to, come to that,' said the Praelector sadly. 'He gets worse by the day.'

'Anno domini,' said the Dean, 'anno domini, I'm afraid.'

'Not a particularly happy expression, Dean,' said the Senior Tutor, who still retained some vestiges of a classical education, 'in the circumstances.'

The Dean looked at him lividly. He disliked the Senior Tutor and found his allusions distinctly trying.

'The year of our Lord,' the Senior Tutor explained. 'I have the notion that our Master sees himself in the role of the creator. We shall have our work cut out preventing him from overexerting himself. We have our faults I daresay but they are not ones I would wish to see Sir Godber Evans remedy.'

'I am sure the Master will allow himself to be guided by our advice,' said the Praelector. 'We have had some obdurate Masters in the past. Canon Bowel had some ill-advised notions about altering the Chapel services, I seem to recall.'

'He wanted compulsory Compline,' said the Dean.

'A fearful thought,' the Senior Tutor agreed. 'It would have interfered with the digestive process.'

'The point was made to him,' the Dean continued, 'after a particularly good dinner. We had had devilled crabs with jugged hare to follow. I think it was the cigars that did it. That and the zabaglione.'

'Zabaglione?' shouted the Chaplain, 'it's a little late but I daresay ...'

'We were talking about Canon Bowel,' the Bursar explained to him.

The Chaplain shook his head. 'Couldn't abide the man,' he said. 'Used to live on poached cod.'

'He had a peptic ulcer.'

'I'm not surprised,' said the Chaplain. 'With a name like that he should have known better.'

'To return to the present Master,' the Senior Tutor said, 'I am not prepared to sit back and allow him to alter our present admissions policy.'

'I don't see how we can afford to,' the Bursar agreed. 'We are not a rich college.'

'The point will have to be made to him,' the Dean said. 'We look to you, Bursar, to see that he understands it.' The Bursar nodded dutifully. His was not a strong constitution and the Dean overawed him.

'I shall do my best,' he said.

'And as far as the College Council is concerned I think the best policy will be one of ... er ... amiable inertia,' the Praelector suggested. 'That has always been one of our strong points.'

'There's nothing like prevarication,' the Dean agreed, 'I have yet to meet a liberal who can withstand the attrition of prolonged discussion of the inessentials.'

'You don't think the Bowel treatment, to coin a phrase?' the Senior Tutor asked.

The Dean smiled and stubbed out his cigar.

'There are more ways of killing a cat than stuffing it with ...'

'Hush,' said the Praelector, but the Chaplain slept on. He was dreaming of the girls in Woolworths.

They left him sitting there and went out into the Court, their gowns wrapped round them against the cold. Like so many black puddings, they made their way to their rooms. Only the Bursar lived out with his wife. Porterhouse was still a very old-fashioned college.

In the Porter's Lodge Skullion sat in front of the gas fire polishing his shoes. A tin of black polish stood on the table beside him and every few minutes he would dip the corner of his yellow duster into the tin and smear the polish on to the toe of his shoe with little circular movements. Round and round his finger would go inside the duster while the toecap dulled momentarily and grew to a new and deeper shine. Every now and then Skullion would spit on the cap and then rub it again with an even lighter touch before picking up a clean duster and polishing the cap until it shone like black japan. Finally he would hold the shoe away from him so that it caught the light and he could see deep in the brilliant polish a dark distorted reflection of himself. Only then would he put the shoe to one side and start on the other.

It was something he had learnt to do in the Marines so many years ago and the ritual still had the satisfying effect it had had then. In some obscure way it seemed to ward off the thought of the future and all the threats implicit in that future, as if tomorrow was always a Regimental

Sergeant-Major and an inspection and change could be propitiated by a gleaming pair of boots. All the time his pipe smoked out of the corner of his mouth and the mantles of the gas fire darkened or glowed in the draught and the snow fell outside. And all the time Skullion's mind, protected by the ritual and the artefacts of habit, digested the import of the Master's speech. Change? There was always change and what good did it do? Skullion could think of nothing good in change. His memory ranged back over the decades in search of certainty and found it only in the assurance of men. Men no longer living or, if not dead, distant and forgotten, ignored by a world in search of effervescent novelty. But he had seen their assurance in his youth and had been infected by it so that now, even now, he could call it up like some familiar from the past to calm the seething uncertainties of the present. Quality, he had called it, this assurance that those old men had. Quality. He couldn't define it or fix it to particulars. They had had it, that was all, and some of them had been fools or blackguards come to that but when they'd spoken there'd been a harshness in their voices as if they didn't give a damn for anything. No doubts, that's what they'd had, or if they had them kept them to themselves instead of spreading their uncertainites about until you were left wondering who or where you were. Skullion spat on his shoe in memory of such men and their assurance and polished his reflection by the fire. Above him the tower clock whirred and rumbled before striking twelve. Skullion put on his shoes and went outside. The snow was falling still and the Court and all the College roofs were white. He went to the postern gate and looked outside. A car slushed by and all the way up King's Parade the lamps shone orange through the falling snow. Skullion went in and shut the door. The outside world was none of his affair. It had a bleakness that he didn't want to know.

He went back into the Porter's Lodge and sat down again with his pipe. Around him the paraphernalia of his office, the old wooden clock, the counter, the rows of pigeonholes, the keyboard and the blackboard with 'Message for Dr Messmer' scrawled on it, were reassuring relics of his tenure and reminders that he was still needed. For forty-five years Skullion had sat in the Lodge watching over the comings and goings of Porterhouse until it seemed he was as much a part of the College as the carved heraldic beasts on the tower above. A lifetime of little duties easily attended to while the world outside stormed by in a maelstrom of change had bred in Skullion a devotion to the changelessness of Porterhouse traditions. When he'd first come there'd been an Empire, the greatest Empire that the world had known, a Navy, the greatest Navy in the world, fifteen battleships, seventy cruisers, two hundred destroyers, and

Skullion had been a keyboard sentry on the *Nelson* with her three for'ard turrets and her arse cut off to meet the terms of some damned treaty. And now there was nothing left of that. Only Porterhouse was still the same. Porterhouse and Skullion, relics of an old tradition. As for the intellectual life of the College, Skullion neither knew nor cared about it. It was as incomprehensible to him as the rigmarole of a Latin mass to some illiterate peasant. They could say or think what they liked. It was the men he worshipped, some at least and fewer these days, their habits and the trappings he associated with that old assurance. The Dean's 'Good morning, Skullion', Dr Huntley's silk shirts, the Chaplain's evening stroll around the Fellows' Garden, Mr Lyons's music evening every Friday, the weekly parcel from the Institute for Dr Baxter. Chapel, Hall, the Feast, the meeting of the College Council, all these occasions like internal seasons marked the calendar of Skullion's life and all the time he looked for that assurance that had once been the hallmark of a gentleman.

Now sitting there with the gas fire hissing before him he searched his mind for what it was those old men signified. It wasn't that they were clever. Some were, but half were stupid, more stupid than the young men coming up these days. Money? Some had a lot and others hadn't. That wasn't what had made the difference. To him at least. Perhaps it had to them. A race apart they were. Helpless half of them. Couldn't make their beds, or wouldn't. And arrogant. 'Skullion this and Skullion that.' Oh, he'd resented it at the time and done it all the same and hadn't minded afterwards because ... because they'd been gentlemen. He spat into the fire affectionately and remembered an argument he'd had once with a young pup in a pub who'd heard him going on about the good old days.

'What gentlemen?' the lad had said. 'A lot of rich bastards with nothing between their ears who just exploited you.'

And Skullion had put down his pint and said, 'A gentleman stood for something. It wasn't what he was. It was what he knew he ought to be. And that's something you will never know.' Not what they were but what they ought to be, like some old battle standard that you followed because it was a symbol of the best. A ragged tattered piece of cloth that stood for something and gave you confidence and something to fight for.

He got up and walked across the Court and through the Screens and down the Fellows' Garden to the back gate. Everywhere the snow had submerged the details of the garden. Skullion's feet on the gravel path were soundless. In a few rooms lights still burned. The Dean's windows were still alight.

'Brooding on the speech,' Skullion thought and glanced reproachfully at the Master's Lodge where all was dark. At the back gate he stood looking up at the rows of iron spikes that topped the wall and the gate. How often in the old days he had stood there in the shadow of the beech-trees watching young gentlemen negotiate those spikes only to step out and take their names. He could remember a good many of those names still and see the startled faces turned towards his as he stepped out into the light.

'Good morning, Mr Hornby. Dean's report in the morning, sir.'

'Oh damn you, Skullion. Why can't you go to bed sometimes?'

'College regulations, sir.'

And they had gone off to their rooms cursing cheerfully. Now no one climbed in. Instead they knocked you up at all hours. Skullion didn't know why he bothered to come and look at the back wall any more. Out of habit. Old habit. He was just about to turn and trudge back to his bed in the Lodge when a scuffling noise stopped him in his tracks. Someone in the street was trying to climb in.

Zipser walked down Free School Lane past the black clunch walls of Corpus. The talk on 'Population Control in the Indian Subcontinent' had gone on longer than he had expected, partly due to the enthusiasm of the speaker and partly to the intractable nature of the problem itself. Zipser had not been sure which had been worse, the delivery, if that was an appropriate word to use about a speech that concerned itself with abortion, or the enthusiastic advocacy of vasectomy which had prolonged the talk beyond its expected limits. The speaker, a woman doctor with the United Nations Infant Prevention Unit in Madras, who seemed to regard infant mortality as a positive blessing, had disparaged the coil as useless, the pill as expensive, female sterilization as complicated, had described vasectomy so seductively that Zipser had found himself crossing and re-crossing his legs and wishing to hell that he hadn't come. Even now as he walked back to Porterhouse through the snow-covered streets he was filled with foreboding and a tendency to waddle. Still, even if the world seemed doomed to starvation, he had had to get out of Porterhouse for the evening. As the only research graduate in the College he found himself isolated. Below him the undergraduates pursued a wild promiscuity which he envied but dared not emulate, and above him the Fellows found compensation for their impotence in gluttony. Besides he was not a Porterhouse man, as the Dean had pointed out when he had been accepted. 'You'll have to live in College to get the spirit of the place,' he had said, and while in other colleges research graduates lived in cheap and comfortable digs, Zipser found himself occupying an exceedingly expensive suite of rooms in Bull Tower and forced to follow the regime of an undergraduate. For one thing he had to be in by twelve or face the wrath of Skullion and the indelicate inquiries next morning of the Dean. The whole system was anachronistic and Zipser wished he had been accepted by one of the other colleges. Skullion's attitude he found particularly unpleasant. The Porter seemed to regard him as an interloper, and lavished a wealth of invective on him normally reserved for tradesmen. Zipser's attempts to mollify him by explaining that Durham was a university and that there had been a Durham College in Oxford in 1380 had failed hopelessly. If anything, the mention of Oxford had increased Skullion's antipathy.

'This is a gentleman's college,' he had said, and Zipser, who didn't claim to be even a putative gentleman, had been a marked man ever since. Skullion had it in for him.

As he crossed Market Hill he glanced at the Guildhall clock. It was twelve thirty-five. The main gate would be shut and Skullion in bed. Zipser slackened his pace. There was no point in hurrying now. He might just as well stay out all night now. He certainly wasn't going to knock Skullion up and get cursed for his pains. It wouldn't have been the first time he had wandered about Cambridge all night. Of course there was Mrs Biggs the bedder to be taken care of. She came to wake him every morning and was supposed to report him if his bed hadn't been slept in but Mrs Biggs was accommodating. 'A pound in the purse is worth a flea in the ear,' she had explained after his first stint of nights wandering, and Zipser had paid up cheerfully. Mrs Biggs was all right. He was fond of her. There was something almost human about her in spite of her size.

Zipser shivered. It was partly the cold and partly the thought of Mrs Biggs. The snow was falling heavily now and it was obvious he couldn't stay out all night in this weather. It was equally clear that he wasn't going to wake Skullion. He would have to climb in. It was an undignified thing for a graduate to do but there was no alternative. He crossed Trinity Street and went past Caius. At the bottom he turned right and came to the back gate in the lane. Above him the iron spikes on top of the wall looked more threatening than ever. Still, he couldn't stay out. He would probably freeze to death if he did. He found a bicycle in front of Trinity Hall and dragged it up the lane and put it against the wall. Then he climbed up until he could grasp the spikes with his hands. He paused for a moment and then with a final kick he was up with one knee on the wall and his foot under the spikes. He eased himself up and swung the other leg over, found a foothold and jumped. He landed softly in the flowerbed and scrambled to his feet. He was just moving off down the path under the beech-trees when something moved in the shadow and a hand fell on his shoulder. Zipser reacted instinctively. With a wild flurry he struck out at his attacker and the next moment a bowler hat was in mid-air and Zipser himself, ignoring the College rules which decreed that only Fellows could walk on the lawns, was racing across the grass towards New Court. Behind him on the gravel path Skullion lay breathing heavily. Zipser glanced over his shoulder as he dashed through the gate into the Court and saw his dark shape on the ground. Then he was in O staircase and climbing the stairs to his rooms. He shut the door and stood in the darkness panting. It must have been Skullion. The bowler hat told him that. He had assaulted a College porter, bashed his face and chopped him down. He went to the window and peered out and it was then that he realized what a fool he had been. His footsteps in the snow would give him away. Skullion would follow them to the Bull Tower. But there was no sign of the Porter. Perhaps he was still lying out there unconscious. Perhaps he had knocked him out. Zipser shuddered at this fresh indication of his irrational nature, and its terrible consequences for mankind. Sex and violence, the speaker had said, were the twin poles of the world's lifeless future, and Zipser could see now what she had meant.

Anyway, he could not leave Skullion lying out there to freeze to death even if going down to help him meant that he would be sent down from the University for 'assaulting a college porter', his thesis on the Pumpernickel as A Factor in the Politics of 16th-Century Westphalia uncompleted. He went to the door and walked slowly downstairs.

Skullion got to his feet and picked up his bowler, brushed the snow off it and put it on. His waistcoat and jacket were covered with patches of snow and he brushed them down with his hands. His right eye was swelling. Young bastard had caught him a real shiner. 'Getting too old for this job,' he muttered, muddled feelings of anger and respect competing in his mind. 'But I can still catch him.' He followed the footsteps across the lawn and down the path to the gate into New Court. His eye had swollen now so that he could hardly see out of it, but Skullion wasn't thinking about his eye. He wasn't thinking about catching the culprit. He was thinking back to the days of his youth. 'Fair's fair. If you can't catch 'em, you can't report 'em,' old Fuller, the Head Porter at Porterhouse had said to him when he first came to the College and what was true then was truc now. He turned left at the gate and went down the Cloister to the Lodge and went through to his bedroom. 'A real shiner,' he said examining the swollen eye in the mirror behind the door.

It could do with a bit of beefsteak. He'd get some from the College kitchen in the morning. He took off his jacket and was unbuttoning his waistcoat when the door of the Lodge opened. Skullion buttoned his waistcoat again and put on his jacket and went out into the office.

Zipser stood in the doorway of O staircase and watched Skullion cross the Court to the Cloisters. Well, at least he wasn't lying out in the snow. Still he couldn't go back to his room without doing something. He had better go down and see if he was all right. He walked across the Court and into the Lodge. It was empty and he was about to turn away and go back to his room when the door at the back opened and Skullion appeared. His right eye was black and swollen and his face, old and veined, had a deformed lop-sided look about it.

'Well?' Skullion asked out of the side of his mouth. One eye peered angrily at Zipser.

'I just came to say I'm sorry,' Zipser said awkwardly.

'Sorry?' Skullion asked as if he didn't understand.

'Sorry about hitting you.'

'What makes you think you hit me?' The lop-sided face glared at him.

Zipser scratched his forehead.

'Well, anyway I'm sorry. I thought I had better see if you were all right.'

'You thought I was going to report you, didn't you?' Skullion asked contemptuously. 'Well, I'm not. You got away.'

Zipser shook his head.

'It wasn't that. I thought you might be ... well ... hurt.'

Skullion smiled grimly.

'Hurt? Me hurt? What's a little hurt matter?' He turned and went back into the bedroom and shut the door. Zipser went out into the Court. He didn't understand. You knocked an old man down and he didn't mind. It wasn't logical. It was all so bloody irrational. He walked back to his room and went to bed.

CHAPTER THREE

The Master slept badly. The somatic effects of the Feast and the psychic consequences of his speech had combined to make sleep difficult. While his wife slept demurely in her separate bed, Sir Godber lay awake reliving the events of the evening with an insomniac's obsessiveness. Had he been wise to so offend the sensibilities of the College? It had been a carefully calculated decision and one which his political eminence had seemed to warrant. Whatever the Fellows might say about him, his reputation for moderate and essentially conservative reform would absolve him of the accusation that he was the advocate of change for change's sake. As the Minister who had made the slogan 'Alteration without Change' so much a part of the recent tax reforms, Sir Godber prided himself on his conservative liberalism or, as he had put it in a moment of self-revelation, authoritarian permissiveness. The challenge he had thrown down to Porterhouse had been deliberate and justified. The College was absurdly old-fashioned. Out of touch with the times, and to a man whose very life had been spent keeping in touch with the times there could be no greater dereliction. An advocate of comprehensive education at no matter what cost, chairman of the Evans Committee on Higher Education which had introduced Sixth Form Polytechnics for the Mentally Retarded, Sir Godber prided himself on the certain knowledge that he knew what was best for the country, and he was supported in this by Lady Mary, his wife, whose family, now staunchly Liberal, still retained the Whig traditions enshrined in the family motto, *Laisser Mieux*. Sir Godber had taken the motto for his own, and associating it with Voltaire's famous dictum had made himself the enemy of the good wherever he found it. 'Be good, sweet maid, and let who will be clever' had no appeal for Sir Godber's crusading imagination. What sweet maids required was a first-rate education and what sleeping dogs needed was a kick up the backside. This was precisely what he intended to administer to Porterhouse.

Lying awake through the still hours of the night listening to the bells of the College clocks and the churches toll the hours, a sound he found medieval and unnecessarily premonitory, Sir Godber planned his campaign. In the first instance he would order a thorough inventory of the College's resources and make the economies needed to finance the alterations he had in mind. In themselves such economies would effect some changes in Porterhouse. The kitchen staff could well do with some thinning out and since so much of the ethos of Porterhouse emanated from the kitchen and the endowments lavished upon it by generations of Porterhouse men, a careful campaign of retrenchment there would do much to alter the character of the College. And such savings would be justified by the building programme and the expansion of numbers. With the experience of hundreds of hours in committees behind him, the Master anticipated the arguments that would be raised against him by the Fellows. Some would object to any changes in the kitchen. Others would deny the need for expansion in numbers. In the darkness Sir Godber smiled happily. It was precisely on such divisions of opinion that he thrived. The original issue would get lost in argument and he would emerge as the arbiter between divided factions, his role as the initiator of dissension quite forgotten. But first he would need an ally. He ran through the Fellows in search of a weak link.

The Dean would oppose any increase in the numbers of undergraduates on the specious grounds that it would destroy the Christian community which he supposed Porterhouse to be and, more accurately, would make discipline difficult to impose. Sir Godber put the Dean to one side. There was no help to be found there except indirectly from the very obduracy of his conservatism, which irritated some of the other Fellows. The Senior Tutor? A more difficult case to assess. A rowing man in his day, he might be inclined to favour a larger intake on the grounds that it would add weight to the College boat and improve Porterhouse's chances in the Bumps. On the other hand he would oppose any changes in the kitchen for fear that the diet of the Boat Club might be diminished. The Master decided a compromise was in order. He would give an absolute assurance that the Boat Club would continue to get its quota of beefsteak no matter what other economies were made in the kitchen. Yes, the Senior Tutur could be persuaded to support expansion. Sir Godber balanced him against the Dean and turned his attention to the Bursar. Here was the key, he thought. If the Bursar could be enlisted on the side of change, his assistance would be invaluable. His advocacy of the financial benefits to be gained from an increase of undergraduate contributions, his demand for frugality in the kitchens, would carry immense weight. Sir Godber considered the Bursar's character and, with that insight into his own nature which had been the cornerstone of his success, recognized opportunism when he saw it. The Bursar, he had no doubt, was an ambitious man and unlikely to be content with the modest attainments of College life. The opportunity to serve on a Royal Commission – Sir Godber's retirement from the Cabinet was sufficiently recent for him to know of several pending – would give him a chance to put this nonentity at the service of the public and give him the recognition which would make amends for his lack of achievement. Sir Godber had no doubt that he could arrange his invitation. There was always a place for a man of the Bursar's contingent character on Royal Commissions. He would concentrate his attention on the Bursar. Satisfied with this plan of campaign, the Master turned on his side and fell asleep.

At seven he was woken by his wife whose insistence that early to bed and early to rise makes a man healthy, comfortably off and wise had never ceased to irritate him. As she bustled about the bedroom with a lack of concern for the feelings of other people which characterized her philanthropy, Sir Godber studied once more those particulars of his wife which had been such a spur to his political ambitions. Lady Mary was not an attractive woman. Her physical angularity made manifest the quality of her mind.

'Time to get up,' she said, spotting Sir Godber's open eye.

'Ours not to reason why, ours but to do or die,' thought the Master, sitting up and fumbling for his slippers.

'How did the Feast go?' Lady Mary asked, adjusting the straps of her surgical corset with a vigour that reminded Sir Godber of a race meeting.

'Tolerably, I suppose,' he said with a yawn. 'We had swan stuffed with some sort of duck. Very indigestible. Kept me awake half the night.'

'You should be more careful about what you eat.' Lady Mary sat down and swung one leg over the other to put on her stockings. 'You don't want to have a stroke.'

'It's called Porterhouse Blue.'

'What is?'

'A stroke,' said Sir Godber.

'I thought it was something you got for rowing,' said Lady Mary. 'That or a cheese. Something on the order of a Stilton – blue and veined –'

Sir Godber lowered his eyes from her legs. 'Well, it isn't,' he said hurriedly, 'it's an apoplectic fit brought on by over-indulgence. An old College tradition, and one I intend to eradicate.'

'And about time too,' said Lady Mary. 'I think it's utterly disgraceful in this day and age that all this good food should go to waste just to satisfy the greed of some old men. When I think of all those ...'

Sir Godber went into the bathroom and shut the door and turned the tap on in the hand basin. Dimly through the door and through the noise of running water he could hear his wife lamenting starving children in India. He looked at himself in the mirror and sighed. Just like the bloody cockcrow, he thought. Starts the day with a dirge. Wouldn't be happy if someone wasn't dying of starvation or drowning in a hurricane or dropping dead of typhus.

He shaved and dressed and went down to breakfast. Lady Mary was reading the *Guardian* with an avidity that suggested a natural disaster of considerable magnitude. Sir Godber refrained from inquiring what it was and contented himself with reading one or two bills.

'My dear,' he said when he had finished, 'I shall be seeing the Bursar this morning and I was thinking of inviting him to dinner on Wednesday.'

Lady Mary looked up. 'Wednesday's no good. I have a meeting on. Thursday would be better,' she said. 'Do you want me to invite anyone else. He's a rather common little man, isn't he?'

'He has his good points,' said the Master. 'I'll see if Thursday suits him.' He went to his study with *The Times*. There were days when his wife's moral intensity seemed to hang like a pall over his existence. He wondered what the meeting on Wednesday was about. Battered babies probably. The Master shuddered.

In the Bursar's office the telephone rang.

'Ah, Master. Yes, certainly. No, not at all. In five minutes then.' He put down the phone with a smile of quiet satisfaction. The bargaining was about to begin and the Master had not invited anyone else. The Bursar's office overlooked the Fellows' Garden and nobody else had taken the path under the beech-trees to the Master's Lodge. As he left his office and walked across the lawn the Bursar reviewed the strategy he had decided on during the night. He had been tempted to put himself at the head of the Fellows in their opposition to any change. There were after all advantages to be gained in the climate of the seventies from adherence to the principles of strict conservatism, and in the event of the Master's retirement or early death the Fellows might well elect him Master in his place out of gratitude. The Bursar rather fancied not. He lacked the carnivorous bonhomie that Porterhouse sought in its Masters. Old Lord Wurford for instance, Skullion's touchstone, or Canon Bowel, whose penchant for Limburger cheese and rugby fanaticism had in a sinister way been interrelated. No, the Bursar could not see himself among their number. It was wiser to follow in his Master's footsteps. He knocked on the door of the Master's Lodge and was admitted by the French au pair.

'Ah, Bursar, so good of you to come,' said the Master, rising from his chair behind the large oak desk that stood in front of the fire. 'Some madeira? Or would you prefer something a little more contemporary?' The Master chuckled. 'A campari, for instance. Something to keep the cold out.' In the background the radiators gurgled gently. The Bursar considered the question.

'I think something contemporary would be fitting, Master,' he said at last.

'So do I, Bursar, so I do indeed,' said the Master, and poured the drinks.

'Now then,' he said when the Bursar had seated himself in an armchair, 'to business.'

'To business,' said the Bursar raising his glass in the mistaken belief that a toast had been proposed. The Master eyed him cautiously.

'Yes. Well,' he said, 'I've asked you here this morning to discuss the College finances. I understand from the Praelector that you and I share responsibility in this matter. Correct me if I am wrong?'

'Quite right, Master,' said the Bursar.

'But of course as Bursar you are the real power. I quite appreciate that,' the Master continued. 'I have no desire to impinge upon your authority in these matters, let me assure you of that.' He smiled genially on the Bursar.

'My purpose in asking you here this morning was to reassure you that the changes I spoke of last night were of a purely general nature. I seek no alterations in the administration of the College.'

'Quite,' said the Bursar, nodding with approval. 'I entirely agree.'

'So good of you to say so, Bursar,' said the Master. 'I had the impression that my little sally had a not altogether unmixed reception from the less ... er ... contemporary Senior Fellows.'

'We are a very traditional college, Master,' said the Bursar.

'Yes, so we are, but some of us, I suspect, are rather less traditional than others, eh, Bursar?'

'I think it's fair to say so, Master,' the Bursar assented.

Like two elderly dogs they circled warily in search of the odour of agreement, sniffing each hesitation for the nuance of complicity. Change was inevitable. Indeed, indeed. The old order. Quite so. Quite so. Those of us in authority. Ah yes. Ah yes. On the mantelpiece the alabaster clock ticked on. It was an hour before the preliminary skirmishes were done and with a second, larger campari Sir Godber relaxed the role of Master.

'It's the sheer animality of so many of our undergraduates I object to,' he told the Bursar.

'We tend to attract the less sensitive, I must admit.' The Bursar puffed his cigar contentedly.

'Academically our results are deplorable. When did we last get a first?'

'In 1956,' said the Bursar.

The Master raised his eyes to heaven.

'In Geography,' said the Bursar, rubbing salt in the wound.

'In Geography. One might have guessed.' He got up and stood looking out of the french windows at the garden covered in snow. 'It is time to change all that. We must return to the Founder's intentions "studiously to engage in learning". We must accept candidates who have good academic records instead of the herd of illiterates we seem to cater for at present.'

'There are one or two obstacles to that,' the Bursar sighed.

'Quite so. The Senior Tutur for one. He is in charge of admissions.'

'I was thinking rather of our, how shall I say, dependence on the endowment subscriptions,' said the Bursar.

'The endowment subscriptions? I've never heard of them.'

'Very few people have, Master, except of course the parents of our less academic undergraduates.'

Sir Godber frowned and stared at the Bursar. 'Do you mean to say that we accept candidates without academic qualifications if their parents subscribe to an endowment fund?' he asked.

'I'm afraid so. Frankly, the College could hardly continue without their contributions,' the Bursar told him.

'But this is monstrous. Why, it's tantamount to selling degrees.'

'Not tantamount, Master. Identical.'

'But what about the Tripos examinations?'

The Bursar shook his head. 'Ah I'm afraid we don't aspire to such heights. Specials are more our mark. Ordinary degrees. Just good plain old-fashioned BAs. We put up the names and they're accepted without question.'

Sir Godber sat down dumbfounded.

'Good God, and you mean to tell me that without these ... er ... contributions ... dammit, these bribes, the College couldn't carry on?'

'In a nutshell, Master,' said the Bursar. 'Porterhouse is broke.'

'But why? What do other colleges do?'

'Ah,' said the Bursar, 'well that's rather different. Most of them have enormous resources. Shrewd investments over the years. Trinity, for instance, is to the best of my knowledge the third largest landowner in the country. Only the Queen and the Church of England exceed Trinity's holdings. King's had Lord Keynes as Bursar. We unfortunately had Lord Fitzherbert. Where Keynes made a fortune, Fitzherbert lost one. You've heard of the man who broke the bank at Monte Carlo?'

The Master nodded miserably.

'Lord Fitzherbert,' said the Bursar.

'But he must have made a fortune,' said the Master.

The Bursar shook his head. 'It wasn't the bank of Monte Carlo he broke, Master, but the bank at Monte Carlo, our bank, the Anglian Lowland Bank. Two million on the spin of the wheel. Never recovered from the blow.'

'I'm not in the least surprised,' said the Master, 'I wonder he didn't blow his brains out on the spot.'

'The bank, Master, not Lord Fitzherbert. He came back and eventually was elected Master,' said the Bursar.

'Elected Master? It seems an odd thing to elect a man who has bankrupted the place. I should have thought he'd have been lynched.'

'Frankly, the College had to depend on him for some time. The revenue from his estate saw us through bad times, I'm told.' The Bursar sighed. 'So you see, Master, while I support you in principle, I'm afraid the ... er ... exigencies of our financial position do impose certain restraints in the way of effecting the changes you have in mind. A case of cutting our coats to suit our cloth.' The Bursar finished his campari and stood up. The Master sat staring out into the garden. It had started to snow again but the Master was not aware of it. His mind was on other things. Looking back over his long career, he was suddenly conscious that the situation he was now facing was a familiar one. The Bursar's arguments had been those of the Treasury and the Bank of England. Sir Godber's ideals had always foundered on the rocks of financial necessity. This time it would be different. The frustrations of a lifetime had come to a head. Sir Godber had nothing left to lose. Porterhouse would change or bust. Inspired by the example of Lord Fitzherbert, Sir Godber stood up and turned to the Bursar. But the Bursar was no longer there. He had tiptoed from the room and could be seen waddling gently across the Fellows' Garden.

CHAPTER FOUR

Zipser overslept. His exertions, both mental and physical, had left him exhausted. By the time he woke, Mrs Biggs was already busy in his outer room, moving furniture and dusting. Zipser lay in bed listening to her. Like something out of Happy Families, he thought. Mrs Biggs the Bedder. Skullion the Head Porter. The Dean. The Senior Tutor. Relics of some ancient childish game. Everything about Porterhouse was like that. Masters and Servants.

Lying there listening to the ponderous animality of Mrs Biggs' movements, Zipser considered the curious turn of events that had forced him into the role of a master while Mrs Biggs maintained an aggressive servility quite out of keeping with her personality and formidable physique. He found the relationship peculiar, and further complicated by the sinister attractions she held for him. It must be that in her fullness Mrs Biggs retained a natural warmth which in its contrast to the artificiality of all else in Cambridge made its appeal. Certainly nothing else could explain it. Taken in her particulars, and Zipser couldn't think of any other way of taking her, the bedder was quite remarkably without attractions. It wasn't simply the size of her appendages that was astonishing but the sheer power. Mrs Biggs' walk was a thing of menacing maternity, while her face retained a youthfulness quite out of keeping with her volume. Only her voice declared her wholly ordinary. That and her conversation, which hovered tenuously close to the obscene and managed to combine servility with familiarity in a manner he found unanswerable. He got out of bed and began to dress. It was one of the ironies of life, he thought, that in a college that prided itself on its adherence to the values of the past, Mrs Biggs' manifest attractions should go unrecognized. In paleolithic times she would have been a princess and he was just wondering at what particular moment of history the Mrs Biggses had ceased to represent all that was finest and fairest in womanhood when she knocked on the door.

'Mr Zipser, are you decent?' she called.

'Hang on. I'm coming,' Zipser called back.

'I shouldn't be at all surprised,' Mrs Biggs muttered audibly.

Zipser opened the door.

'I haven't got all day,' Mrs Biggs said brushing past him provocatively.

'I'm sorry to have kept you,' said Zipser sarcastically.

'Kept me indeed. Listen to who's talking. And what makes you think I'd mind being kept?'

Zipser blushed. 'That's hardly what I meant,' he said hotly.

'Very complimentary I'm sure,' said Mrs Biggs, regarding him with arch disapproval. 'Got out of bed the wrong side this morning, did we?'

Zipser noted the plural with a delicious shudder and lowered his eyes. Mrs Biggs' boots, porcinely tight, entranced him.

'Mr Skullion's got a black eye this morning,' the bedder continued. 'A right purler. Not before time either. I says to him, "Somebody's been taking a poke at you". You know what he says?' Zipser shook his head.

'He says, "I'll thank you to keep your comments to yourself, Mrs Biggs." That's what he says. Silly old fool. Don't know which century he's living in.' She went into the other room and Zipser followed her. He put a kettle on to make coffee while Mrs Biggs bustled about picking things up and putting them down again in a manner which suggested that a great deal of work was being done but which merely helped to emphasize her feelings. All the time she rattled on with her daily dose of inconsequential information while Zipser dodged about the room like a toreador trying to avoid a talkative bull. Each time she brushed past him he was aware of an animal magnetism that overrode considerations of taste and that aesthetic sensibility his education was supposed to have given him. Finally he stood in the corner, hardly able to contain himself, and watched her figure as it walloped about the room. Her words lost all meaning, became mere soothing sounds, waves of accompaniment to the surge of her thighs and the great rollers of her buttocks dimpled and shimmering beneath her skirt. 'Well I says, "You know what you can do ..." ' Mrs Biggs' voice echoed Zipser's terrible thought. She bent over to plug in the vacuum-cleaner and her breasts plunged in her blouse and undulated with a force of attraction Zipser found almost irresistible. He felt himself moved out of his corner like a boxer urged forward by unnatural passion for an enormous opponent. Words crowded into his mouth. Unwanted words. Unspeakable words.

'I want you,' he said and was saved the final embarrassment by the vacuum-cleaner which roared into life.

'What's that you said?' Mrs Biggs shouted above the din. She was holding the suction pipe against a cushion on the armchair. Zipser turned purple.

'Nothing,' he bawled, and fell back into his corner.

'Bag's full,' said Mrs Biggs, and switched the machine off.

In the silence that followed Zipser leant against the wall, appalled at his terrible avowal. He was about to make a dash for the door when Mrs Biggs bent over and undid the clips on the back of the vacuum-cleaner. Zipser stared at the backs of her knees. The boots, the creases, the swell of her thighs, the edge of her stockings, the crescent ...

'Bag's full,' Mrs Biggs said again. 'You can't get any suction when the bag's full.'

She straightened up holding the bag grey and swollen ... Zipser shut his eyes. Mrs Biggs emptied the bag into the wastepaper basket. A cloud of grey dust billowed up into the room.

'Are you feeling all right, dearie?' she asked, peering at him with motherly concern. Zipser opened his eyes and stared into her face.

'I'm all right,' he managed to mutter trying to take his eyes off her lips. Mrs Biggs' lipstick gleamed thickly. 'I didn't sleep well. That's all.'

'Too much work and not enough play makes Jack a dull boy,' said Mrs Biggs holding the bag limply. To Zipser the thing had an erotic appeal he dared not analyse. 'Now you just sit down and I'll make you some coffee and you'll feel better.' Mrs Biggs' hand grasped his arm and guided him to a chair. Zipser slumped into it and stared at the vacuum-cleaner while Mrs Biggs, bending once again and even more revealingly now that Zipser was sitting down and closer to her, inserted the bag into the back of the machine and switched it on. A terrible roar, and the bag was sucked into the interior with a force which corresponded entirely to Zipser's feelings. Mrs Biggs straightened up and went through to the gyp room to make coffee while Zipser shifted feebly in the chair. He couldn't imagine what was happening to him. It was all too awful. He had to get away. He couldn't go on sitting there while she was in the room. He'd do something terrible. He couldn't control himself. He'd say something. He was about to get up and sneak out when Mrs Biggs came back with two cups of coffee.

'You do look funny,' she said, putting a cup into his hand. 'You ought to go and see a doctor. You might be going down with something.'

'Yes,' said Zipser obediently. Mrs Biggs sat down opposite him and sipped her coffee. Zipser tried to keep his eyes off her legs and found himself gazing at her breasts.

'Do you often get taken queer?' Mrs Biggs inquired.

'Queer?' said Zipser, shaken from his reverie by the accusation. 'Certainly not.'

'I was only asking,' said Mrs Biggs. She took a mouthful of coffee with a schlurp that was distinctly suggestive. 'I had a young man once,' she continued, 'just like you. Got took queer every now and then. Used to throw himself about and wriggle something frightful. Took me all my time to hold him down, it did.'

Zipser stared at her frenziedly. The notion of being held down while wriggling by Mrs Biggs was more than he could bear. With a sudden lurch that spilt his coffee Zipser hurled himself out of the chair and dashed from the room. He rushed downstairs and out into the safety of the open air. 'I've got to do something. I can't control myself. First Skullion and now Mrs Biggs.' He walked hurriedly out of Porterhouse and through Clare towards the University Library.

Alone in Zipser's room, Mrs Biggs switched on the vacuum-cleaner and poked the handle round the room. As she worked she sang to herself loudly, 'Love me tender, love me true.' Her voice, raucously off key, was drowned by the roar of the Electrolux.

The Dean spent the morning writing letters to members of the Porterhouse Society. As the Society's secretary he attended the annual dinners in London and Edinburgh and corresponded regularly with members, a great many of whom lived in Australia or New Zealand, and for whom the Dean's letters formed a link with their days at Porterhouse on which they had traded socially ever since. For the Dean himself the very remoteness of most of his correspondents, and particularly their tendency to assume that nothing had changed since their undergraduate days, was a constant reassurance. It allowed him to pretend to an omnipotent conservatism that had little connection with reality. After the new Master's speech it was not easy to maintain that pretence, and the Dean's pen held in his mottled hand crawled slowly across the paper like some literate but decrepit tortoise. Every now and then he would lift his head and look for inspiration into the clear-cut features of the young men whose photographs cluttered his desk and stared with sepia arrogance from the walls of his room. The Dean recalled their athleticism and youthful indiscretions, the shopgirls they had compromised, the tailors they had bilked, the exams they had failed, and from his window he could look down on to the fountain where they had ducked so many homosexuals. It had all been so healthy and naturally violent, so different from the effete aestheticism of today. They hadn't fasted for the good of the coolies in India or protested because an anarchist was imprisoned in Brazil or stormed the Garden House Hotel because they disapproved of the government in Greece. They'd acted in high spirits. Wholesomely. The Dean sat back in his chair remembering the splendid riot on Guy Fawkes Night in 1948. The bomb that blew the Senate House windows out. The smoke bomb down the lavatory in Market Square that nearly killed an old man with high blood pressure. The lamp glass littering the streets. The bus being pushed backwards. The coppers' helmets flying. The car they'd overturned in King's Parade. There'd been a pregnant woman in it, the Dean recalled, and afterwards they'd all chipped in to pay her for the damage. Good-hearted lads. They didn't make them like that any more. Quickened by the recollection, his pen scrawled swiftly across the page. It would take more than Sir Godber Evans to change the character of Porterhouse. He'd see to that. He had just finished a letter and was addressing the envelope when there was a knock on the door.

'Come in,' the Dean called. The door opened and Skullion came in, holding his bowler hat in one hand.

'Morning, sir,' Skullion said.

'Good morning, Skullion,' the Dean said. The ritual of twenty years, the porter's daily report, always began with pleasantries. 'Heavy fall of snow during the night.'

'Very heavy, sir. Three inches at least.'

The Dean licked the envelope and fastened it down.

'Nasty eye you've got there, Skullion.'

'Slipped on the path, sir. Icy,' Skullion said. 'Very slippery.'

'Slippery? Got away, did he?' the Dean asked.

'Yes, sir.'

'Good for him,' said the Dean. 'Nice to know there are still some undergraduates with spirit about. Nothing else to report?'

'No, sir. Nothing to report. Nothing except Cheffy, sir.'

'Cheffy? What's the matter with him?'

'Well, it's not just him, sir. It's all of us. Very upset about the Master's speech,' Skullion said carefully, treading the tightrope between speaking out of turn and rightful protest. There were things you could say to the Dean and there were things you couldn't. Reporting the Chef's sense of outrage seemed a safe way of expressing his own feelings.

The Dean swung his chair round and looked out of the window to evade the difficulty. He relied on Skullion's information but there was always the danger of condoning insubordination or at least encouraging a familiarity detrimental to good discipline. But Skullion wasn't the man to take advantage of the situation. The Dean trusted him.

'You can tell the Chef there'll be no changes,' he said finally. 'The Master was just feeling his way. He'll learn.'

'Yes sir,' said Skullion doubtfully. 'Very upsetting that speech, sir.'

'Thank you, Skullion,' said the Dean dismissively.

'Thank you, sir,' Skullion said and left the room.

The Dean swung his chair round to his desk and took up his pen again. Skullion's resentment had inspired him with a new determination to block Sir Godber's schemes. There were all the OPs, for instance. Their opinion and influence could be decisive properly organized. It might be as well to inform that opinion now.

Skullion went back to the Lodge and sorted out the second mail. His conversation with the Dean had only partially restored his confidence. The Dean was getting old. His voice didn't carry the same weight any more in the College Council. It was the Bursar who was listened to, and

Skullion had his doubts about *him*. He took the *New Statesman* and the *Spectator* and read *The Times*, not the *Telegraph* like the other dons. 'Neither fish, flesh, fowl nor good red herring,' Skullion summed him up with his usual political acumen. If the Master got at him there was no saying which way he'd jump. Skullion began to think it might be time for him to pay a visit to General Sir Cathcart D'Eath at Coft. He usually went there on the first Tuesday of every month, a ritual visit with news of the College and also to have a word with a reliable stable boy in Sir Cathcart's racing stables whose information had in the past done much to supplement Skullion's meagre income. Sir Cathcart had been one of Skullion's Scholars and the debt had never been wholly repaid. 'Taking the afternoon off,' he told Walter the under-porter when he finished sorting the mail and Walter had put Dr Baxter's weekly issue of *The Boy* back into its plain envelope.

'What? Going fishing?' Walter asked.

'Never you mind where I'm going,' Skullion told him. He lit his pipe and went into the back room to fetch his coat and presently was cycling with due care and attention over Magdalene Bridge towards Coft.

Zipser sat on the third floor of the north wing of the University Library trying to bring his mind to bear on The Influence of Pumpernickel on the Politics of 16th-Century Osnabruck but without success. He no longer cared that it had been known as *bonum paniculum* and his interest in Westphalian local politics had waned. The problem of his feelings for Mrs Biggs was more immediate.

He had spent an hour in the stacks browsing feverishly through textbooks of clinical psychology in search of a medical explanation of the symptoms of irrational violence and irrepressible sexuality which had manifested themselves in his recent behaviour. From what he had read it had begun to look as if he were suffering from a multitude of different diseases. On the one hand his reaction to Skullion suggested paranoia, 'violent behaviour as a result of delusions of persecution', while the erotic compulsion of his feelings for Mrs Biggs was even more alarming and seemed to indicate schizophrenia with sado-masochistic tendencies. The combination of the two diseases, paranoid schizophrenia, was apparently the worst possible form of insanity and quite incurable. Zipser sat staring out of the window at the trees in the garden beyond the footpath and contemplated a lifetime of madness. He couldn't imagine what had suddenly occasioned the outbreak. The textbooks implied that heredity had a lot to do with it, but apart from an uncle who had a passion for concrete dwarves in his front garden and who his mother had said was a bit touched in the head, he couldn't think of anyone in the family who was actually and certifiably insane.

The explanation had to lie elsewhere. His feelings for the bedder deviated from every known norm. So for that matter did Mrs Biggs. She bulged where she should have dimpled and bounced when she should have been still. She was gross, vulgar, garrulous and, Zipser had no doubt in his mind, thoroughly insanitary. To find himself irresistibly attracted to her was the worst thing he could think of. It was perfectly all right to be queer. It was positively fashionable. To have constant and insistent sexual desires for French au pair girls, Swedish language students, girls in Boots, even undergraduates at Girton, was normality itself, but Mrs Biggs came into the category of the unmentionable. And the knowledge that but for the fortuitous intervention of the vacuum-cleaner he would have revealed his true feelings for her threw him into a panic. He left his table and went downstairs and walked back into town.

As he reached Great St Mary's the clock was striking twelve. Zipser stopped and studied the posters on the railings outside the church which announced forthcoming sermons.

CHRIST AND THE GAY CHRISTIAN Rev. F. Leaney.

HAS SALT LOST ITS SAVOUR? Anglican attitudes to disarmament. Rev. B. Tomkins.

JOB, A MESSAGE FOR THE THIRD WORLD Right Reverend Sutty, Bishop of Bombay.

JESUS JOKES Fred Henry by permission of ITA & the management of the Palace Theatre, Scunthorpe.

BOMBS AWAY A Christian's attitude to Skyjacking by Flight Lieutenant Jack Piggett, BOAC.

Zipser stared at the University Sermons with a sudden sense of loss. What had happened to the old Church, the Church of his childhood, the friendly Vicar and the helping hand? Not that Zipser has ever been to church, but he had seen them on television and had been comforted by the knowledge that they were still there in *Songs of Praise* and *Saints Alive* and *All Gas and Gaiters*. But now when he needed help there was only this pale parody of the daily paper with its mishmash of politics and sensationalism. Not a word about evil and how to cope with it. Zipser felt betrayed. He went back into Porterhouse in search of help. He'd go and see the Senior Tutor. There was just time before lunch. Zipser climbed the stairs to the Tutor's rooms and knocked on the door.

'The trouble with the Feast,' said the Dean, munching a mouthful of cold beef, 'is that it does tend to run on. Cold beef today. Cold beef tomorrow. Cold beef on Thursday. After that I suppose we'll have stewed beef on Friday and Saturday and cottage pie on Sunday. By next week we should be getting back to normal.'

'Difficult to eat an entire ox at one sitting,' said the Bursar. 'One suspects our predecessors had, shall we say, grosser appetites.'

'I always said it was a mistake to make him Prime Minister,' said the Chaplain.

The Senior Tutor took his place at table. He was looking more than usually austere.

'Talking of gross appetites,' he said grimly, 'I have the gravest doubts about some of our younger members. I have just had a visit from a young man who claims to be under some compulsion to sleep with his bedder.' He helped himself to horseradish.

The Bursar sniggered. 'Which one?' he asked.

'Zipser,' said the Senior Tutor.

'Which bedder?'

'I didn't inquire,' said the Senior Tutor. 'It didn't seem a particularly relevant question.'

The Bursar considered the problem.

'Isn't he in the Tower?' he asked the Dean.

'Who?'

'Zipser.'

'Yes. I think he is,' said the Dean.

'Then it must be Mrs Biggs.'

The Senior Tutor, who had been debating what to do with a long piece of gristle, swallowed it.

'Dear me. Mrs Biggs. I must say I did young Zipser an injustice,' he said with alarm.

'Impossible to do an injustice to anyone with such depraved tastes,' said the Dean firmly.

'Mrs Biggs hardly comes within the category of forbidden fruit,' tittered the Bursar.

'Thank you,' answered the Chaplain, 'I think I will have an apple.'

'Mrs Biggs,' muttered the Tutor. 'No wonder the poor fellow imagined he was going mad.'

'Not really,' said the Chaplain. 'This one is all right at any rate.'

'What advice did you give him?' the Bursar asked.

The Senior Tutor looked at him disbelievingly. 'Advice?' he asked. 'It is hardly my position to offer advice on such questions. I am the Senior Tutor, not a Marriage Guidance Counsellor. As a matter of fact I advised him to see the Chaplain.'

'It's a noble calling,' said the Chaplain, helping himself to a pear. The Senior Tutor sighed and finished his cold beef.

'It only goes to show what happens when you open the doors of the College to research graduates. In the old days such a thing would have been unheard of,' said the Dean.

'Unheard of perhaps but not I think unknown,' said the Bursar.

'With bedders?' the Dean asked angrily. 'With *bedders*? Maintain some sense of proportion, I beg you.'

'No thank you, Dean. I've had quite enough already,' the Chaplain replied.

The Dean was about to say something about old fools when the Senior Tutor intervened. 'In the case of Mrs Biggs,' he said, 'it is precisely the question of proportion that is at stake.'

'We had that last night,' said the Chaplain.

'Oh for God's sake,' the Senior Tutor snarled. 'How the hell can one conduct a serious discussion with him around.'

'My dear fellow,' the Praelector sighed, 'that is a question that has been bothering me for years.'

They finished the meal in silence, each occupied with his own thoughts. It was only when they were assembled in the Combination Room for coffee and the Chaplain had been persuaded to go to his room to write a note inviting Zipser to tea that the discussion began again.

'I think that we should view this matter in the wider context,' the Dean said. 'The Master's speech last night indicated only too clearly that he has in mind an extension of precisely that permissiveness of which this latest incident is indicative. I understand, Bursar, that you had a *tête-à-tête* with Sir Godber this morning.'

The Bursar looked at him unpleasantly. 'The Master phoned to ask me to discuss the College finances with him,' he said. 'I think you might give me credit for having done my best to disabuse him of the changes his speech suggested.'

'You explained that our resources do not allow us to indulge in the liberal extravagances of King's or Trinity?' the Senior Tutor asked. The Bursar nodded.

'And was the Master satisfied?' the Dean asked.

'Stunned, I think, would be the more accurate description of his reaction,' said the Bursar.

'Then we are all agreed that whatever he suggests at the meeting of the College Council tomorrow we shall oppose on principle,' said the Dean.

'I think it would be best to wait to hear what he proposes before deciding on a definite policy,' the Praelector said.

The Senior Tutor nodded. 'We must not appear too inflexible. An appearance of open-mindedness has in my experience a tendency to disarm the radical left. They seem to feel the need to reciprocate. I've often wondered why but it has worked to keep the country on the right lines for years.'

'Unfortunately this time we are dealing with a politician,' the Dean objected. 'I have a shrewd idea the Master is rather more experienced in these affairs than we give him credit for. I still think an undivided front is the best policy.'

They finished their coffee and went about their business. The Senior Tutor went down to the Boathouse to coach the first boat, the Dean slept until teatime, and the Bursar spent the afternoon doodling in his office wondering if he had been wise to tell Sir Godber about the endowment subscriptions. There had been a strength of feeling in the Master's reaction that had surprised the Bursar and had made him wonder if he had gone too far. Perhaps he had misjudged Sir Godber and the vehemence of his ideals.

CHAPTER FIVE

Skullion cycled out along the Barton Road towards Coft. His bowler hat set squarely on his head, his cycle clips and his black overcoat buttoned against the cold gave him an intransigently episcopalian air in the snow-covered landscape. He cycled slowly but relentlessly, his thoughts as dark as his habit and as bitter as the wind blowing unchecked from the Urals. The few bungalows he passed looked insubstantial beside him, transient and rootless in contrast to the black figure on the bicycle in whose head centuries of endured servitude had bred a fierce bigotry nothing would easily remove. Independence he called it, this hatred for change whether for better or worse. In Skullion's view there was no such thing as change for the better. That came under the heading of improvement. He was prepared to give his qualified approval to improvements provided there was no suggestion that it was the past that had been improved upon. That was clearly out of the question and if at the back of his mind he recognized the illogicality of his own argument, he refused to admit it even to himself. It was one of the mysteries of life which he accepted as unquestioningly as he did the great metal spiders's webs strung out across the fields beside the road to catch the radio evidence of stars that had long since ceased to exist. The world of Skullion's imagination was as remote as those stars but it was enough for him that, like the radio telescopes, he was able to catch echoes of it in men like General the Honourable Sir Cathcart D'Eath, KCMG, DSO.

The General had influence in high places and Royalty came to stay at Coft Castle. Skullion had once seen a queen mother dawdling majestically in the garden and had heard royal laughter from the stables. The General could put in a good word for him and more importantly a bad one for the new Master and, as an undergraduate, the then just Hon Cathcart D'Eath had been one of Skullion's Scholars.

Skullion never forgot his Scholars and there was little doubt that though they might have liked to, none of them forgot him. They owed him too much. It had been Skullion who had arranged the transactions and had acted as intermediary. On the one hand idle but influential undergraduates like the Hon Cathcart and on the other impecunious research graduates eking out a living giving supervision and grateful for the baksheesh Skullion brought their way. The weekly essay regularly handed in and startingly original for undergraduates so apparently ill-informed. Two pounds a week for an essay had served to subsidize some very important research. More than one doctorate owed everything to those two pounds. And finally Tripos by proxy, with Skullion's Scholars lounging in a King Street pub while in the Examination School their substitutes wrote answers to the questions with a mediocrity that was unexceptional. Skullion had been careful, very careful. Only one or two a year and in subjects so popular that there would be no noticing an unfamiliar face in the hundreds writing the exams. And it had worked. 'No one will be any the wiser,' he had assured the graduate substitutes to allay their fears before slipping five hundred, once a thousand, pounds into their pockets. And no one had been any the wiser. Certainly the Honourable Cathcart D'Eath had gone down with a two two in History with his ignorance of Disraeli's influence on the Conservative Party unimpaired in spite of having to all appearances written four pages on the subject. But what he had gained on the roundabout he had also gained on the swings and the study of horseflesh he had undertaken during those three years at Newmarket served him well in the future.

His use of cavalry in the Burmese jungle had unnerved the Japanese by its unadulterated lunacy and, combined with his name, had suggested a kamikaze element in the British army they had never suspected. Sir Cathcart had emerged from the campaign with twelve men and a reputation so scathed that he had been promoted to General to prevent the destruction of the entire army and the loss of India. Early retirement and his wartime experience of getting horses to attempt the impossible had encouraged Sir Cathcart to return to his first love and to take up training. His stables at Coft were world-famous. With what appeared to be a magical touch but owed in fact much to Skullion's gift for substitution, Sir Cathcart could transform a broken-winded nag into a winning two-year-old and had prospered accordingly. Coft Castle, standing in spacious grounds, was surrounded by a high wall to guard against intruding eyes and cameras and by an ornate garden in a remote corner of which was a small canning factory where the by-products of the General's stables were given discreet anonymity in Cathcart's Tinned Catfood. Skullion dismounted at the gate and knocked on the lodge door. A Japanese gardener, a prisoner of war, whom Sir Cathcart kept carefully ignorant of world news and who was, thanks to the language barrier, incapable of learning it for himself, opened the gate for him and Skullion cycled on down the drive to the house.

In spite of its name there was nothing remotely ancient about Coft Castle. Staunchly Edwardian, its red brick bespoke a lofty disregard for style and a concern for comfort on a grand scale. The General's Rolls-Royce, RIP 1, gleamed darkly on the gravel outside the front door. Skullion dismounted and pushed his bicycle round to the servants' entrance.

'Come to see the General,' he told the cook. Presently he was ushered into the drawing-room where Sir Cathcart was lolling in an armchair before a large coal fire.

'Not your usual afternoon, Skullion,' he said as Skullion came in, bowler hat in hand.

'No, sir. Came special,' said Skullion. The General waved him to a kitchen chair the cook brought in on these occasions and Skullion sat down and put his bowler hat on his knees.

'Carry on smoking,' Sir Cathcart told him. Skullion took out his pipe and filled it with black tobacco from a tin. Sir Cathcart watched him with grim affection.

'That's filthy stuff you smoke, Skullion,' he said as blue smoke drifted towards the chimney. 'Must have a constitution like an elephant to smoke it.'

Skullion puffed at his pipe contentedly. It was at moments like this, moments of informal subservience, that he felt happiest. Sitting smoking his pipe on the hard kitchen chair in Sir Cathcart D'Eath's drawing-room he felt approved. He basked in the General's genial disdain.

'That's a nice black eye you've got there,' Sir Cathcart said. 'You look as if you've been in the wars.'

'Yes, sir,' said Skullion. He was quite pleased with that black eye.

'Well, out with it, man, what have you come about?' Sir Cathcart said.

'It's the new Master. He made a speech at the Feast last night,' Skullion told him.

'A speech? At the Feast?' Sir Cathcart sat up in his chair.

'Yes, sir. I knew you wouldn't like it.'

'Disgraceful. What did he say?'

'Says he's going to change the College.'

Sir Cathcart's eyes bulged in his head. 'Change the College? What the devil does he mean by that? The damned place has been changed beyond all recognition already. Can't go in the place without seeing some long-haired lout looking more like a girl than a man. Swarming with bloody poofters. Change the College? There's only one change that's needed and that's back to the old ways. The old traditions. Cut their hair off and duck them in the fountain. That's what's needed. When I think what Porterhouse used to be and see what it's become, it makes my blood boil. It's the same with the whole damned country. Letting niggers in and keeping good white men out. Gone soft, that's what's happened. Soft in the head and soft in the body.' Sir Cathcart sank back in his chair limp from his denunciation of the times. Skullion smiled inwardly. It was just such bitterness he had come to hear. Sir Cathcart spoke with an authority Skullion could never have but which charged his own intransigence with a new vigour.

'Says he wants Porterhouse to be an open college,' he said, stoking the embers of the General's fury.

'Open college?' Sir Cathcart responded to the call. 'Open? What the devil does he mean by that? It's open enough already. Half the scum of the world in as it is.'

'I think he means more scholars,' Skullion said.

Sir Cathcart grew a shade more apoplectic.

'Scholars? That's half the trouble with the world today, scholarship. Too many damned intellectuals about who think they know how things should be done. Academics, bah! Can't win a war with thinking. Can't run a factory on thought. It needs guts and sweat and sheer hard work.

If I had my way I'd kick every damned scholar out of the College and put in some athletes to run the place properly. Anyone would think Varsity was some sort of school. In my day we didn't come up to learn anything, we came up to forget all the damned silly things we'd had pumped into us at school. My God, Skullion, I'll tell you this, a man can learn more between the thighs of a good woman than he ever needs to know. Scholarship's a waste of time and public money. What's more, it's iniquitous.' Exhausted by his outburst, Sir Cathcart stared belligerently into the fire.

'What's Fairbrother say?' he asked finally.

'The Dean, sir? He doesn't like it any more than you do, sir,' Skullion said, 'but he's not as young as he used to be, sir.'

'Don't suppose he is,' Sir Cathcart agreed.

'That's why I came to tell you, sir,' Skullion continued. 'I thought you'd know what to do.'

Sir Cathcart sniffed. 'Do? Don't see what I can do,' he said presently. 'I'll write to the Master, of course, but I've no influence in the College these days.'

'But you have outside, sir,' Skullion assured him.

'Well perhaps,' Sir Cathcart assented. 'All right I'll see what I can do. Keep me informed, Skullion.'

'Yes, sir. Thank you, sir.'

'Get Cook to give you some tea before you go,' Sir Cathcart told him and Skullion went out with his chair and took it back to the kitchen. Twenty minutes later he cycled off down the drive, spiritually resuscitated. Sir Cathcart would see there were no more changes. He had influence in high places. There was only one thing that puzzled Skullion as he rode home. Something Sir Cathcart had said about learning more between the thighs of a good woman than ... but Sir Cathcart had never married. Skullion wondered how an unmarried man got between the thighs of a good woman.

Zipser's interview with the Senior Tutor had left him with a sense of embarrassment that had unnerved him completely. His attempt to explain the nature of his compulsion had been fraught with difficulties. The Senior Tutor kept poking his little finger in his ear and wriggling it around and examining the end of it when he took it out while Zipser talked, as if he held some waxy deposit responsible for the flow of obscene information that was reaching his brain. When he finally accepted that his ears were not betraying him and that Zipser was in fact confessing to being attracted by his bedder, he had muttered something to the effect that the Chaplain would expect him for tea that afternoon and that, failing that, a good psychiatrist might help. Zipser had left miserably and had spent the early part of the afternoon in his room trying to concentrate on his thesis without success. The image of Mrs Biggs, a cross between a cherubim in menopause and booted succubus, kept intruding. Zipser turned for escape to a book of photographs of starving children in Nagaland but in spite of this mental flagellation Mrs Biggs prevailed. He tried Hermitsch on *Fall Out & the Andaman Islanders* and even *Sterilization, Vasectomy and Abortion* by Allard, but these holy writs all failed against the pervasive fantasy of the bedder. It was as if his social conscience, his concern for the plight of humanity at large, the universal and collective pity he felt for all mankind, had been breached in some unspeakably personal way by the inveterate triviality and egoism of Mrs Biggs. Zipser, whose life had been filled with a truly impersonal charity – he had spent holidays from school working for SOBB, the Save Our Black Brothers campaign – and whose third worldliness was impeccable, found himself suddenly the victim of a sexual idiosyncrasy which made a mockery of his universalism. In desperation he turned to *Syphilis, the Scourge of Colonialism*, and stared with horror at the pictures. In the past it had worked like a charm to quell incipient sexual desires while satisfying his craving for evidence of natural justice. The notion of the Conquistadores dying of the disease after raping South American Indians no longer had its old appeal now that Zipser himself was in the grip of a compulsive urge to rape Mrs Biggs. By the time it came for him to go to the Chaplain's rooms for tea, Zipser had exhausted the resources of his theology. So too, it seemed, had the Chaplain.

'Ah my boy,' the Chaplain boomed as Zipser negotiated the bric-à-brac that filled the Chaplain's sitting-room. 'So good of you to come. Do make yourself comfortable.' Zipser nudged past a gramophone with a paper-mâché horn, circumvented a brass-topped table with fretsawed legs, squeezed beneath the fronds of a castor-oil plant and finally sat down on a chair by the fire. The Chaplain scuttled backwards and forwards between his bathroom and the teatable muttering loudly to himself a liturgy of things to fetch. 'Teapot hot. Spoons. Milk jug. You do take milk?' 'Yes, thank you,' said Zipser. 'Good. Good. So many people take lemon, don't they? One always forgets these things. Teacosy. Sugar basin.' Zipser looked round the room for some indication of the Chaplain's interests but the welter of conflicting objects, like the addition of random numbers to a code, made interpretation impossible. Apart from senility the furnishings had so little in common that they seemed to indicate a wholly catholic taste.

'Crumpets,' said the Chaplain scurrying out of the bathroom. 'Just the thing. You toast them.' He speared a crumpet on the end of a toasting-fork and thrust the fork into Zipser's hand. Zipser poked the crumpet at the fire tentatively and felt once again that dissociation from reality that seemed so much a part of life in Cambridge. It was as if everyone in the College sought to parody himself, as if a parody of a parody could become itself a new reality. Behind him the Chaplain stumbled over a footrest and deposited a jar of honey with a boom on the brass-topped table. Zipser removed the crumpet, blackened on one side and ice cold on the other, and put it on a plate. He toasted another while the Chaplain tried to spread butter on the one he had half done. By the time they had finished Zipser's face was burning from the fire and his hands were sticky with a mixture of melted butter and honey. The Chaplain sat back in his chair and filled his pipe from a tobacco jar with the Porterhouse crest on it.

'Do help yourself, my dear boy,' said the Chaplain, pushing the jar towards him.

'I don't smoke.'

The Chaplain shook his head sadly. 'Everyone should smoke a pipe,' he said. 'Calms the nerves. Puts things in perspective. Couldn't do without mine.' He leant back, puffing vigorously. Zipser stared at him through a haze of smoke.

'Now then where were we?' he asked. Zipser tried to think. 'Ah yes, your little problem, that's right,' said the Chaplain finally. 'I knew there was something.'

Zipser stared into the fire resentfully.

'The Senior Tutor said something about it. I didn't gather very much but then I seldom do. Deafness, you know?'

Zipser nodded sympathetically.

'The affliction of the elderly. That and rheumatism. It's the damp, you know. Comes up from the river. Very unhealthy living so close to the Fens.' His pipe percolated gently. In the comparative silence Zipser tried to think what to say. The Chaplain's age and his evident physical disabilities made it difficult for Zipser to conceive that he could begin to understand the problem of Mrs Biggs.

'I really think there's been a misunderstanding,' he began hesitantly and stopped. It was evident from the look on the Chaplain's face that there was no understanding at all.

'You'll have to speak up,' the Chaplain boomed. 'I'm really quite deaf.'

'I can see that,' Zipser said. The Chaplain beamed at him.

'Don't hesitate to tell me,' he said. 'Nothing you say can shock me.'

'I'm not surprised,' Zipser said.

The Chaplain's smile remained insistently benevolent. 'I know what we'll do,' he said, hopping to his feet and reaching behind his chair. 'It's something I use for confession sometimes.' He emerged holding a loudhailer and handed it to Zipser. 'Press the trigger when you're going to speak.'

Zipser held the thing up to his mouth and stared at the Chaplain over the rim. 'I really don't think this is going to help,' he said finally. His words reverberated through the room and set the teapot rattling on the brass table.

'Of course it is,' shouted the Chaplain, 'I can hear perfectly.'

'I didn't mean that,' Zipser said desperately. The fronds of the castor-oil plant quivered ponderously. 'I meant I don't think it's going to help to talk about ...' He left the dilemma of Mrs Biggs unspoken.

The Chaplain smiled in absolution and puffed his pipe vigorously. 'Many of the young men who come to see me,' he said, invisible in a cloud of smoke, 'suffer from feelings of guilt about masturbation.'

Zipser stared frantically at the smoke screen. 'Masturbation? Who said anything about masturbation?' he bawled into the loudhailer. It was apparent someone had. His words, hideously amplified, billowed forth from the room and across the Court outside. Several undergraduates by the fountain turned and stared up at the Chaplain's windows. Deafened by his own vociferousness, Zipser sat sweating with embarrassment.

'I understood from the Senior Tutor that you wanted to see me about a sexual problem,' the Chaplain shouted.

Zipser lowered the loudhailer. The thing clearly had disadvantages.

'I can assure you I don't masturbate,' he said.

The Chaplain looked at him incomprehendingly. 'You press the trigger when you want to speak,' he explained. Zipser nodded dumbly. The knowledge that to communicate with the Chaplain at all he had to announce his feelings for Mrs Biggs to the world at large presented him with a terrible dilemma made no less intolerable by the Chaplain's shouted replies.

'It often helps to get these things into the open,' the Chaplain assured him. Zipser had his doubts about that. Admissions of the sort he had to make broadcast through a loudhailer were not likely to be of any help at all. He might just as well go and propose to the wretched woman straightaway and be done with it. He sat with lowered head while the Chaplain boomed on.

'Don't forget that anything you tell me will be heard in the strictest confidence,' he shouted. 'You need have no fears that it will go any further.'

'Oh sure,' Zipser muttered. Outside in the Quad a small crowd of undergraduates had gathered by the fountain to listen.

Half an hour later Zipser left the room, his demoralization quite complete. At least he could congratulate himself that he had revealed nothing of his true feelings and the Chaplain's kindly probings, his tentative questions, had elicited no response. Zipser had sat silently through a sexual catechism only bothering to shake his head when the Chaplain broached particularly obscene topics. In the end he had listened to a lyrical description of the advantages of au pair girls. It was obvious that the Chaplain regarded foreign girls as outside the sexual canons of the Church.

'So much less danger of a permanently unhappy involvement,' he had shouted, 'and after all I often think that's what they come here for. Ships that pass in the night and not on one's own doorstep you know.' He paused and smiled at Zipser salaciously. 'We all have to sow our wild oats at some time or other and it's much better to do it abroad. I've often thought that's what Rupert Brooke had in mind in that line of his about some corner of a foreign field. Mind you, one can hardly say that he was particularly healthy, come to think of it, but there we are. That's my advice to you, dear boy. Find a nice Swedish girl, I'm told they're very good, and have a ball. I believe that's the modern idiom. Yes, Swedes or French, depending on your taste. Spaniards are a bit difficult, I'm told, and then again they tend to be rather hairy. Still, buggers can't be choosers as dear old Sir Winston said at the queer's wedding. Ha, ha.'

Zipser staggered from the room. He knew now what muscular Christianity meant. He went down the dark staircase and was about to go out into the Court when he saw the group standing by the fountain. Zipser turned and fled up the stairs and locked himself in the lavatory on the top landing. He was still there an hour later when First Hall began.

CHAPTER SIX

Sir Godber dined at home. He was still recovering from the gastric consequences of the Feast and in any case the Bursar's revelations had disinclined him to the company of the Fellows until he had formulated his plans more clearly. He had spent the afternoon considering various schemes for raising money and had made several telephone calls to financial friends in the City to ask their advice and to put up proposals of his own but without success. Blomberg's Bank had been prepared to endow several Research Fellowships in Accountancy but even Sir Godber doubted if such generosity would materially alter the intellectual climate of Porterhouse. He had even considered offering the American Phosgene Corp. facilities for research into nerve gas, facilities they had been denied by all American universities, in return for a really large endowment but he suspected that the resultant publicity and student protest would destroy his already tenuous liberal reputation. Publicity was much on his mind. At five o'clock the BBC phoned to ask if he would appear on a panel of leading educationalists to answer questions on financial priority in Education. Sir Godber was sorely tempted to agree but refused on the grounds that he had hardly acquired much experience. He put the phone down reluctantly and wondered what effect his announcement to several million viewers that Porterhouse College was in the habit of selling degrees to rich young layabouts would have had. It was a pleasing thought and gave rise in the Master's mind to an even more satisfying conclusion. He picked up the phone again and spoke to the Bursar.

'Could we arrange a College Council meeting for tomorrow afternoon? Say two-thirty?' he asked.

'It's rather short notice, Master,' the Bursar replied.

'Good. Two-thirty it is then,' Sir Godber said with iron geniality and replaced the receiver. He sat back and began to draw up a list of innovations. Candidates to be chosen by academic achievement only. The kitchen endowment to be cut by three-quarters and the funds reallocated to scholarships. Women undergraduates to be admitted as members. Gate hours abolished. College playing fields open to children from the town. Sir Godber's imagination raced on compiling proposals with no thought for the financial implications. They would have to find the money somewhere and he didn't much care where. The main thing was that he had the Fellows over a barrel. They might protest but there was nothing they could do to stop him. They had placed a weapon in his hands. He smiled to himself at the thought of their faces when he explained the alternatives tomorrow. At six-thirty he went through to the drawing-room where Lady Mary, who had been chairing a committee on Teenage Delinquency, was writing letters.

'Be with you in a minute,' she said when Sir Godber asked her if she would like a sherry. He looked at her dubiously. There were times when he wondered if his wife was ever with him. Her mind followed a wholly independent course and was ever concentrated on the more distressing aspects of other people's lives. Sir Godber poured himself a large whisky.

'Well, I think I've got them by the short hairs,' he said when she finally stopped tapping at her typewriter.

Lady Mary's lean tongue lubricated the flap of an envelope. 'Non-specific urethritis is reaching epidemic proportions among school-leavers,' she said. Sir Godber ignored the interjection. He couldn't for the life of him see what it had to do with the College. He pursued his own topic. 'I'm going to show them that I'm not prepared to be a cipher.'

'Surveys show that one in every five children has . . .'

'I haven't ended my career in politics only to be pushed into a sinecure,' Sir Godber contended.

'That's not the problem,' Lady Mary agreed.

'What isn't?' Sir Godber asked momentarily interested by her assertion.

'Cure. Easy enough. What we've got to get at is the moral delinquency . . .'

Sir Godber drank his whisky and tried not to listen. There were times when he wondered if he would ever have succeeded as a politician without the help of his wife. Without her incessant preoccupation with unsavoury statistics and sordid social problems, late-night sittings in the House might have had less appeal and committees less utility. Would he have made so many passionate speeches or spoken with such urgency if Lady Mary had been prepared to listen to one word he said at home? He rather doubted it. They went into dinner and Sir Godber passed the time as usual by counting the number of times she said Must and Our Duty. The Musts won by fifty-four to forty-eight. Not bad for the course.

After he had heard the Chaplain go down to Hall, Zipser slipped out of the lavatory and went to his room. There was no sign of the little crowd of undergraduates who had been gathered in the Court when he first went down and he hoped no one would find out who had been talking, if that was the right word, to the Chaplain. The tendency he shared with the Master's wife to think in wholly impersonal terms about world issues had quite deserted him. During his hour in the lavatory he had taken the Chaplain's advice and had attempted to interpose the image of a Swedish girl between himself and Mrs Biggs. Every time Mrs Biggs intruded he concentrated on the slim buttocks and breasts of a Swedish actress he had seen once in *Playboy* and to some extent the practice had worked. Not entirely. The Swede tended to swell and to assume unnatural proportions until she was displaced by a smiling Mrs Biggs, but the series of little respites was encouraging and suggested that a substantial Swede might be even more effective. He would take the Chaplain's advice and find an au pair girl or a language student and ... and ... well ... and. Zipser's lack of sexual experience prevented him from formulating at all clearly what he would do then. Well, he would copulate with her. Having arrived at this neat if somewhat abstract conclusion he felt better. It was certainly preferable to raping Mrs Biggs, which seemed the only alternative. As usual Zipser had no doubts about rape. It was a brutal, violent act of assertive masculinity, a loosening of savage instinctual forces, passionate and bestial. He would hurl Mrs Biggs to the floor and thrust himself ... With an effort of will he dragged his imagination back from the scene and thought aseptically about copulating with a Swede.

A number of difficulties immediately presented themselves. First and foremost he knew no Swedes, and secondly he had never copulated with anyone. He knew a great many intense young women who shared his concern for the fate of mankind and who were prepared to talk about birth control into the early hours of the morning but they were all English and their preoccupation with mankind's problems had seemed to preclude any interest in him. In any case Zipser had scruples on aesthetic grounds about asking any of them to act as a substitute Mrs Biggs, and rather doubted their efficacy in the role. It would have to be a Swede. With the abstract calculation that was implicit in his whole approach Zipser decided that he would probably be able to find a promiscuous Swede in the Cellar Bar. He wrote it down and put as an alternative the Ali Baba Discothèque. That dealt with the first problem. He would fill her up with wine, Portuguese white would do, and bring her back to his room. All quite simple. With her cooperation the sexual spectre of Mrs Biggs would lose its force. He went to bed early having set the alarm for seven o'clock so as to be up and out before the bedder arrived – and before he fell asleep realized that he had forgotten an important detail. He would need some contraceptives. He'd go and have his hair cut in the morning and get some.

Skullion sat in front of the gas fire in the Porter's Lodge and smoked his pipe. His visit to Coft Castle had eased his mind. The General would use his influence to see that the Master didn't make any changes. You could rely on the General. One of the old brigade, and rich too. The sort that always gave you a big tip at the end of term. Skullion had had some big tips in his time and he had put them all away in his bank with the shares old Lord Wurford had left him in his will and had never touched them. He lived off his salary and what he earned on his night off as a steward at the Fox Club. There had been some big takings there too in his time; the Maharajah of Indpore had once given him fifty quid after a day at the races, when a tip from Sir Cathcart's stable-boy had paid off. Skullion considered the Maharahjah quite a gent, a compliment he paid to few Indians, but then a Maharahah wasn't a proper Indian, was he? Maharajahs were Princes of the Empire and as far as Skullion was concerned wogs in the Empire were quite different from wogs outside it and wogs in the Fox Club wasn't wogs at all or they wouldn't be members. The intricate system of social classification in Skullion's mind graded everyone. He could place a man within a hair's breadth in the social scale by the tone of his voice or even the look in his eye. Some people thought you could depend on the cut of a man's coat but Skullion knew better. It wasn't externals that mattered, it was something much more indefinable, an inner quality which Skullion couldn't explain but which he recognized immediately. And responded to. It had something to do with assurance, a certainty of oneself which nothing could shake. There were lots of intermediate stages between this ineffable superiority and the manifest inferiority of, say, the kitchen staff, but Skullion could sense them all and put them in the right place. There was money by itself, brash and full of itself but easily deflated. There was two-generation money with a bit of land. Usually a bit pompous, that was. There was County rich and poor. Skullion noted the distinction but tended to ignore it. Some of the best families had come down in the world and so long as the confidence was there, money didn't count, not in Skullion's eyes anyway. In fact confidence without money was preferable, it indicated a genuine quality and was accordingly revered. Then there were various degrees of uncertainty, nuances of self-doubt that went unnoticed by most people but which Skullion spotted immediately. Flickers of residual deference immediately suppressed – but too late to be missed by Skullion. Doctors' and lawyers' sons. Professional classes and treated respectfully. Still public school anyway, and graded from Eton and Winchester downwards. Below public school Skullion lost all interest, according only slight respect if there was money in it for him. But at the top of the scale above all these distinctions there was an assurance so ineffable that it seemed almost to merge into its opposite Real quality, Skullion called it, or even the old aristocracy to distinguish it from mere titular nobility. These were the saints of his calendar, the touchstone against which all other men were finally judged. Even Sir Cathcart was not of their number. In fact Skullion had to admit that he was fundamentally of the fourth rank, though near the top of it, and that was high praise considering how many ranks Skullion had in his mind. No, the real quality were without Sir Cathcart's harshness. There was often an unassuming quality about the saints which less perceptive porters than Skullion mistook for timidity and social insecurity but which he knew to be a sign of breeding, and not to be taken advantage of. It accorded his servility the highest accolade, this helplessness that was quite unforced, and gave him the sure knowledge that he was needed. Under the cover of that helplessness Skullion could have moved mountains, and frequently had to in the way of luggage and furniture, humping it up staircases and round corners and arranging it first here and then there while its owner, graciously indecisive, tried to make up what there was of his mind where it would look best. From such expeditions Skullion would emerge with a temporary lordliness as if touched by grace and would recall such services rendered in years to come with the feeling that he had been privileged to attend an almost spiritual occasion. In Skullion's social hagiography two names stood out as the epitome of the effeteness he worshipped, Lord Pimpole and Sir Launcelot Gutterby, and at moments of contemplation Skullion would repeat their names to himself like some repetitive prayer. He was in the process of this incantation and had reached his twentieth 'Pimpole and Gutterby' when the Lodge door opened and Arthur, who waited at High Table, came in.

'Evening, Arthur,' said Skullion condescendingly.

'Evening,' said Arthur.

'Going off home?' Skullion inquired.

'Got something for you,' Arthur told him, leaning confidentially over the counter.

Skullion looked up. Arthur's attendance at High table was a source of much of his information about the College. He rose and came over to the counter. 'Oh ah,' he said.

'They're in a tizz whizz tonight,' Arthur said. 'Proper tizz-whizz.'

'Go on,' said Skullion encouragingly.

'Bursar come in to dinner all flushed and flummoxy and the Dean's got them high spots on his cheeks he gets when his gander's up and the Tutor don't eat his soup. Not like him to turn up his soup,' Arthur said.

Skullion grunted his agreement. 'So I know something's up.' Arthur paused for effect. 'Know what it is?' he asked.

Skullion shook his head. 'No. What is it?' he said.

Arthur smiled. 'Master's called a College Council for tomorrow. The Bursar said it wasn't convenient and the Master said to call it just the same and they don't like it. They don't like it at all. Put them off their dinner it did, the new Master acting all uppity like that, telling them what to do just when they thought they'd got him where they wanted him. Bursar said he'd told the Master they hadn't got the money for all the changes he has in mind and the Master seemed to have taken it, but then he rings the Bursar up and tells him to call the meeting.'

'Can't call a College Council all of a sudden,' Skullion said, 'Council meets on the first Thursday of every month.'

'That's what the Dean said and the Tutor. But the Master wouldn't have it. Got to be tomorrow. Bursar rang him up and said Dean and Tutor wouldn't attend like they'd told him and Master said that was all right with him but that the meeting would be tomorrow whether they were there or not.' Arthur shook his head mournfully over the Master's wilfulness. 'It ain't right all this telling people what to do.'

Skullion scowled at him. 'The Master come to dinner?' he asked.

'No,' said Arthur, 'he don't stir from the Lodge. Just telephones his orders to the Bursar.' He glanced significantly at the switchboard in the corner. Skullion nodded pensively.

'So he's going ahead with his changes,' he said at last.

'And they thought they'd got him where they wanted him, eh?'

'That's what they said,' Arthur assured him. 'Bursar said he wasn't going to do nothing and then he suddenly calls the meeting.'

'What's the Dean say to all this?' Skullion asked.

'Says they've all got to stick together. Mind you, he didn't have much to say tonight. Too upset by the look of him. But that's what he's said before.'

'Don't suppose the Tutor agrees with him,' Skullion suggested.

'He do now. Didn't before but this being told to attend the meeting has got him on the raw. Don't like that at all, the Tutor don't.'

Skullion nodded. 'Ah well, that's something,' he said. 'It isn't like him to side with the Dean. Bursar agree?'

'Bursar says he does but you never can tell with him, can you?' Arthur said. 'He's a slippery sod, he is. One moment this, the next moment something else. You can't rely on him.'

'Got no bottom, the Bursar,' said Skullion, drawing on the language of the late Lord Wurford for his judgement.

'Ah, is that what it is?' Arthur said. He gathered up his coat. 'Got to be getting along now.'

Skullion saw him to the door. 'Thank you, Arthur,' he said. 'Very useful that is.'

'Glad to be of service,' Arthur said, 'besides I don't want any changes in the College any more than you do. Too old for changes, I am. Twenty-five years I've waited at High Table and fifteen years before that I was ...'

Skullion shut the door on old Arthur's reminiscences and went back to the fire. So the Master was going ahead with his plans. Well it wasn't a bad thing he'd ordered the College Council for tomorrow. It had got the Dean and the Senior Tutor to agree for the first time in years. That was something in itself. They had hated one another's guts for years, ever since the Dean had preached a sermon on the text, 'Many that are first shall be last', when the Tutor had first begun to coach the Porterhouse Boat. Skullion smiled to himself at the memory. The Tutor had come storming out of Chapel with his gown billowing behind him like the wrath of God and had worked the eight so hard they were past their peak by the time of the May Bumps. Porterhouse had been bumped three times that year and had lost the Head of the River. He'd never forgiven the Dean that sermon. Never agreed with him about anything since and now the Master had got their backs up. Well, it was an ill wind that blew no good. And anyway there was always Sir Cathcart in the wings to put his oar in if the Master went too far. Skullion went out and shut the gate and went to bed. Outside it was snowing again. Damp flakes flicked against the windows and ran in runnels of water down the panes. 'Pimpole and Gutterby,' murmured Skullion for the last time, and fell asleep.

Zipser slept fitfully and was awake before the alarm clock went off at seven. He dressed and made himself some coffee before going out and he was just cutting himself some bread in the gyp room when Mrs Biggs arrived.

'You're up early for a change,' she said, easing herself through the door of the tiny gyp room.

'What are you doing here now?' Zipser demanded belligerently. 'You shouldn't come till eight.'

Mrs Biggs, fulsome in a red mackintosh, smiled dreadfully. 'I can come any time I want to,' she said with quite unnecessary emphasis. Zipser needed no telling. He writhed against the sink and stared helplessly into the acres of her smile. Mrs Biggs unbuttoned her mac slowly with one hand like a gargantuan stripper and Zipser's eyes followed her down. Her breasts swarmed in her blouse as she slipped the mac over her shoulders. Zipser's eyes salivated over them.

'Here, help me with the arms,' Mrs Biggs said, wedging herself round so that she had her back to him. Zipser hesitated a moment and then, impelled by a fearful and uncontrollable urge, lunged forward.

'Here,' said Mrs Biggs somewhat surprised by the frenzy of his assistance and the unusual whinnying sounds Zipser was making, 'the arms I said. What do you think you're doing?' Zipser floundered in the folds of her mac unable to think at all let alone what he was doing. His mind was ablaze with overwhelming desire. As he thrust himself into the red inferno of Mrs Biggs's raincoat, the bedder hunched herself and then heaved. Zipser fell back against the sink and Mrs Biggs issued into the hall. Between them on the gyp-room floor, like the plastic afterbirth of some terrible delivery, the disputed raincoat slowly subsided.

'Goodness gracious me,' said Mrs Biggs recovering her composure, 'you want to be more careful. You might give people the wrong idea.'

Zipser huddled in the corner of the gyp room breathing heavily hoped desperately that Mrs Biggs didn't get the right idea.

'I'm sorry,' he mumbled, 'I must have slipped. Don't know what came over me.'

'Wonder you didn't come all over me,' Mrs Biggs said coarsely. 'Throwing yourself about like that.' She plummeted over and picked up the raincoat and, trailing it behind her like a bull fighter's cape, marched into the other room. Zipser stared at her boots with a fresh surge of longing and hurried downstairs. The need for a girl his own age to take his body off the bedder had become imperative. He had to do something to escape the temptation presented by Mrs Biggs's extensive charms or he would find himself before the Dean. Zipser could think of nothing worse than being sent down from Porterhouse for 'the attempted rape of a bedder'. Or only one thing. The successful accomplishment of rape. That would be a police-court matter. He would kill himself sooner than face that humiliation.

'Good morning, sir,' Skullion called out as he passed the Lodge.

'Good morning,' said Zipser and went out of the gate. He had over an hour to wait before the barbers' shops opened. He walked along the river to kill time and envied the ducks, sleeping on the banks, their uncomplicated existence.

Mrs Biggs tucked the sheets under the mattress of Zipser's bed with a practised hand and plumped his pillow with a mitigated force that was almost tender. She was feeling rather pleased with herself. It had been some years since Mr Biggs had passed on, consigned to an early grave by his wife's various appetites, and even longer since anyone had paid her the compliment of finding her attractive. Zipser's clumsy advances had not escaped her attention. The fact that he followed her about from room to room as she worked and that his eyes were seldom off her were signs too obvious to be ignored. 'Poor boy misses his mum,' she had thought at first and had noted Zipser's solitariness as an indication of homesickness. But his recent behaviour had suggested less remote causes for his interest. The bedder's fancy ignored the weather and lumbered to thoughts of love. 'Don't be silly,' she told herself. 'What would he see in you?' But the notion remained and Mrs Biggs' sense of propriety began to adapt itself to the incongruities of the situation. She had begun to dress accordingly and to pay more attention to her looks and even, as she went from room to room and bed to bed, to indulge her imagination a little. The episode in the gyp room had confirmed her best suspicions. 'Fancy now,' she said to herself, 'and him such a nice young fellow too. Who'd have guessed?' She looked at herself in the mirror and primped her hair with a heavy hand.

At nine-fifteen Zipser took his seat in the barber's chair.

'Just a trim,' he told the barber.

The man looked at his head doubtfully.

'Wouldn't like a nice short back and sides, I don't suppose?' he asked mournfully.

'Just a trim, thank you,' Zipser told him.

The barber tucked the sheet into his collar. 'Don't know why some of you young fellows bother to have your hair cut at all,' he said. 'Seem determined to put us out of business.'

'I'm sure you still get lots of work,' Zipser said.

The barber's scissor clicked busily round his ears. Zipser stared at himself in the mirror and wondered once again at the disparity between his innocent apperance and the terrible passion which surged inside him. His eyes moved sideways to the rows of bottles, Eau de Portugal, Dr Linthrop's Dandruff Mixture, Vitalis, a jar of Pomade. Who on earth used Pomade? Behind him the barber was chattering on about football but Zipser wasn't listening. He was eyeing the glass case to his left where a box in one corner suggested the reason for his haircut. He couldn't move his head so that he wasn't sure what the box contained but it looked the right sort of box. Finally when the man moved forward to pick up the clippers Zipser turned his head and saw that he had been eyeing with quite pointless interest a box of razor blades. He turned his head further and scanned the shelves. Shaving creams, razors, lotions, combs, all were there in abundance but not a single carton of contraceptives.

Zipser sat on in a trance while the clippers buzzed on his neck. They must keep the damned things somewhere. Every hairdresser had them. His face in the mirror assumed a new uncertainty. By the time the barber had finished and was powdering his neck and waving a handmirror behind him, Zipser was in no mood to be critical of the result. He got out of the chair and waved the barber's brush away impatiently.

'That'll be thirty pence, sir,' the barber said, and made out a ticket. Zipser dug into his pocket for the money. 'Is there anything else?' Now was the moment he had been waiting for. The open invitation. That 'anything else' of the barber had covered only too literally a multitude of sins. In Zipser's case it was hopelessly inadequate not to say misleading.

'I'll have five packets of Durex,' Zipser said with a strangled bellow.

'Afraid we can't help you,' said the man. 'Landlord's a Catholic. It's in the lease we're not allowed to stock them.'

Zipser paid and went out into the street, cursing himself for not having looked in the window to see if there were any contraceptives on display. He walked into Rose Crescent and stared into a chemist's shop but the place was full of women. He tried three more shops only to find that they were all either full of housewives or that the shop assistants were young females. Finally he went into a barber's shop in Sidney Street where the window display was sufficiently broad-minded.

Two chairs were occupied and Zipser stood uncertainly just inside the door waiting for the barber to attend to him. As he stood there the door behind him opened and someone came in. Zipser stepped to one side and found himself looking into the face of Mr Turton, his supervisor.

'Ah, Zipser, getting your hair cut?' It seemed an unnecessarily inquisitive remark to Zipser. He felt inclined to tell the wretched man to mind his own busines. Instead he nodded dumbly and sat down.

'Next one,' said the barber. Zipser feigned politeness.

'Won't you . . .?' he said to Mr Turton.

'Your need is greater than mine, my dear fellow,' the supervisor said and sat down and picked up a copy of *Titbits*. For the second time that morning Zipser found himself in a barber's chair.

'Any particular way?' the barber asked.

'Just a trim,' said Zipser.

The barber bellied the sheet out over his knees and tucked it into his collar.

'If you don't mind my saying so, sir,' he said, 'but I'd say you'd already had your hair cut this morning.'

Zipser, staring into the mirror, saw Mr Turton look up and his own face turn bright red.

'Certainly not,' he muttered. 'What on earth makes you think that?' It was not a wise remark and Zipser regretted it before he had finished mumbling.

'Well, for one thing,' the barber went on, responding to this challenge to his powers of observation, 'you've still got powder on your neck.' Zipser said shortly that he'd had a bath and used talcum powder.

'Oh quite,' said the barber sarcastically, 'and I suppose all these clipper shavings . . .'

'Listen,' said Zipser conscious that Mr Turton has still not turned back to *Titbits* and was listening with interest, 'if you don't want to cut my hair . . .' The buzz of the clippers interrupted his protest. Zipser stared angrily at his reflection in the mirror and wondered why he was being dogged by embarrassing situations. Mr Turton was eyeing the back of his head with a new interest.

'I mean,' said the barber putting his clippers away, 'some people like having their hair cut.' He winked at Mr Turton and in the mirror Zipser saw that wink. The scissors clicked round his ears and Zipser shut his eyes to escape the reproach he saw in them in the mirror. Everything he did now seemed tinged with catastrophe. Why in God's name should he fall in love with an enormous bedder? Why couldn't he just get on with his work, read in the library, write his thesis and go to meetings of CUNA?

'Had a customer once,' continued the barber remorselessly, 'who used to have his hair cut three times a week. Mondays, Wednesdays and Fridays. Regular as clockwork. I asked him once, when he'd been coming for a couple of years mind you, I said to him, "Tell me, Mr Hattersley, why do you come and have your hair cut so often?" Know what he said? Said it was the one place he could think. Said he got all his best ideas in the barber's chair. Weird when you think about it. Here I stand all day clipping and cutting and right in front of me, under my hand you might say, there's all those thoughts going on unbeknown to me. I mean I must have cut the hair on over a hundred thousand heads in my time. I've been cutting hair for twenty-five years now and that's a lot of customers. Stands to reason some of them must have been having some pretty peculiar thoughts at the time. Murderers and sex maniacs I daresay. I mean there would be, wouldn't there in all that number? Stands to reason.'

Zipser shrank in the chair. Mr Turton had lost all interest in *Titbits* now.

'Interesting theory,' he said encouragingly. 'I suppose statistically you're right. I've never thought of it that way before.'

Zipser said it took all sorts to make a world. It seemed the sort of trite remark the occasion demanded. By the time the barber had finished, he had given up all thought of asking for contraceptives. He paid the thirty pence and staggered out of the shop. Mr Turton smiled and took his place in the chair.

It was almost lunchtime.

CHAPTER SEVEN

'I think we can dispense with formalities,' the Master said sitting forward in his chair and looking down the long mahogany table. On his left the Bursar fiddled with his pen while on his right the Chaplain, accorded this position by virtue of his deafness, nodded his agreement. Down the long table the faces of the Council reflected their displeasure at this sudden meeting.

'It would appear to me,' said the Dean, 'that we have already dispensed with such formalities as we are used to. I can see no virtue in ridding ourselves of the few that are left.'

The Master regarded him closely. 'Bear with me, Dean,' he said, aware that he was relapsing from his carefully rehearsed down-to-earth manner into the vernacular of academic bitchiness. He pulled himself up. 'I have called this meeting,' he continued with a nasty smile, 'to discuss in detail the changes in the College I mentioned in my speech on Tuesday night. I shan't keep you long. When I have finished you can go away and think about my suggestions.' A ripple of indignation at the effrontery of his remark ran round the table. The Dean in particular lost his cool.

'The Master seems to be under some misapprehension as to the purpose of the College Council,' he said. 'May I remind him that it is the governing body of the College. We have been summoned here this afternoon at short notice and we have come at considerable inconvenience to ourselves . . .' The Master yawned. 'Quite so. Quite so,' he murmured. The Dean's face turned a deeper shade of puce. A virtuoso in the art of the discourteous aside, he had never been subjected to such disrespect.

'I think,' said the Senior Tutor stepping into the breach, 'that it should be left to the Council to decide whether or not the Master's proposals merit discussion this afternoon.' He smiled unctuously at the Master.

'As you wish,' said Sir Godber. He looked at his watch. 'I shall be here until three. If after that you have things you wish to discuss, you will have to do so without me.' He paused. 'We can meet again tomorrow or the next day. I shall be available in the afternoon.'

He looked down the table at the suffused faces of the Fellows and felt satisfied. The atmosphere was just what he had wanted for the announcement of his plans. They would react predictably and with a violence that would disarm them. Then when it would appear to be all over he would nullify all their protests with a threat. It was a charming prospect made all the more pleasing by the knowledge that they would misinterpret his motives. They would, they would. Obtuse men, small men for whom Porterhouse was the world and Cambridge the universe. Sir Godber despised them, and it showed.

'If we are all agreed then,' he continued, ignoring the titubation of the Dean who had been nerving himself to protest at the Master's incivility and leave the meeting, 'let me outline the changes I have in mind. In the first place, as you are all aware, Porterhouse's reputation has declined sadly since ... I believe the rot set in in 1933. I have been told there was a poor intake of Fellows in that year. Correct me if I'm wrong.'

It was the turn of the Senior Tutor to stiffen in his seat. 1933 had been the year of his election.

'Academically our decline seems to have set in then. The quality of our undergraduates has always seemed to me to be quite deplorable. I intend to change all that. From now on, from this year of Grace, we shall accept candidates who possess academic qualifications alone.' He paused to allow the information to sink in. When the Bursar ceased twitching in his chair, he continued. 'That is my first point. The second is to announce that the College will become a co-educational institution from the beginning of the forthcoming academic year. Yes, gentlemen, from the beginning of next year there will be women living in Porterhouse.' A gasp, almost a belch of shock, broke from the Fellows. The Dean buried his face in his hands and the Senior Tutor put both his hands on the edge of the table to steady himself. Only the Chaplain spoke.

'I heard that,' he bellowed, his face radiant as if with divine revelation, 'I heard it. Splendid news. Not before time either.' He relapsed into silence. The Master beamed. 'I accept your approval, Chaplain,' he said, 'with thanks. It is good to know that I have support from such an unexpected quarter. Thirdly ...'

'I protest,' shouted the Senior Tutor, half rising to his feet. Sir Godber cut him short.

'Later,' he snapped and the Senior Tutor dropped back into his seat. 'Thirdly, the practice of dining in Hall will be abandoned. A self-service canteen run by an outside catering firm will be established in the Hall. There will be no High Table. All forms of academic segregation will disappear. Yes Dean ...?'

But the Dean was speechless. His face livid and congested he had started to protest only to slump in his chair. The Senior Tutor hurried to his side while the Chaplain, always alert to the possibilities provided by a stricken audience, bellowed words of comfort into the insensible Dean's ear. Only the Master remained unmoved.

'Not, I trust, another Porterhouse Blue,' he said audibly to the Bursar, and looked at his watch, with calculated unconcern. To the Dean Sir Godber's manifest lack of interest in his demise came as a stimulant. His face grew pale and his breathing less sibilant. He opened his eyes and stared with loathing down the table at the Master.

'As I was saying,' continued Sir Godber, picking up the threads of his speech, 'the measures I have proposed will transform Porterhouse at a stroke.' He paused and smiled at the appositeness of the phrase. The Fellows stared at this fresh evidence of gaucherie. Even the Chaplain, imbued with the spirit of goodwill and deaf to the world's wickedness, was appalled by the Master's sang-froid.

'Porterhouse will regain its rightful place in the forefront of colleges,' the Master went on in a manner now recognizably political. 'No longer will we stumble on hamstrung by the obsolescence of outmoded tradition and class prejudice, by the limitations of the past and the cynicism of the present, but inspired by confidence in the future we shall prove ourselves worthy of the great trust that has been bequeathed us.' He sat down, inspired by his own brief eloquence. It was clear that nobody else present shared his enthusiasm for the future. When at last someone spoke it was the Bursar.

'There do appear to be one or two problems involved in this ... er ... transformation,' he pointed out. 'Not insuperable, I daresay, but nevertheless worth mentioning before we all become too enthusiastic.'

The Master surfaced from his reverie. 'Such as?' he said shortly.

The Bursar pursed his lips. 'Quite apart from the foreseeable difficulties of getting this ... er ... legislation accepted by the Council, I use the term advisedly you understand, there is the question of finance to consider. We are not a rich college ...' He hesitated. The Master had raised an eyebrow.

'I am not unused to the argument,' he said urbanely. 'In a long career in government I had heard it put forward on too many occasions to be wholly convinced that the plea of poverty is as formidable as it sounds. It is precisely the rich who use it most frequently.'

The Bursar was driven to interrupt. 'I can assure you ...' he began but the Master overrode him.

'I can only invoke the psalmist and say Cast thy bread upon the waters.'

'Not to be taken literally,' snapped the Senior Tutor.

'To be taken how you wish,' Sir Godber snapped back. The members of the Council stared at him with open belligerence.

'It is precisely that we have no bread to throw,' said the Bursar, trying to pour oil on troubled waters.

The Senior Tutor ignored his efforts. 'May I remind you,' he snarled at the Master, 'that this Council is the governing body of the College and ...'

'The Dean reminded me earlier in the meeting,' the Master interrupted.

'I was about to say that policy decisions affecting the running of the College are taken by the Council as a whole,' continued the Senior Tutor. 'I should like to make it quite clear that I for one have no intention of accepting the changes outlined in the proposals that the Master has submitted to us. I think I can speak for the Dean,' he glanced at the speechless Dean before continuing, 'when I say we are both adamantly opposed to any changes in College policy.' He sat back. There were murmurs of agreement from the other Fellows. The Master leant forward and looked round the table.

'Am I to understand that the Senior Tutor has expressed the general feelings of the meeting?' he asked. There was a nodding of heads round the table. The Master looked crestfallen.

'In that case, gentlemen, there is little I can say,' he said sadly. 'In the face of your opposition to the changes in College policy that I have proposed, I have little choice but to resign the Mastership of Porterhouse.' A gasp came from the Fellows as the Master rose and gathered his notes. 'I shall announce my resignation in a letter to the Prime Minister, an open letter, gentlemen, in which I shall state the reasons for my resignation, namely that I am unable to continue as Master of a college that augments its financial resources by admitting candidates without academic qualifications in return for large donations to the Endowment Subscription Fund and selling degrees.' The Master paused and looked at the Fellows who sat stunned by his announcement. 'When I was nominated by the Prime Minister, I had no idea that I was accepting the Mastership of an academic auction-room nor that I was ending a career marked, I am proud to say, by the utmost adherence to the rules of probity in public life by becoming an accessory to a financial scandal of national proportions. I have the facts and figures here, gentlemen, and I shall include them in my letter to the Prime Minister, who will doubtless pass them on to the Director of Public Prosecutions. Good afternoon, gentlemen.'

The Master turned and stalked out of the room. Behind him the Fellows of Porterhouse sat rigid like embalmed figures round the table, each absorbed in calculating his own complicity in a scandal that must bring ruin to them all. It took little imagination to foresee the public outcry that would follow Sir Godber's resignation and the publication of his open letter, the wave of indignation that would sweep the country, the execrations that would fall on their heads from the other colleges in Cambridge, the denunciations of the other, newer universities. The Fellows of Porterhouse had little imagination but they could foresee all this and more, the demand for public accountability, possibly even prosecutions, even perhaps an inquiry into the sources and size of College funds. What would Trinity and King's say to that? The Fellows of Porterhouse knew the odium they could expect for having precipitated a public inquiry that could put, would put, in jeopardy the vast wealth of the other colleges and they shrank from the prospect. It was the Dean who first broke the silence with a strangled cry.

'He must be stopped,' he gurgled.

The Senior Tutor nodded sympathetically. 'We have little alternative.'

'But how?' demanded the Bursar, who was desperately trying to banish from his mind the knowledge that he had inadvertently provided the Master with the information he was now threatening to disclose. If the other Fellows should ever learn who had provided Sir Godber with this material for blackmail his life in College would not be worth living.

'At all costs the Master must be persuaded to stay on,' said the Senior Tutor. 'We simply cannot afford the scandal that would ensue from the publication of his letter of resignation.'

The Praelector looked at him vindictively. 'We?' he asked. 'I beg not to be included in the list of those responsible for this disgraceful disclosure.'

'And what precisely do you mean by that?' asked the Senior Tutor.

'I should have thought that it was obvious,' said the Praelector. 'Most of us have had nothing to do with the administration of College finances nor with the admissions procedure. We cannot be held responsible for ...'

'We are all responsible for College policy,' shouted the Senior Tutor.

'You are responsible for admissions,' the Praelector shouted back. 'You are responsible for the choice of candidates. You are ...'

'Gentlemen,' the Bursar interposed, 'let us not bicker about individual responsibilities. We are all responsible as members of the Council for the running of the College.'

'Some of us are more responsible than others,' the Praelector pointed out.

'And we shall all share the blame for the mistakes that have been made in the past,' continued the Bursar.

'Mistakes? Who said anything about mistakes?' demanded the Dean breathlessly.

'I think that in the light of the Master's ...' began the Senior Tutor.

'Damn the Master,' the Dean snarled, struggling to his feet. 'Damn the man. Let us stop talking about mistakes. I said he must be stopped. I didn't say we had to surrender to the swine.' He waddled to the head of the table, portly, belligerent and stubborn, like some crimson toad and with all that creature's resilience to the challenges of climate. The Senior Tutor hesitated in the face of his colleague's revitalized obstinacy. 'But ...' he began. The Dean raised a hand for silence.

'He must be stopped,' he said. 'For the time being perhaps we must accept his proposals, but for the time being only. In the short run we must use the tactics of delay, but only in the short run.'

'And then?' the Senior Tutor asked.

'We must buy time,' continued the Dean. 'Time to bring influence to bear upon Sir Godber and time to subject his own career to the scrutiny he has seen fit to apply to the customs and traditions of the College. No man who has spent as long as Sir Godber Evans in public life is wholly without fault. It is our business to discover the extent of his weaknesses.'

'Are you saying that we should ...' the Praelector began.

'I am saying that the Master is vulnerable,' the Dean went on, 'that he is corrupt and that he is open to influence from the powers that be. The tactics he has used this afternoon, tactics of blackmail, are a symptom of the corruption I am referring to. And let us not forget that we have powerful friends.'

The Senior Tutor pursed his lips and nodded. 'True. Very true, Dean.'

'Yes, Porterhouse can justly claim its share of eminent men. The Master may dismiss our protests but we have powerful allies,' said the Dean.

'And in the meantime we must eat humble pie and ask the Master to reconsider his resignation in the light of our acceptance of the changes he has proposed?' said the Senior Tutor.

'Precisely.' The Dean looked round the table at the Fellows for a sign of hesitancy. 'Has anyone here any doubts as to the wisdom of the course I have proposed?' he asked.

'We seem to be left with little choice,' said the Bursar.

'We have no choice at all,' the Dean told him.

'And if the Master refuses to withdraw his resignation?' the Praelector asked.

'There is no possible reason why he should,' the Dean said. 'I propose that we go now in a body to the Master's Lodge and ask him to reconsider.'

'In a body? Is that really wise? Wouldn't it look ... rather ... well ... obsequious?' the Senior Tutor asked doubtfully.

'I don't think this is any time to be thinking about appearances,' said the Dean. 'I am only concerned with results. Humble pie, you said yourself. Very well, if Sir Godber requires humble pie to retract his threat he shall have it. I shall see to it that he eats it himself later on. Besides I should not like him to think that we are in any way divided.' He stared fiercely at the Bursar. 'At a time of crisis it is vital that we present a united front. Don't you agree, Bursar?'

'Oh yes. Absolutely, Dean,' the Bursar assured him.

'Very well, let us go,' said the Dean and led the way out of the Council Chamber. The Fellows trooped after him into the cold.

Skullion listened to their footsteps on the floor above his head and climbed off the chair he had been standing on. It was hot in the boiler-room, hot and dusty, a dry heat that had irritated his nose and made it difficult not to sneeze while he stood on the chair with his ear pressed to a pipe listening to the voices raised in anger in the Council Chamber. He brushed the dust off his sleeve and spread an old newspaper on the seat of the chair and sat down. It wouldn't do to be seen coming out of the boiler-room just yet and besides he wanted to think.

The central heating system wasn't the best conductor of conversations in the world, it tended to parenthesize its own gurgles at important moments, but Skullion had heard enough to startle him. The Master's threat to resign he had greeted with delight, only to feel the sting in its tail with an alarm that equalled that of the Fellows. His thoughts flew to his Scholars and the threat that public exposure of the sort Sir Godber was proposing would do to them. Sir Cathcart must hear this new danger at once – but then the Dean had proposed his own solution and Skullion's heart had warmed to the old man. 'There's life in the old Dean yet,' he said to himself and chuckled at the thought of Sir Godber retracting his resignation only to find that he had been outsmarted. Powerful allies, the Dean had said and Skullion wondered if the old man knew just how powerful some of those allies were, or what a threat the Master's disclosure would pose to them. Cabinet ministers ranked among Skullion's Scholars, cabinet ministers, civil servants, directors of the Bank of England, eminent men indeed. It began to dawn on Skullion that the Master was in a stronger position than he knew. A public inquiry into the academic antecedents of so many public figures would have appalling consequences, and the powerful allies the Dean evidently had in mind were hardly likely to put up more than token opposition to the changes at Porterhouse the Master wanted, if the alternative was a national scandal in which they would figure so prominently. The Dean was barking up the wrong tree after all, and Skullion's premature optimism gave way to a deep melancholy. At this rate there would be women in Porterhouse before the year was out. It was a prospect that infuriated him. 'Over my dead body,' he muttered darkly, and pondered ways and means of frustrating Sir Godber.

CHAPTER EIGHT

Zipser was drunk. Eight pints of bitter, each drunk in a different pub, had changed his outlook on life. The narrow confines of his compulsion had given way to a brighter, broader, more expansive frame of mind. True, his haircuts had left him shorn and practically bald and with an aversion for the company of barbers which would last him a lifetime, but his eyes sparkled, his cheeks had a ruddier, rosier look, and he was in a mood to run the gauntlet of a hundred middle-aged housewives and to face the disapproval of as many chemists in search of an immaculate misconception. In any case a flash of inspiration had robbed him of the need to publicize his requirements. As he had wandered up Sidney Street after his second haircut he had suddenly recalled having seen a contraceptive dispenser in the lavatory of a pub in Bermondsey, and while Bermondsey was rather too far to go in search of a discreet anonymity, it occurred to him that Cambridge pubs must surely offer a similarly sophisticated service for lovers caught as it were on the hop. Zipser's spirits rose with the thought. He went into the first pub he came to and ordered a pint. Ten minutes later he left that pub empty-handed and found another only to be similarly disappointed. By the time he had been to six pubs and had drunk six pints of bitter he was in a mood to point out the deficiency of their service to the bartenders. At the seventh pub he struck gold. Waiting until two elderly men had finished a protracted pee Zipser fumbled with his change and put two coins into the machine. He was about to pull the handle when an undergraduate came in. Zipser went out and finished his seventh pint keeping an eagle eye on the door of the Gents. Two minutes later he was back and tugging at the handle. Nothing happened. He pulled and pushed but the dispenser refused to dispense. He peered into the Money Returned slot and found it empty. Finally he put two more coins in and pulled the handle again. This time his money dropped into the slot and Zipser took it out and looked at it. The damned dispenser was empty. Zipser went back to the bar and ordered an eighth pint.

'That machine in the toilet,' he said conspiratorially to the barman.

'What about it?' the barman asked.

'It's empty,' said Zipser.

'That's right,' said the barman. 'It's always empty.'

'Well, it's got some of my money in it.'

'You don't say.'

'I do say.'

'A gin and tonic,' said a man with a moustache next to Zipser.

'Coming up,' said the barman. Zipser sipped his pint while the barman poured a gin and tonic. Finally when the man with the moustache had taken his drink back to a table by the window, Zipser raised the subject of faulty dispensers again. He was beginning to feel distinctly belligerent.

'What are you going to do about my money?' he asked.

The barman looked at him warily.

'How do I know you put any in?' he asked. 'How do I know you're not just trying it on?'

Zipser considered the question.

'I don't see how I can,' he said finally. 'I haven't got it.'

'Very funny,' said the barman. 'If you've got any complaints to make about that dispenser, you take them to the suppliers.' He reached under the bar and produced a card and handed it to Zipser. 'You go and tell them your problems. They stock the machines. I don't. All right?' Zipser nodded and the man went off down the other end of the counter to serve a customer. Zipser left the pub with the card and went down the road. He found the suppliers in Mill Road. There was a young man with a beard behind the counter. Zipser went in and put the card down in front of him.

'I've come from the Unicorn,' he said. 'The dispenser is empty.'

'What already?' the man said. 'Don't know what happens to them, they go so quickly.'

'I want . . .' Zipser began thickly but the young man had disappeared through a door to the back. Zipser was beginning to feel distinctly light-headed. He tried to think what he was doing discussing wholesale contraceptive sales with a young man with a beard in an office in Mill Road.

'Here you are. Two gross. Sign here,' said the clerk reappearing from the back with two cartons which he plonked on the counter. Zipser stared at the cartons, and was about to explain that he had merely come to ask for his money back when a woman came in. Zipser suddenly felt sick. He picked up the ballpen and signed the slip and then, clutching the two cartons, stumbled from the shop.

By the time he got back to the Unicorn the pub was shut. Zipser tried knocking on the door without result and finally gave it up and went back to Porterhouse.

He weaved his way past the Porter's Lodge and headed across the Court towards his staircase. Ahead of him a line of black figures emerged from the door of the Council Chamber in solemn processional and moved towards him. At the head of them waddled the Dean. Zipser hiccupped and tried to focus on them. It was very difficult. Almost as difficult as trying to stop the world going around. Zipser hiccupped again and was sick on the snow as the column of figures advanced on him.

'Beg your pardon,' he said. 'Shouldn't have done that. Had too much to drink.'

The column stopped and Zipser peered down into the Dean's face. It kept going in and out of focus alarmingly.

'Do you . . . do you . . . know how red your face is?' he asked, waving his head erratically at the Dean. 'Shouldn't have a red face, should you?'

'Out of the way,' snapped the Dean.

'Shertainly,' said Zipser and sat down in the snow. The Dean loomed over him menacingly.

'You, sir, are drunk. Disgustingly drunk,' he said.

'Quite right,' said Zipser. 'Full marks for perspic . . . perspicac . . . ity. Hit the nail on the head firsht time.'

'What is your name?'

'Zhipsher shir, Zhipsher.'

'You're gated for a week, Zipser,' snarled the Dean.

'Yesh,' said Zipser happily, 'I am gated for a week. Shertainly, shir.' He struggled to his feet, still clutching his cartons, and the column of dons moved on across the Court. Zipser wobbled off to his room and collapsed on the floor.

*

Sir Godber watched the deputation of Fellows from his study window. 'Canosssa,' he thought to himself as the procession trudged through the snow to the front door and rang the bell. For a moment it crossed his mind to let them wait but better judgement prevailed. Pope Gregory's triumph had after all been a temporary one. He went out into the hall and let them in.

'Well, gentlemen,' he said when they had filed into his study, 'and what can I do for you now?'

The Dean shuffled forward. 'We have reconsidered our decision, Master,' he said.

Behind him the members of the College Council nodded obediently. Sir Godber looked round their faces and was satisfied. 'You wish me to remain as Master?'

'Yes, Master,' the Dean said.

'And this is the general wish of the Council?'

'It is.'

'And you accept the changes in the College that I have proposed without any reservations?' the Master asked.

The Dean mustered a smile. 'Naturally, we have reservations,' he said. 'It would be asking rather much to expect us to abandon our ... er ... principles without retaining the right to have private reservations, but in the interest of the College as a whole we accept that there may be a need for compromise.'

'My conditions are final,' said the Master. 'They must be accepted as they stand. I am not prepared to attenuate them. I think I should make that plain.'

'Quite so, Master. Quite so.' The Dean smiled weakly.

'In that case I shall postpone my decision,' said Sir Godber, 'until the next meeting of the College Council. That will give us all time to consider the matter at our leisure. Shall we say next Wednesday at the same time?'

'As you wish, Master,' said the Dean. 'As you wish.'

They trooped out and Sir Godber, having seen them to the door, stood at the window watching the dark procession disappear into the winter evening with a new sense of satisfaction. 'The iron fist in the iron glove,' he murmured to himself, conscious that for the first time in a long career of political manoeuvring and compromise he had at long last achieved a clear-cut victory over an apparently intransigent opposition. There had been no doubting the Fellows' obeisance. They had crawled to him and Sir Godber indulged himself in the recollection before going on to consider the implications of their surrender. No one – and who should know better than Sir Godber – crawled quite so submissively without good reasons.

The Fellows' obeisance had been too complete to be without ulterior motive. It was not enough to suppose that his threat had been utter. It had been sufficient to force them to come to heel but there had been no need for the Dean, of all people, to wag his tail so obsequiously. Sir Godber sat down by the fire and considered the character of the Dean for a hint of his motive. And the more he thought the less cause he found for premature self-congratulation. Sir Godber did not underestimate the Dean. The man was an ignorant bigot, with all the persistence of bigotry and all the cunning of the ignorant. 'Buying time,' he thought shrewdly, 'but time for what?' It was an unpleasant notion. Not for the first time since his arrival at Porterhouse, Sir Godber felt uneasy, aware, if only subliminally, that the facile assumptions about human nature upon which his liberal ideals were founded were somehow threatened by a devious scholasticism whose origins were less rational and more obscure than he preferred to think. He got up and stared out into the night at the medieval buildings of the College silhouetted against the orange sky. It had begun to snow again and the wind had risen, blowing the snowflakes hither and thither in sudden ungovernable flurries. He pulled the curtains to shut out the sight of nature's lack of symmetry and settled himself in his chair with his favourite author, Bentham.

At High Table the Fellows dined in moody silence. Even the Chef's poached salmon failed to raise their spirits, dampened by the obduracy of the Master and the memory of their capitulation. Only the Dean remained undaunted, shovelling food into his mouth as if to fuel his determination and mouthing imprecations on Sir Godber simultaneously, his forehead greasy and his eyes bright with the cunning Sir Godber had recognized.

In the Combination Room, as they took their coffee, the Senior Tutor broached the topic of their next move. 'It would appear that we have until Wednesday to circumvent the Master's proposals,' he said, sipping brandy fastidiously.

'A relatively short time, if you don't mind my saying so.'

'Short but enough,' said the Dean tersely.

'I must say I find your confidence a little surprising, Dean,' said the Bursar nervously.

The Dean looked at him with a sudden ferocity. 'No more surprising than I find your lack of discretion, Bursar,' he snapped. 'I hardly imagine that this unfortunate turn of events would have occurred without your disclosure of the financial state of the College.'

The Bursar reddened. 'I was simply trying to point out to the Master that the changes he was proposing would place an intolerable strain on our resources,' he protested. 'If my memory serves me right you were the first to suggest that the finances should be brought to his attention.'

'Certainly I suggested that. I didn't however suggest that he should be made privy to the details of our admissions policy,' the Dean retorted.

'Gentlemen,' said the Senior Tutor, 'the mistake has been made. Nothing is to be gained by post-mortem. We are faced by an urgent problem. It is not in our best interest to apportion blame for past mistakes. If it comes to that we are all culpable. Without the divisions that prevented the election of Dr Siblington as Master, we should have avoided the nomination of Sir Godber.'

The Dean finished his coffee. 'There is some truth in that,' he admitted, 'and a lesson to be learnt. We must remain united in the face of the Master. In the meantime I have already made a move. I have arranged a meeting with Sir Cathcart D'Eath for this evening. His car should be waiting for me now.' He rose to his feet and gathered his gown about him.

'May one inquire the purpose of this meeting?' the Praelector asked. The Dean looked down at the Bursar. 'I should not like to think that our plans are likely to reach Sir Godber's ears,' he said deliberately.

'I can assure you ...' began the Bursar.

'I have requested this meeting because Sir Cathcart as you all know is President of the OPs. I think he should know what changes the Master proposes. Furthermore I think he should know the manner in which the Master has conducted himself in the matter. I fancy that there will be an extraordinary meeting of the Porterhouse Society next Tuesday to discuss the situation and I have high hopes that at that meeting a resolution will be passed censoring Sir Godber for the dictatorial attitude he has adopted in his dealings with the College Council and calling for his immediate resignation from the Mastership.'

'But, Dean, surely that is most unwise,' protested the Senior Tutor thoroughly alarmed. 'If a motion of that sort is passed, the Master is bound to resign and to publish his confounded letter. I really don't see what that is going to accomplish.'

The Bursar put down his coffee-cup with unwonted violence. 'For God's sake, Dean,' he said, 'consider what you are doing.'

The Dean smiled grimly. 'If Sir Godber can threaten us,' he said, 'we can threaten him.'

'But the scandal, think of the scandal. It will involve us all,' muttered the Bursar desperately.

'It will also involve Sir Godber. That is precisely the point of the exercise. We shall get in first by demanding his resignation. The force of his letter to the PM will be dulled by the fact that the College authorites and the Porterhouse Society have both demanded his resignation on the grounds of incompetence and his letter to the press with its so-called disclosures will have the appearance of being the action of a slighted and bitter man. Besides I rather think you over-estimate Sir Godber's political courage. Faced with the ultimatum we shall present at the Council meeting on Wednesday I doubt if he will risk a further confrontation.'

'But if the call for his resignation has already been published . . .'

'It won't have been. The motion will have been passed, I trust unanimously, but its publication will be dependent on Sir Godber's attitude. If he persists in demanding the changes in the College, then we shall publish.'

'And if he resigns without warning?'

'We shall publish all the same,' said the Dean. 'We shall muddy the issue until it is uncertain whether we forced his resignation or not. Oh, we shall stir the pot, gentlemen. Have no fear of that. If there must be dirt let there be lots of it.' The Dean turned and went out, his gown billowing darkly behind him. In the Combination Room the Fellows looked at one another ruefully. Whatever changes the Master proposed appeared minor by comparison with the uproar the Dean seemed bent on provoking.

It was the Chaplain who broke the silence. 'I must say,' he shouted, 'that the Chef excelled himself tonight. That soufflé was delicious.'

Outside the main gate Sir Cathcart's Rolls-Royce waited ostentatiously as the Dean, swaddled in a heavy coat and wearing his blackest hat, hurried past the Porter's Lodge.

Skullion opened the car door for him.

'Good evening, Skullion.'

'Good evening to you, sir,' Skullion murmured humbly.

The Dean clambered in and the car moved off, its wheels slushing through the snow. In the back the Dean stared through the window at the flurries of snowflakes and the passers-by with their heads bent against the driving wind. He felt warm and contented, with none of the uneasy feelings that had driven the Master to his Bentham. This was weather he appreciated, cold bitter weather with the river rising and the biting wind creating once again the divisions of his youth, that hierarchy of rich and poor, good and bad, the comfort and the misery which he longed to preserve and which Sir Godber would destroy in his search for soulless uniformity. 'The old order changeth,' he muttered to himself, 'but damned slowly if I have anything to do with it.'

*

Skullion went back into the Porter's Lodge.

'Going to supper,' he told the under-porter and trudged across the Court to the kitchen. He went down the stone stairs to the kitchen where the Chef had laid a table for two in his pantry. It was hot and Skullion took off his coat before sitting down.

'Snowing again they tell me,' said the Chef taking his seat.

Skullion waited until a younger waiter with a gaping mouth had brought the dishes before saying anything.

'Dean's gone to see the General,' he said finally.

'Has he now?' said the Chef, helping himself to the remains of the poached salmon.

'Council meeting this afternoon,' Skullion continued.

'So I heard.'

Skullion shook his head.

'You aren't going to like this,' he said. 'The Master's changes aren't going to suit your book, I can tell you.'

'Never supposed they would, Mr Skullion.'

'Worse than I expected, Chef, much worse.' Skullion took a mouthful of Ockfener Herrenberg 1964 before going on.

'Self-service in Hall,' he said mournfully.

The Chef put down his knife and fork. 'Never,' he growled.

'It's true. Self-service in Hall.'

'Over my dead body,' said the Chef. 'Over my bloody dead body.'

'Women in College too.'

'What? Living in College?'

'That's it. Living in College.'

'That's unnatural, Mr Skullion. Unnatural.'

'You don't have to tell me that, Chef. You don't have to tell me. Unnatural and immoral. It isn't right, Chef, it's downright wicked.'

'And self-service in Hall,' the Chef muttered. 'What's the world coming to? You know, Mr Skullion, when I think of all the years I've been Chef to the College and all the dinners I've cooked for them, I sometimes wonder what's the meaning of it all. They've got no right to do it.'

'It's not them that's doing it,' Skullion told him. 'It's him that says it's got to change.'

'Why don't they stop him? They're the Council. He can't do it without their say-so.'

'They can't stop him. Threatened to resign if they didn't agree.'

'Why didn't they let him? Good riddance to bad rubbish.'

'Threatened to write to the papers and tell them we've been selling degrees,' Skullion said.

The Chef looked at him with alarm.

'You don't mean he knows about your ...'

'I don't know what he knows and what he don't,' Skullion said. 'I don't think he knows about them. I think he's talking about the ones they let in because they've got money. I think that's what he means.'

'But we've a right to let in who we like,' the Chef protested. 'It's our college. It's not anyone else's.'

'That's not the way he sees it,' Skullion said. 'He's threatened them with a national scandal if they don't toe the line and they've agreed.'

'What did the Dean say? He must have said something.'

'Said they'd got to buy time by seeming to agree. He's gone to see the General now. They'll think of something.'

Skullion finished his wine and smiled to himself. 'He don't know what he's tackled,' he said more cheerfully.

'Thinks he's dealing with the pipsqueaks in Parliament, he does. Wordmongers, that's what MPs are. Think you've only got to say a thing for it to be there next day. They don't know nothing about doing and they don't have nothing to lose, but the Dean's a different kettle of fish. He and the General, they'll do him down. See if they don't.' He grinned knowingly and winked his unblacked eye. The Chef nibbled a grape moodily.

'Don't see how they can,' he said.

'Digging for dirt,' said Skullion. 'Digging for dirt in his past, that's what the Dean said.'

'Dirt? What sort of dirt?'

'Women,' said Skullion.

'Ah,' said the Chef. 'Disreputable women.'

'Precisely, Chef, them and money.'

The Chef pushed his hat back on his head. 'He wasn't what you might call a rich undergrad, was he?'

'No,' said Skullion, 'he wasn't.'

'And he's rich now.'

'Married it,' Skullion told him. 'Lacey money, that's what it is. Lady Mary's money. That's the sort of man he is, Sir Godber.'

'Bony woman. Not my cup of tea,' said the Chef. 'Like something with a bit more meat to it myself. Wouldn't be surprised if he hadn't got a fancy woman somewhere.'

Skullion shook his head doubtfully. 'Not him. Not enough guts,' said Skullion.

'You don't think they'll find anything then?'

'Not that sort of thing. They'll have to bring pressure. Influential friends the College has got, the Dean said. They'll use them.'

'They'd better use something. I'm not staying on to run a self-service canteen and have women in my Hall,' said the Chef.

Skullion got up from the table and put on his coat. 'The Dean'll see to it,' he said and climbed the stairs to the Screens. The wind had blown snow on to the steps and Skullion turned up the collar of his coat. 'Got no right to change things,' he grumbled to himself, and went out into the night.

At Coft Castle the Dean and Sir Cathcart sat in the library, a decanter of brandy half empty on the table beside them and their thoughts bitter with memories of past greatness.

'England's ruin, damned Socialists,' growled Sir Cathcart. 'Turned the country into a benevolent society. Seem to think you can rule a nation with good intentions. Damned nonsense. Discipline. That's what the country needs. A good dose of unemployment to bring the working classes to their senses.'

'Doesn't seem to work these days,' said the Dean with a sigh. 'In the old days a depression seemed to have a very salutary effect.'

'It's the dole. Man can earn more not working than he can at his job. All wrong. A bit of genuine starvation would soon put that right.'

'I suppose the argument is that the wives and children suffer,' said the Dean.

'Can't see much harm in that,' the General continued. 'Nothing like a hungry woman to put some pep into a man. Reminds me of a painting I saw once. Lot of fellows sitting round a table waiting for their dinner and the lady of the house comes in and lifts the cover of the dish. Spur inside, what? Sensible woman. Fine painting. Have some more brandy?'

'That's very kind of you,' said the Dean, proffering his glass.

'Trouble with this Godber Evans fellow is he comes from poor stock,' continued Sir Cathcart when he had filled their glasses. 'Doesn't understand men. Hasn't got generations of county stock behind him. No leadership qualities. Got to have lived with animals to understand men, working men. Got to train them properly. A whack on the arse if they do something wrong and a pat on the head if they get it right. No use filling their heads with a whole lot of ideas they can't use. Bloody nonsense, half this education lark.'

'I quite agree,' said the Dean. 'Educating people above their station has been one of the great mistakes of this century. What this country requires is an educated elite. What it's had in fact, for the past three hundred years.'

'Three meals a day and a roof over his head and the average man has nothing to grumble about. Stout fellows. The present system is designed to create layabouts. Consumer society indeed. Can't consume what you don't make. Damned tommyrot.'

The Dean's head nodded on his chest. The fire, the brandy and the ubiquitous central heating in Coft Castle mingled with the warmth of Sir Cathcart's sentiments to take their toll of his concentration. He was dimly aware of the rumble of the General's imprecations, distant and receding like some tide going out across the mudflats of an estuary where once the fleet had lain at anchor. All empty now, the ships gone, dismantled, scrapped, the evidence of might deplenished, only a sandpiper with Sir Godber's face poking its beak into the sludge. The Dean was asleep.

CHAPTER NINE

Zipser stirred on the floor of his room. His face in contact with the carpet felt sore and his head throbbed. Above all he was cold and stiff. He turned on his side and stared at the window, where an orange glow from the sky over Cambridge shone dimly through the falling snow. Slowly he gathered himself together and got to his feet. Feeling distinctly weak and sick he went to the door and turned on the light and stood blinking at the two large cartons on the floor. Then he sat down hurriedly in a chair and tried to remember what had happened to him and why he was the possessor of two gross of guaranteed electronically tested three-teat vending machine pack contraceptives. The details of the day's events slowly returned to him and with them the remembrance of his misunderstanding with the Dean. 'Gated for a week,' he murmured and realized the implications of his predicament. He couldn't deliver the beastly things to the Unicorn now and he had signed the slip at the wholesale office. Inquiries would be made. The barman at the Unicorn would identify him. So would the wretched clerk at the wholesale office. The police would be informed. There would be a search. He'd be arrested. Charged with being in felonious possession of two gross of ... Zipser clutched his head in his hands and tried to think what to do. He'd have to get rid of the things. He looked at his watch. Eleven o'clock. Got to hurry. Burn them? He looked at the gas fire and gave up the idea. Out of the question. Flush them down the lavatory? Better idea. He threw himself at the cartons and began to open them. First the outer carton, then the inner one, then the packet itself and finally the foil wrapper. It was a laborious job. He'd never do it. He'd got to do it.

Beside him on the carpet a pile of empty packets slowly grew and with it a pile of foil and a grotesque arrangement of latex rings looking like flattened and translucent button mushrooms. Lubricated with sensitol, his hands were sticky, which made it even more difficult to tear the foil. Finally after an hour he had emptied one carton. It was twelve o'clock. He gathered the contraceptives up and took a handful out on to the landing and into the lavatory. He dropped them into the pan and pulled the chain. A rush of water, swirls, bubbles, gone? The water subsided and he stared down at two dozen rubber rings floating defiantly in the pan. 'For God's sake,' said Zipser desperately and waited until the cistern had filled again. He waited a minute after the water had stopped running and pulled the chain again. Two dozen contraceptives smiled up at him. One or two had partially unfurled and were filled with air. Zipser stared at the things frantically. Got to get them to go down somehow. He reached behind the pan and grabbed the cleaning brush and shoved it down on them. One or two disappeared round the U bend but for the most part they resisted his efforts. Three even had the audacity to adhere to the brush itself. Zipser picked them off with fastidious disgust and dropped them back into the water. By this time the cistern had filled again, gurgling gently and ending with a final swish. Zipser tried to think what to do. If buying the damned things had been fraught with appalling difficulties, getting rid of them was a nightmare.

He sat down on the lavatory seat and considered the intractability of matter. A tin of lavatory cleanser caught his attention. He picked it up and wondered if it would dissolve rubber. Then he got off the seat and emptied the contents on to the rings floating in the water. Whatever chemical action the cleanser promised failed altogether. The contraceptives remained unaffected. Zipser grabbed the brush again and plunged it into the pan. Wafts of disinfectant powder irritated his nose. He sneezed loudly and clutched the chain. For the third time the cistern flushed and Zipser was just studying the subsidence and counting the six contraceptives which remained immune to chemistry and the rush of water when someone knocked on the door.

'What the hell's going on in there?' a voice asked. It was Foxton, who lived in the room next door.

Zipser looked hauntedly at the door. 'Got diarrhoea,' he said weakly.

'Well, must you pull the bloody chain so often?' Foxton asked. 'Making a bloody awful noise and I'm trying to sleep.' He went back to his room and Zipser turned back to the pan and began fishing for the six contraceptives with the lavatory brush.

Twenty minutes later he was still searching for some method of disposing of his incriminating evidence. He had visited six lavatories on neighbouring staircases and had found a method of getting the things to disappear by first filling them with water from a tap and tying the ends. It was slow and cumbersome and above all noisy and when he had tried six at a time on J staircase he had to spend some time unblocking the U pipe. He went back to his room and sat shivering with cold and anxiety. It was one o'clock and so far he had managed to rid himself of thirty-eight. At this rate he would still be flushing lavatories all over the College when Mrs Biggs arrived in the morning. He stared at the pile of foil and the packets. Got to get rid of them too. Put them behind the gas fire and burn them he thought and he was just wrestling with the gas fire and trying to make space behind it when the howling draught in the chimney gave him a better idea. He went to the window and looked out into the night. In the darkness outside snowflakes whirled and scattered while the wind battered at the window pane. Zipser opened the window and poked his head out into the storm before wetting his finger and holding it up to the wind. 'Blowing from the East,' he muttered and shut the window with a smile of intense satisfaction. A moment later he was kneeling beside the gas fire and undoing the hose of his gas ring and five minutes afterwards the first of 250 inflated contraceptives bounced buoyantly against the sooty sides of the medieval chimney and disappeared into the night sky above. Zipser rushed to the window and gazed up for a glimpse of the winsome thing as it whirled away carrying its message of abstinence far away into the world, but the sky was too dark and there was nothing to see. He went back and fetched a torch and shone it up the chimney but apart from one or two errant snowflakes the chimney was clear. Zipser turned cheerfully back to the gas ring and inflated five more. Once again the experiment was entirely successful. Up the chimney they floated, up and away. Zipser inflated twenty and popped them up the chimney with equal success. He was just filling his hundredth when the gas gave out, with a hideous wheeze the thing deflated. Zipser rummaged in his pockets for a shilling and finally found one. He put it into the meter and the contraceptive assumed a new and satisfactory shape. He tied the end and stuffed it up the chimney. The night wore on and Zipser acquired a wonderful dexterity. On to the tube, gas on, gas off, a knot in the end and up the chimney. Beside him on the floor the cartons filled with discarded foil and Zipser was just wondering if there were schoolchildren who collected used contraceptive containers like milk-bottle tops when he became aware that something had gone wrong in the chimney. The bloated and strangulated rear of his last contraceptive was hanging suspended in the fireplace. Zipser gave it a shove of encouragement but the poor thing merely bulged dangerously. Zipser pulled it out and peered up the chimney. He couldn't peer very far. The chimney was crowded with eager contraceptives. He extracted another, smeared with soot, and put it down on the floor. He extracted a third and thrust it behind him. Then a fourth and a fifth, both deeply encrusted with soot. After that he gave up. The rest were too high to reach. He clambered out of the fireplace and sat on the floor wondering what to do. At least he had disposed of all two gross, even if some were lodged in the chimney stack. They were well hidden there – or would be once he had put the gas fire back in place. He would think of some way of disposing of them in the morning. He was too tired to think of anything now. He turned to reach for the five he had managed to extract only to find that they had disappeared. 'I put them down on the carpet. I'm sure I did,' he muttered lightheadedly to himself and was about to look under the bookcase when his eye caught sight of a movement on the ceiling. Zipser looked up. Five sooty contraceptives had lodged themselves in a corner by the door. Little bits of soot marked the ceiling where they had touched.

Zipser got wearily to his feet and climbed on to a chair and reached up. He could just manage to get his fingers on to the belly of one of the things but the sensitol made it impossible to get a grip. Zipser squeezed and with a coy squeak the contraceptive evaded his grasp and lumbered away across the room, leaving a track of soot behind it. Zipser tried again on another with the same result. He moved the chair across the room and reached up. The contraceptive waddled gently into the corner by the window. Zipser moved the chair again but the contraceptive rolled away. Zipser climbed down and stared maniacally at his ceiling. It was covered in delicate black trails as if some enormous snail had called after a stint of coal-heaving. The self-control Zipser had been exercising began to slip. He picked up a book and lobbed it at a particularly offensive-looking contraceptive, but apart from driving it across the room to join the flock in the corner by the door the gesture was futile. Zipser crossed to the desk and pushed it over to the door. Then he fetched the chair and stood it on the desk and climbed precariously up and seized a contraceptive by its knotted tail. He climbed down and thrust it up the chimney. Five minutes later all five were back in place and although the last one still protruded below the lintel, when he pushed the gas fire back into position it was invisible. Zipser collapsed on to his sofa and stared at the ceiling. All that remained was to clean the soot off the plaster. He went out into the gyp room and fetched a duster and spent the next half hour pushing his desk round the room and climbing on to it to dust the ceiling. Traces of soot still remained but they were less noticeable now. He pushed the desk back into its corner and looked round the room. Apart from a noticeable smell of gas and the more intransigent stains on the ceiling there was nothing to connect him with two gross of contraceptives fraudulently obtained from the wholesalers. Zipser opened the window to clear the room of gas and went through to his bedroom and went to bed. In the eastern sky the first light of dawn was beginning to appear, but Zipser had no eyes for the beauties of nature. He fell into a restless sleep haunted by the thought that the logjam in his chimney might break during the coming day to issue with shocking ebullience above the unsuspecting College. He need not have worried. Porterhouse was already infested. The falling snow had seen to that. As each porcine sensitol-lubricated protective had emerged from the chimney stack the melting snow had ended its night flight almost abruptly. Zipser had not foreseen the dangers of icing.

The Dean arrived back at Porterhouse in Sir Cathcart's Rolls-Royce at two o'clock. He was spiritually restored though physically taxed by the day's excitements and Sir Cathcart's brandy. He knocked on the main gate and Skullion, who had been waiting up obediently for him, opened the postern and let him in.

'Need any help, sir,' Skullion asked as the Dean tottered through.

'Certainly not,' said the Dean thickly and set off across the Court. Skullion followed him at a distance like a good dog and saw him through the Screens before turning back to his Porter's Lodge and bed. He had already shut the door and gone through into his backroom when the Dean's strangled cry sounded from the New Court. Skullion heard nothing. He took off his collar and tie and climbed between the sheets. 'Drunk as a lord,' he thought fondly, and closed his eyes.

The Dean lay in the snow and cursed. He tried to imagine what he had slipped on. It certainly wasn't the snow. Snow didn't squash like that. Snow certainly didn't explode like that and even in these days of air pollution snow didn't smell of gas like that. The Dean eased himself on to a bruised hip and peered into the darkness. A strange rustling sound in which a sort of wheeze and the occasional squeak were intermingled came from all sides. The Court seemed to be alive with turgid and vaguely translucent shapes which gleamed in the starlight. The Dean reached out tentatively towards the nearest one and felt it bounce delicately away from him. He scrambled to his feet and kicked another. A ripple of rustling, squeaking, jostling shapes issued across the Court. 'That damned brandy,' muttered the Dean. He waded through the mass to the door of his staircase and stumbled upstairs. He was feeling distinctly ill. 'Must be my liver,' he thought, and slumped into a chair with the sudden resolution to leave brandy well alone in future. After a bit he got up and went to the window and looked out. Seen from above the Court looked empty, white with snow but otherwise normal. The Dean shut the window and turned back into the room. 'I could have sworn there were ...' He tried to think just what he could have sworn the Court was filled with, but couldn't think of anything appropriate. Balloons was as near as he could get, but balloons didn't have that awful translucent ectoplasmic quality about them.

He went into his bedroom and undressed and put on his pyjamas and got into bed but sleep was impossible. He had dozed too long at Sir Cathcart's, and besides, he was haunted by his recent experience. After an hour the Dean got out of bed again and put on his dressing-gown and went downstairs. At the bottom he peered out into the Court. There was the same indelicate squeaking sound but apart from that the night was too dark to see anything clearly. The Dean stepped out into the Court and banged into one of the objects. 'They *are* there after all,' he muttered and reached down to pick whatever it was up. The thing has a soft vaguely oily feel about it and scuttled away as soon as the Dean's finger's tightened on it. He tried another and missed and it was only at the third attempt that he managed to obtain a grip. Holding the thing by its tail the Dean took it into the lighted doorway and looked at it with a growing sense of disgust and outrage. He held it head down and the thing righted itself and turned head up. Holding it thus he went out into the Court and through the Screens to Old Court and the Porter's Lodge.

To Skullion, emerging sleepily from his backroom, the sight of the Dean in his dressing-gown holding the knotted end of an inflated contraceptive had about it a nightmare quality that deprived him of his limited amount of speech. He stood staring wild-eyed at the Dean while on the periphery of his vision the contraceptive wobbled obscenely.

'I have just found this in New Court, Skullion,' said the Dean, suddenly conscious that there was a certain ambiguity about his appearance.

'Oh ah,' said Skullion in the tone of one who has his private doubts. The Dean let go of the contraceptive hurriedly.

'As I was saying ...' he began only to stop as the thing slowly began to ascend. Skullion and the Dean watched it, hypnotized. The contraceptive reached the ceiling and hovered there. Skullion lowered his eyes and stared at the Dean.

'There seem to be others of that ilk,' continued the Dean.

'Oh ah,' said Skullion.

'In the New Court,' said the Dean. 'A great many others.'

'In the New Court?' said Skullion slowly.

'Yes,' said the Dean. In the face of Skullion's evident doubts he was beginning to feel rather heated. So was the contraceptive. The draught from the door had nudged it next to the light bulb in the ceiling and as the Dean opened his mouth to say that the New Court was alive with the things, the one above their heads touched the bulb and exploded. In fact there were three explosions. First the contraceptive blew. Then the bulb, and finally and most alarmingly of all the gas ignited. Blinded momentarily by the flash and bereft of the light of the bulb, the Dean and Skullion stood in darkness while fragments of glass and rubber descended on them.

'There are more where that one came from,' said the Dean finally, and led the way out into the night air. Skullion groped for his bowler and put it on. He reached behind the counter for his torch and followed the Dean. They passed through the Screens and Skullion shone his torch into New Court.

Huddled like so many legless animals, some two hundred contraceptives gleamed in the torchlight. A light dawn breeze had risen and with it some of the more inflated contraceptives, so that it seemed as though they were attempting to mount their less active neighbours while the whole mass seethed and rippled. One or two were to be seen nudging the windows on the first floor.

'Gawd,' said Skullion irreverently.

'I want them cleared away before it gets light, Skullion,' said the Dean. 'No one must hear about this. The College reputation, you understand.'

'Yes, sir,' said Skullion. 'I'll clear them away. Leave it to me.'

'Good, Skullion,' said the Dean and with one last disgusted look at the obscene flock went up the stairs to his rooms.

Mrs Biggs had a bath. She had poured bath salts into the water and the pink suds matched the colour of her frilly shower cap. Bath night for Mrs Biggs was a special occasion. In the privacy of her bathroom she felt liberated from the constraints of commonsense. Standing on the pink bath mat surveying her reflection in the steamed-up mirror it was almost possible to imagine herself young again. Young and fancy free, and she fancied Zipser. There was no doubt about it and no doubt too that Zipser fancied her. She dried herself lovingly and put on her nightdress and went through to her bedroom. She climbed into bed and set the alarm clock for three. Mrs Biggs wanted to be up early. She had things to do.

In the early hours she left the house and cycled across Cambridge. She locked the bicycle by the Round Church and made her way on foot down Trinity Street to the side entrance of Porterhouse and let herself in with a key she had used in the old days when she had bedded for the Chaplain. She passed through the passage by the Buttery and came out by the Screens and was about to make her way across New Court when a strange sound stopped her in her tracks. She peered round the archway. In the early morning light Skullion was chasing balloons. Or something. Not chasing. Dancing seemed more like it. He ran. He leapt. He cavorted. His outstretched arms reached yearningly towards whatever it was that floated jauntily beyond his reach as if to taunt the Porter. Backwards and forwards across the ancient court the strange pursuit continued until just as it seemed the thing was about to escape over the wall into the Fellows' Garden there was a loud pop and whatever it was or had been hung limp and tatterdemalion upon the branches of a climbing rose like some late-flowering bloom. Skullion stopped, panting, and stared up at the object of his chase and then, evidently inspired by its fate, turned and hurried towards the Screens. Mrs Biggs retreated into the darkness of the Buttery passage as Skullion hurried by and then, when she could see him heading for the Porter's Lodge, emerged and tiptoed through the contraceptives to the Bull Tower. Around her feet the contraceptives squeaked and rustled. Mrs Biggs climbed the staircase to Zipser's room with a fresh sense of sexual excitement brought on by the presence of so many prophylactics. She couldn't remember when she had seen so many. Even the American airmen with whom she had been so familiar in the past had never been quite so prolific with their rubbers, and they'd been generous enough in all conscience if her memory served her aright. Mrs Biggs let herself into Zipser's room and sported the oak. She had no intention of being disturbed. She crossed to Zipser's bedroom and went inside. She switched on the bedside light.

Zipser awoke from his troubled sleep and blinked. He sat up in bed and stared at Mrs Biggs brilliant in her red coat. It was evidently morning. It didn't feel like morning but there was Mrs Biggs so it must be morning. Mrs Biggs didn't come in the middle of the night. Zipser levered himself out of bed.

'Sorry,' he mumbled groping for his dressing-gown. 'Must have overslept.' Zipser's eye caught the alarm clock. It seemed to indicate half-past three. Must have stopped.

'Shush,' said Mrs Biggs with a terrible smile. 'It's only half-past three.'

Zipser looked at the clock again. It certainly said half-past three. He tried to equate the time with Mrs Biggs's arrival and couldn't. There was something terribly wrong with the situation.

'Darling,' said Mrs Biggs, evidently sensing his dilemma. Zipser looked up at her open-mouthed. Mrs Biggs was taking off her coat. 'Don't make any noise,' she continued, with the same extraordinary smile.

'What the hell is going on?' asked Zipser. Mrs Biggs went into the other room.

'I'll be with you in a minute,' she called out in a hoarse whisper.

Zipser stood up shakily. 'What are you doing?' he asked.

There was a rustle of clothes in the other room. Even to Zipser's befuddled mind it was evident that Mrs Biggs was undressing. He went to the door and peered out into the darkness.

'For God's sake,' he said, 'you mustn't do that.'

Mrs Biggs emerged from the shadows. She had taken off her blouse. Zipser stared at her enormous brassière.

'Darling,' she said. 'Go back to bed. You mustn't stand and watch me. It's embarrassing.' She gave him a push which sent him reeling on to the bed. Then she shut the door. Zipser sat on his bed shaking. The sudden emergence of Mrs Biggs at half-past three in the morning from the shadows of his own private fantasies into a real presence terrified him. He tried to think what to do. He couldn't shout or scream for help. Nobody would believe he hadn't invited her to ... He'd be sent down. His career would be finished. He'd be disgraced. They'd find the French letters up the chimney. Oh God. Zipser began to weep.

In the front room Mrs Biggs divested herself of her bra and panties. It was terribly cold. She went to the window to shut it when a faint popping noise from below startled her. Mrs Biggs peered out. Skullion was running round the Court with a stick. He appeared to be spearing the contraceptives. 'That'll keep him busy,' Mrs Biggs thought happily, and shut the window. Then she crossed to the gas fire and lit it. 'Nice to get dressed in the warm,' she thought, and went into the bedroom. Zipser had got back into bed and had switched off the light.

'Wants to spare me,' Mrs Biggs thought tenderly and climbed into bed. Zipser shrank from her but Mrs Biggs had no sense of his reluctance.

Grasping him in her arms she pressed him to her vast breasts. In the darkness Zipser squeaked frantically and Mrs Biggs's mouth found his. To Zipser it seemed that he was in the grip of a great white whale. He fought desperately for air, surfaced for a moment and was engulfed again.

Skullion, who had returned from the Porter's Lodge armed with a broom handle to which he had taped a pin, hurled himself into the shoal and struck about him with a fury that was only partially explained by having to work all night. It was rather the effrontery of the things that infuriated him. Skullion had little use for contraceptives at the best of times. Unnatural, he called them, and placed them in the lower social category of things along with elastic-sided boots and made-up bow ties. Not the sort of attire for a gentleman. But even more than their humble origins, he was infuriated by the insult to Porterhouse that the presence of so great and so inflated a number represented. The Dean's admonition that news of the infestation must not leak out was wasted on Skullion. He needed no telling. 'We'd be the laughing-stock of the University,' he thought, lancing a particularly large one. By the time dawn broke over Cambridge Skullion had cleared New Court. One or two had escaped into the Fellows' Garden and he went through the archway in the wall and began spiking the remainder. Behind him the Court was littered with tattered latex, almost invisible against the snow. 'I'll wait until it's a bit lighter to pick them up,' he muttered. 'Can't see them now.' He had just run a small but agile one to earth in the rose garden when a dull rumbling noise at the top of the Tower made him turn and look up. Something was going on in the old chimney. The chimney pot at the top was shaking. The brickwork silhouetted against the morning sky appeared to be bulging. The rumbling stopped, to be succeeded by an almighty roar as a ball of flame issued from the chimney and billowed out before ascending above the College. Below it the chimney toppled sideways, crashed on to the roof of the Tower and with a gradually increasing rumble of masonry the fourteenth-century building lost its entire façade. Behind it the rooms were clearly visible, their floors tilted horribly and sagging. Skullion stood mesmerized by the spectacle. A bed on the first floor slid sideways and dropped on to the masonry below. Desks and chairs followed suit. There were shouts and screams. People poured out of doorways and windows opened all round the Court. Skullion ignored the screams for help. He was busy chasing the last few remaining contraceptives when the Master, clad in his dressing-gown, emerged from the Master's Lodge and hurried to the scene of the disaster. As he rushed across the garden he found Skullion trying to spear a contraceptive floating in the fishpond.

'Go and open the main gates,' the Master shouted at him.

'Not yet,' said Skullion taciturnly.

'What do you mean, not yet?' the Master demanded. 'The ambulance men and the fire brigade will want to get in.'

'Not having any strangers in College till I've cleared these things up. Wouldn't be right,' said Skullion.

The Master stared at the floating contraceptive furiously. Skullion's obstinacy enraged him. 'There are injured people in there,' he screamed.

'So there are,' said Skullion, 'but there's the College reputation to be thought of too.' He leant across the pond and burst the floating bubble. Sir Godber turned and ran on to the scene of the accident. Skullion turned and followed him slowly. 'Got no sense of tradition,' he said sadly, and shook his head.

CHAPTER TEN

'These sweetbreads are delicious,' said the Dean at dinner. 'The coroner's inquest has given me a considerable appetite.'

'Very tactfully handled,' said the Senior Tutor. 'I must admit I had anticipated a less magnanimous verdict. As it is, suicide never hurt anyone.'

'Suicide?' shouted the Chaplain. 'Did I hear someone say suicide?' He looked up expectantly. 'Now there's a topic we could well consider.'

'The Coroner has already done so at some length, Chaplain,' the Bursar bawled in his ear.

'Very good of him too,' said the Chaplain.

'The Senior Tutor has just made that point,' the Bursar explained.

'Has he now? Very interesting,' said the Chaplain, 'and about time too. Haven't had a decent suicide in College for some years now. Most regrettable.'

'I must say I can't see why the decline of the fashion should be so regrettable, Chaplain,' said the Bursar.

'I think I'll have a second helping of sweetbreads,' said the Dean.

The Chaplain leant back in his chair and looked at them over his glasses. 'In the old days hardly a week went by without some poor fellow taking the easy way out. When I first came here as Chaplain I used to spend half my time attending inquests. Come to think of it, there was a time when we were known as the Slaughterhouse.'

'Things have changed for the better since then,' said the Bursar.

'Nonsense,' said the Chaplain. 'The fall in the number of suicides is the clearest indication of the decline of morality. Undergraduates don't seem to be as conscience-stricken as they were in my young days.'

'You don't think it has to do with the introduction of natural gas?' asked the Senior Tutor.

'Natural gas? No such thing,' said the Dean. 'I agree with the Chaplain. Things have gone to pot.'

'Pot,' shouted the Chaplain. 'Did I hear somebody say pot?'

'I was merely saying ...' began the Dean.

'At least nobody has suggested that young Zipser was on drugs,' interrupted the Bursar. 'The police made a very thorough investigation, you know, and they found nothing.'

The Dean raised his eyebrows. 'Nothing?' he asked. 'To the best of my knowledge they took away an entire sackful of ... er ... contraceptives.'

'I was talking of drugs, Dean. There was the question of motive, you understand. The police seemed to think Zipser was in the grip of an irrational impulse.'

'From what I heard he was in the grip of Mrs Biggs,' said the Senior Tutor. 'I suppose you can call Mrs Biggs an irrational impulse. Certainly a very tasteless one. And as for the other things, I must admit I find a predilection for gas-filled contraceptives quite unaccountable.'

'According to the police, there were two hundred and fifty,' said the Bursar.

'No accounting for tastes,' said the Dean, 'though for my part I prefer ... to regard the whole deplorable affair as being politically motivated. This fellow Zipser was clearly an anarchist. He had a lot of left-wing literature in his rooms.'

'I understood him to be doing research into pumpernickel,' said the Bursar. 'Its origins in sixteenth-century Germany.'

'He also belonged to a number of subversive societies,' the Dean continued.

'I'd hardly call the United Nations Association subversive, Dean,' the Bursar protested.

'I would,' said the Dean. 'All political societies are subversive. Must be. Stands to reason. Wouldn't exist if they weren't trying to subvert something or other.'

'Certainly a most extraordinary way of going about things,' said the Bursar. 'And it still doesn't explain the presence of Mrs Biggs.'

'I'm inclined to agree with the Dean,' said the Senior Tutor. 'Anyone who could go to bed with Mrs Biggs must have been either demented or motivated by a grossly distorted sense of social duty and to have launched two hundred and fifty lethal contraceptives on an unsuspecting world argues a fanaticism ...'

'On the other hand,' said the Bursar, 'he had been to see you about his ... er ... compulsion for the good woman. You mentioned it at the time.'

'Yes, well, perhaps he did,' the Senior Tutor admitted, 'though I'd question your use of good as far as Mrs Biggs was concerned. In any case, I sent him on to the Chaplain.'

They looked at the Chaplain questioningly. 'Mrs Biggs good?' shouted the Chaplain. 'I should say so. Splendid woman.'

'We were wondering if Zipser gave you any hint as to his motives,' the Bursar explained.

'Motives?' said the Chaplain. 'Perfectly obvious. Good old-fashioned lust.'

'That hardly explains the explosive nature of his end,' said the Senior Tutor.

'You can't put new wine in old bottles,' said the Chaplain.

The Dean shook his head. 'Whatever his motives,' he said, 'Zipser has certainly made our own position extremely awkward. It is difficult to argue against the need for change when members of the College make such an exhibition of themselves. The meeting of the Porterhouse Society has been cancelled.'

The Fellows looked at him in amazement.

'But I understood the General had agreed to call it,' said the Senior Tutor. 'He's surely not backing down now.'

'Cathcart has proved himself a broken reed,' said the Dean mournfully. 'He phoned me this morning to say that he thought we should wait until this whole affair had blown over. An unfortunate phrase but one sees his point. The College can hardly afford another scandal just yet.'

'Damn Zipser,' said the Senior Tutor. The Fellows finished their dinner in silence.

In the Master's Lodge Sir Godber and Lady Mary mourned the passing of Zipser more austerely over scrambled eggs. As was ever the case, tragedy had lent Lady Mary a fresh vitality, and the strange circumstances of Zipser's end had given a fillip to her interest in psychology.

'The poor boy must have had a fetish,' she said, peeling a banana with a dispassionate interest that reminded Sir Godber of his honeymoon. 'Just like that case of the boy who was found inside a plastic bag in the lavatory on a railway train.'

'Seems an odd place to be,' said Sir Godber, helping himself to some tinned raspberries.

'Of course, that was a much clearer case of the mother complex at work,' continued Lady Mary. 'The plastic bag was obviously a substitute placenta.'

Sir Godber pushed his plate away. 'I suppose you're going to tell me that filling contraceptives with gas is a sure indication that the poor fellow had penis envy,' he said.

'Boys don't have penis envy, Godber,' said Lady Mary austerely. 'That's a girls' complaint.'

'Is it? Well, perhaps the bedder suffered from it then. I mean there's no indication that Zipser was actually responsible for stuffing them up the chimney. We know that he obtained the things, but for all we know Mrs Biggs filled them with gas and put them up the chimney.'

'And that's another thing,' Lady Mary said. 'The Dean's remarks about Mrs Biggs were in the worst of taste. He seemed to find the fact that the boy was having an affair with his bedder proof that Zipser was insane. A more glaring example of class prejudice it would be hard to imagine, but then I've always thought the Dean was a singularly common little man.'

Sir Godber looked at his wife with open admiration. The illogicality of her attitudes never ceased to amaze him. Lady Mary's egalitarianism stemmed from a sense of innate superiority which not even her marriage to Sir Godber had diminished. There were times when he wondered if her acceptance of his proposal had not been yet another political decision, a demonstration of her liberal pretensions. He brushed aside this domestic reverie and thought about the consequences of Zipser's death.

'It's going to be very difficult to quell the Dean now,' he said thoughtfully. 'He's already maintaining that this whole affair is a result of sexual permissiveness.'

Lady Mary snorted. 'Absolute nonsense,' she snapped predictably. 'If there had been women in College this thing would never have happened.'

'In the Dean's view, it was precisely the presence of Mrs Biggs in Zipser's rooms that caused the disaster,' Sir Godber pointed out.

'The Dean,' said Lady Mary with feeling, 'is a male chauvinist pig. A sensible policy of coeducation would avoid the sexual repressions that result in fetishism. You must make the point at the next Council meeting.'

'My dear,' said Sir Godber wearily, 'you don't seem to understand the difficulty I am in. I can hardly resign the Mastership now. It would look as if I was admitting some responsibility for what has happened. As it is my time is going to be taken up raising money for the Restoration Fund. It's going to cost a quarter of a million to repair the Tower.'

Lady Mary regarded him sternly. 'Godber,' she said, 'you must not weaken now. You must not compromise your principles. You must stick to your guns.'

'Guns, my dear?'

'Guns, Godber, guns.'

Sir Godber raised his eyebrows doubtfully. What guns he had had, and, in the light of Lady Mary's pacifism, he doubted if the metaphor was morally appropriate, appeared to have been effectively spiked by Zipser's tragic act.

'I really can't see what I can do,' he said finally.

'Well, in the first place, you can see that contraceptives are freely available in the College.'

'I can what?' shouted Sir Godber.

'You heard me,' snapped his wife. 'King's College has a dispenser in the lavatory. So do some of the other colleges. It seems a most wholesome precaution.'

The Master shuddered. 'King's has them, eh? Well I daresay it needs them. The place is a hotbed of homosexuality.'

'Godber,' said Lady Mary warningly. Sir Godber stopped short. He knew Lady Mary's views on homosexuals. She held them in the same sort of esteem as foxes, and her views on foxhunting were intemperate to say the least.

'All I meant was that King's have them for a purpose,' he said.

'I hardly imagine that ...' Lady Mary began when the French au pair girl brought in coffee.

'As I was saying ...'

'Pas devant les doméstiques,' said his wife.

'Oh quite,' said Sir Godber hastily. 'All I meant was that they have them pour encourager les autres.'

The girl went out and Lady Mary poured coffee.

'What others?' she asked.

'Others?' said Sir Godber, who by this time had lost the thread of the conversation.

'You were saying that King's had installed a dispenser to encourage the others.'

'Precisely. I know how you feel about homosexuality, my dear, but one can have enough of a good thing,' he explained.

'Godber, you are prevaricating,' said Lady Mary firmly. 'I insist that for once in your life you do what you say you're going to do. When I marrried you, you were filled with splendid ideals. Now when I look at you, I sometimes wonder what happened to the man I married.'

'My dear, you seem to forget that I have spent a lifetime in politics,' Sir Godber protested. 'One learns to compromise. It's a depressing fact but there it is. Call it the death of idealism if you will, at least it saves a lot of people's lives.' He took his coffee cup and went through to his study and sat morosely by the fire and wondered at his own pusillanimity.

He could remember a time when he had shared his wife's enthusiasm for social justice, but time had dimmed ... or rather since Lady Mary remained vigorous over the years, not time itself but something had dimmed his zeal – if zeal could be dimmed. Sir Godber wondered about it and was struck by his preoccupation with the question. If not time then what? The intractability of human nature. The sheer inertia of Englishmen for whom the past was always sacred and inviolable and who prided themselves on their obstinacy. 'We didn't win the war,' thought Sir Godber, 'we just refused to lose it.' Stirred to a new belligerency, he reached for the poker and poked the fire angrily and watched the sparks fly upwards into the darkness. He was damned if he was going to be put upon by the Dean. He hadn't spent a lifetime in high office to be frustrated by an ageing academic with a taste for port. He got up and poured himself a stiff whisky and paced the room. Lady Mary was right. A dispenser would be a move in the right direction. He'd speak to the Bursar in the morning. He glanced out of the window towards the Bursar's rooms and saw the lights burning. It wasn't late. He'd pay him a social call now. He finished his drink and went out into the hall and put on his overcoat.

The Bursar lived out. He dined in College as frequently as possible, thanks to his wife's cooking, and it was only by chance that he had stayed on in his rooms after dinner. He had things to think about. The Dean's pessimism, for one thing, and his failure to solicit the help of Sir Cathcart. It might be as well, he thought, to consider transferring his tenuous loyalties to Sir Godber after all. The Master had already shown himself to be a man of some determination – the Bursar had not forgotten his ultimatum to the College Council – and properly handled might well reward him for services rendered. After all it had been the Bursar who had given him the information which Sir Godber had used to browbeat the Council. It was worth considering. He got up to put on his coat and go home when footsteps on the stairs suggested a late caller. The Bursar sat down at his desk again and pretended business. There was a knock on the door.

'Come in,' said the Bursar. Sir Godber peered round the door.

'Ah, Bursar,' he said. 'I hope I'm not disturbing you. I was crossing the Court when I saw your light and I thought I would pop up.'

The Bursar rose to greet him with warm obsequiousness. 'How good of you to come, Master,' he said, hurrying to take Sir Godber's coat. 'I was about to drop you a line asking if I could see you.'

'In that case, I am delighted to have saved you the trouble,' said Sir Godber.

'Do take a seat.' Sir Godber sat in an armchair by the fire and smiled genially. The warmth of the Bursar's welcome and the atmosphere of indigence in the furnishings of his rooms were to his taste. He looked round approvingly at the worn carpet and the second-rate prints on the walls, from an almanac by the look of them, and felt the broken spring in the chair beneath him. Sir Godber recognized the importunity of it all. His years in office had given him a nose for dependency, and Sir Godber was not a man to withhold favours.

'Would you care for a little something?' the Bursar asked, hovering uncertainly near a decanter of indifferent port. Sir Godber hesitated a moment. Port on top of whisky? He thrust the considerations of his liver aside in favour of policy.

'Just a small glass, thank you,' he said, taking out his pipe and filling it from a worn pouch. Sir Godber was not an habitual pipe smoker; he found it burnt his tongue, but he had learnt the value of the common touch.

'A bad business about poor Zipser,' said the Bursar bringing the port. 'It's going to be a costly business restoring the Tower.'

Sir Godber lit his pipe. 'One of the topics I wanted to consult you about, Bursar. We'll have to set up a Restoration Fund, I imagine.'

'I'm afraid so, Master,' the Bursar said sadly.

Sir Godber sipped his port. 'In the ordinary way,' he said, 'and if the College were only less . . . er shall we say . . . less antiquated in its attitudes, I daresay I could use my influence in the City to raise a substantial sum, but as it is I find myself in an ambiguous position.' He trailed off airily, leaving the Bursar with a sense of infinite financial connections. 'No, we shall simply have to fall back on our own resources.'

'We have so few,' said the Bursar.

'We shall have to make what use we can of them,' Sir Godber continued, 'until such time as the College decides to give itself a more contemporary image. I'll do what I can of course, but I'm afraid it will be an uphill battle. If only the Council would see the importance of change.' He smiled and looked at the Bursar. 'But then I daresay you agree with the Dean?'

It was the moment the Bursar had been waiting for. 'The Dean has his own views, Master,' he said, 'and they are not ones I share.'

Sir Godber's eyebrows expressed encouragement with reservations.

'I have always felt that we were falling behind the times,' continued the Bursar, anxious to win the full approval of those eyebrows, 'but as Bursar I have been concerned with administration and it does tend to leave little time for policy. The Dean's influence is quite remarkable, you know, and of course there is Sir Cathcart.'

'I gather Sir Cathcart intends to call a meeting of the Porterhouse Society,' said Sir Godber.

'He's cancelled it since the Zipser affair,' the Bursar told him.

'That's interesting. So the Dean is on his own, is he?'

The Bursar nodded. 'I think some of the Council have had second thoughts too. The younger Fellows would like to see changes, but they don't carry much weight. So few of them too, but then we've never been noted for our Research Fellowships. We have neither the money nor the reputation to attract them. I have suggested ... but the Dean ...' he waved his hands helplessly.

Sir Godber gulped his port. In spite of it he was glad he had come. The Bursar's change of tune was encouraging and Sir Godber was satisfied. It was time to talk frankly. He knocked out his pipe and leant forward.

'Between ourselves I think we can circumvent the Dean,' he said, tapping the Bursar on the knee with a forefinger with a vulgar assurance. 'You mark my words. We'll have him where we want him.'

The Bursar stared at Sir Godber in startled fascination. The man's crudity, the change from an assumed urbanity to this backstair forcefulness took him by surprise, and Sir Godber noted his astonishment with satisfaction. The years of calling working men whom he despised 'Brother' had not been wasted. There was no doubting the menace in his grim bonhomie. 'He won't know his arse from his elbow by the time we've finished with him,' he continued. The Bursar nodded meekly. Sir Godber hitched his chair forward and began to outline his plans.

Skullion stood in the Court and wondered at the lights burning in the Bursar's room.

'He's staying late,' he thought. 'Usually home by nine, he is.' He walked through to the back gate and locked it, glancing hopefully at the spiked wall as he did so. Then he turned and made his way through the Fellows' Garden to New Court. He walked slowly and with a slight limp. The exertions of the chase had left him stiff and aching and he had still not recovered from the shock of the explosion in the Tower. 'Getting old,' he muttered and stopped to light his pipe, and as he stood in the shadow of a large elm the light in the Bursar's room went out. Skullion sucked at his pipe thoughtfully and tamped the tobacco down with his thumb. He was about to leave the shelter of the elm when a crunch of gravel on the path caused him to hesitate. Two figures had emerged from New Court and were coming towards him deep in conversation. Skullion recognized the Master's voice. He moved back into the shadows as the two figures passed him.

'No doubt the Dean will object,' Sir Godber was saying, 'but faced with a *fait accompli* there won't be anything he can do about it. I think we can take it that the days of the Dean's influence are numbered.'

'Not before time,' said the Bursar. The two figures disappeared round the side of the Master's Lodge. Skullion emerged from the shadow and stood on the path peering after them, his mind furiously occupied. So the Bursar had gone over to Sir Godber. Skullion wasn't surprised. He had never had much time for the Bursar. The man wasn't out of the top drawer for one thing and for another he was responsible for the wages of the College servants. Skullion regarded him more as a foreman than a genuine Fellow, a paymaster, and a mean one at that, and held him responsible for the pittance he received. And now the Bursar had gone over to Sir Godber. Skullion turned and made his way into New Court with a fresh sense of grievance and some perplexity. The Dean should be told but Skullion knew better than to tell him. The Dean didn't approve of eavesdropping. He was a proper gentleman. Skullion wondered what a fate accomplee was. He'd have to think of some way of warning the Dean in the morning. He went through the Screens and across to the Porter's Lodge and made himself some cocoa. 'So the Dean's days are numbered, are they?' he thought bitterly. 'We'll see about that.' It would take more than Sir Godber Evans and the miserable Bursar to change things. There was always Sir Cathcart. He'd see they didn't get their way. He had great faith in Sir Cathcart. At midnight he got up and went outside to close the front gate. During the day the thaw had set in and the snow had begun to melt but the wind had changed during the evening and it had begun to freeze again. Skullion stood in the doorway for a moment and stared out into the street. A middle-aged man slipped on the pavement opposite and fell. Skullion regarded his fall without interest. What happened outside Porterhouse was none of his affair. With a sudden wish that the Master would slip and break his neck, Skullion went back into the College and shut the door. Above him in the Tower the clock struck twelve.

CHAPTER ELEVEN

On the towpath by the river the Dean stood huddled in his overcoat against the wind. Behind him the willows shuddered and shook and the hedgerow rustled. In front the eights rowed through choppy water, each with its coterie of coaches and supporters splashing through the puddles on their bicycles and shouting orders and encouragement. On every stroke the coxes jerked backwards and the boats leapt forwards, each in pursuit of the eight ahead and each in turn in flight from the eight behind. Occasionally a sudden burst of cheering signalled a bump as one eight touched the boat in front and the two pulled into the side of the river and the victors broke off a willow branch and stuck it into the bow. There were gaps in the procession where bumps had been achieved, spaces of empty water and then another eight would appear round the bend still trying desperately to catch the boat at least two lengths ahead and overbump. Jesus. Porterhouse. Lady Margaret. Pembroke. Trinity. St Catherine's. Christ's. Churchill. Magdalene. Caius. Clare. Peterhouse. Historic names, hallowed names like so many prayers on a rosary of racing boats to be repeated twice yearly at Lent and after Easter. To the Dean the ritual was holy, a sacred occasion to be attended, no matter how cold or wet the weather, in memory of the healthy athleticism of the past and the certainties of his youth ... The Bumps were a time of renewal for him. Standing on the towpath he felt once more the innocence, the unquestioning innocence of his own rowing days and the fitness of things then. Yes, fitness, a fitness not simply of body, or even of mind, but of things in general, an acceptance of life as it was without the insidious subversion of questions or the dangerous speculations which had gained momentum since. A guiltless time, that, a golden age of assurance before the Great War when there was honey still for tea and a servant to bring it too. In memory of that time the Dean braved the wind and the cold and stood on the towpath while the bicycles splashed mud on to his shoes and the eights rowed by. When it was all over he turned and trudged back to the Pike and Eel where his car was parked. Behind him and in front, strung out along the path, old men like himself turned up the collars of their overcoats and headed home, their heads bent against the wind but with a new sprightliness in their step. The Dean had reached the railway bridge when he was aware of a familiar figure in front. 'Afternoon, Skullion. We rowed over again,' he said. Skullion nodded. 'Jesus never looked like catching us,' the Dean said, 'and we should bump Trinity tomorrow. It was the choppy water that stopped us today.'

They walked on in silence while the Dean recalled other Bumps and famous crews and Skullion tried to think of some way of broaching the subject of the Bursar's treachery without offending the Dean's sense of what was proper for College servants to say. It wasn't easy even to walk beside the Dean. Not his place, and presently Skullion gave up the unequal struggle with his conscience and gradually fell back a pace or two behind the old man. At the Pike and Eel the Dean, still lost in thought, unlocked his car and climbed in. Skullion fetched his bicycle and wheeled it across the footbridge. Behind him the Dean sat in his car and waited for the traffic to clear. He had forgotten Skullion. He had forgotten even the Bumps and the youth they had recalled to him. He was thinking about Sir Godber and the glibness of his modernity and the threat to Porterhouse he represented. His feet were cold and the joints in his knees ached. He was an old man, bitter at the loss of his power. When the last of the other cars had gone he started the engine and drove home through the factory workers coming out of Pye's television factory. Cars pulled out of the factory gates in front of him. Men on bicycles ignored him and girls ran across the road to catch their buses. The Dean eyed them angrily. In the old days he would have blown his horn and cleared them off the road. Now he had to sit and wait. He found himself staring at an advertisement. 'Watch with Carrington on Pye', it said and a face smiled at him from a television screen. A familiar face. A face he knew. 'Carrington on Conservation. The Nation's Heritage at Stake.' The Dean stared at the face and was suddenly conscious of new hope. Behind him someone hooted importunately and the Dean put his car in gear and moved forward. He drove steadily home, unaware now of the traffic and of the present.

He left his car in the garage behind Phipps Building and went up to his room and presently he was sitting at his desk checking the Porterhouse Register for Cornelius Carrington's name. There it was, 1935–8. The Dean closed the book and sat back contentedly. A nasty piece of work, Cornielius Carrington, but effective for all that. The Jeremiah of the BBC, they called him, and certainly his romantic Toryism was popular. Not even politically divisive, just good-hearted nostalgia for the best that was British and with immense family appeal. The Dean did not often watch television but he had heard of Cornelius Carrington's programmes.

'Jewels of the Empire' had been one such series, with the ubiquitous Carrington expatiating on the architectural treasures of Poona and Lucknow. Another programme had been devoted to the need to preserve the rum ration in the Royal Navy, and Carrington had made himself the spokesman for past privileges wherever they were threatened. He was, the Dean felt sure, capable of extolling the virtues of any subject you chose and certainly there was no doubting the effectiveness of his appearance. Elicit Cornelius Carrington's interest and you were sure of an audience. And the wretched fellow was a Porterhouse man. The Dean smiled to himself at the thought of Carrington's publicizing the threat that Sir Godber's innovations posed to the College. It was a nice thought. He would have to speak to Sir Cathcart about it. It would depend on the outcome of the College Council meeting in the morning.

Skullion was at his waterpipe in the boiler-room when the meeting began. With the usual interruptions from the central heating system he could hear much of what was said. Most of the discussion centred on the cost of repairing the damage done to the Tower by Zipser's experiment in the mass disposal of prophylactics. Sir Godber, it seemed, had very definite views on the subject.

'It is time,' he was saying, 'that the College recognized the need to act in accordance with the principles which appear to have motivated the members of this Council in the past. The changes which I proposed at our last meeting met with opposition on the grounds that Porterhouse is a self-sufficient and independent college, a self-governing body whose interests are internal and without reference to the world at large. For myself as you know, that view is without foundation, but I am prepared to accept it since it appears to represent the views of the majority of this Council.' The Master paused, evidently looking round the Fellows for approval. In the boiler-room Skullion tried to digest the import of his words without much success. It seemed too much to hope that Sir Godber had changed his mind.

'Are we to understand that you have conceded that there is no need for the changes you proposed at our last meeting?' the Dean asked.

'The point I am conceding, Dean,' continued the Master, 'is that the College is responsible for its own internal affairs. I am prepared to accept the views of the Council that we should not look for guidance or assistance from the public.'

'I should certainly hope not,' said the Senior Tutor fervently.

'That is all I am conceding and since that is the case the full responsibility for the recent tragic events must be borne by the College.

In particular the cost of the repairs to the Tower must be met out of our own resources.'

A murmur of astonishment greeted the Master's statement.

'Impossible,' said the Dean angrily, 'out of the question. In the past we have had recourse to a Restoration Fund. There seems to be no good reason why we should not set up such a fund in this case.'

In the boiler-room Skullion followed the argument with difficulty. The Master's tactics evaded him.

'I must say, Dean, that I find your attitude a little difficult to understand,' Sir Godber continued. 'On the one hand you are opposed to any changes that would bring Porterhouse into line with contemporary standards of education ...' There was an angry interjection from the Dean. '... and on the other you seem only too ready to appeal to public subscription to avoid the necessary economies required to rebuild the Tower ...' At this point the central heating system interjected and it was some time before Skullion could catch the drift of the discussion again. By then they had got on to the details of the economies Sir Godber had in mind. Not surprisingly they seemed to embody just those changes in College policy he had suggested at the previous meeting but this time the Master was arguing less from policy than from financial necessity.

Through the gurgles in the pipe Skullion caught the words 'Self-service system in Hall ... coeducation ... and the sale of College properties.' He was about to climb down from his perch when Rhyder Street was mentioned. Skullion lived in Rhyder Street. Rhyder Street was College property. In the boiler-room Skullion's interest in the proceedings taking place above his head took on a new and more personal touch.

'The Bursar and I have calculated that the cost of the repairs can be met by the economies I have outlined,' Skullion heard. 'The sale of Rhyder Street in particular will provide something in the region of £150,000 at today's inflated prices. It is slum property, I know, but ...' Skullion slid down the pipe and sat on the chair. Slum property, he called it. Rhyder Street where he lived in Number 41. Slum property. The Chef lived there too. The street was filled with the houses of College servants. They couldn't sell it. They'd got no right to. A new fury possessed Skullion, a bitterness against Sir Godber that was no longer a concern for the traditions of the College he had served so long but a sense of personal betrayal. He'd been going to retire to Rhyder Street. It had been one of the conditions of his employment. The College had provided a house at a nominal rent. Skullion hadn't worked for forty-five years at a pittance a week to be evicted from a house that had been sold over his head by Sir Godber. Without waiting to hear more he got up from the chair and lurched out of the boiler-room into the Old Court in search of the Chef. Above his head a new violence of debate had broken out in the Council Chamber. Sir Godber had announced the proposed installation of a contraceptive dispenser.

The Dean erupted from the meeting with a virulence that stemmed from the knowledge that he had been outmanoeuvred. The Master's appeal to principle had placed him in a false position and the Dean was conscious that his arguments against the Master's proposed economies had lacked the force of conviction. 'To cap it all,' he muttered to himself as he swept from the room, 'a damned contraceptive machine.' The Bursar's sudden change of allegiance had infuriated him too. With his support Sir Godber could manipulate the College finances as he pleased, and the Dean cursed the Bursar viciously as he climbed the stairs to his room. There remained only Sir Cathcart and already he had shown himself pusillanimous in the matter of calling a meeting of the Porterhouse Society. Well, there were others who could be relied on to bring influence to bear. 'I'll see Sir Cathcart this afternoon,' he decided, and poured himself a glass of sherry.

Sir Godber left the meeting with the Bursar. He was feeling distinctly pleased with his morning's work.

'Why don't you lunch with us at the Lodge?' he said with a sudden generosity. 'My wife has been asking to meet you.'

'That's very kind of you,' said the Bursar, glad to escape the hostile reception he was likely to meet at High Table. They strolled across the lawn past a group of Fellows who were conferring at the entrance to the Combination Room. In the Screens they saw Skullion scowling darkly in the shadows.

'I must say I find Skullion's manner a trifle taciturn,' Sir Godber said when they were out of earshot. 'Even as an undergraduate I found him unpleasant to deal with, and age hasn't improved his manners.'

The Bursar sympathized with Sir Godber. 'Not a very likeable fellow but he's very conscientious and he is a great favourite of the Dean.'

'I can imagine that they get on well together,' said Sir Godber. 'All the same, Porterhouse may be the name of the College but it doesn't mean that the Head Porter is in charge. On the night of the ... er ... accident Skullion was distinctly disrespectful. I told him to open the main gates for the ambulancemen and he refused. One of these days I daresay I shall have to ask you to give him notice.'

The Bursar blanched at the thought. 'I think that would be most inadvisable, Master,' he said. 'The Dean would be most upset.'

'Well,' said Sir Godber, 'the next time I have any insolence from him out he goes and no mistake.' With the silent thought that it was time such relics of the past got their marching orders, the Master led the way into the Lodge.

Lady Mary was waiting in the drawing-room. 'I've asked the Bursar to lunch, my dear,' said Sir Godber, his voice a shade less authoritative in the presence of his wife.

'I'm afraid you'll just have to take pot luck,' Lady Mary told the Bursar. 'My husband tells me that you treat yourselves lavishly at High Table.'

The Bursar simpered apologetically. Lady Mary ignored these signs of submission. 'I find it quite deplorable that so much good money should be wasted on maintaining the ill-health of a number of elderly scholars.'

'My dear,' Sir Godber intervened, 'you'll be glad to hear that the Council has accepted our proposals.'

'And not before time,' said Lady Mary, studying the Bursar with distaste. 'One of the most astonishing things about the educational institutions of this country is the way they have resisted change. When I think how long we've been urging the abolition of private education I'm amazed. The public schools seem to go from strength to strength.'

To the Bursar, himself the product of a minor public school on the South Downs, Lady Mary's words verged on the blasphemous. 'You're surely not suggesting public schools should be abolished,' he said. From the table where Sir Godber was pouring sherry there came the sound of rattled glass. Lady Mary assumed a new hauteur.

'Am I to infer from that remark that you are in favour of private education?' she asked.

The Bursar groped for a conciliatory reply. 'Well, I think there is something to be said for it,' he mumbled finally.

'What?' asked Lady Mary.

But before the Bursar could think of anything to recommend the Public School system without offending his hostess, Sir Godber had come to his rescue with a glass of sherry. 'Very good of you, Master,' he said gratefully and sipped his drink. 'And a very pleasant sherry, if I may say so.'

'We don't drink South African sherry,' Lady Mary said. 'I hope the College doesn't keep any in stock.'

'I believe we have some for the undergraduates,' said the Bursar, 'but I know the Senior Members don't touch the stuff.'

'Quite right too,' said Sir Godber.

'I was not thinking of the question of taste,' Lady Mary continued, 'so much as the moral objections to buying South African products. I have always made a point of boycotting South African goods.'

To the Bursar, long accustomed to the political opinions expressed at High Table by the Dean and the Senior Tutor, Lady Mary's views were radical in the extreme and the fact that they were expressed in a tone of voice which suggested that she was addressing a congregation of unmarried mothers unnerved him. He stumbled through the thorny problems of world poverty, the population explosion, abortion, the Nicaraguan earthquake, strategic arms limitation talks, and prison reform until a gong sounded and they went into lunch. Over a sardine salad that would have served as an *hors d'oeuvre* in Hall his discomfiture took a more personal turn.

'You're not by any chance related to the Shropshire Shrimptons?' Lady Mary asked.

The Bursar shook his head sorrowfully.

'My family came originally from Southend,' he said.

'How very unusual,' said Lady Mary. 'I only asked because we used to stay with them at Bognorth before the war. Sue Shrimpton was up with me at Somerville and we served together on the Needham Commission.'

The Bursar acknowledged Lady Mary's social distinction in silence. He would put his present humiliation to good use in the future. At sherry parties for years to come he would be able to say 'Lady Mary was saying to me only the other day ...' or 'Lady Mary and I ...' and establish his own superiority over lesser men and their wives. It was in such small achievements that the Bursar's satisfactions were found. Sir Godber ate his sardines in silence too. He was grateful to the Bursar for providing a target for his wife's conversation and moral rectitude. He dreaded to think what would happen if the injustices on which Lady Mary vented her moral spleen ever disappeared. 'The poor are always with us, thank God,' he thought and helped himself to a piece of cheddar.

It was left to Skullion to represent the college on the towpath that afternoon. The Dean had driven over to Coft to see Sir Cathcart and Skullion stood alone in the biting wind watching Porterhouse row over for the second day running. The terrible sense of wrong that he had felt in the boiler-room when he heard the proposed sale of Rhyder Street had not left him. It had been augmented by the news Arthur had brought him from High Table after lunch.

'He's put the cat among the pigeons now, the Master has,' Arthur said breathlessly. 'He's got under their skin something terrible this time.'

'I don't wonder,' said Skullion, thinking bitterly of Rhyder Street.

'I mean you wouldn't want one in your own home, would you? Not one of them things.'

'What things?' Skullion asked, all too conscious of the fact that he was unlikely to have a home to put anything in if Sir Godber had his way.

'Well I don't rightly know what they're called,' Arthur said. 'Not exactly, that is. You put your money in and ...'

'And what?' Skullion asked irritably.

'And you get these things out. Three I think. Not that I've ever had occasion to use them.'

'What things?'

'Frenchies,' said Arthur, looking round to make sure no one was listening.

'Frenchies?' said Skullion. 'What Frenchies?'

'The Frenchies that Zipser gentleman exploded himself with,' Arthur explained. Skullion looked at him in disgust. 'You mean to tell me they're going to bring one of those filthy things into the College?'

Arthur nodded. 'In the men's toilet. That's where it's going.'

'Over my dead body,' said Skullion. 'I'm not staying here as Head Porter with one of those things in the toilet. This isn't a bloody chemist's shop.'

'Some of the other colleges have them,' Arthur told him.

'Some of the other colleges may have them. Doesn't mean we've got to. It isn't right. Encourages immorality, French letters do. You'd have thought they'd have learnt that from what happened to that Zipser bloke. Preyed on his mind, all those FLs did.'

Arthur shook his head sorrowfully. ''Tisn't right,' he said, ''tisn't right, Mr Skullion. I don't know what the College is coming to. Senior Tutor is particularly upset. He says it will affect the rowing.'

Standing on the towpath Skullion agreed with the Senior Tutor. 'All this business about sex,' he muttered. 'It doesn't do anybody any good. It isn't right.'

When the Porterhouse Eight rowed past Skullion raised a feeble cheer and then stumped off after them. Around him bicycles churned the muddy puddles as they overtook him but, like the Dean the day before, Skullion was lost in thought and bitterness.

His anger, unlike the Dean's, was tainted with a sense of betrayal. The College whose servant he was and his ancestors before him had let him down. They had no right to let Sir Godber sell Rhyder Street. They should have stopped him. That was their duty to him, just as his duty to the College had been for forty-five years to sit in the Porter's Lodge all day and half the night for a miserable pittance a week, the guardian of privilege and of the indiscretions of the privileged young. How many drunken young gentlemen had Skullion helped to their rooms? How many secrets had he kept? How many insults had he suffered in his time? He could not begin to recall them but in the back of his mind the debits had balanced the credits and he had been secure in the knowledge that the College would always look after him now and in his old age. He had been proud of his servility, the Porter of Porterhouse, but what if the College's reputation was debased? What would he be then? A homeless old man with his memories. He wasn't having it. They'd got to see him right. It was their duty.

CHAPTER TWELVE

In the library at Coft Castle, the Dean put the same point to Sir Cathcart.

'It's our duty to see these damnable innovations are stopped,' he said. 'The man seems intent on changing the entire character of the College. For years, damn it for centuries, we've been famous for our kitchens and now he's proposing a self-service canteen and a contraceptive dispenser.'

'A what?' Sir Cathcart gasped.

'A contraceptive dispenser.'

'Good God, the man's insane!' shouted Sir Cathcart. 'Can't have one of those damned things in College. When I was an undergraduate you got sent down if your were caught riveting a dolly!'

'Quite,' said the Dean, who had a shrewd suspicion that in his time the General had been a steam-hammer if the imagery of his language was anything to go by. 'What you don't seem to appreciate, Cathcart,' he continued, before the General could indulge in any further mechanical memories, 'is that the Master is undermining something very fundamental. I'm not thinking simply of the College now. The implications are rather wider than that. Do you take my meaning?'

Sir Cathcart shook his head. 'No, I don't,' he said bluntly.

'This country,' said the Dean with a new intensity, 'has been run for the past three hundred years by an oligarchy.' He paused to see if the General understood the word.

'Quite right, old boy,' said Sir Cathcart. 'Always has been, always will be. No use denying it. Good thing.'

'An elite of gentlemen, Cathcart,' continued the Dean. 'Now don't mistake me, I'm not suggesting they started off as gentlemen. They didn't, half of them, they came from all walks of life. Take Peel for instance, grandson of a mill hand, ended up a gentleman though, and a damned fine Prime Minister. Why?'

'Can't think,' said Sir Cathcart.

'Because he had a proper education.'

'Ah. Went to Porterhouse eh?'

'No,' said the Dean. 'He was an Oxford man.'

'Good God. And still a gentleman? Extraordinary.'

'The point I'm trying to make, Cathcart,' said the Dean solemnly, 'is that the two Universities have been the forcing-house of an intellectual aristocracy with tastes and values that had nothing whatever to do with their own personal backgrounds. How many of our Prime Ministers over the last hundred and seventy years have been to Oxford or Cambridge?'

'Good Lord, don't ask me,' said the General. 'Got no idea.'

'Most of them,' said the Dean.

'Quite right too,' said Sir Cathcart. 'Can't have any Tom, Dick or Harry running the affairs of state.'

'That is precisely the point I have been trying to make,' said the Dean. 'The business of the older Universities is to take Toms and Dicks and Harrys and turn them into gentlemen. We have been doing that very successfully for the past five hundred years.'

'Mind you,' said Sir Cathcart doubtfully, 'I knew some bounders in my time.'

'I daresay you did,' said the Dean.

'Used to duck 'em in the Fountain. Did them no end of good.' Sir Cathcart reminisced cheerfully.

'What Sir Godber proposes,' the Dean continued, 'means the end of all that. In the name of so-called social justice the man intends to turn Porterhouse into a run-of-the-mill college like Selwyn or Fitzwilliam.'

Sir Cathcart snorted.

'Take more than Godber Evans to do that,' he said. 'Selwyn! Full of religious maniacs in my time, and Fitzwilliam wasn't a college at all. A sort of hostel for townies.'

'And what do you think Porterhouse will be with a self-service canteen instead of Hall and a contraceptive dispenser in every lavatory? There won't be a decent family prepared to pay a penny towards the Endowment Fund, and you know what that means.'

'Oh come now, can't be as bad as that,' said Sir Cathcart, 'I mean to say we've survived worse crises in the past. There was the business over the Bursar . . . what was his name?'

'Fitzherbert.'

'Enough to ruin another college, that was.'

'Enough to ruin us,' said the Dean. 'If it hadn't been for him we wouldn't be dependent on wealthy parents now.'

'But we got over it all the same,' Sir Cathcart insisted, 'and we'll get over this present nonsense. Just fashion, all this equality. Here today, gone tomorrow. Have a drink.' He got up and went over to the Waverley Novels. 'Scotch?' The Dean regarded the set in some bewilderment.

'Scott?' he asked. He had never regarded Sir Cathcart as a man with even remotely literary tastes and this sudden change in the conversation seemed unduly inconsequential.

'Or sherry? if you prefer,' said Sir Cathcart, indicating a handsomely bound copy of *Lavengro*. The Dean shook his head irritably. There was something extraordinarily vulgar about Sir Cathcart's travesty of a library.

'*Romany Rye* perhaps?' The Dean shook his head. 'Nothing, thank you,' he said. Sir Cathcart helped himself to *Rob Roy* and sat down.

'Proust,' he said, raising his glass. The Dean stared at him angrily. Sir Cathcart's flippancy was beginning to get on his nerves. He hadn't come out to Coft Castle to be regaled with the liquid contents of the library.

'Cathcart,' he said firmly, 'we have got to do something to stop the rot.'

The General nodded. 'Absolutely. Couldn't agree more.'

'It needs more than agreement to stop Sir Godber,' continued the Dean. 'It needs action. Public pressure. That sort of thing.'

'Difficult to get any public sympathy when you've got undergraduates running round blowing up buildings. Extraordinary thing to do really. Fill all those contraceptives with gas. Practical joke I suppose. Went wrong.'

'Very wrong,' said the Dean, who didn't want to get side-tracked.

'Mind you,' said Sir Cathcart, 'I can remember getting up to some pretty peculiar pranks. When I first went in the Army, great thing was to fill a French letter with water and stick it down someone's bed when he was out. Top bunk, you follow. Comes back. Gets into bed. Puts his toe through the thing. Fellow below gets drenched.'

'Very amusing,' said the Dean grimly.

'That's only the beginning,' said the General. 'Fellow below thinks fellow on top has wet his bed. Gets up and clobbers him. Damned funny.

Two fellows fighting like that.' He finished his whisky and got up to replenish his glass. 'Sure you won't change your mind,' he asked.

The Dean studied the shelves pensively. He was beginning to feel the need for some sort of restorative.

'A pink gin,' he said finally, with a malicious gleam in his eye.

'Zola,' said the General promptly and reached up for a copy of *Nana*. The Dean tried to collect his thoughts. Sir Cathcart's flippancy had begun to erode his fervour. He sipped his gin in silence while the General lit a cheroot.

'Trouble with you academic wallahs,' said Sir Cathcart finally, evidently sensing the Dean's confusion, 'is you take things too seriously.'

'This is a serious matter,' said the Dean.

'Didn't say it wasn't,' Sir Cathcart told him. 'What I said was you take it seriously. Bad mistake. Ever hear the joke Goering told his psychiatrist in the prison at Nuremburg?'

The Dean shook his head.

'About different nationalities. Very revealing,' Sir Cathcart went on. 'Take one German and what have you got?'

'And what have you got?'

'A good worker. Take two Germans and you've got a Bund. Three Germans and you've a war.'

The Dean smiled obediently. 'Very amusing,' he said, 'but I really don't see what this has to do with the College.'

'Haven't finished yet. Take one Italian and you've a tenor. Two Italians a retreat. Three Italians unconditional surrender. Take one Englishman and you've an idiot. Two Englishmen a club and three Englishmen an Empire.'

'Very funny,' said the Dean, 'but a little out of date, don't you think? We seem to have mislaid the Empire en route.'

'Forgot to be idiots,' said Sir Cathcart. 'Great mistake. Did bloody well when we were chinless wonders. Done bloody badly since. The Sir Godbers of this world have upset the applecart. Look serious and are fools. Different in the old days. Looked fools and were serious. Confused the foreigners. Ribbentrop came over to London. Heil Hitlered the King. Went back to Germany convinced we were decadent. Got a thrashing for his pains in '40. Hanged for that slip-up. Should have looked a bit closer. Mind you, it wouldn't have helped him. Went on appearances.' Sir Cathcart chuckled to himself and eyed the Dean.

'You may be right at that,' said the Dean grudgingly. 'And certainly the Master is a fool.'

'Clever fellows often are,' Sir Cathcart said. 'Got one-track minds.

Have to have, I suppose, to do so well. Great handicap, though. In life I mean. Get so carried away with what's going on inside their own silly heads they can't cope with what's going on outside. Don't know about life. Don't know about people. Got no nose for it.'

The Dean sipped his gin and tried to follow the train of Sir Cathcart's thoughts. A new mellowness had begun to steal over him and he had the feeling, it was no more than a mere glimmer, that somewhere in the General's rambling and staccato utterances there was a thread that was leading slowly to an idea. Something about the General's manner as he helped himself to a third whisky and the Dean to a second gin and bitters suggested it. Something like a sparkle of cunning in the bloodshot eyes and a twitch of his veined snout and the bristles of his ginger whiskers which reminded the Dean of an old animal, scarred but undefeated. The Dean began to suspect that he had underestimated Sir Cathcart D'Eath. He accepted one of the General's cheroots and puffed it slowly.

'As I was saying,' Sir Cathcart continued, settling once more into his chair, 'we've forgotten the natural advantages of idiocy. Puts the other fellow off you see. Can't take you seriously. Good thing. Then when he's off guard you give it to him in the goolies. Never fails. Out like a light. Want to do the same with this Godber fellow.'

'I really hadn't visualized going to quite such lengths,' said the Dean doubtfully.

'Shouldn't think he's got any,' said the General. 'Wife certainly doesn't look up to much. Scrawny sort of woman. Bad complexion. Not fond of boys, is he.'

The Dean shuddered. 'That at least we've been spared,' he said.

'Pity,' said Sir Cathcart. 'Useful bait, boys.'

'Bait?' asked the Dean.

'Bait the trap.'

'Trap?'

'Got to have a trap. Weak spot. Bound to have one. What?' said the General. 'Bleating of the sheep excites the tiger. *Stalky*. Great book.' He got up from his chair and crossed to the window and stared out into the darkness while the Dean, who had been trying to keep up with his train of thought, wondered if he should tell Sir Cathcart that *Lavengro* had nothing to do with Spain. On the whole he thought not. Sir Cathcart was too set in his ways.

'I forgot to mention it earlier,' he said at last, 'but the Master also intends to put Rhyder Street up for sale.'

Sir Cathcart, who had become immersed in his own reflection in the window, turned and stood glowering down at him. 'Rhyder Street?'

'He wants to use the money for the restoration of the Tower,' the Dean explained. 'It's old College property and rather run down. The College servants live there.'

The General sat down and fiddled with his moustache. 'Skullion live there?' he asked. The Dean nodded. 'Skullion, the Chef, the under-porter, the gardener, people like that.'

'Can't have that. Got to stable them somewhere,' said the General. He helped himself to a fourth whisky. 'Can't turn them out into the street. Old retainers. Wouldn't look good,' and his eyes which a moment before had been dark suddenly glittered. 'Not a bad idea either.'

'I must say, Cathcart,' said the Dean, 'I do wish you would not jump about so. What do you mean? "Wouldn't look good" and "Not a bad idea either". The two statements don't go together.'

'Looks bad for Sir Godber,' said the General. 'Bad publicity for a socialist. Headlines. See them now. Wouldn't dare. Got him.'

Slowly and dimly, through the shrapnel of Sir Cathcart's utterances, the Dean perceived the drift of his thought.

'Ah,' he said.

The General winked a dreadful eye. 'Something there, eh?' he asked.

The Dean leant forward eagerly. 'Have you ever heard of a fellow called Carrington? Cornelius Carrington? Conservationist. TV personality.'

He was aware that the infection of the General's staccato had finally taken hold of him but the thought was lost in the excitement of the moment. Sir Cathcart's eyes were gleaming brightly now and his nostrils were flared like those of a bronze warhorse.

'Just the fellow. An OP. Up his street. Couldn't do better. Nasty piece of work.'

'Right,' said the Dean. 'Can you arrange it?'

'Invite him up. Delighted to come. Snob. Give him the scent and off he'll go.'

The Dean finished his gin with a contented smile.

'It's just the sort of situation he likes,' he said, 'and although I deplore the thought of any more publicity – that wretched fellow Zipser gave us a lot of trouble in that direction you know – I rather fancy friend Carrington will give Sir Godber cause for thought. You definitely think he'll come?'

'Jump at the opportunity. I'll see to that. Same club. Can't think why. Should have been blackballed,' said the General. 'Fix it tomorrow.'

By the time the Dean left Coft Castle that evening he was a happier man. As he tottered out of his car in time for dinner and passed the

Porter's Lodge he noticed Skullion sitting staring into the gas fire. 'Must ask him how we did,' the Dean muttered and went into the Porter's Lodge.

'Ah, Skullion,' he said as the porter got to his feet, 'I wasn't able to be at the Bumps this afternoon. How did it go?'

'Rowed over, sir,' said Skullion dejectedly.

The Dean shook his head sadly.

'What a pity,' he said, 'I was rather hoping we'd do better today. Still there is always a chance in May.'

'Yes, sir,' Skullion said, but without, it seemed to the Dean, the enthusiasm that had been his wont.

'Getting old, poor fellow,' the Dean thought as he stumbled past the red lanterns that guarded the fallen debris of Zipser's climacteric.

CHAPTER THIRTEEN

Cornelius Carrington travelled to Cambridge by train. It accorded with the discriminating nostalgia which was the hallmark of his programmes that he should catch the Fenman at Liverpool Street and spend the journey in the dining-car speculating on the suddenness of Sir Cathcart's invitation, while observing his fellow travellers and indulging in British Rail's high tea. As the train rattled past the tenements and factories of Hackney and on to Ponders End, Carrington recoiled from the harshness of reality into the world of his own choosing and considered whether or not to have a second toasted tea cake. His was a soft world, fuzzy with private indecisions masked by the utterance of public verities which gave him the appearance of a lenient Jeremiah. It was a reassuring image and a familiar one, appearing at irregular but timely intervals throughout the year and bringing with it a denunciation of the present, made all the more acceptable by his approval of the recent past. If pre-stressed concrete and high-rise apartments were anathemas to Cornelius Carrington, to be condemned on social, moral and aesthetic grounds, his adulation of pebble-dash, pseudo-Tudor and crazy paving asserted the supreme virtues of the suburbs and reassured his viewers that all was well with the world in spite of the fact that nearly everything was wrong. Nor were his crusades wholly architectural. With a moral fervour which was evidently religious, without being in any way denominational, he espoused hopeless causes and gave viewers a vicarious sense of philanthropy that was eminently satisfying. More than one meths drinker had been elevated to the status of an alcoholic thanks to Carrington's intervention, while several heroin addicts had served an unexpected social purpose by suffering withdrawal symptoms in the company of Carrington, the camera crew, and several million viewers. Whatever the issue, Cornelius Carrington managed to combine moral indignation with entertainment and to extract from the situation just those elements which were most disturbing, without engendering in his audience a more than temporary sense of hopelessness which his own personality could render needless. There was about the man himself a genuinely comforting quality, epitomizing all that was sure and certain and humane about the British way of life. Policemen might be shot (and if his opinion was anything to go by they were being massacred daily across the country) but the traditions of the law remained unimpaired and immune to the rising tide of violence. Like some omniscient Teddy Bear, Cornelius Carrington was ultimately comforting.

As he sat in the dining car savouring the desultory landscape of Broxbourne, Carrington's thoughts turned from teacakes to the ostensible reasons for his visit. Sir Cathcart's invitation had come too abruptly both in manner and in time to convince him that it was wholly ingenuous. Carrington had listened to the General's description of the recent events in Porterhouse with interest. His ties with his old college had been tenuous, to put it mildly, and he shared with Sir Godber some unpleasant memories of the place and his time as an undergraduate. At the same time he recognized that the changes Sir Cathcart regretted in other colleges and feared in Porterhouse might have a value for a series on Cambridge. Carrington on Cambridge. It was an excellent title and the notion of a personal view of the University by 'An Old Freshman' appealed to him. He had declined the General's invitation and had come unannounced to reconnoitre. He would visit Porterhouse, certainly, but he would stay more comfortably at the Belvedere Hotel. More comfortably and less fettered by obligation. No one should say that Cornelius Carrington had bit the hand that fed him.

By the time the train reached Cambridge, he had already begun to organize the programme in his mind. The railway station would make a good starting point and one that pointed a moral. It had been built so far from the centre of the town on the insistence of the University Authorities in 1845 who had feared its malign influence. Foresight or the refusal to accept change? The viewer could take his pick. Carrington was impartial. Then shots of College gateways. Eroded statues. Shields. Heraldic animals. Chapels and gilded towers. Gowns. Undergraduates.

The Bridge of Sighs. It was all there waiting to be explored by Carrington at his most congenial.

He took a taxi and drove to the Belvedere Hotel. It was not what he remembered. The old hotel, charming in a quiet opulent way, was gone and in its place there stood a large modern monstrosity, as tasteless a monument to commercial cupidity as any he had ever seen. Cornelius Carrington's fury was aroused. He would definitely make the series now. Rejecting the anonymous amenities of the Belvedere, he cancelled his room and took the taxi to the Blue Boar in Trinity Street. Here too things had changed, but at least from the outside the hotel looked what it had once been, an eighteenth-century hostelry, and Carrington was satisfied. After all, it is appearances that matter, he thought as he went up to his room.

At any previous time in his life Skullion would have agreed with him but now that his house in Rhyder Street was up for sale, and the College's reputation threatened by the Master's flirtation with the commercial aspects of birth control, Skullion was less concerned with appearances. He skulked in the Porter's Lodge with a new taciturnity in marked contrast to the gruff deference he had accorded callers in the past. No longer did he appear at the door to greet the Fellows with a brisk 'Good morning, sir' and anyone calling for a parcel was likely to be treated to a surly indifference and a churlishness which defeated attempts at conversation. Even Walter, the under-porter, found Skullion difficult. He had never found him easy but now his existence was made miserable by Skullion's silence and his frequent outbursts of irritation. For hours Skullion would sit staring at the gas fire mulling over his grievances and debating what to do. 'Got no right to do it,' he would suddenly say out loud with a violence that made Walter jump.

'No right to do what?' he asked at first.

'None of your business,' Skullion snapped back and Walter gave up the attempt to discuss whatever it was that had put the Head Porter's back up. Even the Dean, never the most sensitive of men when it came to other people's feelings, noticed the change in Skullion when he called each morning to make his report. There was a hangdog look about the Porter that caused the Dean to wonder if it wasn't time he was put down before recalling that Skullion was after all a human being and that he had been misled by the metaphor. Skullion would sidle into the room with his hat in his hand and mutter, 'Nothing to report, sir,' and sidle out again leaving the Dean with a sense of having been rebuked in some unspoken way. It was an uncomfortable feeling after so many years of approval and the Dean felt aggrieved. If Skullion couldn't be put down, it was perhaps time he retired before this new churlishness tarnished his previously unspotted reputation for deference. Besides, the Dean had enough to worry about in Sir Godber's plans without being bothered with Skullion's private grievances.

If Skullion accorded the Dean scant respect, his attitude to the other Fellows was positively mutinous. The Bursar in particular suffered at his hands, or at least his tongue, whenever he had the misfortune to have to call in at the Porter's Lodge for some unavoidable reason.

'What do you want?' Skullion would ask in a tone that suggested that he would like the Bursar to ask for a black eye. It was the only thing Skullion, it appeared, was prepared to give him. His mail certainly wasn't. It regularly arrived two days late and Skullion's inability on the telephone switchboard to put the Bursar's calls through to the right number exacerbated the Bursar's sense of isolation. Only the Master seemed happy to see him now and the Bursar spent much of his time in consultation with Sir Godber in the Master's Lodge, conscious that even here he was not wholly welcome, if Lady Mary's manner was anything to go by. Between the Scylla of Skullion and the Charybdis of Lady Mary, not to mention the dangers of the open sea in the shape of the Fellows at High Table, the Bursar led a miserable existence made no less difficult by Sir Godber's refusal to accept the limitations placed on his schemes by the financial plight of the College. It was during one of their many wrangles about money that the Bursar mentioned Skullion's new abruptness.

'Skullion costs us approximately a thousand pounds a year,' he said. 'More if you take the loss on the house in Rhyder Street. Altogether the College servants mean an annual outflow of £15,000.'

'Skullion certainly isn't worth that,' said the Master, 'and besides I find his attitude decidedly obnoxious.'

'He has become very uncivil,' agreed the Bursar.

'Not only that but I dislike the proprietary attitude he takes to the College,' the Master said. 'Anyone would think he owns the place. He'll have to go.'

For once the Bursar did not disagree. As far as he was concerned Porterhouse would be a pleasanter place when Skullion no longer exercised his baleful influence in the Porter's Lodge.

'He'll be reaching retiring age in a few years' time,' he said. 'Do you think we should wait ...'

But Sir Godber was adamant. 'I don't think we can afford to wait,' he said. 'It's a simple question of redundancy. There is absolutely no need for two porters, just as there is no point in employing a dozen mentally deficient kitchen servants where one efficient man could do the job.'

'But Skullion is getting on. He's an old man,' said the Bursar, who saw looming before him the dreadful task of telling Skullion that his services were no longer required.

'Precisely my point. We can hardly sack the under-porter, who is young, simply to satisfy Skullion, who, as you say yourself, will be retiring in a few years' time. We really cannot afford to indulge in sentimentality, Bursar. You must speak to Skullion. Suggest that he look around for some other form of employment. There must be something he can do.'

The Bursar had no doubts on that score and he was about to suggest deferring Skullion's dismissal until they should see what the sale of Rhyder Street raised by way of additional funds when Lady Mary put a spoke in his wheel.

'I can't honestly see why the porter's job shouldn't be done by a woman,' she said. 'It would mark a significant break with tradition and really the job is simply that of a receptionist.'

Both Sir Godber and the Bursar turned and stared at her.

'Godber, don't goggle,' said Lady Mary.

'My dear ...' Sir Godber began, but Lady Mary was in no mood to put up with argument.

'A woman porter,' she insisted, 'will do more than anything else to demonstrate the fact that the College has entered the twentieth century.'

'But there isn't a college in Cambridge with a female porter,' said the Bursar.

'Then it's about time there was,' Lady Mary snapped. The Bursar left the Master's Lodge a troubled man. Lady Mary's intervention had ended once and for all his hopes of deferring the question of Skullion until the Porter had either made himself unpopular with the other Fellows by his manner or had come to his senses. The thought of having to tell the Head Porter that his services were no longer required daunted the Bursar. For a brief moment he even considered consulting the Dean but he was hardly likely to get any assistance from that quarter. He had burnt his bridges by siding with the Master. He could hardly change sides again. He entered his office and sat at his desk. Should he send Skullion a letter or speak to him personally? He was tempted by the idea of an impersonal letter but his better feelings prevailed over his natural timidity. He picked up the phone and dialled the Porter's Lodge.

'Best to get it over with quickly,' he thought, waiting patiently for Skullion to answer.

The summons to the Bursar's office caught Skullion in a rare mood of melancholy and self-criticism. The melancholy was not rare, but for once Skullion was not thinking of himself so much as of the College. Porterhouse had come down in the world since he had first come to the Porter's Lodge and in his silent commune with the gas fire Skullion had come to feel that he had been a little unjust in his treatment of the Dean and Fellows. They couldn't help what Sir Godber did. It was all the Master's fault. No one else was to blame. It was in this brief mood of contrition that he answered the phone.

'Wonder what he wants?' he muttered as he crossed the Court and knocked on the Bursar's door.

'Ah, Skullion,' said the Bursar with a nervous geniality, 'good of you to come.'

Skullion stood in front of the desk and waited. 'You wanted to see me,' he said.

'Yes, yes. Do sit down,' Skullion chose a wooden chair and sat down.

The Bursar shuffled some papers and then looked fixedly at the doorknob which he could see slightly to the left of the porter.

'I don't really know how to put this,' he began, with a delicacy of feeling that was wasted on Skullion.

'What?' said the Porter.

'Well to put the matter in perspective, Skullion, the College financial resources are not all that they should be,' the Bursar said.

'I know that.'

'Yes. Well, for some years now we've been considering the advisability of making some essential economies.'

'Not in the kitchen I hope.'

'No. Not in the kitchen.'

Skullion considered the matter. 'Wouldn't do to touch the kitchen,' he said. 'Always had a good kitchen the College has.'

'I can assure you that I am not talking about the kitchen,' said the Bursar, still apparently addressing the doorknob.

'You may not be talking about it but that's what the Master has in mind,' said Skullion. 'He's going to have a self-service canteen. Told the College Council he did.'

For the first time the Bursar looked at Skullion. 'I really don't know where you get your information from ...' he began.

'Never you mind about that,' said Skullion. 'It's true.'

'Well ... perhaps it is. There may be something in what you say but that's not ...

'Right,' interrupted Skullion. 'And it's all wrong. He shouldn't be allowed to do it.'

'To be perfectly honest, Skullion,' said the Bursar, 'there are some changes envisaged on the catering side.'

Skullion scowled. 'Told you so,' he said.

'But I really didn't ask you here to discuss . . .'

'Could always raise money in the old days by asking the Porterhouse Society. Haven't tried that yet, have you?'

The Bursar shook his head.

'Lot of rich gentlemen still,' Skullion assured him. 'They wouldn't want to see changes in the kitchen. They'd chip in if they knew he was going to put a canteen in. You ask them before you do anything.'

The Bursar tried to think how to bring the conversation back to its original object.

'It isn't simply the kitchen, you know. There are other economies we have to make.'

'Like selling Rhyder Street I suppose,' said Skullion.

'Well, there's that and . . .'

'Wouldn't have done that in Lord Wurford's time. He wouldn't have stood for it.'

'We simply haven't got the money to do anything else,' said the Bursar lamely.

'It's always money,' Skullion said. 'Everything gets blamed on money.' He got up and walked to the door. 'Doesn't mean you've got the right to sell my home. Wouldn't have happened in the old days.' He went out and shut the door behind him. The Bursar sat at his desk and stared after him. He sighed. 'I'll simply have to write him a letter,' he thought miserably and wondered what it was about Skullion that was so daunting. He was still sitting there ten minutes later when there was a knock on the door and the Head Porter reappeared.

'Yes, Skullion?' the Bursar asked.

Skullion sat down again on the wooden chair. 'I've been thinking about what you said.'

'Really?' said the Bursar, trying to think what he had said. He had been under the impression that Skullion had done all the talking.

'I'm prepared to help the College,' Skullion said.

'Well, that's very good of you, Skullion,' said the Bursar, 'but . . .'

'It isn't very much but it's all I can do,' Skullion continued. 'You'll have to wait till tomorrow for it till I've been to the bank.'

The Bursar looked at him in astonishment.

'The bank? You don't mean . . .'

'Well it's college property really. Lord Wurford left it to me in his will. It's only a thousand pounds but if it ...'

'My dear Skullion, really this is ... Well, it's extremely good of you but I ... we couldn't possibly accept a gift from you,' the Bursar stuttered.

'Why not?' said Skullion.

'Well ... well it's out of the question. You'll need it yourself. For your retirement ...'

'I ain't retiring,' Skullion said firmly.

The Bursar stood up. The situation was getting quite beyond him. He must take a firm line.

'It's about your retirement that I wanted to see you,' he said with a determined harshness. 'It has been decided that it would be in your own interest if you were to seek other employment.' He stopped and stared out of the window. Behind him Skullion had sagged on the chair.

'Sacked,' he said, with a hiss of air that sounded as if he were expiring with disbelief.

The Bursar turned reassuringly.

'Not sacked, Skullion,' he said cheerfully. 'Not sacked, just ... well ... for your own sake, for everyone's sake it would be better if you looked around for another job.'

Skullion stared at him with an intensity that alarmed the Bursar. 'You can't do it,' he said, rising to his feet. 'You've got no right. No right at all.'

'Skullion,' the Bursar began warningly.

'You've sacked me,' Skullion roared, and his face which had been briefly pale flushed to a new and terrible red. 'After all these years I've given to the College you've sacked me.'

To the Bursar it seemed that Skullion had swollen to a fearful size which filled his office and threatened him. 'Now, Skullion,' he began, as the Porter loomed at him, but Skullion only stared a moment and then turned on his heel and rushed from the office slamming the door behind him. The Bursar subsided into his chair limp and exhausted.

To Skullion, stumbling blindly across the Court, the Bursar's words were impossible. Forty years. Forty-five years he had served the College. He reeled into the Screens and stood clutching the lintel of the Buttery counter for support. The sense of being needed, of being as much a support to the College as the stone lintel he clutched was to the wall above it, all this had left him or was leaving him as waves of realization swept over him and eroded his absolute conviction that he was still and would forever be the Porter of Porterhouse. Breathing deeply Skullion heaved himself on down the steps into the Old Court and walked woodenly towards the Porter's Lodge and the consolation of his gas fire. There he brushed past Walter and sat slumped in his chair, unable even now to accept the enormity of the Bursar's words. There had been Skullions at Porterhouse since the College was founded. He had Lord Wurford's word for it and with such a continuity of possession behind him, it was as though he stood upon the edge of the world with only an abyss before him. Skullion recoiled from the oblivion. It was impossible to conceive. In a state of numbed disbelief he heard Walter moving about the Lodge as if it were somewhere distant.

'Gutterby and Pimpole,' Skullion muttered, invoking the saints of his calendar almost automatically in his agony.

'Yes, Mr Skullion?' said Walter. 'Did you say something?' But Skullion said nothing and presently Walter went out leaving the Head Porter muttering dimly to himself.

'Going off his head, old bugger,' he thought without regret. But Skullion was mad only in a figurative sense. As the full extent of his deprivation dawned on him, the anger which had been gathering in him since Sir Godber became Master broke through the barrier of his deference and swept like a flash flood down the arid watercourse of his feelings. For years, for forty years, he had suffered the arrogance and the impertinent assumptions of privileged young men and had accorded them in turn a quite unwarranted respect and now at last, released from all his obligations, the anger he had suppressed at so many humiliations added to the momentum of his present fury. It was almost as though Skullion welcomed the ruin of his pretensions, had secretly hoarded the memories of his afflictions against such an eventuality so that his freedom, when and if it came, should be complete and final. Not that it was or could be. The habits of a lifetime remained unaltered. An undergraduate came in for a parcel and Skullion rose obediently and brought it to the counter but without the rancour that had been the emblem of his servitude. His anger was all internal. Outwardly Skullion seemed subdued and old, shuffling about his office in his bowler hat and muttering to himself, but inwardly all was altered. The deep divisions in his mind, like the two separate lobes of his brain, his allegiance to the College and his self-interest, were sundered and Skullion's anger at his lot in life could run unchecked.

When Walter returned at six o'clock, Skullion put on his overcoat.

'Going out,' he said and left Walter dumbfounded. It wasn't his night on duty. Skullion went out of the gate and turned down Trinity Street towards the Round Church. On the corner he hesitated and looked down towards the Baron of Beef but it wasn't the pub for his present mood. He wanted something less tainted by change. He walked on down Sidney Street towards King Street. The Thames Boatman was better. He hadn't been there for some time. He went in and ordered a Guinness and sat at a table in the corner and lit his pipe.

CHAPTER FOURTEEN

Cornelius Carrington spent the day in rehearsal. With a cultivated eccentricity he wandered through the colleges singling out the architectural backdrops against which his appearance would be most effective. He adored King's College Chapel though only briefly. It was too well-known, hackneyed he thought and, more important, it dwarfed his personality. Conscious of his own limitations he sought the less demanding atmosphere of Corpus Christi and stood in the Old Court admiring its medieval charms. He pottered on through St Catherine's and Queens' over the wooden bridge and shuddered at the desecration of concrete that had been erected over the river. In Pembroke he lamented Waterhouse's library for its Victorian vulgarity before changing his mind and deciding that it was an ornamental classic of its time. Glazed brick was preferable to concrete after all, he thought, as he made his way down Little St Mary's Lane towards the Graduate Centre.

He had morning coffee in the Copper Kettle, lunch in the Whim, and all the time his mind revolved around the question which had been bothering him since his arrival. The programme as he visualized it lacked the human touch. It was not enough to conduct a million viewers on a guided tour of Cambridge colleges. There had to be a moral in it somewhere, a human tragedy that touched the heart and raised the Carrington Programme from the level of aesthetic nostalgia to the heights of drama. He'd find it somewhere, somehow. He had a nose for the undiscovered miseries of life.

In the afternoon he continued his pilgrimage through Trinity and John's and fulminated at the huge new building there. He minced through Magdalene and it wasn't until half-past three that he found himself in Porterhouse. Here, if anywhere in Cambridge, time stood still. No hint of concrete here. The blackened walls of brick and clunch were as they had been in his day. The cobbled court with its chapel in the Gothic style, its lawns and the great Hall through whose stained-glass windows the winter sun glowed richly: all was as he remembered. And with the memory there came the uneasy feeling of his own inadequacy, which had been his mood in those days, and which, in spite of his renown, he had never wholly eradicated. Steeling himself against this recrudescence of inferiority he climbed the worn steps to the Screens and stood for a moment studying the notices posted in the glass cases there. Here too nothing had changed. The Boat Club. Rugger. Squash. Fixture lists. With a shudder Carrington turned away from this reminder that Porterhouse was a rowing college and stood in the archway looking down into New Court with astonishment. Here things had changed. Plastic sheeting covered the front of the Tower and broken masonry lay heaped on the flags below. Carrington gaped at the extent of the destruction and was about to go down to make a closer examination when a small figure, heavily muffled in an overcoat, panted up the steps behind him and he turned to find himself face to face with the Dean.

'Good afternoon,' Carrington said, relapsing suddenly into a deference he thought he had outgrown. The Dean stopped and looked at him.

'Good afternoon,' he said, suppressing the glint of recognition in his eye. Carrington's face was familiar from the hoardings, but the Dean preferred to pretend to an infallible memory for Porterhouse men. 'We haven't seen you for a long time, have we?'

Carrington shrank a little at the supposition that his viewers, however numerous elsewhere, did not include the Senior Members of his old college.

'To my knowledge you haven't been back since ... um ... er,' the Dean fabricated a tussle with his memory, 'nineteen ... er thirty-eight, wasn't it?'

Carrington agreed humbly that it was, and the Dean, secure now in his traditional role as the ward of an ineffable superiority, led the way towards his rooms.

'You'll join me for tea,' he asked and Carrington, already reduced to a submissiveness that infuriated him, thanked him for the offer.

'I'm told,' said the Dean as they climbed the narrow staircase, 'by those who know about these things, that you have made something of a name for yourself in the entertainment industry.'

Carrington found himself simpering a polite denial.

'Come, come, you're too modest,' said the Dean, rubbing salt into the wound. 'Your opinion matters, you know.'

Carrington doubted it.

'You must be one of the few distinguished members the College has produced in recent years,' the Dean continued, leading the way down the corridor from whose walls there stared the faces of Porterhouse men whose expressions left Carrington in little doubt that whatever they might think of him distinguished was not the word.

'You just sit down while I put the kettle on,' said the Dean and Carrington left for a moment tried hard to restore the dykes of his self-esteem. The room did not help. It was filled with reminders of past excellence in which he had no share. As an undergraduate Carrington had shone at nothing and even the knowledge that these peers of his youth who stared unwrinkled from their frames, singly or in teams, had failed to sustain the promise of their early brilliance did nothing to console him. They were probably substantial men, if hardly known, and Carrington for all his assumed arrogance was conscious of the ephemeral nature of his own reputation. He was not and would never be a substantial man, a man with Bottom, as the eighteenth century and no doubt the Dean would phrase it, and Carrington was enough of an Englishman to resent his inadequacy. It was probably this sense of having failed as a good fellow, a solid dependable sort of a chap, which give to his practised nostalgia for the twenties and thirties its quality of genuine emotion as if he pined for a time as mediocre as himself. He was rescued from his self-pity by the Dean who emerged with a tray from his tiny kitchen.

'Harrison,' said the Dean of the photograph Carrington had been studying self-critically.

'Ah,' he agreed noncommitally.

'Brilliant scrum-half. Scored that try at Twickenham in ... now when was it?'

'I've no idea,' said Carrington.

'Thirty-six? About your time. I'm surprised you don't remember.'

'I was never a great rugby man.'

The Dean looked at him critically. 'No, now I come to think of it you weren't, were you? Was it rowing, you were interested in?'

'No,' said Carrington, uncomfortably aware that the Dean knew it already.

'You must have done something in your years in College. Mind you, a lot of the young fellows who come up these days don't do anything very much. I sometimes wonder what they come to University for. Sex, I suppose, though why they can't indulge their sordid appetites somewhere else I can't imagine.' He shuffled into his kitchen and returned with a plate of rock cakes.

'I was looking at the damage to the Tower,' Carrington began when the Dean had poured tea.

'Come to make capital out of our misfortunes, I suppose,' said the

Dean. 'You journalist fellows seem to be the carrion crows of contemporary civilization.' He sat back smiling at the happy alliteration of his insult.

'I wouldn't really regard myself as a journalist,' Carrington demurred.

'Wouldn't you? How every interesting,' said the Dean.

'I see myself more as a commentator.'

The Dean smiled. 'Of course. How stupid of me. One of the lords of the air. A maker of opinion. How very interesting.' He paused to allow Carrington to savour his indifference. 'Don't you often feel embarrassed at the amount of influence you wield? I know I should. But then of course nobody listens to what I have to say. I suppose you might say I lack the common touch. Do have some more tea.'

In his chair Carrington regarded the old man angrily. He had had enough of the Dean's hospitality, the polite insults and the delicate depreciation of everything he had achieved. Porterhouse had not changed. Not one iota. The place, the man, were anachronisms beyond the compassion of his nostalgia.

'One of the things that amazes me,' he said finally, 'is to find that in a University that prides itself on scholarship and research, Porterhouse remains so resolutely a sporting college. I was glancing at the notices just now. No mention of scholarships or academic work. Just the old rugby lists ...'

'And what did you get? A double first, was it?' the Dean inquired sweetly.

'A two two,' said Carrington.

'And look where it's got you,' said the Dean. 'It speaks for itself really. Let's just say that we haven't succumbed to the American infection yet.'

'The American infection?'

'Doctoratitis. The assumption that a man's worth is to be measured by mere diligence. A man spends three years minutely documenting documents if you understand my meaning, anyway investigating issues that have escaped the notice of more discriminating scholars, and emerges from the ordeal with a doctorate which is supposed to be proof of his intelligence. Than which I can think of nothing more stupid. But there you are, that's the modern fashion. It comes, I suppose, from a literal acceptance of the ridiculous dictum that genius is an infinite capacity for taking pains. These fellows seem to think that if you can demonstrate an appetite for indigestible and trivial details for three years you must be a genius. In my opinion genius is by definition a capacity to jump the whole process of taking infinite pains, but then as I say, nobody listens to me. I mean there must be millions of people taking whatever these infinite pains are without a spark of intelligence let alone genius between them. And then again you have a silly fellow like Einstein who can't even count ... it depresses me, it really does, but it's the fashion.'

The Dean waved his hands as if to exorcize the evil spirit of his time and Carrington ventured to intervene.

'But surely research does pay off ...' he suggested.

'Pay?' said the Dean, 'I daresay it does. It certainly earns some colleges a great deal of money. Again you have this absurd assumption that provided you purchase enough sows' ears one of them is bound to turn into a silk purse. Utter nonsense, of course. It's the quality that counts not the quantity but then I don't expect you to sympathize with my old-fashioned point of view. When all's said and done it's quantity that's made your reputation, isn't it?'

'Quantity?'

'Megaviewers,' said the Dean. 'It seems an appropriate if nasty expression.'

By the time Cornelius Carrington left the Dean's rooms the erosion of his self-respect was almost complete and the comfortable acceptance of himself as the spokesman of a wholesome public concern quite gone. In the Dean's eyes he was clearly a parvenu, a jack in the box, he had suggested with a smile, and Carrington had found himself sharing the Dean's opinion. He walked out of Porterhouse envying the man his assurance and cursing himself for his inability to cope. What concrete and system-built housing was for him, he clearly was for the Dean, evidence of a facile and ugly commercialism. What had the Dean said? That he found the ephemeral distasteful, and there had been no doubt that of all ephemera he found television commentators the least to his liking. Carrington walked down Senate House Lane debating the source of the Dean's assurance. The man's lifetime spanned the coming of pebble-dash and the mock-Tudor suburbs Carrington found so appealing. He belonged to an earlier tradition. The Toby Jug Englishman, Squarsons and squires who didn't give a tuppenny damn what the world thought of them and bloodied the world's nose when it got in their way. In this mood of self-recrimination at his unalterable deference to such men, Carrington found himself in King Street. He wasn't at all sure how he had got there and at first found it difficult to recognize. King Street had changed more than any other part of Cambridge. The houses and shops that had stood huddled together down the narrow street were gone. A concrete multi-storied car park, a row of ugly brick arcades. And where were all the pubs? Walking down the street Carrington forgot his own demolition. A sense of righteous anger gripped him. The old King Street had been shabby and dishevelled but it had been entertaining. Now it was bleak, impersonal and grim. A little further on he came to some remnants. An antique shop that had odds and ends of vases and bad paintings in its windows. A coffee-shop cluttered with percolators and the more intricate jugs that undergraduates still evidently cultivated. But for the most part the developers had done their damnedest. Finally he came to the Thames Boatman and grateful to find it still standing he went inside.

'A pint of bitter, please,' he told the barman with his usual sense of place. Gin and tonic in a King Street pub would have been unthinkable. He took his beer to a table by the window.

'Seem to have been a lot of changes since I was here last,' he said, having taken a large swig from his beer glass. He didn't usually take large swigs. In fact he didn't usually drink beer at all, but beer in large swigs was, he remembered, customary in King Street.

'Knocking the whole street down,' said the barman laconically.

'Must be bad for business,' Carrington suggested.

''Tis and it isn't,' the barman agreed.

Carrington gave up the attempt to make conversation and turned his attention to the more responsive decorations of the bar-room.

A short time later a man in a bowler hat entered the bar and ordered a Guinness. Carrington studied his back and found a vague familiarity there. The dark overcoat, the highly polished shoes, the solid neck and above all the square set of the bowler hat, all these were tokens of a college porter. But it was the pipe, the jutting bulldog pipe, that woke his memory and told him this was Skullion. The porter paid for his Guinness and took it to the table in the corner and lit his pipe. A waft of blue smoke reached Carrington. He sniffed, and in that sniff the years receded and he was back in the Porter's Lodge in Porterhouse. Skullion. He had forgotten the man and his stiff, wooden almost military ways. Skullion standing like some heraldic beast at the College gate or seen from his rooms above the Hall, a dark helmeted figure marching across the Court in the early morning, his attendant shadow jutting above the crenellations cast by the morning sunlight on the lawn. The pipe at the gates of dawn, Carrington had once called him but there was nothing of the dawn about the Porter now. He sat over his Guinness and sucked his pipe and scowled unseeingly. Carrington studied the heavy features and was struck by the grim strength of the face below the brim of the bowler hat. If the Dean had prompted the thought of Toby Jugs, Skullion called to mind an older type that than. Something almost Chaucerian about the man, Carrington thought, relying for his assessment on vague memories of *The Prologue*. Certainly medieval. But above all it was the impressiveness of the man that struck him most. Impressive was the word for the face that stared out across the bar. Carrington drank his beer and ordered another. As he waited for it he crossed to the table where Skullion sat.

'It's Skullion, isn't it?' he asked. Skullion looked up at him doubtfully. 'What if it is?' he asked, adopting the impersonal pronoun as if to avoid an intrusion on his privacy.

'I thought I recognized you,' Carrington went on. 'You probably wouldn't remember me, Carrington. I was up at Porterhouse in the thirties.'

'Yes, I remember you. You had rooms over the Hall.'

'Let me get you another drink. Guinness, isn't it?' And before Skullion could say anything Carrington had returned back to the barman and was ordering a Guinness. Skullion regarded him morosely. He remembered Carrington all right. Bertie they used to call him. Flirty Bertie. Not a gentleman. He'd been something in the Footlights. Skullion hadn't approved of him.

Carrington brought the glasses across and sat down. 'I suppose you've retired now,' he asked presently.

'Not what you might call retired,' Skullion said grimly.

'You mean you're still Head Porter after all these years? My goodness, you have been there a long time.' He spoke with the affected eagerness of an interviewer, and indeed something about Skullion had awoken in him the feeling that there was a story here. Carrington had a nose for these things.

'Forty-five years,' said Skullion and drank his stout.

'Forty-five years,' echoed Carrington. 'Remarkable.'

Skullion grunted and lifted a bushy eyebrow. There was nothing remarkable about it to him.

'And now you've retired?' Carrington persisted. Skullion sucked his pipe slowly and said nothing. Carrington drank another mouthful of beer, and changed the subject.

'I don't suppose they have the King Street Run anymore,' he said. 'Now that they've knocked down so many of the old pubs.'

Skullion nodded. 'Used to be fourteen and a pint in every one in half an hour. Took some doing.' He relapsed into silence. Carrington had caught the mood. The old ways were passed and with them the Head Porter. That partially explained the old man's grim expression but there was something more behind it. Carrington changed his tack.

'The College doesn't seem to have changed much anyway.'

Skullion's scowl deepened. 'Changed more than you know,' he grunted.

'Going to change out of recognition now.' He made a move as if to spit on the floor but turned back and smelt the bowl of his pipe.

'You mean the new Master?' Carrington inquired.

'Him and all the rest of them. Women in college. Self-service canteen in Hall. And what about us as served the College all our lives! Out on the street like dogs.' Skullion drank his beer and banged the glass down on the table. Carrington was silent. He sat still almost invisible with interest like a predator that sees its prey. Skullion lit his pipe and blew smoke.

'Forty-five years I've been a porter,' he said presently. 'A lifetime, wouldn't you say?' Carrington nodded solemnly. 'I've sat in that Lodge and watched the world go by. When I was a boy we used to wait at the Catholic Church for the young gentlemen's cabs to come by from the station. "Carry your bags, sir," we'd shout and run beside the horses all the way to the College and carry their trunks up to their rooms for sixpence. That's how we earned some money in those days. Running a mile and carrying trunks into College. For sixpence.' Skullion smiled at the memory and for a moment it seemed to Carrington that the intensity had gone out of him. But there was something more than mere memory there, a sense of wrong that Carrington could sense and which in a remote way matched his own feelings. And his own feelings? It was difficult to define them, to say precisely what it was that he had found so monstrous in the Dean's delicate contempt. Except an insufferable arrogance that viewed him distantly as if he had been a microbe squirming convulsively upon a slide. Carrington acknowledged his own infirmity of spirit but his anger remained. He turned to Skullion as to an ally.

'And now they've turned you out?' he asked.

'Who said they had?' Skullion asked belligerently. Carrington prevaricated. 'I thought you said something about being made redundant,' he murmured.

'Got no right to do it,' he said almost to himself. 'They wouldn't have done it in the old days.'

'I seem to remember in my day that the College had rather a good reputation among the servants.'

Skullion looked at him with new respect. 'Yes, sir,' he said, 'Porterhouse was known for its fairness.'

'That's what I thought,' said Carrington, adopting the lordly manner which was evidently what Skullion required of him.

'Old Lord Wurford wouldn't have dreamt of turning the Head Porter into the streets,' Skullion continued. 'When he died he left me a thousand pounds. Offered it to the Bursar, I did, to help the College out. Turned me down. Would you believe it? Turned my offer down.'

'You offered him a thousand pounds to help the College out?' Carrington asked.

Skullion nodded. 'I did that. "Oh no," he says, "wouldn't dream of taking it" and the next second he gives me notice. It's not credible is it?'

To Carrington credibility hardly mattered. The story was enough.

'They're selling Rhyder Street too,' Skullion went on.

'Rhyder Street?'

'Where all the College servants live. Turning us all out.'

'Turning you out? They can't do that.'

'They are,' Skullion said. 'Chef, the head gardener, Arthur, all of us.'

Carrington finished his beer and bought two more. He had the human touch he had been seeking and with it the knowledge that his visit had not been wasted after all. He had his story now.

CHAPTER FIFTEEN

The Dean smiled. He had enjoyed his tea with Carrington. It was seldom nowadays that he had the opportunity to put his gifts for malice to good use. 'Nothing like a goad for making a man prove himself,' he thought, recalling his happy days as coach to the Porterhouse crew, and the insults he had used to drive the Eight to victory. And Carrington had suffered the gibes in silence. They would fester in him and give him the edge that was needed. He would do the programme on Porterhouse. His coming to Cambridge had proved his interest in the College in spite of his refusal of Sir Cathcart's invitation. And that refusal was an advantage too. Nobody could say now that he had been put up to it. As for the content of the programme, the Dean felt secure in the knowledge that Carrington was the high priest of nostalgia. Sir Godber's plans would be the bait. Tradition sullied. The old and proven ways under threat. The curse of modernism. The Dean could hear the clichés now, rolling off Carrington's tongue to stir the millions hungry for the good old days. And what of Sir Godber himself? Carrington would make mincemeat of the man's pretensions. The Dean helped himself to sherry with the air of a man well content, if not with the world, at least with that corner of it over which he was guardian. He went down to dinner in high spirits. They were having Caneton à l'orange and the Dean was fond of duck. He entered the Combination Room and was surprised to find the Master already there talking to the Senior Tutor. The Dean had forgotten that Sir Godber dined in Hall occasionally.

'Good evening, Master,' he said.

'Good evening, Dean,' Sir Godber replied. 'I have just been discussing this business of the restoration fund with the Senior Tutor. It seems that we've had an offer for Rhyder Street from Mercantile Properties. They've offered one hundred and fifty thousand. I must say I'm inclined to accept. What's your opinion?'

The Dean grasped his gown and frowned. His objections to the sale of Rhyder Street were tactical. He opposed what Sir Godber proposed on principle but now it was useful that the Master should commit himself to an act whose lack of charity Cornelius Carrington could emphasize.

'Opinion? Opinion?' he said finally. 'I have no opinions on the matter. I regard the sale of Rhyder Street as a betrayal of our trust to the College servants. That is not an opinion. It is a matter of fact.'

'Ah well,' said Sir Godber, 'we shall just have to differ, won't we?'

The Senior Tutor was conciliatory. 'It's a hard decision to make. I do see that,' he said. 'On the one hand the servants have to be considered and on the other there is no doubt that the restoration fund needs the money. A difficult decision.'

'Not one that I apparently am called to make,' said the Dean. They trooped into Hall and in the absence of the Chaplain, whose deafness had in no way improved since the explosion in the tower, the Dean said grace. They ate in silence for a while, Sir Godber munching his duck and congratulating himself on the change in the Senior Tutor's attitude, due possibly to the poor showing of the College in the Bumps, and one or two unfortunate remarks by the Dean. Eager to exploit the rift, Sir Godber set out to cultivate the Senior Tutor. He passed the salt without being asked for it. He told two amusing stories about the Prime Minister's secretary and finally, when the Senior Tutor ventured the opinion that he thought such goings-on were due to the entry into the Common Market, launched into a detailed account of an interview he had once had with de Gaulle. Throughout it all the Dean remained patently uninterested, his eyes fixed on tables where the undergraduates sat talking noisily, and his mind entertained by the fuse that had been lit in Cornelius Carrington. Towards the end of the meal the Master, having exhausted the eccentricities of de Gaulle, turned the monologue to matters nearer home.

'My wife is most anxious that you should dine with us one evening,' he fabricated. 'She is concerned to know your views on the question of lady tutors for our female undergraduates.'

'Lady tutors?' said the Senior Tutor. 'Lady tutors?'

'Naturally as a coeducational college we shall require some female Fellows,' the Master explained.

'Charming,' said the Dean nastily.

'This comes as something of a shock, Master,' said the Senior Tutor.

Sir Godber helped himself to stilton. 'There are some matters, Senior Tutor, that are essentially feminine if you see what I mean. You would hardly want a young woman coming to you for advice about an abortion.'

The Senior Tutor disengaged himself from a mango precipitately. 'Certainly not,' he spluttered.

'It's an eventuality we have to consider, you know,' continued Sir Godber. 'These things do happen, and since they do it would be as well to have a Lady Tutor.'

Down the table the Dean smiled happily. 'And possibly a resident surgeon?' he suggested.

The Master flushed. 'You find the topic amusing, Dean?' he inquired.

'Not the topic, Master, so much as the contortions of the liberal conscience,' said the Dean, settling back in his chair with relish. 'On the one hand we have an overwhelming urge to promote the equality of the sexes. We admit women to a previously all-male college on the grounds that their exclusion is clearly discriminatory. Having done so much we find it necessary to provide a contraceptive dispenser in the Junior lavatory and an abortion centre doubtless in the Matron's room. Such a splendid prospect for parents to know that the welfare of their daughters is so well provided for. No doubt in time there will be a College crèche and a clinic.'

'Sex is not a crime, Dean.'

'In my view pre-marital intercourse comes into the category of breaking and entering,' said the Dean. He pushed back his chair and they stood while he said grace.

As he walked back through the Fellows' Garden the Master felt again that sense of unease which dining in Hall always seemed to give him. There had been a confidence about the Dean that he distrusted. Sir Godber couldn't put his finger on it exactly but the feeling persisted. It wasn't simply the Dean's manner. It had something to do with the Hall itself. There was something vaguely barbarous about the Hall, as if it were a shrine to appetite and hallowed by the usage of five hundred years. How many carcases had been devoured within its walls? And what strange manners had those buried generations had? Pre-Renaissance men, pre-scientific men, medieval men had sat and shouted and thought ...

Sir Godber shuddered at the superstitions they had entertained as if he could undo the thread of time that linked him to their animality. He willed his separation from them. He was a rational man. The contradiction in the phrase alarmed him suddenly. A rational man, free of the absurd and ignorant restrictions that had limited those men whose speculations on the nature of angels and devils, on alchemy and Aristotle, seemed now to verge on the insane. Sir Godber halted in the garden, astonished at the idea that he was the product of such a strange species. They were as remote to him as prehistoric animals and yet he inhabited buildings which they had built. He ate in the same Hall in which they had eaten and even now was standing on ground where they had walked. Alarmed at this new apprehension of his pedigree, Sir Godber peered around him in the darkness and hurried down the path to the Master's Lodge. Only when he had closed the door and was standing in the hall beneath the electric light did he feel reassured. He went into the drawing-room where Lady Mary was watching a film on television about the problems of senility. Sir Godber allowed himself to be conducted through several geriatric wards before becoming uncomfortably aware that his simple equation of progress with improvement did not apply to the ageing process of the human body. With the silent thought that if that was what the future held in store for him he would prefer to return to the past, he took himself up to bed.

Skullion returned from the Thames Boatman at closing time. He had had no supper and eight pints of Guinness had done nothing to improve his opinion that he had been shamefully treated. He staggered into the Porter's Lodge and, ignoring Walter's protest that his wife had been expecting him home for supper at seven o'clock and it was now eleven and what was he supposed to tell her, stumbled through to the back room and lay on the bed. It was a long time since he had had eight pints of anything and it was this more than his innate sense of duty that got him off the bed to close the front gate at twelve o'clock. In the intervals between tottering through to the lavatory Skullion lay in the darkness, while the room revolved around him, trying to sort out what he should do from what that television chap had said to him. Go and see the General in the morning. Apppear on the box with Carrington. Programme on Cambridge. Finally he got to sleep and woke late for the first time in forty-five years. It no longer mattered. His days as Head Porter of Porterhouse were over.

By the time Walter arrived Skullion had made up his mind. He took his coat down from the hook and put it on. 'Going out,' he told the astonished under-porter (Skullion hadn't been known to go out in the morning since he had been his assistant) and fetched his bicycle. The thaw had set in and this time as Skullion pedalled out to Coft the fields around him were piebald. Head bent against the wind, Skullion concentrated on what he was going to say and failed to notice the Dean's car as it swept past him. By the time he reached Coft Castle the bitterness that had been welling in him since his interview with the Bursar had bred in him an indifference to etiquette. He left his bicycle beside the front door of the house and knocked heavily on the door knocker. Sir Cathcart answered the door himself and was too astonished to find Skullion glowering at him from the doorstep to remind him that he was expected to use the kitchen door. Instead he found himself following the Porter into his drawing-room where the Dean, already ensconced in an armchair in front of the fire, had been telling him the news about Cornelius Carrington. Skullion stood inside the door and stared belligerently at the Dean while Sir Cathcart wondered if he should ring for the cook to bring a kitchen chair.

'Skullion, what on earth are you doing here?' asked the Dean. There was nothing hangdog about the Porter now.

'Come to tell the General about being sacked,' said Skullion grimly.

'Sacked? What do you mean? Sacked?' The Dean rose to his feet, and stood with his back to the fire. It was a good traditional stance for dealing with truculent servants.

'What I say,' said Skullion, 'I've been sacked.'

'Impossible,' said the Dean. 'You can't have been sacked. Nobody's told me anything about this. What for?'

'Nothing,' said Skullion.

'There must be some mistake,' said the General. 'You've got hold of the wrong end of . . .'

'Bursar sent for me. Told me I'd got to go,' Skullion insisted.

'Bursar? He's got no authority to do a thing like that,' said the Dean.

'Well, he's done it. Yesterday afternoon,' Skullion continued. 'Told me to find other employment. Says the College can't afford to keep me on. Offered him money too, to help out. Wouldn't take it. Just gave me the sack.'

'This is scandalous. We can't have College servants treated in this high-handed fashion,' said the Dean. 'I'll have a word with the Bursar when I get back.'

Skullion shook his head sullenly. 'That won't do any good. The Master put him up to it.'

The Dean and Sir Cathcart looked at one another. There was in that glance a hint of triumph which grew as Skullion went on. 'Turned out of my own house. Sacked after all the years I've given to the College. It isn't right. Not standing for it, I'm not. I'm going to complain.'

'Quite right,' said the General. 'Absolutely scandalous behaviour on the part of the Master.'

'I want my job back now or else,' Skullion muttered. The Dean turned and warmed his hands at the fire. 'I'll put in a good word for you, Skullion. You need have no fear on that score.'

'I'm sure the Dean will do his best for you, Skullion,' said Sir Cathcart, opening the door for him. But Skullion stood his ground.

'Going to need more than words,' he said defiantly. The Dean turned round sharply. He wasn't used to being spoken to in that tone of voice by servants.

'You heard what I said, Skullion,' he said peremptorily. 'We'll do what we can for you. Can't promise more than that.'

Still Skullion stood where he was.

'Got to do better than that,' he muttered.

'I beg your pardon, Skullion,' said the Dean. But Skullion was not to be intimidated.

'It's my right to be porter,' he maintained. 'I've not done anything wrong. Forty-five years ...'

'Yes, we know all that, Skullion,' said the Dean.

'I'm sure this is just a misunderstanding,' interposed Sir Cathcart. 'The Dean and I will see what we can do to put the matter right. I'll see the Master personally if necessary. Can't have this sort of thing going on in a college like Porterhouse.'

Skullion looked at him gratefully. The General would see him right. He turned to the door and went out. The General followed him into the hall. 'Ask Cook to give you some tea before you go,' he said, reverting to his old routine, but Skullion had already gone. Planting his bowler hat firmly on his head he mounted his bicycle and pedalled off down the drive.

Sir Cathcart went back into the drawing-room. 'What price Sir Godber now?' he said.

The Dean rubbed his hands happily. 'I think we've got the rod we need,' he said. 'The Master is going to rue the day he sacked Skullion. That's one of the nice things about these damned socialists. The first people to get hurt by their rage for social justice are the working classes.'

'He's certainly got old Skullion's back up,' said Sir Cathcart. 'Well, I suppose we had better get in touch with the Bursar and see what we can do.'

'Do? My dear Cathcart, we do precisely nothing. If Sir Godber is fool enough to have the Bursar sack Skullion, I for one am not going to rescue him from his folly.'

Sir Cathcart stared uneasily at the receding figure of the Porter. Seen through the glass of the mullioned window Skullion had assumed a new amorphous aspect, dwindling but at the same time unsettling. He wondered briefly how much the Dean knew about Skullion's amendment of the examination process. It seemed a question better left unasked. Doubtless the whole business would blow over.

'After all, Cathcart,' said the Dean, 'you were the one who said the bleating of the sheep excites the tiger. Carrington is going to love this. He's staying at the Blue Boar. I think I'll drop in and have a word with him on the way back. Invite him to dine in Hall.'

General Sir Cathcart D'Eath sighed. It was one of the few good things about the affair that he didn't have to share his house with Cornelius Carrington.

CHAPTER SIXTEEN

Cornelius Carrington spent the morning in his room organizing his thoughts. It was one of his characteristics as a spokesman for his times that he seldom knew what to think about any particular issue. On the other hand he had an unerring instinct about what not to think. It was for instance unthinkable to approve of capital punishment, of government policy, or of apartheid. These were always beyond the pale and on a par with Stalin, Hitler and the Moors murderers. It was in the middle ground that he found most difficulty. Comprehensive schools were terrible but then so was the eleven-plus. Grammar schools were splendid but he despised their products. The unemployed were shiftless unless they were redundant. Miners were splendid fellows until they went on strike, and the North of England was the heart of Britain to be avoided at all costs. Finally Ireland and Ulster. Cornelius Carrington's mind boggled when he tried to find an opinion on the topic. And since his existence depended upon his capacity to appear to hold inflexible opinions on nearly every topic under the sun without at the same time offending more than half his audience at once, he spent his life in a state of irresolute commitment.

Even now, faced with the simple case of Skullion's sacking, he needed to decide which side the angels were on. Skullion was irrelevant, the object of an issue and superbly telegenic, but otherwise unimportant. He would be paraded before the cameras, encouraged to say a few inarticulate but moving sentences, and sent home with his fee to be forgotten. It was the issue that bothered Carrington. Who to blame for the injustice done to the old retainer? What aspect of Cambridge life to deplore? The old or the new? Sir Godber, who was evidently doing his best to turn Porterhouse into an academic college with modern amenities in an atmosphere of medieval monasticism? Or the Dean and Fellows, whose athletic snobbery Carrington found personally so insufferable? On the surface Sir Godber was the culprit but there was much to be said for lambasting the Dean without whose obstinacy the economies which necessitated sacking the Head Porter could have been avoided. He would have to see Sir Godber. It was necessary in any case to get his permission to do the programme. Carrington picked up the phone and dialled the Master's Lodge.

'Ah, Sir Godber,' he said when the Master answered, 'my name is Carrington, Cornelius Carrington.' He paused and listened to the Master's voice change tone from indifference to interest. Sir Godber was evidently a man who knew his media, and rose accordingly in Carrington's estimation.

'Of course. Come to lunch. We can have it here or in Hall as you prefer,' Sir Godber gushed. Carrington said he'd be delighted to. He left the Blue Boar and walked towards Porterhouse.

Sir Godber sat in his study invigorated. A programme on Porterhouse by Cornelius Carrington. It was an unexpected stroke of luck, a chance for him to appear once more in the public eye, and a golden opportunity to propound his philosophy of education. Come to think of it, he cut a good figure on television. He rather doubted if the Dean would come across as well, always supposing the old fool was prepared to appear on anything quite so new fangled. He was still engrossed in composing an unrehearsed account of the changes he had in mind for the College when the doorbell rang and the au pair girl announced Cornelius Carrington. The Master rose to greet him.

'How very nice of you to come,' he said warmly and led Carrington into the study. 'I had no idea you were an old Porterhouse man and to be perfectly honest I still find it hard to believe. I don't mean that in any derogatory sense, I assure you. I'm a great admirer of yours. I thought that thing you did on Epilepsy in Flintshire was excellent. It's just that I've come to associate the College with a rather less concerned approach to contemporary problems.' Conscious that he was perhaps being a little too effusive, the Master offered him a drink. Carrington looked round the room appreciatively. There were no photographs here to remind him of the insignificance of his own youth and Sir Godber's adulation came as a pleasant change from the Dean's polite asperity.

'This programme of yours on the College is a splendid idea,' Sir Godber continued when they were seated. 'Just the sort of thing the College needs. A critical look at old traditions and an emphasis on the need for change. I imagine you have something of that sort in mind?' Sir Godber looked at him expectantly.

'Quite,' said Carrington. Sir Godber's generalities left every option open. 'Though I don't imagine the Dean will approve.'

Sir Godber looked at him keenly. The hint of malice he detected was most encouraging. 'A wonderful character, the Dean,' he said, 'though a trifle hidebound.'

'A genuine eccentric,' agreed Carrington drily. It was evident from his manner that the Dean did not command his loyalty. Reassured, the Master launched into an analysis of the function of the college system in the modern world while Carrington toyed with his glass and considered the invincible gullibility of all politicians. Sir Godber's faith in the future was almost as insufferable as the Dean's condescension and Carrington's erratic sympathies veered back towards the past. Sir Godber had just finished describing the advantages of coeducation, a subject that Carrington found personally distasteful, when Lady Mary arrived.

'My dear,' said Sir Godber, 'I'd like you to meet Cornelius Carrington.'

Carrington found himself gazing into the arctic depths of Lady Mary's eyes.

'How do you do?' said Lady Mary, her sympathies strained by the evident ambiguities of Carrington's sexual nature.

'He's thinking of doing a programme on the College,' Sir Godber said, pouring the driest of sherries.

'How absolutely splendid,' Lady Mary barked. 'I found your programme on spina bifida most invigorating. It really is time we put some backbone into those people at the Ministry of Health.'

Carrington shivered at the forcefulness of Lady Mary's enthusiasm. It filled him with that nostalgia for the nursery that was the hidden counterpart of his own predatory nature. The nursery with Lady Mary as the nanny. Even the thin mouth thrilled him, and the yellow teeth.

'Of course it's the same with the dental service,' Lady Mary snarled telepathically. 'We should put some teeth into it.' She smiled and Carrington glimpsed the dry tongue.

'I imagine you must find this a great change from London,' he said.

'It's quite extraordinary,' said Lady Mary still blossoming under the warmth of his asexual attention. 'Here we are only fifty miles from

London and it seems like a thousand.' She pulled herself together. He was still a man for all that.

'What sort of thing were you thinking of doing on the College?' she asked. On the sofa Sir Godber blended with the loose cover.

'It's really a question of presentation,' Carrington said vaguely. 'One has to show both sides, naturally ...'

'I'm sure you'll do that very well,' said Lady Mary.

'And leave it to the viewers to make up their own minds,' Carrington went on.

'I think you'll have difficulty persuading the Dean and the Fellows to cooperate. You've no idea what a reactionary lot they are,' Lady Mary said. Carrington smiled.

'My dear,' said Sir Godber. 'Carrington is a Porterhouse man himself.'

'Really,' said Lady Mary, 'in that case I must congratulate you. You've come out of it very well.' They went in to lunch and Lady Mary talked enthusiastically about her work with the Samaritans over a pilchard salad while Carrington slowly wilted. By the time he left the Lodge carrying with him their benediction on the programme Carrington had begun to feel he understood the Master's longing for a painless, rational and fully automated future free from disease, starvation and the miseries of war and personal incompatibility. There would be no place in it for Lady Mary's terrifying philanthropy.

He dawdled throughout the College grounds, gazed at the goldfish in the pond, patted the busts in the library, and posed in front of the reredos in the chapel. Finally he made his way to the Porter's Lodge to reassure himself that Skullion was still agreeable to stating his grievances before three million viewers. He found the Porter less pessimistic than he'd hoped.

'I told them,' he said, 'I told them they'd got to do something.'

'Told whom?' Carrington asked, grammatically influenced by his surroundings.

'Sir Cathcart and the Dean.'

Carrington breathed a sigh of relief. 'They should certainly see that you're reinstated,' he said, 'but just in case they don't, you can always find me at the Blue Boar.'

He left the office and made his way to the hotel. There was really nothing to worry about. An appeal by the Dean to Sir Godber's better feelings was hardly likely to advance the Porter's cause but, just in case, Carrington phoned the *Cambridge Evening News* and announced that the Head Porter of Porterhouse had been dismissed for objecting to the proposed installation of a contraceptive dispenser in the Junior lavatory.

'You can confirm it with the Domestic Bursar,' he told the sub-editor, and replaced the receiver.

A second call to the Students Radical Alliance announcing the victimization of a college servant for joining a trade union, and a third to the Bursar himself, conducted this time in pidgin English, and complaining that the UNESCO expert on irrigation in Zaire expected his diplomatic immunity to protect him from being ejected with obscenities by the guardian of the Porterhouse gate, completed the process of ensuring that Skullion's dismissal should become public knowledge, the centre of left-wing protest, and irrevocable. Feeling fully justified, Carrington lay back on his bed with a smile. It had been a long time since he had been ducked in the fountain in New Court but he had never forgotten it. In the Bursar's office the telephone rang and rang again. The Bursar answered, refused to comment, demanded to know where the sub-editor had got his information, denied that a contraceptive dispenser had been installed in the Junior lavatory, admitted that one was going to be, refused to comment, denied any knowledge of sexual orgies, agreed that Zipser's death had been caused by the explosion of gas-filled prophylactics, asked what that had to do with the Head Porter's dismissal, admitted that he had been sacked and put the phone down. He was just recovering when the Students Radical Alliance phoned. This time the Bursar was brief and to the point. Having relieved his feelings by telling the Radical Students what he thought of them he replaced the receiver with a bang only to hear it ring again. The ensuing conversation with the delegate from Zaire, marked as it was by frequent references to the Secretary of State for Foreign Affairs and the Race Relations Board and punctuated by apologies from the Bursar and the assurance that the porter in question had been dismissed, completed his demoralization. He put the phone down, picked it up again and sent for Skullion. He was waiting for him when the Dean entered.

'Ah, Bursar,' he said, 'just wanted a word with you. What's all this I hear about Skullion being sacked?' The Bursar looked at him vindictively. He had had about all he could take of Skullion for one afternoon.

'It would appear that you have been misinformed,' he said with considerable restraint, 'Skullion has not been sacked. I have merely suggested to him that it is time he looked round for other employment. He's getting on and he's due for retirement shortly. If he can find another job in the meantime it would be sensible for him to take it.' He paused for a moment to allow the Dean to digest this version before continuing. 'However, that was yesterday. What has happened today puts the matter in an entirely different light. I have sent for Skullion and I do intend to sack him.'

'You do?' said the Dean, who had never before seen the Bursar so forthright.

'I have just received a complaint from a diplomat from Zaire who says that he was thrown out of the College by Skullion, who, if I understood him aright, called him among other things a nigger.'

'Quite right and proper,' said the Dean, who had been trying to figure out where Zaire was. 'The College is private property and Skullion doubtless had good reasons for chucking the blighter out. Probably committing a public nuisance.'

'He called him a nigger,' said the Bursar.

'If the man is a nigger, I see no reason why Skullion shouldn't call him one.'

'The Race Relations Board might not view the matter quite so leniently.'

'Race Relations Board? What the devil has it got to do with them?' asked the Dean.

'The fellow said he was going to complain to them. He also mentioned the Foreign Secretary.'

The Dean capitulated. 'Dear me,' he muttered, 'we can't have the College involved in a diplomatic incident.'

'We certainly can't,' said the Bursar. 'Skullion will just have to go.'

'I suppose you're right,' said the Dean, and took his leave. Outside in the Court he found the Porter waiting in the rain.

'This is a bad business, Skullion,' he said mournfully. 'A very bad business. There's nothing I can do for you now I'm afraid. A bad business,' and still shaking his head he made his way across the lawn to his staircase. Behind him Skullion stood in the falling dusk with a new and terminal sense of betrayal. There was evidently no point in seeing the Bursar. He turned and plodded back to the Porter's Lodge and began to pack his odds and ends.

The Bursar sat on in his office waiting. He phoned the Porter's Lodge but there was no reply. Finally he typed a letter to Skullion and posted it on the way home.

It was still raining when Skullion left the Porter's Lodge with his few belongings in a battered suitcase. The rain gathered on his bowler and flecked his face so that it was difficult even for him to know if there were tears running down his nose or not. If there were they were not for himself but for the past whose representative he had ceased to be. He stopped every now and then to make sure that none of the labels on the suitcase had come off in the rain. The bag had belonged to Lord Wurford and the stickers from Cairo and Cawnpore and Hong Kong were like relics from some Imperial pilgrimage. He crossed the Market Square, where the stalls were empty for the night. He went down Petty Curie and through Bradwell's Court and across Christ's Piece towards Midsummer Common. It was already dark and his feet squelched in the mud of the cycle track. Like the wind that blew in his face, swerved to left and right and suddenly propelled him forward, Skullion's feelings seemed to have no fixed direction. There was no calculation in them; the years of his subservience had robbed him of self-interest. He was a servant with nothing left to serve. No Master, no Dean, not even an undergraduate to whom he could attach himself, grudgingly, rudely, to disguise from himself the totality of his dependence. Above all, no College to protect him from the welter of experience. It wasn't the physical college that mattered. It was the idea and that had gone with his dismissal and the betrayal it represented.

Skullion crossed the iron footbridge and came to Rhyder Street. A tiny street of terraced houses hidden among the large Victorian villas of Chesterton so that even here Skullion could feel himself not far removed from the boathouses and the homes of professors. He went inside and took off his coat and put the suitcase on the kitchen table. Then he sat down and took his shoes off. He made a pot of tea and sat at the kitchen table wondering what to do. He'd go and see the bank manager in the morning about his legacy from Lord Wurford. He fetched a tin of boot polish and a duster and began to polish the toecaps of his shoes. And slowly, as each toecap began to gather lustre under the gentle circling of his finger, Skullion lost the sense of hopelessness that had been with him since the Dean had left him standing in New Court. Finally, taking a clean duster, he gave a final polish to the shoes and held them up to the light and saw reflected in their brilliance something remote that he knew to be his face. He got up and put the duster and the tin of polish away and made himself some supper. He was himself again, the Porter of Porterhouse and with this restoration of his own identity there came a new stubbornness. He had his rights. They couldn't turn him out of his own home and his job. Something would happen to stop them. As he moved about the house his mind became obsessed with Them. They had always been there hedged with respect and carrying an aura of authority and trust so that he had felt himself to be safe from Them but it was different now. The old loyalty was gone and Skullion had lost all sense of obligation to Them. Looking back over the years since the war he could see that there'd been a steady waning of respect. There'd been no real gentlemen since then, none that he'd had much time for, but if each succeeding year had disillusioned him a little more with the present, it had added a deal of deference to the more distant past. It was as though the war had been the fulcrum of his regard. Lord Wurford, Dr Robson, Professor Dunstable, Dr Montgomery, they had gained in lustre out of sheer contrast with the men who had come after them. And Skullion himself had been exalted with them because he had known and served them.

At ten o'clock he went to bed and lay in the darkness unable to sleep. At midnight he got up and shuffled downstairs almost automatically and opened the front door. It had stopped raining and Skullion shut the door again after peering up and down the street. Then, reassured by this act of commemoration, he lit the gas fire in the front room and made himself a pot of tea. At least he had still got his legacy. He'd go to the bank in the morning.

The bank manager saw Skullion at ten o'clock. 'Shares?' he said. 'We have an investment department and we could advise you of course.' He looked down at the details of Skullion's deposit account. 'Yes, five thousand pounds is quite sufficient but don't you think it would be wiser to put the money into something less speculative?'

Skullion shifted his hat on his knees and wondered why no one seemed to listen to what he said. 'I don't want to buy any shares. I want to buy a house,' he said.

The manager looked at him approvingly. 'A much better idea. Put your money in property especially in these days of inflation. You have a property in mind?'

'It's in Rhyder Street,' said Skullion.

'Rhyder Street?' The manager raised his eyebrows and pursed his mouth. 'That's a different matter. It's being sold as a lot, you know. You can't buy individual houses in Rhyder Street, and quite frankly I don't suppose your five thousand would match some of the other bids.' He permitted himself a chuckle. 'In fact it's doubtful if five thousand would get you anything in Cambridge. You'd have to raise a mortgage, and at your age that's not an easy matter.'

Skullion produced the envelope containing his shares. 'I know that,' he said. 'That's why I want to sell these shares. There are ten thousand. I think they're worth a thousand pounds.'

The manager took the envelope. 'We must just hope they're worth a little more than that,' he said. 'Now then ...' His condescendingly cheerful tone stuttered out. 'Good God!' he said, and stared at the sheaf of shares before him. Skullion shifted guiltily on his chair, as if he personally took the blame for whatever it was about the pieces of paper that caused the manager to stare in such amazement. 'Amalgamated Universal Stores. But this is quite extraordinary. How many did you say?' the manager was on his feet now twittering.

'Ten thousand,' said Skullion.

'Ten thousand?' The manager sat down again. He picked up the phone and rang the investment department. 'Amalgamated Universal Stores. What's the current selling price?' There was a pause while the manager studied Skullion with a new incredulous respect. 'Twenty five and a half?' He put the phone down and stared at Skullion.

'Mr Skullion,' he said at last, 'this may come as something of a shock to you. I don't quite know how to put it, but you are worth a quarter of a million pounds.'

Skullion heard the words, but they had no visible effect upon him. He sat unmoved upon his chair and stared numbly at the bank manager. It was the manager himself who seemed most affected by the sudden change in Skullion's status. He laughed nervously and with a slight hysteria.

'I don't think there's much doubt that you can make a bid for Rhyder Street now,' he said at last but Skullion wasn't listening. He was a rich man. It was something he had never dreamed of being.

'There must have been dividends,' said the manager. Skullion nodded. 'In the building society.' He got up and put the chair back against the wall. He looked at the shares which represented his fortune. 'You'd better put them back into the safe,' he said.

'But ...' began the manager. 'Now Mr Skullion, sit down and let's discuss this matter. Rhyder Street? There's no need to think of Rhyder Street now. We can sell these shares and ... or at least some of them and you can purchase a decent property and settle down to a new life.'

Skullion considered the suggestion. 'I don't want a new life,' he said grimly, 'I want my old one back.'

He left the manager standing behind his desk and went out into Sydney Street. In his office the bank manager sat down, his mind crowded with cheap images of wealth, cruises and cars and bright suburban bungalows, ideas he had thought disreputable before. To Skullion, standing on the pavement, such things meant nothing. He was a rich man and the knowledge did nothing to ease his resentment. If anything it increased it. He had been cheated somehow. Cheated by his own ignorance and the loyalty he had given Porterhouse. The Master, the Dean, even General Sir Cathcart D'Eath, were the legatees of his new bitterness.

They had misused him. He was free now, without the fear of dismissal or unemployment to mitigate his hatred. He went down Green Street towards the Blue Boar.

CHAPTER SEVENTEEN

During the next two days Cornelius Carrington was intensely busy. His dapper figure trotted across lawns and up staircases with a retinue of cameramen and assistants. Corners of Porterhouse that had remained obscure for centuries were suddenly illuminated by the brightest of lights as Carrington adorned his commentary with architectural trimmings. Everyone cooperated. Even the Dean, convinced that he was heaping coals of fire on the Master's head, consented to discuss the need for conservatism in the intellectual climate of the present day. Standing beneath a portrait of Bishop Firebrace, Master 1545–52, who had, as Carrington was at some pains to point out in his added commentary, played a notable role in suppressing Kett's Rebellion, the Dean launched into a ferocious attack on permissive youth and extolled the celibacy of previous generations of undergraduates. In contrast, the Chaplain was driven to admit that what many supposed to have been a nunnery before it was burnt down in 1541 had in fact been a brothel during the fifteenth century. The camera dwelt at length on foundations of the 'nunnery' still visible in parts in the Fellows' Garden while Carrington expressed surprise that a college like Porterhouse should have allowed such sexual laxity so many centuries before. The Senior Tutor was filmed cycling along the towpath by Fen Ditton coaching an eight, and was then interviewed in Hall on the dietary requirements of athletes. Carrington wheedled out of him the fact that the annual Feast cost over £2,000 and then went on to ask if the College made any contribution to Oxfam. At this point, forgetful of his electronic audience, the Senior Tutor told him to mind his own business and stalked out of the Hall trailing the broken lead of his throat microphone. Sir Godber was treated more gently. He was allowed to stroll across New Court and through the Screens discoursing on the need for a progressive and humanitarian role for Porterhouse. Pausing to look far-sightedly across the thirty feet that separated him from the end wall of the library, the Master spoke of the emotional-intellectual symbiosis that was a part of university experience, he lowered his head and addressed a crocus on the catharsis of sexual union, he raised his eyes to a fifteenth-century chimney and esteemed the compassion of the young, their energetic concern and the rightness of their revulsion at the outmoded traditions that ... He waxed eloquent on meaningful relationships and urged the abolition of exams. Above all he praised youth. The elderly, by which he evidently meant anyone over thirty-five, must not stand in the way of young men and women whose minds and bodies were open ... Even Sir Godber faltered at this point and Carrington steered him back to the subject of social compassion, which he saw as the true benefit of a university education. The Master agreed that a sense of social justice was indeed the hallmark of the educated mind. Carrington stopped the cameras and Sir Godber made his way back to the Master's Lodge, certain that he had ended on the right note. Carrington thought so too. While his cameramen took close-ups of the heraldic beasts on the front of the main gate and panned along the spikes that guarded the back wall, Carrington drove over to Rhyder Street and spent an hour closeted with Skullion. 'All I want you to do is to come back to the College and talk about your life as Head Porter,' he told him. Skullion shook his head. Carrington tried again. 'We'll take some shots of you outside the main gate and then you can stand in the street and I'll ask you a few questions. You don't have to go into the College itself.' Skullion remained adamant.

'You'll do me in London or you won't do me at all,' he insisted.

'In London?'

'Haven't been to London for thirteen years,' said Skullion.

'We can take you up to London for a day if you like but it would be much better if we filmed the interview here. We can do it here in your own home.' Carrington looked round the dingy kitchen approvingly. It had just that element of pathos he required.

'Wouldn't look good,' said Skullion. Under his breath Carrington cursed the old fool.

'I'm not having myself on film either,' Skullion continued.

'Not having yourself on film?'

'I want to go out live,' said Skullion.

'Live?'

'In a studio. Like they do on *Panorama*. Always wanted to see what it was like in a studio,' Skullion went on. 'It's more natural, isn't it?'

'No,' said Carrington, 'it's extremely unnatural. It's hot and you have large cameras ...'

'That's the way I want it,' Skullion said, 'I'm not doing it any other way. Live.'

'All right,' Carrington said finally, 'if you insist. We'll have to rehearse it first, of course. I'll put questions to you and you'll reply. We'll run through it so that there aren't any mistakes.' He left the house in some annoyance, troubled by Skullion's persistence and conscious that without Skullion the programme would lack dramatic impact. If Skullion wanted to go to London and if, in his superstitious way, he objected to being 'put on film' he would have to be placated. In the meantime the cameramen could film Rhyder Street and at least the exterior of the Head Porter's home. He drove back to Porterhouse and collected the camera crew. Only one interview left now, that with General Sir Cathcart D'Eath at Coft Castle.

A week later Carrington and Skullion travelled to London together. Carrington had spent the week editing the film and adding his commentary but all the time he had been harassed by a nagging suspicion that there was something wrong, not with the programme as he had finally concocted it but with Skullion. The petulance that had attracted Carrington to him in the first place had gone out of him. In its stead there was a stillness and an impression of strength. It was as though Skullion had gained in stature since his dismissal and was pursuing interests he knew to be his own and no one else's. Carrington did not mind the change. In its own way it would heighten the effect Skullion would have on the millions who would watch him. Carrington had even found reason to congratulate himself on the Porter's insistence that he appear live in the studio. His rugged face, with its veined nose and heavy eyebrows, would stand out against the artificiality of the studio and give his appearance a sense of immediacy that was lacking in the interviews filmed in Cambridge. Above all, Skullion's inarticulate answers would stir the hearts of his audience. Across the country men and women would sit forward in their chairs to listen to his pitiable story, conscious that they were witnessing an authentic human drama. Coming after the radical platitudes of Sir Godber and the reactionary vehemence of the Dean, Skullion's transparent honesty would emphasize the homely virtues in which they and Cornelius Carrington placed so much faith. And finally there would come the master-stroke. From the gravel drive in front of Coft Castle, General Sir Cathcart D'Eath would offer Skullion a home and the camera would pan to a bungalow where the Head Porter could see his days out in peace. Carrington was proud of that scene. Coft Castle was suburbia inflated and transplanted to the countryside and the General himself the epitome of a modern English gentleman. It had taken a good deal of editing to achieve that result, but Carrington's good sense had prevailed over Sir Cathcart's wilder flights of abuse. He had to admit that the Sealyham had helped to inject a note of sympathy into Sir Cathcart's conversation.

Carrington had spotted the dog playing on the lawn and had asked the General if he was fond of dogs.

'Always been fond of 'em,' Sir Cathcart had replied. 'Loyal friend, obedient, go anywhere with you. Nothing to touch 'em.'

'If you found a stray you'd give him a home?'

'Certainly,' said Sir Cathcart. 'Glad to. Couldn't leave him to starve. Plenty of room here. Have the run of the place. Decent quarters.'

Since in the edited version Sir Cathcart's hospitality appeared to refer to Skullion, Carrington felt that he could congratulate himself on a brilliant performance. All it had needed had been the substitution of 'If Skullion needed a place to live you'd offer him a home?' for 'If you found a stray you'd give him a home?' The General was unlikely to deny his invitation. The consequences to his image as a public benefactor would be too enormous.

As they drove to London Carrington coached Skullion in his role. 'Remember to look straight into the camera. Just answer my questions simply.' In the darkness Skullion nodded silently.

'I'll say "When did you first become a porter?" and you'll say "In 1928". You don't have to elaborate. Do you understand?'

'Yes,' said Skullion.

'Then I'll say, "You've been the Head Porter of Porterhouse since 1945?" and you'll say "Yes".'

'Yes,' said Skullion.

'Then I'll go on, "So you've been a College servant for forty-five years?" and you'll say "Yes". Is that clear?'

'Yes,' said Skullion.

'Then I'll say, "And now you've been sacked?" and you'll say "Yes". I'll say "Have you any idea why you've been sacked?" What will you say to that?'

'No,' said Skullion. Carrington was satisfied. The General might just as well have been talking about Skullion when he said that dogs were obedient. Carrington relaxed. It was going to go well.

They crossed London to the studio and Skullion was shepherded by an assistant to the entertainment room in the basement while Carrington disappeared into a lift. Skullion looked around him suspiciously. The room looked like a rather large air-raid shelter.

'Do sit down, Mr Skullion,' said the young man. Skullion sat on the plastic sofa and took off his bowler hat, while the young man unlocked what looked like a built-in wardrobe and wheeled out a large box. Skullion scowled at the box.

'What's that?' he inquired.

'It's a sort of portable bar. It helps to have a drink before one goes up to the studio.'

'Ah,' said Skullion and watched the young man unlock the box. A formidable array of bottles gleamed in the interior.

'What would you care for? Whisky, gin?'

'Nothing,' said Skullion.

'Really,' twittered the young man. 'That's most unusual. Most people need a drink especially if they're going on live.'

'You have one if you want one,' Skullion said. 'Mind if I smoke?' He took out his pipe and filled it slowly. The young man looked doubtfully at the portable bar.

'Are you sure you wouldn't care for a drink?' he asked. 'It does help, you know.'

Skullion shook his head. 'Have one afterwards,' he said, and lit his pipe. The young man locked the bar and put it back into the wardrobe.

'Is this your first time?' he asked, evidently anxious to put Skullion at his ease.

Skullion nodded and said nothing.

He was still saying nothing when Cornelius Carrington came down to collect him. The room was filled with the acrid smoke from Skullion's pipe and the young man was sitting at the far end of the plastic sofa in a state of considerable agitation.

'He won't drink anything,' he whispered. 'He won't say anything. He just sits there smoking that filthy pipe.' Carrington looked at Skullion with some alarm. Visions of Skullion drying up in the middle of the interview began to seem a distinct possibility.

'Are you all right?' he asked.

Skullion looked at him sourly. 'Never felt better,' he said. 'But I can't say I like the company.' He glowered at the young man.

Carrington escorted him out into the corridor. 'Poofter,' said Skullion as they went up in the lift. Carrington shuddered. There was something disturbing about the Head Porter's new attitude. He lacked the eagerness to please that seemed to affect most people who came to be interviewed, a nervous geniality that made them pliable and stimulated in Carrington a dominance he was unable to satisfy outside the artificial environs of the studio. If anyone was likely to dry up, he admitted to himself, it seemed more likely to be Cornelius Carrington than Skullion. He ushered the Porter into the brilliantly lit studio and sat him in the chair before hurrying out and having two quick slugs of whisky. By the time he had returned Skullion was telling a young make-up woman to keep her paws to herself.

Carrington took his seat and smiled at Skullion. 'One thing you must try to avoid is kicking the mike,' he said. Skullion said he'd try not to. The cameras moved round him. Young men came and went. In the next room behind a large darkened window the producer and the technicians arranged themselves at the console. Carrington on Cambridge was on the air. 9.25. Peak-hour viewing.

In Porterhouse dinner was over. It had, for a change, been an equable affair without any of the verbal infighting that usually occurred whenever the Fellows were gathered together. Instead a strange goodwill prevailed. Even the Master dined in Hall and the Dean sitting on his right managed to refrain from being offensive. It was as though a truce had been declared.

'I've done my best to see that more influential members of the Porterhouse Society have been informed about the programme,' he told the Master.

'Excellent,' said Sir Godber. 'I'm sure we all owe you a debt of gratitude, Dean.' The Dean forebore from sniggering. 'One does one's best,' he said. 'After all it's for the good of the College. We should get one or two fairly healthy subscriptions for the restoration fund as a result of young Carrington's efforts.'

'I found him a most sympathetic man,' said Sir Godber. 'Unusually perceptive, I thought, for ...' He was about to say an old Porterhouse man but thought better of it.

'Flirty Bertie, they used to call him, when he was an undergraduate,' shouted the Chaplain.

'Ah well, he seems to have changed a good deal since those days,' said Sir Godber.

'They ducked him in the fountain,' the Chaplain continued. It was the only ominous remark of the whole meal.

Afterwards they sat in the Combination Room over coffee and cigars, glancing occasionally at the large colour television set that had been installed for the occasion. At nine they switched it on and watched the news, while Arthur, the waiter, was told to bring some more brandy. Sir Cathcart arrived at the invitation of the Dean and when the Carrington Programme began all those who had some part in it were present in the Combination Room. All except Skullion, who sat in the studio with the suggestion of a smile softening imperceptibly the harsh lines of his face.

In the Combination Room Cornelius Carrington's voice broke through the last bars of the Eton Boating Song which had accompanied the opening shots of the Backs and King's College Chapel. 'To many people

Cambridge is one of the great centres of learning, the birthplace of science and of culture. Here the great English poets had their education. Milton was a scholar of Christ's College.' The interior of Milton's room appeared upon the screen. 'Wordsworth and Tennyson, Byron and Coleridge were all Cambridge men.' The camera skipped briefly from an upper window in St John's to Trinity and Jesus, before settling on the seated figure of Tennyson in Trinity Chapel. 'Here Newton,' Newton's statue glowed on the screen, 'first discovered the laws of gravity, and Rutherford, the father of the atom bomb, first split the atom.' A corner of the Cavendish Laboratory, discreetly photographed to avoid any sign of modernity, appeared.

'I must say friend Carrington has a way of leaping the centuries fairly rapidly,' said the Dean.

'What's the Eton Boating Song got to do with King's?' asked Sir Cathcart.

Carrington continued. Cambridge was the Venice of the Fens. Shots of the Bridge of Sighs. Punts. Grantchester. Undergraduates pouring out of the lecture rooms in Mill Lane. Carrington's emollient voice proclaimed the glory that was Cambridge.

'But tonight we are going to look at a college that is unique even in the unchanging world of Cambridge.'

The Master sat forward and stared at the College crest on the tower above the main gate. Around him the Fellows stirred uneasily in their chairs. The invasion of their privacy had begun. And it continued. Carrington asked his audience to consider the anachronism that was his old college. The balm had left his voice. A new strident note of alarm had crept in suggesting to his audience that what they were about to see might well shock and surprise them. There was an implication that Porterhouse was something more than a mere college and that the crisis which had developed there was somehow symbolic of the choice that confronted the country. In the Combination Room the Fellows gaped at the screen in amazement. Even Sir Godber shivered at the new emphasis. Malaise was hardly a word he'd expected to hear applied to the condition of the College and when, after floating through Old Court and the Screens, the camera zoomed in on the plastic sheeting of the Tower there was a unanimous gasp in the Combination Room.

'What drove a brilliant young scholar to take his life and that of an elderly woman in this strange fashion?' Carrington asked, and proceeded to describe the circumstances of Zipser's death in a manner which fully justified his earlier warning that viewers must expect to be shocked and surprised.

'Good God,' shouted Sir Cathcart, 'what's the bastard trying to do?' The Dean closed his eyes and Sir Godber took a gulp of brandy.

'I asked the Dean his opinion,' Carrington continued and the Dean opened his eyes to peer at his own face as it appeared on the screen.

'It's my opinion that young men come up today with their heads filled with anarchist nonsense. They seem to think they can change the world by violent means,' the Dean heard himself telling the world.

'He did nothing of the sort,' shouted the Dean. 'He never mentioned Zipser!'

Carrington issued his denial. 'So you see this as an act of self-destructive nihilism on the part of a young man who had been working too hard?' he asked.

'Porterhouse has always been a sporting college. In the past we have tried to achieve a balance between scholarship and sport,' the Dean replied.

'He never put that question to me,' yelled the real Dean. 'He's taking my words out of context.'

'You don't see this as an act of sexual aberration?' Carrington interrupted.

'Sexual promiscuity plays no part in college life,' the Dean asserted.

'You've certainly changed your tune, Dean,' shouted the Chaplain. 'The first time I've heard you say that.'

'I didn't say that,' screamed the Dean. 'I said ...'

'Hush,' said Sir Godber, 'I'm trying to hear what you did say.'

The Dean turned purple in the darkness as Carrington continued.

'I interviewed the Chaplain of Porterhouse in the Fellows' Garden,' he told the world. The Dean and Bishop Firebrace had disappeared to be replaced by the rockeries and elms and two tiny figures walking on the lawn.

'I never realized the Fellows' Garden was so large,' said the Chaplain, peering at his remote figure.

'It's distorted by the wide-angle lens ...' Sir Cathcart began to explain.

'Distorted?' snarled the Dean. 'Of course it's distorted, the whole bloody programme's a distortion.'

The camera zoomed in on the Chaplain.

'The College used to have a brothel, you know. People like to pretend it was a nunnery but it was actually a whorehouse. In the fifteenth century it was quite the normal thing,' the Chaplain's voice echoed across the lawn. 'Burnt down in 1541. A great pity really. Mind you I'm not saying there weren't nuns. The Catholics have always been broadminded about such things.'

'So much for the ecumenical movement,' muttered the Senior Tutor.

'So you don't agree with the Dean that . . .' Carrington began.

'Agree with the Dean, dear me no,' the Chaplain shouted. 'Never did. Peculiar fellow, the Dean. All those photographs of young men in his room. And he's getting on in years now. We all are. We all are.' The camera moved away slowly, leaving the Chaplain a distant figure in a landscape with his voice growing fainter like the distant cawing of rooks.

The Chaplain turned to the Senior Tutor. 'That was rather nice. Seeing oneself on the screen like that. Most enlightening.' In the corner a strangled sound issued from the Dean. The Senior Tutor was breathing hard too, and staring at the river at Fen Ditton. An eight was swinging round Grassy Corner and an aged youth in a blazer and cap cycled busily after them. As the eight approached and disappeared the screen filled with the perspiring face of the Senior Tutor. He stopped and dismounted his bicycle. Carrington's voice interrupted his panting.

'You've been coach now for twenty years and in that time you must have seen some extraordinary changes in Porterhouse. What do you think of the type of young man coming up to Cambridge today?'

'I've seen some lily-livered swine in my time,' the Senior Tutor bawled, 'but nothing to equal this. A more disgraceful exhibition of gutlessness I've never seen.'

'Would you put this down to pot-smoking?' Carrington inquired.

'Of course,' said the Senior Tutor, and promptly disappeared from the screen.

In the Combination Room the Senior Tutor was speechless with rage. 'He didn't ask me any questions like that. He wasn't even there,' he managed to gasp. 'He told me they were simply going to film me on the river.'

'It's poetic licence,' said the Chaplain, and relapsed into silence as Carrington and the Senior Tutor reappeared in Hall and strolled between the tables. The camera focused on the several portraits of obese Masters before returning to the Senior Tutor.

'Porterhouse has enjoyed a long reputation for good living,' Carrington said. 'Would you say that the sort of expense involved in providing caviar and truffled duck paté was really necessary for scholastic achievement?'

'I think much of our success has been due to the balanced diet we provide in Porterhouse,' said the Senior Tutor. 'You can't expect people to do well unless they are adequately fed.'

'But I understand that you spend fairly large sums on the annual Feast. Would you say that £2,000 on a single meal was a fair estimate?' Carrington inquired.

'We do have an endowed kitchen,' the Senior Tutor admitted.

'And I suppose the College makes a large contribution to Oxfam,' said Carrington.

'That's none of your damned business,' shouted the Senior Tutor. The camera followed his figure out of Hall.

As the devastating disclosures continued the Fellows sat dumbfounded in the Combination Room. Carrington waxed eloquent on Porterhouse's academic shortcomings, interviewed several undergraduates who sat with their backs to the camera to preserve their anonymity and claimed that they were afraid they would be sent down if their identities were known to the Senior Members of the College. They accused the College authorities of being hidebound and violently reactionary in their politics, and ... On and on it went. Sir Godber put his case for social compassion as the hallmark of the educated mind and suddenly the scene changed. The images of Cambridge disappeared and the Fellows found themselves staring lividly at Skullion who sat firmly in his seat in the studio. The camera switched to Carrington. 'In the interviews we have already shown tonight we have heard a good deal to justify, and some would say to condemn, the role of institutions such as Porterhouse. We have heard the old traditions defended. We have heard privilege attacked by the progressive young and we have heard a great deal about social compassion, but now we have in the studio a man who more than any other has an intimate knowledge of Porterhouse and whose knowledge extends over four decades. Now you, Mr Skullion, have been for some forty years the Porter of Porterhouse.'

Skullion nodded. 'Yes,' he said.

'You first became a porter in 1928?'

'Yes.'

'And in 1945 you were made Head Porter?'

'That's right.'

'So really you've been in the College long enough to have seen some quite remarkable changes?' Skullion nodded obediently.

'And now I understand you've been sacked?' said Carrington. 'Have you any idea why this has happened?'

Skullion paused while the camera moved in for a close-up.

'I have been dismissed because I objected to the installation of a contraceptive dispenser in the College for the use of the young gentlemen,' Skullion told three million viewers. There was a pause while the camera swung back to Carrington, who was looking suitably shocked and surprised.

'A contraceptive dispenser?' he asked. Skullion nodded. 'A contraceptive dispenser. I don't think it's right and proper for Senior Members of a college like Porterhouse to encourage young men to behave like that.'

'Oh my God,' said the Master. Beside him the Senior Tutor was staring at the screen with bulging eyes while the Dean appeared to be in the throes of some appalling paroxysm. Throughout the Combination Room the Fellows gazed at Skullion as if they were seeing him for the first time, as if the caricature that they had known had suddenly come alive by virtue of the very apparatus which separated him from them. Skullion's presence filled the room. Even Sir Cathcart took note of the change and sat rigidly to attention. Beside him the Bursar whimpered. Only the Chaplain remained unmoved. 'Skullion's remarkably fluent,' he said, 'and making some interesting points too.'

Carrington too seemed to have shrunk to a less substantial role. 'You think the attitude of the authorities is wrong?' he asked lamely.

'Of course it's wrong,' said Skullion. 'Young people shouldn't be taught to think that they've a right to do what they want. Life isn't like that. I didn't want to be a porter. I had to be one to earn my living. Just because a man's been to Cambridge and got a degree doesn't mean life's going to treat him any different. He's still got to earn a living, hasn't he?'

'Quite,' said Carrington, desperately trying to think of some way of getting the discussion back to the original topic. 'And you think –'

'I think they've lost their nerve,' said Skullion. 'They're frightened. They call it permissiveness. It isn't that. It's cowardice.'

'Cowardice?' Carrington had begun to dither.

'It's the same all over. Give them degrees when they haven't done any work. Let them walk about looking like unwashed scarecrows. Don't send them down when they take drugs. Let them come in at all hours of the night and have women in their rooms. When I first started as a porter they'd send an undergrad down as soon as look at him and quite right too, but now, now they want them to have an FL machine in the gents to keep them happy. And what about queers?' Carrington blanched.

'You ought to know about that,' said Skullion. 'Used to duck them in the fountain, didn't they? Yes I remember the night they ducked you. And quite right too. It's all cowardice. Don't talk to me about permissiveness.' Carrington gazed frantically at the programme controller behind the dark glass but the programme remained on the air.

'And what about me?' Skullion asked the camera in front of him. 'Worked for a pittance for forty years and they sack me for nothing. Is that fair? You want permissiveness? Well, why can't I be permitted to work? A man's got a right to work, hasn't he? I offered them money to keep me on. You ask the Bursar if I didn't offer him my savings to help the College out.'

Carrington grasped at the straw. 'You offered the Bursar your life savings to help the College out?' he asked with as much enthusiasm as the recent revelations about his sex life had left him.

'He said they couldn't afford to keep me on as Porter,' Skullion explained. 'He said they were having to sell Rhyder Street to pay for the repairs to the Tower.'

'And Rhyder Street is where you live?'

'It's where all the College servants live. They've got no right to turn us out of our own homes.'

In the Combination Room the Master and Fellows of Porterhouse watched the reputation of the College disintegrate as Skullion pressed on with his charges. This was no longer Carrington on Cambridge. Skullion had taken over with a truer and more forceful nostalgia. While Carrington sat pale and haggard beside him, Skullion ranged far and wide. He spoke of the old virtues, of courage and loyalty, with an inarticulate eloquence that was authentically English. He praised gentlemen long dead and castigated men still alive. He asserted the value of tradition in college life against the shoddy innovations of the present. He expressed his admiration for scholarship and deplored research. He extolled wisdom and refused to confuse it with knowledge. Above all he claimed the right to serve and with it the right to be treated fairly. There was no petulant whine about Skullion's appeal. He held a mirror up to a mythical past and in a million homes men and women responded to the appeal.

By the time the programme ended, the switchboard at the BBC was jammed with calls from people all over the country supporting Skullion in his crusade against the present.

CHAPTER EIGHTEEN

In the Combination Room the Fellows sat looking at the blank screen long after Skullion's terrible image had disappeared and the Bursar had switched the set off. It was the Chaplain who finally broke the appalled silence.

'Very interesting point of view, Skullion's,' he said, 'though I must admit to having some doubts about the effect on the restoration fund. What did you think of the programme, Master?'

Sir Godber suppressed a torrent of oaths. 'I don't suppose,' he said with a desperate attempt at composure, 'that many people will take much note of what a college porter has to say. The public have very short memories, I'm glad to say.'

'Damned scoundrel,' snarled Sir Cathcart. 'Ought to be horsewhipped.'

'What? Skullion?' asked the Senior Tutor.

'That swine Carrington,' shouted the General.

'It was your idea in the first place,' said the Dean.

'Mine?' screamed Sir Cathcart. 'You put him up to this.'

The Chaplain intervened. 'I always thought it was a mistake to duck him in the fountain,' he said.

'I shall consult my solicitor in the morning,' said the Dean. 'I think we have adequate grounds for suing. There's such a thing as slander.'

'I must say I can hardly see any justification for going to law,' said the Chaplain. Sir Godber shuddered at the prospect.

'He deliberately fabricated questions to answers I had already given,' said the Senior Tutor.

'He may have done that,' the Chaplain agreed, 'but I think you'll have difficulty in proving it. In any case if I were asked I should have to say that he did manage to convey the spirit of our opinions if not the actual letter. I mean you do think the modern generation of undergraduates are ... what was the expression? ... a lot of lily-livered swine. The fact that you have now said it in public may be regrettable but at least it's honest.'

They were still fulminating an hour later when the Master, exhausted by the programme and by the terrible animosity it had provoked among his colleagues, finally left the Combination Room and made his way across the Fellows' Garden to the Master's Lodge. As he stumbled across the lawn he was still uncertain what effect the programme would have.

He tried to console himself with the thought that public opinion was essentially progressive and that his record as a reforming politician would carry him safely through the outcry that was bound to follow. He tried to recall what it was about his own appearance on the screen that had so alarmed him. For the first time in his life he had seen himself as others saw him, an old man mouthing clichés with a conviction that was wholly unconvincing. He went into the Lodge and shut the door.

Upstairs in the bedroom Lady Mary disembarked from her corset languidly. She had watched the programme by herself and had found it curiously stimulating. It had confirmed her opinion of the College while at the same time she had been aroused once again by the warm hermaphroditism of Cornelius Carrington himself. Age and the Rubicon of menopause had stimulated Lady Mary's appetite for such men and she found herself moved by his vulnerable mediocrity. As ever with Lady Mary's affections, distance lent enchantment to the view, and for one brief self-indulgent moment she saw herself the intimate patroness of this idol of the media. Sir Godber, she had to admit, was a spent force whereas Carrington was still an influence. She smothered the impulse with cold cream but there was enough vivacity left to surprise Sir Godber when he came to bed.

'I thought it went rather well, didn't you?' she asked as the Master wearily untied his shoes. Sir Godber lifted his head balefully.

'Well of course there was that awful creature at the end,' Lady Mary conceded. 'I can't imagine why he had to appear.'

'I can,' said Sir Godber.

'Otherwise I enjoyed it. It showed the Dean up in a very foolish light.'

'It showed us all up in a perfectly terrible light,' said Sir Godber.

'He gave you fair warning,' Lady Mary pointed out. 'He said he had to show both sides of the problem.'

'He didn't say he had to show it from underneath,' Sir Godber snapped. 'He made us all look like complete idiots and as for Skullion, anybody would think we had done the damned man an injustice.'

'Aren't you being a bit extreme?' Lady Mary said. 'After all anyone could see he was a dreadful oaf.'

Sir Godber went through to the bathroom and did his teeth while Lady Mary settled down comfortably with the latest statistics on juvenile crime.

At Shepherd's Bush Skullion sat on smoking his pipe and drinking whisky while Carrington screamed at the programme producer.

'You had no right to let him continue,' he shouted. 'You should have cut him off.'

'It's your programme, sweetie,' said the producer. The telephone rang. 'Anyway I don't know what you're worried about,' said the producer, 'the public loved him. The phone's been ringing non-stop.' He listened for a moment and turned to Carrington. 'It's Elsie. She wants to know if he's available for an interview.'

'Elsie?'

'Elsie Controp. The *Observer* woman,' said the producer.

'No, he isn't,' shouted Carrington.

'Yes, he is still here,' the producer said into the phone. 'If you come over now you'll probably get him.' He put the phone down.

'Do you realize he is likely to involve us in a legal action,' Carrington asked. The phone rang. 'Yes,' said the controller. He turned to Carrington. 'They want him for *Talk-In* on Monday. Is that all right?'

'For God's sake,' shouted Carrington.

'He says that's fine,' said the producer.

Skullion sat in the entertainment room with Elsie Controp. It was past eleven but Skullion was not feeling tired. His appearance had invigorated him and the whisky was helping. 'You mean the College authorities accept candidates who have taken no entrance examination and who have no A-levels?' Miss Controp asked. Skullion drank some more whisky and nodded.

'And their parents subscribe to an Endowment Fund?' Skullion nodded again. Miss Controp's pencil flitted across her pad.

'And this is quite a normal procedure at Porterhouse?' she asked. Skullion agreed that it was.

'And other colleges admit candidates in the same way?'

'If you're rich enough you can usually get into a college,' Skullion told her. 'I don't say they subscribe to any funds like in Porterhouse but they get in all the same.'

'But how do they get degrees if they can't pass the exams?'

Skullion smiled. 'Oh, they fail the Tripos. Then they give them pass degrees. College recommends someone for a pass degree and they get it. It's a fiddle.'

'You can say that again,' said Miss Controp fervently. Skullion spent the night in a hotel in Bayswater. On Saturday he went to the Zoo and on Sunday he stayed in bed reading the *News of the World* and then went down to Greenwich to look at the *Cutty Sark*.

*

Sir Godber came down to breakfast on Sunday to find Lady Mary engrossed in the *Observer*. He could see from her expression that a disaster had struck some part of the world.

'Where is it this time?' he asked wearily. Lady Mary did not reply. 'It must be a simply appalling catastrophe,' Sir Godber thought and helped himself to toast. He sat munching noisily and looking out of the window. Saturday had been an unpleasant day. There had been a number of calls from old Porterhouse men who wanted to say how much they resented the sacking of Skullion and who hoped that the Master would think again before making any changes to the College. He had been asked for his opinions by several leading London papers. He had been approached by the BBC to appear on *Talk-In*. He had even received a phone call from the League of Contraception complimenting him on his stand. Altogether the Master was in no mood to face Lady Mary's sympathy for some wretched population stricken by disease, destitution, or natural disaster at the other end of the globe. He could have done with some sympathy himself.

He looked up from a piece of toast to find her regarding him with unusual severity.

'Godber,' she said, 'this is simply dreadful.'

'I rather imagined it must be,' said the Master.

'You've got to do something about it immediately.'

Sir Godber put down his piece of toast. 'My dear,' he said, 'my capacity for doing anything about the inhumanity of man to man or of nature to man or of man to nature is strictly limited. That much I have learnt. Now whatever it is that's causing you such exquisite pain and suffering for the plight of mankind this morning, I am not in any position to do anything about it. I have enough trouble trying to do something about this College –'

'I am talking about the College,' Lady Mary interrupted. She thrust the paper across the table to him and Sir Godber found himself staring at headlines that read, CAMBRIDGE COLLEGE SELLS DEGREES. PORTER ALLEGES CORRUPTION, by Elsie Controp. A photograph of Skullion appeared below the headlines and several columns were devoted to an analysis of Porterhouse's financial affairs. The Master breathed deeply and read.

'Porterhouse College, one of Cambridge's socially more exclusive colleges, has been in the habit of selling pass degrees to unqualified sons of wealthy parents, according to the college porter, Mr James Skullion.'

'Well?' said Lady Mary before Sir Godber could read any further.

'Well what?' said the Master.

'You've got to do something about it. It's outrageous.'

The Master peered vindictively at his wife. 'If you would give me time to read the article I might be able to think of something to do about it. As it is I have had time neither to digest its import nor what little breakfast –'

'You must issue a press statement denying the allegations,' said Lady Mary.

'Quite,' said Sir Godber. 'Which, since as far as I have been able to read, seem to be perfectly true, would do nobody least of all me, any good whatsoever. I suppose Skullion might benefit by being awarded damages for being called a liar.'

'Are you trying to tell me that you've been condoning the sale of degrees?'

'Condoning?' shouted the Master. 'Condoning? What the hell do you –'

'Godber,' said Lady Mary threateningly. The Master lapsed into a stricken silence and tried to finish the article while Lady Mary launched into a sermon on the iniquities of bribery and corruption, public schools and the commercial ethics, or lack of them, of the middle classes. By the end of breakfast the Master was feeling like a battered baby.

'I think I'll take a walk,' he said, and left the table. Outside the sun was shining and in the Fellows' Garden the daffodils were out. So were the pickets. Outside the main gate several youths were sitting on the pavement with placards which read REINSTATE SKULLION. The Master walked past them with his head lowered and headed for the river wondering why it was that his well-meaning efforts to effect a radical change should always provoke the opposition of those in whose interests he was acting. Why should Skullion, whose ideas were archaic in the extreme and who would have chased those long-haired youths away from the main gate, elicit their sympathy now? There was something perverse about English political attitudes that defeated logic. Looking back over his lifetime Sir Godber was filled with a sense of injustice. 'It's the Right wot gets the power. It's the Left wot gets the blame,' he thought. 'Ain't it all a blooming shame?' He wandered on along the path across Sheep's Green towards Lammas Land, dreaming of a future in which all men would be happy and all problems solved. Lammas Land. The land of the day that would never come.

The Dean didn't read the *Observer*. He found its emphasis on the malfunction of the body politic and the body physical not at all to his taste. In fact none of the Sunday papers appealed to him. He preferred his agnosticism straight and accordingly attended morning service in the

College chapel where the Chaplain could be relied upon to maintain the formalities of religious observance in a tone loud enough to make good the deficiency of his congregation and with an irrelevance to the ethical needs of those few who were present that the Dean found infinitely reassuring. He was therefore somewhat surprised to find that the Chaplain had chosen his text from Jeremiah 17:11. 'As the partridge sitteth on eggs, and hatcheth them not; so he that getteth riches, and not by right, shall leave them in the midst of his days, and at his end shall be a fool.' Fortunately for the Dean, he was so preoccupied with the problem of the continuing existence of partridges in spite of their evident shortcomings as parents that he missed a great deal of what the Chaplain had to say. He awoke from his reverie towards the end of the sermon to find the Chaplain in a strangely outspoken way criticizing the college for admitting undergraduates whose only merit was that they belonged to wealthy families. 'Let us remember our Lord's words, "It is easier for a camel to go through the eye of a needle, than for a rich man to enter into the Kingdom of God",' shouted the Chaplain. 'We have too many camels in Porterhouse.' He climbed down from the pulpit and the service ended with 'As pants the hart . . .' The Dean and the Senior Tutor left together.

'A most peculiar service,' said the Dean. 'The Chaplain seemed obsessed with various forms of wild life.'

'I think he misses Skullion,' said the Senior Tutor.

They walked down the Cloisters with a speculative air. After that dreadful programme I would hardly go so far as to say that I missed him,' the Dean said, 'though I daresay he's a great loss to the College.'

'In more ways than one,' said the Senior Tutor. 'I dined in Emmanuel last night.' He shuddered at the recollection.

'Very commendable,' said the Dean. 'I try to avoid Emmanuel. I had some cutlets there once that disagreed with me.'

'I hardly noticed the food,' said the Senior Tutor. 'It was the conversation I found disagreeable.'

'Carrington, I suppose?'

'There was some mention,' said the Senior Tutor. 'I did my best to play it down. No, what I really had in mind was something old Saxton there told me. Apparently there is a not unsubstantial rumour going around that Skullion's assertion that he offered the College his life savings was not without foundation.'

The Dean waded through the morass of double negatives towards some sort of assertion. 'Ah,' he said finally, uncertain how far to commit himself.

'I understood Saxton to say he had it on the highest authority that Skullion was worth a good deal more than one might have supposed.'

'I always said Skullion was invaluable,' said the Dean.

'The sum mentioned was in the region of a quarter of a million pounds,' said the Senior Tutor.

'Out of the question to accept ... What?' said the Dean.

'A quarter of a million pounds.'

'Good God!'

'Lord Wurford's legacy to him,' explained the Senior Tutor.

'And the bloody Bursar turned it down,' stuttered the Dean.

'It puts a rather different complexion on the matter, doesn't it?'

It had certainly put a different complexion on the Dean who stood in the Cloister trying to get his breath.

'My God, a quarter of a million pounds. And the Master sacked him,' he gasped. The Senior Tutor helped him down the Cloisters.

'Come and have a little something in my rooms,' he said. They passed the main gate where a youth was holding a placard.

'Reinstate Skullion,' said the Dean. 'For once I think the protestors are right.'

'The danger is that some other college will bag him before we get the chance,' said the Senior Tutor.

'Do you really think so?' asked the Dean anxiously. 'The dear old fellow was ... is such a loyal College servant.' Even to the Dean's ears the word 'servant' had a hollow ring to it now.

In the Senior Tutor's rooms the bric-à-brac of a rowing man hung like ancient weapons on the walls, an arsenal of trophies. The Dean sipped his sherry pensively.

'I blame Carrington entirely,' he said. 'The programme was a travesty. Cathcart should never have invited him.'

'I had no idea he had,' said the Senior Tutor. The Dean changed direction.

'As a matter of fact I found myself agreeing with a great deal of what Skullion had to say. Most of his accusations applied only to the Master. And Sir Godber is entirely responsible for the whole disgraceful affair. He should never have been nominated. He has done irreparable damage to the reputation of the College.'

The Senior Tutor stared out of the window at the damage done to the Tower. The animosity he had felt for the Dean, an antagonism which had taken the place of the transitory attachments of his youth, had quite left him. Whatever the Dean's faults, and over the years the Senior Tutor had catalogued them all meticulously, no one could accuse him of being an intellectual. Together, though never in unison, they had steered Porterhouse away from the academic temptations to which all other Cambridge colleges had succumbed and had preserved that integrity of ignorance which gave Porterhouse men the confidence to cope with life's complexities which men with more educated sensibilities so obviously lacked. Unlike the Dean, whose lack of scholarship was natural and unforced, the Senior Tutor had once possessed a mind and it had only been by the most rigorous discipline that he had suppressed his academic leanings in the interests of the College spirit. His had been an intellectual decision founded on his conviction that if a little knowledge was a dangerous thing, a lot was lethal. The damage done to the Tower by Zipser's researches confirmed him in his belief.

'Has it occurred to you,' he said, at last turning from his contemplation of the dangers of intellectualism, 'that it might be possible to turn this affair of Carrington's programme and Skullion's sacking to some advantage?'

The Dean agreed that he had hoped it might unnerve the Master. 'It's too late for that now,' he said. 'We have been exposed to ridicule. All of us. It may be College policy to suffer fools gladly but I am afraid the public has other views about university education.'

The Senior Tutor shook his head. 'I think you may be unduly pessimistic,' he said. 'My reading of the situation differs from yours. We have certain advantages on our side. For one thing we have Skullion.' The Dean began to protest but the Senior Tutor held up his hand. 'Hear me out, Dean, hear me out. However ludicrous we may have been made to appear by friend Carrington, Skullion made an extremely favourable impression.'

'At our expense,' the Dean pointed out.

'Certainly, but the fact remains that public sympathy is on his side. Let us assume for a moment that we – and by we I mean the College Council – all excepting the Master, agree to demand Skullion's reinstatement. Sir Godber would naturally resist and would be seen to resist such a move. We should appear as the champions of the underdog and the Master would find himself in an extremely difficult position. If further we present a reasoned case for our admissions policy –'

'Impossible,' said the Dean. 'No one is going to –'

'I haven't finished,' said the Senior Tutor. 'There is a sound case to be made for admitting candidates without suitable academic qualifications. We provide a natural outlet for those without apparent ability. No other college performs such a necessary function. Only the clever people get in to King's or Trinity. Certainly New Hall admits candidates under, to put it mildly, peculiar circumstances, but that's a women's college.'

The Dean sniffed disparagingly.

'Quite,' said the Senior Tutor. 'My point is this: that a properly articulated appeal on behalf of the scholastically crippled might win a great deal of public support. Couple it to demands on our part for Skullion's reinstatement and we could well turn what appears to be defeat into victory.' The Senior Tutor fetched the decanter and poured more sherry while the Dean considered his words.

'There may something in what you say,' he admitted. 'It has always seemed to me to be decidedly inequitable that only the intelligent minority should be allowed to benefit from a university education.'

'My point exactly,' said the Senior Tutor. 'We cease to be the college of privilege, we become the college of the intellectually deprived. It is simply a question of emphasis. What is more, since we are not dependent on grant-assisted undergraduates, it is self-evident that we are saving public money. The question remains how to present this new image to the public. I confess the problem baffles me.'

'The first essential is to call an urgent meeting of the College Council and get some degree of unanimity about reinstating Skullion,' said the Dean.

The Senior Tutor picked up the telephone.

CHAPTER NINETEEN

The College Council met at ten on Monday morning. Several Fellows were unable to attend but signified their readiness to vote by proxy through the Dean. Even the Master, who was not fully informed of the agenda, welcomed the meeting. 'We must thrash this affair out once and for all,' he told the Bursar, as they made their way to the Council Chamber. 'The allegations in yesterday's *Observer* have made it essential to make a clean break with the past.'

'They've certainly made things very awkward for us,' said the Bursar.

'They've made it a damned sight more awkward for the old fogeys,' said Sir Godber.

The Bursar sighed. It was evidently going to be an acrimonious meeting.

It was. The Senior Tutor led the attack.

'I am proposing that we issue a statement rescinding the dismissal of Skullion,' he told the Council when the preliminaries had been dealt with.

'Out of the question,' snapped the Master. 'Skullion has chosen to draw the attention of the public to facts about College policy which I am sure we all agree have put the reputation of Porterhouse in jeopardy.'

'I can't agree,' said the Dean.

'I certainly don't,' said the Senior Tutor.

'But the whole world knows now that we sell degrees,' Sir Godber insisted.

'That portion of the world that happens to read the *Observer*, perhaps,' said the Senior Tutor, 'but in any case allegations are not facts.'

'In this case they happen to be facts,' said the Master. 'Unadulterated facts. Skullion was speaking no more than the truth.'

'In that case I can't see why you should object to his reinstatement,' said the Senior Tutor.

They argued for twenty minutes but the Master remained adamant.

'I suggest we put the motion to the vote,' said the Dean finally. Sir Godber looked round the table angrily.

'Before we do,' he said, 'I think you should consider some further matters. I have been examining the College statutes over the past few days and it appears that as Master I am empowered, should I so wish, to take over admissions. In the light of your refusal to agree to a change in College policy regarding the sort of candidates we admit, I have decided to relieve the Senior Tutor of his responsibilities in this sphere. From now on I shall personally choose all Freshmen. It also lies within my power to select College servants and to dismiss those I consider unsatisfactory. I shall do just that. However you may vote in Council, I shall not, as Master, reinstate Skullion.'

In the Council Chamber a momentary silence followed the Master's announcement. Then the Senior Tutor spoke.

'This is outrageous,' he shouted. 'The statutes are out of date. The position of the Master is a purely formal one.'

'I admire your consistency,' snapped the Master. 'As the upholder of outmoded traditions you should be the first to congratulate me for reassuming powers that are a legacy of the past.'

'I am not prepared to stand by and see College traditions flouted,' shouted the Dean.

'They are not being flouted, Dean,' said Sir Godber, 'they are being applied. As to your standing by, if by that you mean that you wish to resign your fellowship, I shall be happy to accept your resignation.'

'I did not say anything ...' stuttered the Dean.

'Didn't you?' interrupted the Master, 'I thought you did. Am I to understand that you withdraw your –'

'He never made it,' the Senior Tutor was on his feet now. 'I find your behaviour quite unwarranted. We, sir, are not some pack of schoolboys that you can dictate to –'

'If you behave like schoolboys, you may expect to be treated like schoolboys. In any case the analogy was yours not mine. Now if you would be so good as to resume your seat the meeting may continue.' The Master looked icily at the Fellows and the Senior Tutor sat down.

'I shall take this opportunity, gentlemen,' said Sir Godber after a long pause, 'to enlighten you on my views about the function of the College in the modern world. I must confess that I am astonished to find that you seem unaware of the changes that have taken place in recent years. Your attitude suggests that you regard the College as part of a private domain of which you are custodians. Let me disabuse you of that notion. You are part of the public realm, with public duties, obligations and public functions. The fact that you choose to ignore them and to conduct the affairs of the College as though they are your personal property indicates to me that you are acting in abuse of your powers. Either we live in a society that is free, open and wholly equalitarian or we do not. As Master of this College I am determined that we shall extend the benefits of education to those who merit it by virtue of ability, irrespective of class, sex, financial standing or race. The days of rotten boroughs are over.' Sir Godber's voice was strident with idealism and threat. Not since the days of the Protectorate had the Council Chamber of Porterhouse known such vehemence, and the Fellows sat staring at the Master as at some strange animal that had assumed the shape of a man. By the time he had exhausted his theme he had left them in no doubt as to his intentions. Porterhouse would never be the same again. To the long catalogue of changes he had proposed at earlier meetings, he had now added the creation of a student council, with executive powers to decide College appointments and policy. He left the Council Chamber emotionally depleted but satisfied that he had made his point. Behind him the Fellows sat aghast at the crisis they had precipitated. It was a long time before anyone spoke.

'I don't understand,' said the Dean pathetically, 'I simply don't understand what these people want.' It was clear that in his mind Sir Godber's eloquence had elevated or possibly debased him from an individual to a class.

'Their own way,' said the Senior Tutor bitterly.

'The Kingdom of Heaven,' shouted the Chaplain.

'The Bursar said nothing. His multiple allegiances left him speechless.

Lunch was a mournful occasion. It was the end of term and the Fellows at High Table ate in a silence made all the more noticeable by the lack of conversation from the empty tables below them. To make matters worse, the soup was cold and there was cottage pie. But it was the knowledge of their own dispensability that cast gloom over them. For five hundred years they and their predecessors had ordained at least some portion of the elite that had ruled the nation. It had been through the sieve of their indulgent bigotry that young men had squeezed to become judges and lawyers, politicians and soldiers, men of affairs, all of them imbued with a corporate complacency and an intellectual scepticism that desiccated change. They were the guardians of political inertia and their role was done. They had succumbed at last to the least effectual of politicians.

'A student council to run the College. It's monstrous,' said the Senior Tutor, but there was no hope in his protest. Despite his cultivated mediocrity of mind, the Senior Tutor had seen change coming. He blamed the sciences for reestablishing the mirage of truth, and still more the pseudomorph subjects like anthropology and economics whose adepts substituted inapplicable statistics for the ineptness of their insights. And finally there was sociology with its absurd maxim, The Proper Study of

Mankind is Man, which typically it took from a man the Senior Tutor would have rejected as unfit to cox the rugger boat. And now with Sir Godber triumphant, and the Senior Tutor, at least privately, admitted the Master's victory, Porterhouse would lose even the semblance of the College he had loved. Sickly unisex would replace the healthy cheerful louts who had helped to preserve the inane innocence and the athleticism that were his only safeguards against the terrors of thought.

'There must be something we can do,' said the Dean.

'Short of murder I can think of nothing,' the Senior Tutor answered.

'Is he really entitled by statute to take over admissions?'

The Senior Tutor nodded. 'Tradition has it so,' he answered mournfully.

'There's only one thing they can do now,' said Sir Godber to Lady Mary over coffee.

'And what is that, dear?'

'Surrender,' said the Master. Lady Mary looked up. 'How very martial you do sound, Godber,' she said, invoking the ancient spirit of Sir Godber's pacifism. The Master resisted the call.

'I sounded a good deal more belligerent in the Council,' he said.

'I'm sure you did, dear,' Lady Mary parried.

'I should have thought you would have approved,' Sir Godber said. 'After all, if they had their way the College would continue to sell degrees, and exclude women.'

'Oh, don't think for a moment I am criticizing you,' said Lady Mary. 'It's just that power changes one.'

'It has been said before,' Sir Godber replied wearily. His wife's insatiable dissatisfaction subdued him. Looking into her earnest face he sometimes wondered what she saw in him. It must be something pretty harrowing, he thought. They'd been happily married for twenty-eight years.

'I'll leave you to your little victory,' Lady Mary said, getting up and putting her cup on the tray. 'I shan't be in this evening for dinner. It's my night as a Samaritan.' She went out and Sir Godber poked the fire lethargically. He felt depressed. As usual there had been something in what his wife had said. Power did change one, even the power to dominate a group of elderly Fellows in a fourth-rate college.And it was a little victory after all. Sir Godber's humanity prevailed. It wasn't their fault that they opposed the changes that he wanted. They were creatures of habit, comfortable and indulgent habits. Bachelors too – he was thinking of the Dean and the Senior Tutor – without the goad of an empty marriage to spur them to attainment. Good-hearted in their way. Even their personal animosities and petty jealousies sprang from a too constant companionship. When he examined his own motives he found them rooted in inadequacy and personal pique. He would go and speak to the Senior Tutor again and try to establish a more rational ground for disagreement. He got up and carried the coffee cups through to the kitchen and washed up. It was the au pair's day off. Then he put on his coat and went out into the spring sunshine.

Skullion lay in bed and stared at the pale blue ceiling of his hotel room. He felt uncomfortable. For one thing the bed was strange and the mattress too responsive to his movements. It wasn't hard enough for him. There was something indefinite about the whole room which left him feeling uneasy and out of place. It wasn't anything he could put his finger to but it reminded him of a whore he'd once had in Pompey. Too eager to please so that what had started out as a transaction, impersonal and hard, had turned into an encounter with his own feelings. It was the same with this room. The carpet was too thick. The bed too soft. There was too much hot water in the basin. There was nothing to grumble about and in the absence of anything particular to assert himself against, Skullion's resentment was turned in on himself. He was out of place.

His tour of monuments had unsettled him too. He wasn't interested in the *Cutty Sark* or even in *Gypsy Moth*. They too were out of place, set high and dry for kids to run about on and pretend that they were sailors. Skullion had no such romantic illusions. He couldn't pretend even for a moment that he was other than he was, a college servant out of work. The knowledge that he was a rich man only aggravated his sense of loss. It seemed to justify his dismissal by robbing him of his right to feel hard done by. Skullion even regretted his appearance on the Carrington Programme. They'd said how good he was but who were they? A lot of brown-hatters and word-merchants he had no time for, giggling and squeaking and rushing about like blue-arsed flies. They could keep their bleeding compliments to themselves, Skullion didn't need them.

He got out of bed and went through to the bathroom and shaved. They had even bought him a new razor and aerosol of shaving foam and the very ease with which he shaved robbed him of his own ritual in the matter. He put on his collar and tie and did up his waistcoat. He'd had enough. He'd said his piece and he'd been inside a television studio. That was sufficient, he decided. He'd go back to Cambridge. They could have their talk-in without him. He collected his things together and went down to the desk and paid his bill. Two hours later Skullion was sitting in the train smoking his pipe and looking out at the flat fields of Essex. The monotony of the landscape pleased him and reminded him of the Fens. He could buy a bit of land in the Fens now if he wanted to, and grow vegetables like his stepfather had done. Skullion considered the idea only to reject it. He didn't want a new life. He wanted his old one back.

When the train stopped at Cambridge Station Skullion had made up his mind. He would make one last appeal, this time not to the Dean or Sir Cathcart. He'd speak to the Master himself. He walked out of the station and down Station Road wondering why he hadn't thought of it before. He had his pride, of course, and he'd put his trust in the Dean but the Dean had let him down. Besides, he despised Sir Godber, according him only that automatic respect that went with the Mastership. At the corner of Lensfield Road he hesitated under the spire of the Catholic Church. He could turn right across Parker's Piece to Rhyder Street or left to Porterhouse. It was only twelve o'clock and he hadn't eaten. He'd walk into town and have a bite to eat in a pub and think about it. Skullion trudged on down Regent Street and went into the Fountain and ordered a pint of Guinness and some sandwiches. Sitting at a table by the door he drank his beer and tried to imagine what the Master would say. He could only turn him down. Skullion considered the prospect and decided it was worth trying even if it meant risking his self-respect. But was he risking it? All he was asking for was his rights and besides he had a quarter of a million pounds to his name. He didn't need the job. Nobody could accuse him of grovelling. It was simply that he wanted it, wanted his good name back, wanted to go on doing what he had always done for forty-five years, wanted to be the Porter of Porterhouse. Buoyed by the good sense of his own argument Skullion finished his beer and left the pub. He threaded his way through the shoppers towards the Market Hill, his mind still mulling over the wisdom of his action. Perhaps he should wait a day or two. Perhaps they had already changed their mind and a letter was waiting for him at home offering him his job back. Skullion dismissed the idea. And all the time there was the nagging fear that he was putting in jeopardy his self-respect by asking. He silenced the fear but it remained with him, as constant as the natural tendency of his steps to lead towards Porterhouse. Twice he decided to go home and twice changed his mind, postponing the decision by walking down Sydney Street towards the Round Church instead of going on down Trinity Street. He tried to fortify his resolve by thinking about Lord Wurford's legacy but the idea of all that money was as unreal to him as the experience of the past few days. There was no consolation to be found in money. It couldn't replace the cosiness of his Porter's Lodge with its pigeonholes and switchboard and the sense that he was needed. The sum was almost an affront to him, its fortuity robbing his years of service of their sense. He needn't have been a porter. He could have been anything he wanted, within reason. The realization increased his sense of purpose. He would speak to the Master. He hesitated at the Round Church. He wouldn't go in the Main Gate, he'd knock at the Master's Lodge. He turned and went back the way he'd come.

The Master's sudden decision to seek some ground of understanding with the Senior Tutor left him almost as soon as he had crossed the Fellows' Garden. Any sort of overture now would be misinterpreted, he realized, taken as evidence of weakness on his part. He had established his authority. It would not do to weaken it now. But having come out he felt obliged to continue his walk. He went into town and browsed in Heffer's for an hour before buying Butler's *Art of the Possible.* It was not a maxim with which he had much sympathy. It smacked of cynicism but Sir Godber was sufficient of a politician still to appreciate the author's sense of irony. He wandered on debating his own choice of a title for his autobiography. *Future Perfect* was probably the most appropriate, combining as it did his vision with a modicum of scholarship. Catching sight of this reflection in a shop window he found it remarkable that he was as old as he looked. It was strange that his ideals had not altered with his appearance. The methods of their attainment might mellow with experience but the ideals remained constant. That was why it was so important to see that the undergraduates who came up to Porterhouse should be free to form their own judgements, and more important still that they should have some judgements to form. They should rebel against the accepted tenets of their elders and, in Sir Godber's opinion, their worse. He stopped at the Copper Kettle for tea and then made his way back to Porterhouse and sat in his study reading his book. Outside the sky darkened, and with it the College. Out of term it was empty and there were no room lights on to brighten the Court. At five the Master got up and pulled the curtains and he was about to sit down again when a knock at the front door made him stop and go down the corridor into the hall. He opened the door and peered out into the darkness. A dark familiar shape stood on the doorstep.

'Skullion?' said Sir Godber as if questioning the existence of the shape. 'What are you doing here?'

To Skullion the question emphasized his misery. 'I'd like a word,' he said.

Sir Godber hesitated. He didn't want words with Skullion. 'What about?' he asked. It was Skullion's turn to hesitate. 'I've come to apologize,' he said finally.

'Apologize? What for?' Skullion shook his head. He didn't know what for. 'Well, man? What for?'

'It's just that ...'

'Oh for goodness sake,' said Sir Godber, appalled at Skullion's inarticulate despair. 'Come on in.' He turned and led the way to his study with Skullion treading gently behind him.

'Well now, what is it?' he asked when they were in the room.

'It's about my dismissal, sir,' Skullion said.

'Your dismissal?' Sir Godber sighed. He was a sympathetic man who had to steel himself with irritation. 'You should see the Bursar about that. I don't deal with matters of that sort.'

'I've seen the Bursar,' said Skullion.

'I don't see that I can do anything,' the Master said. 'And in any case I really don't think that you can expect much sympathy after what you said the other night.'

Skullion looked at him sullenly. 'I didn't say anything wrong,' he muttered. 'I just said what I thought.'

'It might have paid you to consider what you did think before ...' Sir Godber gave up. The situation was most unfortunate. He had better things to do with his time than argue with college porters. 'Anyway there's nothing more to be said.'

Skullion stirred resentfully. 'Forty-five years I've been a porter here,' he said.

Sir Godber's hand brushed the years aside. 'I know. I know,' he said. 'I'm aware of that.'

'I've given my life to the College.'

'I daresay.'

Skullion glowered at the Master. 'All I ask is to be kept on,' he said.

The Master turned his back on him and kicked the fire with his foot. The man's maudlin appeal annoyed him. Skullion had exercised a baleful influence on the College ever since he could remember. He stood for everything Sir Godber detested. He'd been rude, bullying and importunate all his life and the Master hadn't forgotten his insolence on the night of the explosion. Now here he was, cap in hand, asking to be taken back. Worst of all he made the Master feel guilty.

'I understand from the Bursar that you have some means,' he said callously. Skullion nodded. 'Enough to live on?'

'Yes.'

'Well then, I really can't see what you're complaining about. A lot of people retire at sixty. Haven't you got a family?' Skullion shook his head. Again Sir Godber felt a tremor of unreasonable disgust. His contempt showed in his face, contempt as much for his own vulnerable sensibilities as for the pathetic man before him. Skullion saw that contempt and his little eyes darkened. He had swallowed his pride to come and ask but it rode up in him now in the face of the Master's scorn. It rose up out of the distant past when he'd been a free man and it overwhelmed the barriers of his reference. He hadn't come to be insulted even silently by the likes of Sir Godber. Without knowing what he was doing he took a step forward. Instinctively Sir Godber recoiled. He was afraid of Skullion and, like his contempt a moment before, it showed. He'd been afraid of Skullion all his life, the little Skullions who lived in drab streets he'd had to pass to go to school, who chased him and threw stones and wore grubby clothes.

'Now look here,' he said with an attempt at authority, but Skullion was looking. His bitter eyes stared at Sir Godber and he too was in the grip of the past and its violent instincts. His face was flushed and unknown to him his fists were clenched.

'You bastard!' he shouted and lunged at the Master. 'You bloody bastard!' Sir Godber staggered backwards and tripped against the coffee table. He fell against the mantelpiece and clutched at the edge of the armchair and the next moment he had fallen back into the fireplace. Beneath his feet a rug gently slid away and Sir Godber subsided on to the study floor. His head had hit the corner of the iron grate. Above him Skullion stood dumbfounded. Blood oozed on to the parquet. Skullion's fury ebbed. He stared down at the Master for a moment and turned and ran. He ran down the passage and out the front door into the street. It was empty. Skullion turned to the right and hurried along the pavement. A moment later he was in Trinity Street. People passed him but there was nothing unusual about a college porter in a hurry.

In the Master's Lodge Sir Godber lay still in the flickering light of his fire. The blood running fast from his scalp formed in a pool and dried. An hour passed and Sir Godber still bled, though more slowly. It was eight before he recovered consciousness. The room was blurred and distant and clocks ticked noisily. He tried to get to his feet but couldn't. He knelt against the fireplace and reached for the armchair. Slowly he crawled across the room to the telephone. He'd got to ring for help. He reached up and pulled the phone down on to the floor. He started to dial emergency but the thought of scandal stopped him. His wife? He put the receiver back and reached for the pad with the number of the

Samaritans on it. He found it and dialled. While he waited he stared at the notice Lady Mary had pinned on the pad. 'If you are in Despair or thinking of Suicide, Phone the Samaritans.'

The dialling tone stopped. 'Samaritans here, can I help you?' Lady Mary's voice was as stridently concerned as ever.

'I'm hurt,' said Sir Godber indistinctly.

'You're what? You'll have to speak up.'

'I said I'm hurt. For God's sake come ...'

'What's that?' Lady Mary asked.

'Oh God, oh God,' Sir Godber moaned feebly.

'All right now, tell me all about it,' said Lady Mary with interest. 'I'm here to help you.'

'I've fallen in the grate,' Sir Godber explained.

'Fallen from grace?'

'Not grace,' said Sir Godber desperately. 'Grate.'

'Great?' Lady Mary inquired, evidently convinced she was dealing with a disillusioned megalomaniac.

'The hearth. I'm bleeding. For God's sake come ...' Exhausted by his wife's lack of understanding Sir Godber fell back upon the floor. Beside him the phone continued to squeak and gibber with Lady Mary's exhortations.

'Are you there?' she asked. 'Are you still there? Now there's no need to despair.' Sir Godber groaned. 'Now don't hang up. Just stay there and listen. Now you say you've fallen from grace. That's not a very constructive way of looking at things, is it?' Sir Godber's stentorian breathing reassured her. 'After all what is grace? We're all human. We can't expect to live up to our own expectations all the time. We're bound to make mistakes. Even the best of us. But that doesn't mean to say we've fallen from grace. You mustn't think in those terms. You're not a Catholic, are you?' Sir Godber groaned. 'It's just that you mentioned bleeding hearts. Catholics believe in bleeding hearts, you know.' Lady Mary was adding instruction to exhortation now. It was typical of the bloody woman, Sir Godber thought helplessly. He tried to raise himself so that he could replace the receiver and shut out forever the sound of Lady Mary's implacable philanthropy but the effort was too much for him.

'Get off the line,' he managed to moan. 'I need help.'

'Of course you do and that's what I'm here for,' Lady Mary said. 'To help.'

Sir Godber crawled away from the receiver, spurred on by her obtuseness. He had to get help somehow. His eye caught the trays of drinks near the door. Whisky. He crawled towards it and managed to get the bottle. He drank some and still clutching the bottle reached the side door. Somehow he opened it and dragged himself out into the Fellows' Garden. If only he could reach the Court, perhaps he could call out and someone would hear him. He drank some more whisky and tried to get to his feet. There was a light on in the Combination Room. If only he could get there. Sir Godber raised himself on his knees and fell sideways on to the path.

CHAPTER TWENTY

It was Sir Cathcart's birthday and as usual there was a party at Coft Castle. On the gravel forecourt the sleek cars bunched in the moonlight like so many large seals huddled on the foreshore. Inside the animal analogy continued. In the interests of several Royal guests and uninhibited debauchery, masks were worn if little else. Sir Cathcart typically adopted the disguise of a horse, its muzzle suitably foreshortened to facilitate conversation and his penchant for fellatio. Her Royal Highness the Princess Penelope sought anonymity as a capon and deceived no one. A judge from the Appellate Division was a macaw. There was a bear, two gnus, and a panda wearing a condom. The Loverley sisters sported dildos with stripes and claimed they were zebras and Lord Forsyth, overzealous as a labrador, urinated against a standard lamp in the library and had to be resuscitated by Mrs Hinkle, who was one of the judges at Crufts. Even the detectives mingling with the crowd were dressed as pumas. Only the Dean and the Senior Tutor came as humans, and they were not invited.

'Cathcart's the only man I know who could do it,' the Dean had said suddenly during dinner in the empty Hall.

'Do what?' asked the Senior Tutor.

'See the PM,' said the Dean. 'Get him to rescind the Master's nomination.'

The Senior Tutor lacerated a shinbone judiciously and wiped his fingers. 'On what grounds?'

'General maladministration,' said the Dean.

'Difficult to prove,' said the Senior Tutor.

The Dean helped himself to devilled kidneys and Arthur replenished his wine glass. 'Let us review the facts. Since his arrival the College has seen the deaths of one undergraduate, a bedder, the total destruction of a building classified as a national monument, charges of peculation and a scandal involving the admission of unqualified candidates, the sacking of Skullion and now, to cap it all, the assumption of dictatorial powers by the Master.'

'But surely –'

'Bear with me,' said the Dean. 'Now you and I may know that the Master is not wholly responsible, but the general public thinks otherwise. Have you seen today's *Telegraph*?'

'No,' said the Senior Tutor, 'but I think I know what you mean. *The Times* has three columns of letters, all of them supporting Skullion's statement on the box.'

'Exactly,' said the Dean. 'The *Telegraph* also has a leading article calling for a stand against student indiscipline and a return to the values Skullion so eloquently advocated. Whatever the merits of the Carrington Programme, it has certainly provoked a public reaction against the dismissal of Skullion. Porterhouse may have been blackguarded but it is Sir Godber who takes the blame.'

'As Master, you mean?'

'Precisely,' continued the Dean. 'He may claim –'

'As Master he must accept full responsibility,' said the Senior Tutor.

'Still, I don't see that the Prime Minister would willingly dismiss him. It would reflect poorly on his own judgement in the first place.'

'The Government's position is not a particularly healthy one just at the moment,' said the Dean. 'It only needs a nudge . . .'

'A nudge? From whom?'

The Dean smiled and signalled to Arthur to make himself scarce. 'From me,' he said when the waiter had shuffled off into the darkness of the lower hall.

'You?' said the Senior Tutor. 'How?'

'Have you ever heard of Skullion's Scholars?' the Dean asked. His bloated face glowed in the light of the candles.

'That old story,' said the Senior Tutor. 'An old chestnut surely?'

The Dean shook his head. 'I have the names and the dates and the sums involved,' he said. 'I have the names of the graduates who wrote the papers. I have even some examples of their work.' He put the tips of his fingers together and nodded. The Senior Tutor stared at him.

'No,' he muttered.

'Yes,' the Dean assured him.

'But how?'

The Dean withdrew a little. 'Let's just say that I have,' he said. 'There was a time when I disapproved of the practice. I was young in those days and full of foolishness but I changed my mind. Fortunately I did not destroy the evidence. You see now what I mean by a nudge?'

The Senior Tutor gulped some wine in his amazement. 'Not the PM?' he muttered.

'Not,' admitted the Dean, 'but one or two of his colleagues.' The Senior Tutor tried to think which ministers were Porterhouse men.

'I have some eighty names,' said the Dean, 'some eighty *eminent* names. I think they're quite sufficient.'

The Senior Tutor mopped his forehead. There was no doubt in his mind about the sufficiency of the Dean's information. It would bring the Government down. 'Could you rely on Skullion to substantiate,' he asked.

The Dean nodded. 'I hardly think it will come to that,' he said, 'and if it does I am prepared to stand as scapegoat. I am an old man. I no longer care.'

They sat in silence. Two old men together in the isolated candlelight under the dark rafters of the Hall. Arthur, standing obediently by the green baize door, watched them fondly.

'And Sir Cathcart?' asked the Senior Tutor.

'And Sir Cathcart,' agreed the Dean.

They stood up and the Dean said grace, his voice tremulous in the vastness of the silent Hall. They went out into the Combination Room and Arthur shuffled softly up to the High Table and began to collect the dishes.

Half an hour later they drove out of the College car park in the Senior Tutor's car. Coft Castle was blazing with Edwardian brilliance when they arrived.

'It seems an inopportune moment,' said the Senior Tutor doubtfully surveying the shoal of cars.

'We must strike while the iron is hot,' said the Dean. Inside they were accosted by a puma.

'Do we look like gatecrashers?' the Dean asked severely. The puma shook its head.

'We have urgent business with General Sir Cathcart D'Eath,' said the Senior Tutor. 'Be so good as to inform him that the Dean and Senior Tutor have arrived. We shall wait for him in the library.'

The puma nodded dutifully and they pushed their way through a crush of assorted beasts to the library.

'I must say I find this sort of thing extremely distasteful,' said the Dean. 'I am surprised that Cathcart allows such goings on at Coft Castle. One would have thought he had more taste.'

'He always did have something of a reputation,' said the Senior Tutor. 'Of course he was before my time but I did hear one or two rather unsavoury stories.'

'Youthful excess is one thing,' said the Dean, 'but mutton dressed as lamb is another.'

'They say the leopard doesn't change its spots,' said the Senior Tutor. He sat down in a club easy while the Dean idly examined a nicely bound copy of Stendhal. It contained, as he had expected from the title, a bottle of liqueur.

Outside the puma stalked Sir Cathcart. He found it extremely difficult. He tried the billiard-room, the smoking-room, the morning-room, and the dining-room without success. In the kitchen he asked the cook if she had seen him.

'I wouldn't know him if I had,' the cook said primly. 'All I know is that he's gone as a horse.'

The detective went back into the menagerie and asked several guests who were wearing horsey masks if they were Sir Cathcart. They weren't. He helped himself to champagne and tried again. Finally he ran Sir Cathcart to ground in the conservatory with a well-known jockey. The detective surveyed the scene with disgust.

'Two gentlemen to see you in the library,' he said. Sir Cathcart got to his feet.

'What do you mean?' he said indistinctly. 'What are they doing there? I said nobody was to go in the library.' He staggered off down the passage and into the library where the Dean had just discovered a copy of *A Man and A Maid* inside an early edition of *Great Expectations*.

'What the hell . . .?' Sir Cathcart began before realizing who they were.

'Cathcart?' inquired the Dean, staring doubtfully at the General.

'Who?' said Sir Cathcart.

'We are waiting to speak to Sir Cathcart D'Eath,' said the Dean.

'Isn't here. Gone to London,' said the General, slurring his voice deliberately and hoping that his mask was a sufficient proof against identity. The Dean was unpersuaded. He recognized the General's fetlocks.

'I am prepared to accept the explanation,' he said grimly. 'We have not come here to pry.' He returned to copy of *Great Expectations* to its place. 'We simply wanted to inform Sir Cathcart that the matter of Skullion's Scholars is about to receive a public airing.'

'Damnation,' shouted the General, 'how the hell did . . .?' He stopped and regarded the Dean bitterly.

'Quite,' said the Dean. He sat down behind the desk and the General sank into a chair. 'The matter is urgent, otherwise we shouldn't be here. We have no desire to abuse your hospitality, if that were possible, any longer than we have to. Let us assume that Sir Cathcart is in London for the moment.'

The General nodded his agreement with this tactful proposition. 'What do you want?' he asked.

'Things have reached a crisis,' said the Senior Tutor rising from his club easy. 'We simply want the Prime Minister to be informed that Sir Godber's Mastership must be rescinded.'

'Must?' said the General. The word had an authoritarian ring about it that he was unused to.

'Must,' said the Dean.

Sir Cathcart inside his mask looked doubtful. 'It's a tall order.'

'No doubt,' said the Dean. 'The alternative is possibly the fall of the Government. I am prepared to place my information in the hands of the press. I think you follow the likely consequences.'

Sir Cathcart did. 'But why, for God's sake?' he asked. 'I don't understand. If this got out it would ruin the College.'

'If the Master stays there will be no college to ruin,' said the Dean. 'There will be a hostel. I have some eighty names, Cathcart.'

Sir Cathcart peered through his mask bitterly. '*Eighty*? And you're prepared to put their reputations at risk?'

The Dean's mouth curved upwards in a sneer. 'In the circumstances I find that question positively indecent,' he said.

'Oh, come now,' said the General. 'We all have our little peccadilloes. A fellow's entitled to a little fun.'

On the way out they were importuned by a fowl. 'These gentlemen are just leaving,' said Sir Cathcart hurriedly.

'Before me?' cackled the capon. 'It's against protocol.'

They drove back to Porterhouse in silence. What they had just witnessed had left them with a new sense of disillusionment.

'The whole country is going to the dogs,' said the Senior Tutor as they crossed New Court. As if in answer there was a low moan from the Fellows' Garden.

'What on earth was that?' said the Dean. They turned and peered into the darkness. Under the elms a shadow darker than the rest struggled to its feet and collapsed. They crossed the lawn cautiously and stood staring down at the figure on the ground.

'A drunk,' said the Senior Tutor. 'I'll fetch the Porter,' but the Dean had already struck a match. In the small flare of light they looked down into the ashen face of Sir Godber.

'Good God,' said the Dean, 'it's the Master.'

They carried him slowly and with difficulty down the gravel path to the Master's Lodge and laid him on the sofa.

'I'll get an ambulance,' said the Senior Tutor, and picked the phone off the floor and dialled. While they waited the Dean sat staring down into the Master's face. It was evident Sir Godber was dying. He struggled to speak but the words wouldn't come.

'He's trying to tell us something,' said the Senior Tutor softly. There was no bitterness now. In extremis the Master had regained the Senior Tutor's loyalty.

'He must have been drunk,' said the Dean, who could smell the whisky on Sir Godber's feeble breath.

The Master shook his head. An indefinite future awaited him now in which he would only be a memory. It must not be sullied by false report.

'Not drunk,' he managed to mutter, gazing pitifully into the Dean's face. 'Skullion.'

The Dean and Senior Tutor looked at one another. 'What about Skullion?' the Senior Tutor asked but the Master had no answer for him.

They waited for the ambulance before leaving. It had been impossible to contact Lady Mary. She was on the phone to a depressive who was threatening to end his life. On the way back through the Fellows' Garden the Dean retrieved the whisky bottle.

'I don't think we need mention this to the police,' he said. 'He was obviously drunk and fell into the fireplace. A tragic end.'

The Senior Tutor was lost in thought. 'You realize what he's done?' he asked.

'Only too well,' said the Dean. 'I'll phone Sir Cathcart and tell him to cancel the ultimatum. There's no need for it now. We shall have to elect a new Master. Let us see to it that he has the true interests of the College at heart. We mustn't make another mistake.'

The Senior Tutor shook his head. 'There can be no question of an election, Dean,' he said. 'The Master has already nominated his own successor.'

In the darkness the two old men stared at one another digesting the extraordinary import of Sir Godber's last word. it was unthinkable but yet . . .

They went into the Combination Room to deliberate. The ancient panelled walls, the plaster ceiling decorated with heraldic devices and grotesque animals, the portraits of past Masters, and the silver candlesticks all combined to urge considerations of the past upon their present dilemma.

'There are precedents,' said the Senior Tutor. 'Thomas Wilkins was a pastrycook.'

'He was also an eminent theologian,' said the Dean.

'Dr Cox began his career as a barber,' the Senior Tutor pointed out. 'He owed his election to his wealth.'

'I take your point,' said the Dean. 'In the present cicumstances it is one that cannot be ignored.'

'There is also the question of public opinion to consider,' the Senior Tutor continued. 'In the present climate it would not be an unpopular appointment. It would disarm our critics entirely.

'So it would,' said the Dean. 'It would indeed. But the College Council –'

'Have no say in the matter,' said the Senior Tutor. 'Tradition has it that the Master's dying words constitute an unalterable decision.'

'If uttered in the presence of two or more of the Senior Fellows,' agreed the Dean. 'So it is up to us.'

'There is little doubt that he would be malleable,' the Senior Tutor continued after a long pause. The Dean nodded. 'I confess to finding the argument unanswerable,' he said. They rose and snuffed the candles.

Skullion sat in the darkness of his kitchen, shivering. It was a cold night but Skullion was unconscious of the cold. His tremors had other causes. He had threatened the Master. He had in all probability killed him. The memory of Sir Godber lying in a pool of blood in the fireplace haunted Skullion. He could not think of sleep. He sat there at the kitchen table shivering with fright. He couldn't begin to think what to do. The law would find him. Skullion's innate respect for authority rejected the possibility that his crime would go undetected. It was almost as monstrous a thought as the knowledge that he was a murderer. He was still there when the Dean and the Senior Tutor knocked on his door at eight o'clock. They had brought the Praelector with them. As usual his was a supernumerary role.

Skullion listened to the knocking for some minutes before his instincts as a porter got the better of him. He got up and went down the dingy hall and opened the door. He stood blinking in the sunlight, his face purple with strain but with a solemnity that befitted the occasion.

'If we could just have a word with you, Mr Skullion,' the Dean said.

To Skullion the addition of the title had the effect of confirming his worst fears. It suggested the polite formalities of the hangman. He turned and led the way into his front parlour where the sun, shining through the lace curtains, dappled the antimacassars with a fresh embroidery.

The three Fellows removed their hats and sat awkwardly on the Victorian chairs. Like most of the furniture in the house they had been salvaged from the occasional refurbishment of Porterhouse.

'I think it would be better if you sat down,' said the Dean when Skullion continued to stand before them. 'What we are about to tell you may come as something of a shock.'

Skullion sat down obediently. Nothing that they could tell him would comee as a shock, he felt sure. He had prepared himself for the worst.

'We have come here this morning to tell you that the Master has died,' said the Dean. Skullion's face remained impassively suffused. To the three Fellows his evident self-control augured well for the future.

'On his deathbed Sir Godber named you as his successor,' said the Dean slowly. Skullion heard the words but his expectations deprived them of their meaning. What had seemed unthinkable to the Dean and Senior Tutor at first hearing was inconceivable to Skullion. He stared uncomprehendingly at the Dean.

'He nominated you as the new Master of Porterhouse,' continued the Dean. 'We have come here this morning on behalf of the College Council to ask you to accept this nomination.' He paused to allow the Porter to consider the proposal. 'Naturally we understand that this must come as a very great surprise to you, as indeed it did to us, but we would like to know your answer as soon as possible.'

In the silence that followed this announcement, Skullion underwent a terrible change. A tremor ran down his body and his face, already purple, became darker still. He wrestled with the terrible inconsequentiality of it all. He had murdered the Master and they were offering him the Mastership. There were no just rewards in life, only insane inversions of the scheme of things in which he had trusted. It seemed for a moment that he was going mad.

'We must have your answer,' said the Dean. Skullion's body acted uncontrollably as he went into apoplexy. His head nodded frantically.

'Then we may take it that you accept?' asked the Dean. Skullion's head nodded without stop.

'Then let me be the first to congratulate you, Master,' said the Dean and seizing Skullion's hand shook it convulsively. The Praelector and the Senior Tutor followed suit.

*

'The poor fellow was quite overcome,' said the Dean as they climbed back into the car. 'It seemed to leave him speechless.'

'Hardly surprising, Dean,' said the Praelector, 'I find it difficult to voice my feelings even now. Skullion as the Master of Porterhouse. That it should come to this.'

'At least we shan't have any speeches at the Feast,' said the Senior Tutor.

'I suppose there is that to be said for it,' said the Praelector.

In the front parlour of his old home the new Master of Porterhouse lay still in his chair and stared calmly at the linoleum. A new peace had come to Skullion out of the chaos of the last few minutes. There were no contradictions now between right and wrong, master and servant, only a strange inability to move his left side.

Skullion had suffered a Porterhouse Blue.

CHAPTER TWENTY-ONE

'A stroke of luck really,' said the Dean at lunch after the formal ceremony in the Council Chamber at which the new Master had presided before being wheeled back by Arthur to the Master's Lodge.

'I must say I don't follow you, Dean,' said the Praelector with distaste. 'If you are referring to the Master's affliction –'

'I was merely trying to draw your attention to the advantages of the situation,' said the Dean. 'The Master is not without his comforts after all, and we . . .'

'Enjoy the administration of policy?' the Senior Tutor suggested.

'Precisely.'

'I suppose that is one way of looking at it. Certainly Sir Godber's reforms have been frustrated. I thought Lady Mary behaved extremely badly.'

The Dean sighed. 'Liberals tend to overreact, in my experience. There seems to be something inherently hysterical about progressive opinion,' he said. 'Still, there was no excuse whatsoever for accusing the police of incompetence. Nothing could be more absurd than her suggestion that Sir Godber had been murdered. For one moment I thought she was going to accuse the Senior Tutor and myself.'

'I suppose he was drunk,' said the Praelector.

'Not according to the coroner,' said the Bursar.

The Dean sniffed. 'I have never placed much faith in expert opinion,' he said. 'I smelt the fellow's breath. He was as drunk as a lord.'

'It's certainly the only rational explanation of his choice of Skullion,' said the Praelector. 'To my knowledge he loathed the man.'

'I'm afraid I have to agree with you,' said the Bursar. 'Lady Mary –'

'Accused us of lying,' said the Dean and the Senior Tutor simultaneously.

'As you said yourself, Dean, she was hysterical,' said the Praelector. 'She wasn't herself.'

The Dean scowled down the table. Lady Mary's accusation still rankled. 'Damned woman,' he said, 'she's a disgrace to her sex.' He took his irritation out on the new waiter. 'These potatoes are burnt.'

'Now you come to mention it,' said the Senior Tutor, 'what went wrong at the crematorium? There seemed an inordinately long delay.'

'There was a power cut,' the Dean said, 'on account of the strike.'

'Ah, was that it?' said the Senior Tutor. 'A sympathy strike no doubt.'

They finished their meal and took coffee in the Combination Room.

'There's still the question of Sir Godber's portrait to be considered,' said the Senior Tutor. 'I suppose we should decide on a suitable artist.'

'There's only Bacon,' said the Dean, 'I can think of no one else who could portray a more exact likeness.'

The Fellows of Porterhouse had regained their vivacity.

In the Master's Lodge Skullion's life followed its inexorable pattern. He was wheeled from room to room to catch the sun so that it was possible to tell the time of day from his position at the windows, and every afternoon Arthur would take him out through the Fellows' Garden and across New Court to the main gate. Occasionally late at night the wheel chair, with its dark occupant wearing his bowler hat, could be seen in the shadows by the back gate waiting and watching with an implacable futility of purpose the spiked wall over which the undergraduates no longer climbed. But if Skullion's horizons were limited to the narrow confines of the College they were celestial in time. Each corner of Porterhouse held memories for him that made good the infirmities of the present. It was as if his stroke had sutured the gaps in his memory so that in his immobility he was left free at last to haunt the years as once he had patrolled the courtyards and the corridors of Porterhouse. Sitting in New Court he would recall the occupants of every room, their names and faces, even the counties they came from, so that the Court assumed a new dimension, at once recessional and mute. Each staircase was a warren in his mind alive with men no longer living who had once conferred the honour of their disregard upon him. 'Skullion,' they had shouted, and the shouts still echoed in his mind with their call to a service he would never know again. Instead they called him Master now and Skullion suffered their respect in silence.

Around him the life of the College went on unaltered. Lord Wurford's legacy helped to restore the Tower and Skullion had signed the papers with his thumbprint unprotestingly. As a sop to scholarship there were a few research fellows, mainly in law and the less controversial sciences, but apart from these concessions, little changed. The undergraduates kept later hours, grew longer hair and sported their affectations of opinion as trivially as ever they had once seduced the shopgirls. But in essentials they were just the same. In any case, Skullion discounted thought. He'd known too many scholars in his time to think that they would alter things. It was the continuity of custom and character that counted. What men were, not what they said, and looking round him he was reassured. The faces that he saw and the voices he heard, though now obscured by hair and the borrowed accents of the poor, had still the recognizable attributes of class, and if the old unfeeling arrogance had been replaced by a kindliness and gentle quality that he despised, it was still Them and Us even in the privilege of sympathy. And when an undergraduate would offer to wheel the Master for a walk, he would be deterred by the glint in Skullion's eyes which betrayed a contempt that made a mockery of his dependence.

Occasionally the Senior Tutor would smother his revulsion for the physically inadequate and visit the Master for tea to tell him how the Eight was doing or what the Rugger fifteen had won, and every day the Dean would waddle to the Master's Lodge to report the day's events. Skullion did not enjoy this strange reversal of roles but it seemed to afford the Dean some little satisfaction. It was as if this mock subservience assuaged his sense of guilt.

'We owe it to him,' he told the Senior Tutor who asked him why he bothered.

'But what do you find to say to him?'

'I ask after his health,' said the Dean gaily.

But he can't reply,' the Senior Tutor pointed out.

'I find that most consoling,' said the Dean. 'And after all no news is good news isn't it?'

On Thursday nights the Master dined in Hall, wheeled in by Arthur at the head of the Fellows to sit at the end of the table and watch the ancient ritual of Grace and the serving of the dishes with a critical eye.

While the Fellows gorged themselves, Skullion was fed a few, choice morsels by Arthur. It was his worst humiliation. That, and the fact that his shoes lacked the brilliance that his patient spit and polish had once given them.

It was left to the Dean, unfeeling to the end, to say the last word in the Combination Room after one such meal. 'He may not have been born with a silver spoon in his mouth, but by God he's going to die with one.'

In his corner by the fire the Master was seen to twitch deferentially at this joke at his own expense, but then Skullion had always known his place.

BLOTT ON THE LANDSCAPE

CHAPTER ONE

Sir Giles Lynchwood, Member of Parliament for South Worfordshire, sat in his study and lit a cigar. Outside his window tulips and primroses bloomed, a thrush pecked at the lawn and the sun shone down out of a cloudless sky. In the distance he could see the cliffs of the Cleene Gorge rising above the river.

But Sir Giles had no thoughts for the beauties of the landscape. His mind was occupied with other things; with money and Mrs Forthby and the disparity between things as they were and things as they might have been. Not that the view from his window was one of uninterrupted beauty. It held Lady Maud, and whatever else she might be, nobody in his right mind would ever have described her as beautiful. She was large and ponderous and possessed a shape that someone had once aptly called Rodinesque – certainly Sir Giles, viewing her as dispassionately as six years of marriage allowed, found her monumentally unattractive. Sir Giles was not particularly fussy about external appearances. His fortune had been made by recognizing potential advantage in unprepossessing properties and he could justly claim to have evicted more impecunious tenants than any other anonymous landlord in London. Maud's appearance was the least of his marital problems. It was rather the cast of her mind, her outspoken self-assurance, that infuriated him. That, and the fact that for once in his life he was lumbered with a wife he could not leave and a house he could not sell.

Maud was a Handyman and Handyman Hall had always been her family home. A vast rambling building with twenty bedrooms, a ballroom with a sprung floor, a plumbing system that held fascinations for industrial archaeologists but which kept Sir Giles awake at night, and a central heating system that had been designed to consume coke by the ton, and now seemed to gulp oil by the megagallon, Handyman Hall had been built in 1899 to make manifest in bricks, mortar and the more hideous furnishings of the period the fact that the Handyman family had arrived. Theirs had been a brief social season. Edward the Seventh had twice paid visits to the house, on each occasion seducing Mrs Handyman in the mistaken belief that she was a chambermaid (a result of the diffidence which left her speechless in the presence of Royalty). In recompense for this royal gaffe, and for services rendered, her husband Bulstrode was raised to the Peerage. From that brief moment of social acceptance the Handymans had sunk to their present obscurity. Borne to prominence on a tide of ale – Handyman Pale, Handyman Triple XXX and Handyman West Country had been famous in their time – they had succumbed to a taste for brandy. The first earl of Handyman had died, a suspicious husband and an understandably ardent republican, in time to achieve posthumous fame as the first cadaver to incur Lloyd George's exorbitant death duties. He had been followed almost immediately by his eldest son Bartholomew, whose reaction to the taxman's summons had been to drink himself to death on two bottles of his father's Trois Six de Montpellier.

The outbreak of the First World War had completed the decline in the family fortunes. Boothroyd, the second son, had returned from France with his taste buds so irreparably impaired by taking a swig from a bottle of battery acid to steady his nerves before going over the top that his efforts to restore Handyman Ale to its pre-war quality and popularity had quite the contrary effect. For the first time the title 'Brewers Extraordinary to his Majesty the King' accurately reflected the character of the beer dispensed by the Handyman Brewery. During the twenties and thirties sales dropped until they were confined to a dozen tied houses in Worfordshire whose patrons were forced to consume Boothroyd's appalling concoctions out of a sense of loyalty to the family and by the refusal of the local magistrates (Boothroyd among them) to grant licences to sell spiritous liquors to anyone else. By that time the Handymans had been reduced to living in one wing of the great house and had celebrated the outbreak of the Second World War by offering the rest of their home to the War Office. Boothroyd had died on Home Guard duty to be succeeded by his brother Busby, Maud's father, and the Hall had served first as a home for General de Gaulle's chief of staff and the entire Free French army of that time and later as an Italian prisoner-of-war camp. The fourth Earl had done what he could to restore Handyman Ale to its previous popularity by reverting to the original recipe, and to restore the family fortune by using his influence to see that the War Office paid a quite disproportionately high rent for a building they didn't want.

It had been that influence, the Handyman influence, which had persuaded Sir Giles that he could do worse than marry Lady Maud and through her acquire a seat in Parliament. Looking back over the years Sir Giles was inclined to think that he had paid too high a price for the Hall and social acceptance. A marriage of convenience he had called it at the time, but the term had proved singularly inappropriate. Nothing about Maud's appearance had suggested an unduly fastidious attitude to sex and Sir Giles had been surprised, not to say pained, by her too literal interpretation of his suggestion on their honeymoon that she should tie him to the bed and beat him. Sir Giles' screams had been audible a quarter of a mile along the Costa Brava and had led to an embarrassing interview with the hotel manager. Sir Giles had stood all the way home and ever since had sought refuge in a separate bedroom and in Mrs Forthby, in whose flat in St John's Wood he could at least be assured of moderation. To make matters worse there was no possibility of a divorce. Their marriage settlement included a reversionary clause whereby the Hall and the Estate, for which he had had to pay one hundred thousand pounds to Maud, would revert to her in the event of his death without heirs or of misconduct on his part leading to a divorce case. Sir Giles was a rich man but one hundred thousand pounds was too high a price to pay for freedom.

He sighed and glanced out of the window. Lady Maud had disappeared but the scene was no pleasanter for her going. Her place had been taken by Blott, the gardener, who was plodding across the lawn towards the kitchen garden. Sir Giles studied the squat figure with distaste. For a gardener, for an Italian gardener *and* an Ex-PoW, Blott had an air of contentment that grated on Sir Giles' nerves. He liked his servants to be obsequious and there was nothing obsequious about Blott. The wretched fellow seemed to think he owned the place. Sir Giles watched him disappear through the door in the wall of the kitchen garden and considered ways and means of getting rid of Blott, Lady Maud and Handyman Hall. He had just had an idea.

So had Lady Maud. As she lumbered about the garden, uprooting here a dandelion and there a chickweed, her mind was occupied with thoughts of maternity.

'It's now or never,' she murmured as she squashed a slug. Between her legs she could see Sir Giles in his study and wondered once again why it was that she should have married a man with so little sense of duty. In her view there was no higher virtue. It was out of duty to her family that she had married him. Left to herself she would have chosen a younger, more attractive man, but young attractive men with fortunes were in short supply in Worfordshire and Maud too plain to seek them out in London.

'Coming out?' she had shouted at her mother when Lady Handyman had suggested she should be presented at court. 'Coming out? But I've already been.'

And it was true. Lady Maud's moment of beauty had been premature. At fifteen she had been lovely. At twenty-one the Handyman features, the prominent nose in particular, had made themselves and her plain.

At thirty-five she was a Handyman all over and only acceptable to someone with Sir Giles' depraved taste and eye for hidden advantage. She had accepted his proposal without illusions, only to discover too late that his long bachelorhood had left him with a set of habits and fantasies which made it impossible for him to fulfil his part of the bargain. Whatever else Sir Giles was cut out for it was not paternity. After the unfortunate experience of their honeymoon, Maud had attempted a reconciliation, but without result. She had resorted to drink, to spicy foods, to oysters and champagne, to hard-boiled eggs, but Sir Giles had remained obdurately impotent. Now on this bright spring day when everything about her was breaking out or sprouting or proclaiming the joys of parenthood from every corner of the estate, Lady Maud felt distinctly wanton. She would make one more effort to make Sir Giles see reason. Straightening her back she marched across the lawn to the house and went down the passage.

'Giles,' she said entering the study without knocking, 'it's time we had this thing out.'

Sir Giles looked up from his *Times*. 'What thing?' he asked.

'You know very well what I'm talking about. There's no need to beat about the bush.'

Sir Giles folded the paper. 'Bush, dear?' he said doubtfully.

'Don't prevaricate,' said Lady Maud.

'I'm not prevaricating,' Sir Giles protested, 'I simply don't know what you are talking about.'

Lady Maud put her hands on the desk and leant forward menacingly. 'Sex,' she snarled.

Sir Giles curdled in his chair. 'Oh that,' he murmured. 'What about it?'

'I'm not getting any younger.'

Sir Giles nodded sympathetically. It was one of the few things he was grateful for.

'In another year or two it will be too late.'

Thank God, thought Sir Giles, but the words remained unspoken. Instead he selected a Ramon Allones from his cigarbox. It was an unfortunate move. Lady Maud leant forward and twitched it from his fingers.

'Now you listen to me, Giles Lynchwood,' she said, 'I didn't marry you to be left a childless widow.'

'Widow?' said Sir Giles flinching.

'The operative word is childless. Whether you live or die is of no great moment to me. What is important is that I have an heir. When I married you it was on the clear understanding that you would be a father to my children. We have been married six years now. It is time for you to do your duty.'

Sir Giles crossed his legs defiantly. 'We've been through all this before,' he muttered.

'We have never been through it at all. That is precisely what I am complaining about. You have steadfastly refused to act like a normal husband. You have—'

'We all have our little problems, dear,' Sir Giles said.

'Quite,' said Lady Maud, 'so we do. Unfortunately my problem is rather more pressing than yours. I am over forty and as I have already pointed out, in a year or two I will be past the childbearing age. My family has lived in the Gorge for five hundred years and I do not intend to go to my grave with the knowledge that I am the last of the Handymans.'

'I don't really see how you can avoid that whatever happens,' said Sir Giles. 'After all, in the unlikely event of our having children, their name would be Lynchwood.'

'I have always intended,' said Lady Maud, 'changing the name by deed poll.'

'Have you indeed? Well then let me inform you that there will be no need,' said Sir Giles. 'There will be no children by our marriage and that's final.'

'In that case,' said Lady Maud, 'I shall take steps to get a divorce. You will be hearing from my solicitors.'

She left the room and slammed the door. Behind her Sir Giles sat in his chair shaken but content. The years of his misery were over. He would get his divorce and keep the Hall. He had nothing more to worry about. He reached for another cigar and lit it. Upstairs he could hear his wife's heavy movements in her bedroom. She was no doubt going out to see Mr Turnbull of Ganglion, Turnbull and Shrine, the family solicitors in Worford. Sir Giles unfolded *The Times* and read the letter about the cuckoo once again.

CHAPTER TWO

Mr Turnbull of Ganglion, Turnbull and Shrine was sympathetic but unhelpful. 'If you initiate proceedings on grounds as evidently insubstantial as those you have so vividly outlined,' he told Lady Maud, 'the reversionary clause becomes null and void. You might well end up losing the Hall and the Estate.'

'Do you mean to sit there and tell me that I cannot divorce my husband without losing my family home?' Lady Maud demanded.

Mr Turnbull nodded. 'Sir Giles has only to deny your allegations,' he explained, 'and frankly I can hardly see a man in his position admitting them. I'm afraid the Court would find for him. The difficulty about this sort of case is that you can't produce convincing proof.'

'I should have thought my virginity was proof enough,' Lady Maud told him bluntly. Mr Turnbull suppressed a shudder. The notion of Lady Maud presenting her maidenhead as Exhibit A was not one that appealed to him.

'I think we should need something a little more orthodox than that. After all, Sir Giles could claim that you had refused him his conjugal rights. It would simply be his word against yours. Of course, you could still get your divorce, but the Hall would remain legally his.'

'There must be something I can do,' Lady Maud protested. Looking at her, Mr Turnbull rather doubted it but he was tactful enough not to say so.

'And you say you have attempted a reconciliation?'

'I have told Giles that he must do his duty by me.'

'That's not quite what I meant,' Mr Turnbull told her. 'Marriage is after all a difficult relationship at the best of times. Perhaps a little tenderness on your part would . . .'

'Tenderness?' said Lady Maud. 'Tenderness? You seem to forget that my husband is a pervert. Do you imagine that a man who finds satisfaction in being—'

'No,' said Mr Turnbull hurriedly. 'I take your point. Perhaps tenderness is the wrong word. What I meant was . . . well . . . a little understanding.'

Lady Maud looked at him scornfully.

'After all *tout comprendre, c'est tout pardonner*,' continued Mr Turnbull, relapsing into the language he associated with sophistication in matters of the heart.

'I beg your pardon,' said Lady Maud.

'I was merely saying that to understand all is to pardon all,' Mr Turnbull explained.

'Coming from a legal man I find that remark astonishing,' said Lady Maud, 'and in any case I am not interested in either understanding or in pardon. I am simply interested in bearing a child. My family have lived in the Gorge for five hundred years and I have no intention of being responsible for their not living there for another five hundred. You may find my insistence on the importance of my family romantic. I can only say that I regard it as my duty to have an heir. If my husband refuses to do his duty by me I shall find someone who will.'

'My dear Lady Maud,' said Mr Turnbull, suddenly conscious that he might be in danger of becoming the first object of her extramarital attentions, 'I beg you not to do anything hasty. An act of adultery on your part would certainly allow Sir Giles to obtain a divorce on grounds which would invalidate the reversionary clause. Perhaps you would like me to have a word with him. It sometimes helps to have a third party, someone entirely impartial you understand, to bring about a reconciliation.'

Lady Maud shook her head. She was thinking about adultery.

'If Giles were to commit adultery,' she said finally, 'would I be right in supposing that the Estate would revert to me?'

Mr Turnbull beamed at the prospect. 'No difficulties at all in that case,' he said. 'You would have an absolute right to the Estate. It's in the settlement. No difficulties at all.'

'Good,' said Lady Maud, and stood up. She went downstairs, leaving Mr Turnbull with the distinct impression that Sir Giles Lynchwood was in for a nasty surprise and, better still, that the firm of Ganglion, Turnbull and Shrine could look forward to a protracted case with substantial fees.

Outside Blott was waiting in the car.

'Blott,' said Lady Maud climbing into the back seat, 'what do you know about telephone tapping?'

Blott smiled and started the car. 'Easy,' he said, 'all you need is some wire and a pair of headphones.'

'In that case stop at the first radio shop you come to and buy the necessary equipment.'

By the time they returned to Handyman Hall, Lady Maud had laid her plans.

So had Sir Giles. The first moment of elation at the prospect of a divorce had worn off and Sir Giles, weighing the matter up in his mind, had recognized some ugly possibilities. For one thing he did not relish the thought of being cross-examined about his private life by some eminent barrister. The newspapers, particularly one or two of the Sundays, would have a ball with Lady Maud's description of their honeymoon. Worse still, he would be unable to issue writs for libel. The story could be verified by the hotel manager and while Sir Giles might well win the divorce case and retain the Hall he would certainly lose his public reputation. No, the matter would have to be handled in some less conspicuous manner. Sir Giles picked up a pencil and began to doodle.

The problem was a simple one. The divorce, if and when it came, must be on the grounds on his own choosing. He must be free from any breath of scandal. It was too much to hope that Lady Maud would find a lover, but desperation might drive her to some act of folly. Sir Giles rather doubted it, and besides, her age, shape and general disposition made it seem unlikely. And then there was the Hall and the one hundred thousand pounds he had paid for it. He drew a cat and was just considering that there were more ways of making a profit from property than selling it or burning it to the ground when the shape of his drawing, an eight with ears and tail, put him in mind of something he had once seen from the air. A flyover, a spaghetti junction, a motorway.

A moment later he was unfolding an ordnance survey map and studying it with intense interest. Of course. Why hadn't he thought of it before? The Cleene Gorge was the ideal route. It lay directly between Sheffingham and Knighton. And with motorways there came compulsory purchase orders and large sums paid in compensation. The perfect solution. All it needed was a word or two in the right ear. Sir Giles picked up the phone and dialled. By the time Lady Maud returned from Worford he was in excellent humour. Hoskins at the Worfordshire Planning Authority had been most helpful, but then Hoskins had always been helpful. It paid him to be and it certainly paid for a rather larger house than his salary would have led one to expect. Sir Giles smiled to himself. Influence was a wonderful thing.

'I'm going down to London this afternoon,' he told Lady Maud as they sat down to lunch. 'One or two business things to fix up. I daresay I shall be tied up for a couple of days.'

'I shouldn't be at all surprised,' said Lady Maud.

'If you need me for anything, leave a message with my secretary.'

Lady Maud helped herself to cottage pie. She was in a good humour. She had no doubt whatsoever that Sir Giles indulged his taste for restrictive practices with someone in London. It might take time to find out the name of his mistress but she was prepared to wait.

*

'Extraordinary woman, Lady Maud,' Mr Turnbull said as he and Mr Ganglion sat in the bar of the Four Feathers in Worford.

'Extraordinary family,' Mr Ganglion agreed. 'I don't suppose you remember her grandmother, the old Countess. No, you wouldn't. Before your time. I remember drawing up her will in ... now when can it have been ... must have been in March 1936. Let's see, she died in June of that year so it must have been in March. Insisted on my inserting the fact that her son, Busby, was of partially royal parentage. I did point out that in that case he was not entitled to inherit but she was adamant. "Royal Blood," she kept saying. In the end I got her to sign several copies of the will but it was only in the top one that any mention was made of the royal bastardy.'

'Good Lord,' said Mr Turnbull, 'do you think there was anything in it?'

Mr Ganglion looked over the top of his glasses at him. 'Between ourselves, I must admit it was not outside the bounds of possibility. The dates did match. Busby was born in 1905 and the Royal visit took place in '04. Edward the Seventh had quite a reputation for that sort of thing.'

'It certainly goes some way to explain Lady Maud's looks,' Mr Turnbull admitted. 'And her arrogance, come to that.'

'These things are best forgotten,' said Mr Ganglion sadly. 'What did she want to see you about?'

'She's seeking a divorce. I dissuaded her, at least temporarily. Seems that Lynchwood has a taste for flagellation.'

'Extraordinary what some fellows like,' said Mr Ganglion. 'It's not as though he went to public school either. Most peculiar. Still, I should have thought Maud could have satisfied him if anyone could. She's got a forearm like a navvy.'

'I got the impression that she had rather overdone it,' Mr Turnbull explained.

'Splendid. Splendid.'

'The main trouble seems to be non-consummation. She wants an heir before it's too late.'

'The perennial obsession of these old families. What did you advise? Artificial insemination?'

Mr Turnbull finished his drink. 'Certainly not,' he muttered. 'Apparently she's still a virgin.'

Mr Ganglion sniggered. 'There was an old virgin of forty, whose habits were fearfully naughty. She owned a giraffe whose terrible laugh ... or was it distaff? I forget now.'

They went into lunch.

*

Blott finished his lunch in the greenhouse at the end of the kitchen garden. Around him early geraniums and chrysanthemums, pink and red, matched the colour of his complexion. This was the inner sanctum of Blott's world where he could sit surrounded by flowers whose beauty was proof to him that life was not entirely without meaning. Through the glass windows he could look down the kitchen garden at the lettuces, the peas and beans, the redcurrant bushes and the gooseberries of which he was so proud. And all around the old brick walls cut out the world he mistrusted. Blott emptied his thermos flask and stood up. Above his head he could see the telephone wires stretching from the house. He went outside and fetched a ladder and presently was busily engaged in attaching his wires to the line above. He was still there when Sir Giles left in the Bentley. Blott watched him pass without interest. He disliked Sir Giles intensely and it was one of the advantages of working in the kitchen garden that they seldom came into contact. He finished his work and fitted the headphones and bell. Then he went into the house. He found Lady Maud washing up in the kitchen.

'It's ready,' he said, 'we can test it.'

Lady Maud dried her hands, 'What do I do?'

'When the bell rings put the headphones on,' Blott explained.

'You go into the study and ring a number and I'll listen,' said Lady Maud. Blott went into the study and sat behind the desk. He picked up the phone and tried to think of someone to call. There wasn't anyone he knew to call. Finally his eye fell on a number written in pencil on the pad in front of him. Beside it there was some doodles and a drawing of a cat. Blott dialled the number. It was rather a long one and began with 01 and he had to wait for some time for an answer.

'Hullo, Felicia Forthby speaking,' said a woman's voice.

Blott tried to think of something to say. 'This is Blott,' he said finally.

'Blott?' said Mrs Forthby. 'Do I know you?'

'No,' said Blott.

'Is there anything I can do for you?'

'No,' said Blott.

There was an awkward silence and then Mrs Forthby spoke. 'What do you want?'

Blott tried to think of something he wanted. 'I want a ton of pig manure,' he said.

'You must have the wrong number.'

'Yes,' said Blott and put the phone down.

In the greenhouse Lady Maud was delighted with the experiment. 'I'll soon find out who's beating him now,' she thought and took the headphones off. She went back to the house.

'We shall take it in turns to monitor all telephone calls my husband makes,' she told Blott. 'I want to find out who he's visiting in London. You must write down the name of anyone he talks to. Do you understand?'

'Yes,' said Blott and went back to the kitchen garden happily. In the kitchen Lady Maud finished washing up. She'd meant to ask Blott who he had been talking to. Never mind, it wasn't important.

CHAPTER THREE

Sir Giles got back from London rather sooner than he had expected. Mrs Forthby's period had put her in a foul mood and Sir Giles had enough on his plate without having to put up with the side-effects of Mrs Forthby's menstrual tension. And besides, Mrs Forthby in the flesh was a different kettle of fish to Mrs Forthby in his fantasies. In the latter she had a multitude of perverse inclinations, which corresponded exactly with his own unfortunate requirements, while possessing a discretion that would have done credit to a Trappist nun. In the flesh she was disappointingly different. She seemed to think, and in Sir Giles opinion there could be no greater fault in a woman, that he loved her for herself alone. It was a phrase that sent a shudder through him. If he loved her at all, and it was only in her absence that his heart grew even approximately fonder, it was not for Mrs Forthby's self. It was precisely because as far as he could make out she lacked *any* self that he was attracted to her in the first place.

Externally Mrs Forthby had all the attributes of desirable womanhood, rather too many for more fastidious tastes, and all confined with corsets, panties, suspender belts and bras that inflamed Sir Giles' imagination and reminded him of the advertisements in women's magazines on which his sexual immaturity had first cut its teeth. Internally Mrs Forthby was a void if her inconsequential conversation was anything to go by and it was this void that Sir Giles, ever hopeful of finding a lover with needs as depraved as his own, sought to fill. And here he had to admit that Mrs Forthby fell far short of his expectations. Broad-minded she might be, though he sometimes doubted that she had a mind, but she still lacked enthusiasm for the intricate contortions and strangleholds that constituted Sir Giles' notions of foreplay. And besides she had an unfortunate habit of giggling at moments of his grossest concentration and of interjecting reminiscences of her Girl Guide training while tightening the granny knots which so affected him. Worst of all was her absent-mindedness (and here he had no quarrel with the term). She had been known to leave him trussed to the bed and gagged for several hours while she entertained friends to tea in the next room. It was at such moments of enforced contemplation that Sir Giles was most conscious of the discrepancies between his public and his private posture and hoped to hell the two wouldn't be brought closer together by some damned woman looking for the lavatory. Not that he wouldn't have welcomed some intervention into his fantasy world if only he could be certain that he wouldn't be the laughing-stock of Westminster. After one such episode he had threatened to murder Mrs Forthby and had only been restrained by his inability to stand upright even after she had untied him.

'Where the hell have you been?' he shouted when she returned at one o'clock in the morning.

'Covent Garden,' Mrs Forthby said. '*The Magic Flute*. A divine performance.'

'You might have told me. I've been lying here in agony for six hours.'

'I thought you liked that,' Mrs Forthby said. 'I thought that's what you wanted.'

'Wanted?' Sir Giles screamed. 'Six hours? Nobody in his right mind wants to be trussed up like a spring chicken for six hours.'

'No, dear,' Mrs Forthby said agreeably. 'It's just that I forgot. Shall I get you your enema now?'

'Certainly not,' shouted Sir Giles, in whom some measure of self-respect had been induced by his confinement. 'And don't meddle with my leg.'

'But it shouldn't be there, dear. It looks unnatural.'

Sir Giles stared violently out of the corner of his right eye at his toes. 'I know it shouldn't be there,' he yelled. 'And it wouldn't be if you hadn't been so damned forgetful.'

Mrs Forthby had tidied up the straps and buckles and had made a pot of tea. 'I'll tie a knot in my handkerchief next time,' she said tactlessly, propping Sir Giles up on some pillows so that he could drink his tea.

'There won't be a next time,' he had snarled and had spent a sleepless night trying desperately to assume a less contorted posture. It had been an empty promise. There was always a next time. Mrs Forthby's absent shape and her ready acceptance of his revolting foibles made good the lapses of her memory and Sir Giles returned to her flat whenever he was in London, each time with the fervent prayer that she wouldn't leave him hooded and bound while she spent a month in the Bahamas.

*

But if Sir Giles had difficulties with Mrs Forthby there were remarkably few as far as the motorway was concerned. The thing was already on the drawing board.

'It's designated the Mid-Wales Motorway, the M101,' he was told when he made discreet inquiries of the Ministry of the Environment. 'It has been sent up for Ministerial approval. I believe there have been some doubts on conservation grounds. For God's sake don't quote me.' Sir Giles put the phone down and considered his tactics. Ostensibly he would have to oppose the scheme if only to keep his seat as member for South Worfordshire but there was opposition and opposition. He invested heavily in Imperial Cement, who seemed likely to benefit from the demand for concrete. He had lunch with the Chairman of Imperial Motors, dinner with the Managing Director of Motorway Manufacturers Limited, drinks with the Secretary of the Amalgamated Union of Roadworkers, and he pointed out to the Chief Whip the need to do something to lower the rate of unemployment in his constituency.

In short he was the catalyst in the chemistry of progress. And with it all no money passed hands. Sir Giles was too old a dog for that. He passed information. What companies were on the way to making profits, what shares to buy, and what to sell, these were the tender of his influence. And to insure himself against future suspicions he made a speech at the annual dinner of the Countryside Conservation League in which he urged eternal vigilance against the depredations of the property speculator. He returned to Handyman Hall in time to be outraged by the news of the proposed motorway.

'I shall demand an immediate inquiry,' he told Lady Maud when the requisition order arrived. He reached for the phone.

In the greenhouse Blott had his time cut out listening to Sir Giles' telephone calls. He had no sooner settled down to deal with some aphids on the ornamental apple trees that grew against the wall than the bell rang. Blott dashed in and listened to General Burnett fulminating from the Grange about blackguards in Whitehall, red tape, green belts and blue-stockings, none of which he fully understood. He went back to his aphids when the phone rang again. This time it was Mr Bullett-Finch phoning to find out what Sir Giles intended to do about stopping the motorway.

'It's going to take half the garden,' he said. 'We have spent the last six years getting shipshape and now for this to happen. It's too much. It's not as though Ivy's nerves can stand it.'

Sir Giles sympathized unctuously. He was, he said, organizing a protest committee. There was bound to be an Inquiry. Mr Bullett-Finch could rest assured that no stone would be left unturned. Blott returned to the aphids puzzled. The English language still retained its power to baffle him, and Blott occasionally found himself trapped in some idiom. Shipshape? There was nothing vaguely in the shape of a ship about Mr Bullett-Finch's garden. But then Blott had to admit that the English themselves remained a mystery to him. They paid people more when they were unemployed than when they had to work. They paid bricklayers more than teachers. They raised money for earthquake victims in Peru while old-age pensioners lived on a pittance. They refused Entry Permits to Australians and invited Russians to come and live in England. Finally they seemed to take particular pleasure in being shot at by the Irish. All in all they were a source of constant astonishment to him and of reassurance. They were only happy when something dreadful happened to them, be it flood, fire, war or some appalling disaster, and Blott, whose early life had been a chapter of disasters, took comfort from the fact that he was living in a community that actually enjoyed misfortunes.

Born when, of whom, where, he had no idea. The date of his discovery in the Ladies Room in the Dresden railway station was as near as he could get to a birthday and since the lady cleaner had disclaimed any responsibility for his appearance there, although hard pressed by the authorities to do so, he had no idea who his mother was – let alone his father. He couldn't even be sure his parents had been Germans. For all he and the authorities knew they might have been Jews, though even the Director of the Race Classification Bureau had had the illogical grace to admit that Jews did not make a habit of abandoning their offspring in railway cloakrooms. Still, the notion lent a further element of uncertainty to Blott's adolescence in the Third Reich and he had got no help from his appearance. Dark, hook-nosed pure Aryans there doubtless were, but Blott, who had taken an obsessive interest in the question, found few who were happy to discuss their pedigree with him. Certainly no one was prepared to adopt him, and even the orphanage tended to push him into the background when there were visitors. As for the Hitler Youth ... Blott preferred to forget his adolescence and even the memory of his arrival in England still filled him with uneasiness.

It had been a dark night and Blott, who had been put in to stiffen the resolve of the crew of an Italian bomber, had taken the opportunity to emigrate. Besides, he had a shrewd suspicion that his squadron leader had ordered him to volunteer as navigator to the Italians in the hope that he would not return. It seemed the only explanation for his choice and Blott, whose previous experience had been as a rear-gunner where his only contribution to the war effort had been to shoot down two Messerschmidt 109s that were supposed to be escorting his bomber squadron, had fulfilled his squadron leader's expectations to the letter. Even the Italian airmen, pusillanimous to a man, had been surprised by Blott's insistence that Margate was situated in the heart of Worcestershire. After a heated argument they dropped their bombs over Exmoor and headed back for Pas de Calais across the Bristol Channel before running out of fuel over the mountains of North Wales. It was at this point that the Italians decided to bale out and were attempting to explain the urgency of the situation to Blott, whose knowledge of Italian was negligible, when they were saved the bother by the intervention of a mountain which, according to Blott's bump of direction, should not have been there. In the ensuing holocaust Blott was the sole survivor and since he was discovered naked in the wreckage of an Italian bomber by a search party next morning it was naturally assumed that he must be Italian. The fact that he couldn't speak a word of his native tongue deceived nobody, least of all the Major in charge of the prisoner-of-war camp to which Blott was sent, for the simple reason that he couldn't speak Italian either and Blott was his first prisoner. It was only much later, with the arrival of some genuine Italian prisoners from North Africa, that doubts were cast on his nationality, but by that time Blott had established his bona fides by displaying no interest in the course of the war and by resolutely demonstrating a reluctance to escape that was authentically Italian. Besides, his claim to have been born the son of a shepherd in the Tyrol explained his lack of Italian.

In 1942 the camp had been moved to Handyman Hall and Blott had made the place his home. The Hall and the Handyman family appealed to him. They were both the epitome of Englishness and in Blott's view there could be no higher praise. To be English was the supreme virtue and being a prisoner in England was better than being free anywhere else. If he had had his way the war would have continued indefinitely. He lived in a great house, he had a park to walk in, a river to fish in, a kitchen garden to grow things in, and the run of an idyllic countryside full of woods and hills and fair women whose husbands were away fighting to save the world from people like Blott. Even at night when the camp gates were closed it was perfectly easy to scale the walls and go where he liked. There were no air-raids, no sudden alarms and the whole question of earning a living was taken care of. Even the food was good, supplemented as it was by his poaching and his husbandry in the kitchen garden. To Blott the place was paradise and his only worry was that Germany might win the war. It was an eventuality he dreaded. It had been bad enough being a German in Germany. He couldn't imagine what it would be like to be an Italian who was a German who looked like a Jew in conquered Britain, and the notion of trying to explain how he came to be what he was where he was to the German occupying authorities appalled him. It was one of the nicest things about the English that they didn't seem to worry about such details, but he knew his own countrymen too well to imagine that they would be satisfied with his evasions. Layer by layer, they would peel off his equivocations until the nothing that was the essential Blott was revealed quite naked and then they would shoot what was left for desertion. Blott had no doubt about his fate, and what made matters worse was that as far as he could tell the British were quite incapable of winning the war. Half the time they seemed oblivious of the fact that there was a war on, and for the rest conducted it with an inefficiency that astonished him. Shortly after his arrival at the Hall, Western Command had conducted manoeuvres in the Cleene Forest and Blott had watched the chaos that ensued with horror. If these were the men on whose fighting qualities he had to depend for his captivity, he would have to look for his salvation elsewhere. He found it in a nearby ammunition dump which was, quite typically, unguarded and Blott, determined that if the English wouldn't defend him he would, slowly acquired a small arsenal which he buried in the forest. Two-inch mortars, Bren guns, rifles, boxes of ammunition, all disappeared without notice and were cached, carefully greased and watertight, under the bracken in the hills behind the Hall. By 1945 Blott was in a position to fight a guerrilla war in South Worfordshre. And then the war ended and new problems arose.

The prospect of being repatriated to Italy was not one that appealed to him and he couldn't see himself settling down in Naples after so many agreeable years in England. On the other hand he had no intention of returning to what remained of Dresden. It was in the Russian Zone and Blott had no desire to swop the comforts of life in Worfordshire for the rigours of existence in Siberia. Besides, he rather doubted if even a defeated Fatherland would welcome home a man who had spent five years masquerading as an Italian PoW. It seemed far wiser to stay where he was, and here his devotion to the Handyman family paid off.

Lord Handyman had been a man of enthusiasms. Long before it was generally fashionable he had conceived the notion that the world's resources were on the verge of extinction and had sought to avoid the personal consequences by saving everything. He had been particularly keen on compost and Blott had dug enormous pits in the kitchen garden into which all household refuse of an organic sort was thrown.

'Nothing must be wasted,' the Earl had declared, and nothing was. Under his direction the Hall's sewage system had been diverted to empty into the compost pits and Blott and the Earl had spent happy hours observing the layers of cabbage stalks, potato peelings, and excrement which made up the day's leavings. As each pit filled Blott dug another one and the process began again. The results were quite astonishing. Enormous cabbages and alarming marrows and cucumbers proliferated. So, in summer, did the flies until the situation became intolerable and Lady Handyman, who had lost her appetite since the recycling began, put her foot down and insisted that either the flies went or she would. Blott diverted the sewage system back to its proper place while the Earl, evidently inspired by the rate of reproduction of the flies, turned his attention to rabbits. Blott had constructed several dozen hutches built one above the other on the lines of apartment buildings in which the Earl installed the largest rabbits he could buy, a breed called Flemish Giants. Like all the Earl's schemes, the rabbits had not been an unqualified success. They consumed enormous quantities of vegetation and the family had developed an aversion for rabbit pie, roast rabbit, rabbit stew and lapin à l'orange, while Blott had been driven to distraction trying to keep pace with their voracious appetites. To add to his problems Maud, then ten, had identified her father with Mr McGregor and had aided and abetted the rabbits to escape. As peace broke out in Europe the Gorge was overrun with Flemish Giants. By then Lord Handyman's enthusiasm had waned. He turned to ducks and particularly to Khaki Campbells, a species which had the advantage that they were largely self-supporting and produced an abundance of eggs.

'Can't go wrong with ducks,' he had said cheerfully as the family switched from a diet of rabbit to duck eggs. As usual with his prophecies this one had proved unfounded. It was all too easy to go wrong with ducks, as the family found out when the Earl succumbed to a lethal egg that had been laid too close to one of his old compost pits. Passing away as peacefully as ptomaine poisoning allowed, he had left Maud and her mother to manage alone. It was largely thanks to his death that Blott had been allowed to stay on at the Hall.

CHAPTER FOUR

Over the next few weeks Lady Maud was intensely active. She took legal advice from Mr Turnbull daily. She canvassed opposition to the proposed motorway from every quarter of South Worfordshire and she sat almost continuously on committees. In particular she made her considerable presence felt on the Committee for the Preservation of the Cleene Gorge. General Burnett of the Grange, Guildstead Carbonell, was elected President but as Secretary Lady Maud was the driving force. Petitions were organized, protest meetings held, motions proposed, seconded and passed, money raised and posters printed.

'The price of justice is eternal publicity,' she said with an originality that startled her hearers, but which in fact she had found in *Bartlett's Familiar Quotations*. 'It is not enough to protest, we must make our protest known. If the Gorge is to be saved it will not be by words alone but by action.' On the platform beside her Sir Giles nodded his apparent approval, but inwardly he was alarmed. Publicity was all very well, and justice was fine when it applied to other people but he didn't want public attention focused too closely on his role in the affair. He had expected the motorway to upset Lady Maud; he had not foreseen that she would turn into a human tornado. He certainly hadn't supposed that his seat would be jeopardized by the uproar she seemed bent on provoking.

'If you don't see that the Hall is saved,' Lady Maud told him, 'I'll see to it that you don't sit for South Worfordshire at the next election.' Sir Giles took the threat seriously and consulted Hoskins at the Planning Authority in Worford.

'I thought you wanted the thing to go through the Gorge,' Hoskins told him as they sat in the bar of the Handyman Arms.

Sir Giles nodded unhappily. 'I do,' he admitted, 'but Maud has gone berserk. She's threatening . . . well, never mind.'

Hoskins was reassuring. 'She'll get over it. They always do. Got to give them time to get used to the idea.'

'It's all very well for you to talk,' said Sir Giles, 'but I have to live with the beastly woman. She's up half the night thundering about the bloody house and I'm having to cook for myself. Besides, I don't like the way she keeps cleaning her father's shotgun in the kitchen.'

'You know she took a potshot at one of the surveyors last week,' Hoskins said.

'Can't you have her charged?' Sir Giles asked eagerly. 'That would take the heat off for a bit. Haul her up before the local beaks.'

'She *is* a local magistrate,' Hoskins pointed out, 'and anyway there's no proof. She would just claim she was shooting rabbits.'

'And that's another thing. She's got the house full of bloody great Alsations. Hired them from some damned security firm. I tell you I can't go down the passage for a pee in the night without running the risk of being bitten.' He ordered another two whiskies and considered the problem. 'There'll have to be an Inquiry,' he said finally. 'Promise them an Inquiry and they'll calm down a bit. Secondly, offer the Inquiry a totally unacceptable alternative. Like we did with the block of flats in Shrewton.'

'You mean give planning permission for a sewage farm?'

'That's what we did there. Worked like a charm,' Sir Giles said. 'Now if we could come up with an alternative route which nobody in his right mind would accept ...'

'There's always Ottertown,' said Hoskins.

'What about Ottertown?'

'It's ten miles out of the way and you'd have to go through a council estate.'

Sir Giles smiled. 'Right through the middle?'

'Right through the middle.'

'It sounds promising,' Sir Giles agreed. 'I think I shall be the first to advocate the Ottertown route. You're quite sure it's unacceptable?'

'Quite sure,' said Hoskins. 'And, by the way, I'll take my fee in advance.'

Sir Giles looked round the bar. 'My advice is to buy ...' he began.

'Cash this time,' said Hoskins, 'I lost on United Oils.'

Sir Giles returned to Handyman Hall in a fairly good humour. He disliked parting with money but Hoskins was worth it and the Ottertown idea was the sort of strategy he liked. It would take Maud's mind off eternal publicity. Tempers would cool and the Inquiry would decide in favour of the Gorge. By then it would be too late to inflame public opinion once again. Inquiries were splendid soporifics. He ran the gauntlet of the guard dogs and spent the evening in his study writing a letter to the Minister of the Environment demanding the setting up of an Inquiry. No one could say that the Member of Parliament for South Worfordshire had not got the interests of his constituents at heart.

While Sir Giles connived and Lady Maud committeed, Blott in the kitchen garden had his work cut out trying to do his conflicting duties.

He would settle down to weed the lettuces only to be interrupted by the bell in the greenhouse. Blott spent hours listening to long conversations between Sir Giles and officials at the Ministry, between Sir Giles and members of his constituency or his stockbroker or his business partners, but never between Sir Giles and Mrs Forthby. Sir Giles had been forewarned. Mrs Forthby's remark that she had received a call from someone called Blott who had ordered a ton of pig manure had alarmed Sir Giles. There was obviously some mistake though how Blott could have got hold of the number in the first place he couldn't imagine. It wasn't in the telephone index on his desk. He kept it in his private diary and the diary was in his pocket. Sir Giles memorized the number and then erased it from the diary. There would be no more calls to Mrs Forthby from Handyman Hall.

When Sir Giles wasn't on the telephone, Lady Maud was, issuing orders, drumming up support or hurling defiance at the authorities with a self-assurance that amazed and delighted Blott. You knew where you were with her and Blott, who prized certainty above all else, emerged from the greenhouse after listening to her with the feeling that all was well with the world and would remain so. Handyman Hall, the Park, the Lodge, a great triumphal arch at the bottom of the drive where Blott lived, the kitchen garden, all those things to which he had grafted his own anonymity in a hostile world, would remain safe and secure if Lady Maud had anything to do with it. Sir Giles' calls left a different impression. His protests were muted, too polite and too equivocal to satisfy Blott, so that he came away with the feeling that something was wrong. He couldn't put his finger on it, but whenever he took the earphones off after listening to Sir Giles he felt uneasy. There was too much talk about money for Blott's liking, and in particular about ample compensation for the Hall. The sum most frequently mentioned was a quarter of a million pounds. As he went down the rows of lettuces with his hoe, Blott shook his head. 'Money talks,' Sir Giles had told his caller but it had said nothing to Blott. There were more important words in his vocabulary. On the other hand his hours of listening to Sir Giles had done wonders for his accent. With the headphones on Blott had sat practising Sir Giles' pronunciation. In his study Sir Giles said, 'Of course, my dear fellow, I absolutely agree with you . . .' In the greenhouse Blott repeated the words. By the end of a week his imitation was so exact that Lady Maud, coming into the kitchen garden to collect some radishes and spring onions for lunch one day, had been astonished to hear Sir Giles' voice issuing from among the geraniums. 'I looked upon the whole thing as an infringement of the rules of conservation,' he was saying. 'My dear General, I shall do my damnedest to see that the matter is raised in the House.' Lady Maud stood and gazed into the greenhouse and was just considering the possibility that Blott had rigged up a loudspeaker there when he emerged, beaming triumphantly.

'You like it, my pronunciation?' he asked.

'Good heavens, was that you? You gave me quite a start,' Lady Maud said.

Blott smirked proudly. 'I have been practising correct English,' he said.

'But you speak English perfectly.'

'I don't. Not like an Englishman.'

'Well, I'd be glad if you didn't go round speaking like my husband,' said Lady Maud. 'It's bad enough having one of him about the place.'

Blott smiled happily. These were his sentiments exactly.

'Which reminds me,' she continued, 'I must see that the TV people cover the Inquiry. We must get the maximum publicity.'

Blott collected his hoe and went back to his lettuces while Lady Maud, having collected her radishes, returned to the kitchen. He was rather pleased with himself. It wasn't often he got a chance to demonstrate his ability to mimic people. It was a skill that had developed from his earliest days at the orphanage. Not knowing who he was, Blott had tried out other people's personalities. It had come in handy poaching, too. More than one gamekeeper had been startled to hear his employer's voice issuing from the darkness to tell him to stop making an ass of himself while Blott made good his escape. Now as he worked away at the weeds he tried out Sir Giles again. 'I demand that there be an Inquiry into this whole business,' he said. Blott smiled to himself. It sounded quite authentic. And there was going to be an Inquiry too. Lady Maud had said so.

CHAPTER FIVE

The Inquiry was held in the Old Courthouse in Worford. Everyone was there – everyone, that is, whose property stood on the proposed route through the Cleene Gorge. General Burnett, Mr and Mrs Bullett-Finch, Colonel and Mrs Chapman, Miss Percival, Mrs Thomas, the Dickinsons, all seven of them, and the Fullbrooks who rented a farm from the General. There were also a few other influential families who were quite unaffected by the motorway but who came to support Lady Maud. She sat in front with Sir Giles and Mr Turnbull and behind them the seats were all filled. Blott stood at the back. On the other side of the aisle the seats were empty except for a solicitor representing the Ottertown Town Council. It was quite clear that nobody seriously supposed that Lord Leakham would decide in favour of Ottertown. The thing was a foregone conclusion – or would have been but for the intervention of Lady Maud and the intransigence of Lord Leakham, whose previous career as a judge had been confined to criminal cases in the High Court. The choice of venue was unfortunate, too. The Old Courthouse resembled too closely the courtrooms of Lord Leakham's youth for the old man to deal at all moderately with Lady Maud's frequent interruption of the evidence.

'Madam, you are trying the court's patience,' he told her when she rose to her feet for the tenth time to protest that the scheme as outlined by Mr Hoskins for the Planning Board was an invasion of individual liberty and the rights of property. Lady Maud bristled in tweeds.

'My family has held land in the Cleene Gorge since 1472,' she shouted. 'It was entrusted to us by Edward the Fourth who designated the Handyman family custodians of the Gorge—'

'Whatever His Majesty Edward the Fourth may have done,' said Lord Leakham, 'in 1472 has no relevance to the evidence being presented by Mr Hoskins. Be so good as to sit down.'

Lady Maud sat down. 'Why don't you two men do something?' she demanded loudly. Sir Giles and Mr Turnbull shifted uncomfortably in their seats.

'You may continue, Mr Hoskins,' said the judge.

Mr Hoskins turned to a large relief model of the county which stood on a table. 'As you can see from this model South Worfordshire is a particularly beautiful county,' he began.

'Any fool with eyes in his head can see that,' Lady Maud commented loudly. 'It doesn't require a damnfool model.'

'Continue, Mr Hoskins, continue,' Lord Leakham said with a restraint that suggested he had in mind giving Lady Maud rope to hang herself with.

'Bearing this in mind the Ministry has attempted to preserve the natural amenities of the area to the greatest possible extent—'

'My foot,' said Lady Maud.

'We have here,' Mr Hoskins went on, pointing to a ridge of hills that ran north and south of the Gorge, 'the Cleene Forest, an area of designated natural beauty noted for its wild life ...'

'Why is it,' Lady Maud inquired of Mr Turnbull, 'that the only species that doesn't seem to be protected is the human?'

By the time the Inquiry adjourned for lunch Mr Hoskins had presented the case for the Ministry. As they went downstairs Mr Turnbull had to admit that he was not optimistic.

'The snag as I see it lies in those seventy-five council houses in Ottertown. If it weren't for them I think we would stand a good chance, but quite frankly I can't see the Inquiry deciding in favour of demolishing them. The cost would be enormous and in any case there is the additional ten miles to be taken into account. Frankly, I am not hopeful.'

It was market day in Worford and the town was full. Outside the courtroom two TV cameras had been set up.

'I have no intention of being evicted from my home,' Lady Maud told the interviewer from the BBC. 'My family have lived in the Cleene Gorge for five hundred years and ...'

Mr Turnbull turned away sadly. It was no good. Lady Maud might say what she liked, it would make no difference. The motorway would still come through the Gorge. In any case Lady Maud had made a bad impression on Lord Leakham. He waited for her to finish and then they made their way through the market stalls to the Handyman Arms.

'I wonder where Giles has got to,' she said as they entered the hotel.

'I think he's gone over to the Four Feathers with Lord Leakham,' Mr Turnbull told her. 'He said something about putting him in a more mellow mood.'

Lady Maud looked at him furiously. 'Did he indeed? Well, I'll see about that,' she snapped and leaving Mr Turnbull in the foyer she went into the manager's office and phoned the Four Feathers. When she came out there was a new glint of malice in her eye.

They went into the dining-room and sat down.

At the Four Feathers Sir Giles ordered two large whiskies in the lounge before sending for the menu.

Lord Leakham took his whisky doubtfully.

'I really shouldn't at this time of the day,' he said. 'Peptic ulcer you know. Still, it's been a tiring morning. Who was that ghastly woman in the front row who kept interrupting?'

'I think I'll have prawns to start with,' said Sir Giles hurriedly.

'Reminded me of the assizes in Newbury in '28,' Lord Leakham continued. 'Had a lot of trouble with a woman there. Kept getting up in the dock and shouting. Now what was her name?' He scratched his head with a mottled hand.

'Lady Maud is rather outspoken,' Sir Giles agreed. 'She has something of a reputation in this part of the world.'

'I can well believe it,' said the Judge.

'She's a Handyman, you know.'

'Really?' said Lord Leakham indifferently. 'I should have thought she could have afforded to employ one.'

'The Handyman family have always been very influential,' Sir Giles explained. 'They own the brewery and a number of licensed premises. This is a Handyman House, as a matter of fact.'

'Elsie Watson,' said Lord Leakham abruptly. 'That's the name.' Sir Giles looked doubtful.

'Poisoned her husband. Kept shouting abuse from the dock. Didn't make the slightest difference. Hanged her just the same.' He smiled at the recollection. Sir Giles studied the menu wistfully and tried to think what to recommend for someone with a peptic ulcer. Oxtail à la Handyman or consommé? On the other hand, he was delighted at the way things had gone at the Inquiry. Maud's display had clinched the matter. Finally he ordered Tournedos Handyman for himself, and Lord Leakham ordered fish.

'Fish is off,' said the head waiter.

'Off?' said Sir Giles irritably.

'Not on, sir,' the man explained.

'What on earth is Bal de Boeuf Handyman?' asked the Judge.

'Faggot.'

'I beg your pardon.'

'Meatball.'

'And Brandade de Handyman?' Lord Leakham inquired.

'Cod balls.'

'Cod? That sounds all right. Yes I think I'll have that.'

'Cod's off,' said the waiter.

Lord Leakham looked desperately at the menu. 'Is anything on?'

'I can recommend the Poule au Pot Edward the Fourth,' said Sir Giles.

'Very appropriate,' said Lord Leakham grimly. 'Oh well I suppose I'd better have it.'

'And a bottle of Chambertin,' Sir Giles said indistinctly. He wasn't very happy with his French.

'Extraordinary way to run an hotel,' said Lord Leakham. Sir Giles ordered two more whiskies to hide his irritation.

In the kitchen the chef took their order. 'You can forget the chicken,' he said. 'He can have Lancashire hotpot or faggots à la me.'

'But it's Lord Leakham and he ordered chicken,' the waiter protested. 'Can't you do something?'

The chef took a bottle of chilli powder off the shelf. 'I'll fix something,' he said.

The wine waiter meanwhile was having difficulty finding a Chambertin. In the end he took the oldest bottle he could find. 'Are you sure you want me to serve him this?' he asked the manager, holding up a bottle filled with a purple cloudy fluid that looked like a post-mortem specimen.

'That's what her ladyship instructed,' said the manager. 'Just change the label.'

'It seems a bloody peculiar thing to do.'

The manager sighed. 'Don't blame me,' he muttered. 'If she wants to poison the old bugger that's her affair. I'm just paid to do what she tells me. What is it anyway?'

The wine waiter wiped the bottle. 'It says it's crusted port,' he said doubtfully.

'Crusted's about the word,' said the manager and went back to the kitchen, where the chef was crumbling some leftover faggots on to half a fried chicken. 'For God's sake don't let anyone else have a taste of that stuff,' he told the chef.

'Serve him right for poking his nose into our affairs,' said the chef, and poured sauce from the Lancashire hotpot on to the dish. The manager went upstairs and signalled to the head waiter. Sir Giles and Lord Leakham finished their whiskies and went through into the dining-room.

At the Handyman Arms Lady Maud finished her lunch and ordered coffee. 'One can place too much reliance on the law,' she said. 'My family didn't get where they did by appealing to the courts.'

'My dear Lady Maud,' said Mr Turnbull, 'I implore you not to do anything foolish. The situation is already fraught with difficulty and quite frankly your interruptions this morning didn't help. I'm afraid Lord Leakham may have been prejudiced against us.'

Lady Maud snorted. 'If he isn't he soon will be,' she said. 'You don't seriously suppose that I intend to accept his judgement? The man is a buffoon.'

'He is also a retired judge of considerable reputation,' said Mr Turnbull doubtfully.

'His reputation is only just beginning,' Lady Maud replied. 'It has been perfectly obvious from the beginning that he was going to decide to recommend that the motorway be put through the Gorge. The Ottertown route is not an alternative. It's a red herring. Well, I for one am not going to put up with that.'

'I don't really see what you can do.'

'That, Henry Turnbull, is because you are a lawyer and hold the law in high regard. I don't. And since the law is an ass I intend to see that everyone is aware of the fact.'

'I wish I could see some way out of the situation,' said Mr Turnbull sadly.

Lady Maud stood up. 'You will, Henry, you will,' she said. 'There are more ways of killing a cat than choking it with cream.' And leaving Mr Turnbull to meditate on the implications of this remark she stalked out of the dining-room.

At the Four Feathers Lord Leakham would have understood at once, though given the choice he would have chosen cream every time. The prawn cocktail which he had not ordered but which had been thrust on him by the head waiter appeared to have been marinated in tabasco, but it was as nothing to the Poule au Pot Edward the Fourth. His first mouthful left him speechless and with the absolute conviction that he had swallowed some appalling corrosive substance like caustic soda.

'That chicken looks good,' said Sir Giles as the Judge struggled to get his breath. 'It's a speciality of the maison, you know.'

Lord Leakham didn't know. With starting eyes he reached for his glass of wine and took a large swig. For a moment he cherished the illusion that the wine would help. His hope was short-lived. His palate, in spite of being cauterized by the Poule au Pot, was still sufficiently sensitive to recognize that whatever it was he was in the process of swallowing it most certainly wasn't Chambertin '64. For one thing it appeared to be filled with some sort of gravel which put him in mind of ground glass and for another what he could taste of the muck seemed to be nauseatingly sweet. Stifling the impulse to vomit he held the glass up to the light and stared into its opaque depths.

'Anything the matter?' asked Sir Giles.

'What did you say this was?' asked the Judge.

Sir Giles looked at the label on the bottle. 'Chambertin '64', he muttered. 'Is it corked or something?'

'It's certainly something,' said Lord Leakham who wished the stuff had never been bottled, let alone corked.

'I'll get another bottle,' said Sir Giles and signalled to the wine waiter.

'Not on my account I beg you.'

But it was too late. As the wine waiter hurried away Lord Leakham, distracted by the strange residue under his upper dentures, absent-mindedly took another mouthful of Poule au Pot.

'I thought it looked a bit dark myself,' said Sir Giles ignoring the desperate look in Lord Leakham's bloodshot eyes. 'Mind you I have to admit I'm not a connoisseur of wines.'

Still gasping for air, Lord Leakham pushed his plate away. For a moment he resisted the temptation to quench the flames with crusted port but the certain knowledge that unless he did something he would never speak again swept aside all considerations of taste. Lord Leakham drained his glass.

In the public bar of the Handyman Arms Lady Maud announced that drinks were on the house. Then she crossed the Market Square to the Goat and Goblet and repeated the order before making her way to the Red Cow. Behind her the bars filled with thirsty farmers and by two o'clock all Worford was drinking Lady Maud's health and damnation to the motorway. Outside the Old Courthouse she stopped to chat with the TV men. A crowd had assembled and Lady Maud was cheered as she went inside.

'I must say we do seem to have the public on our side,' said General Burnett as they went upstairs. 'Mind you I thought things looked pretty grim this morning.'

Lady Maud smiled to herself. 'I think you will find they liven up this afternoon,' she said and swept majestically into the courtroom where Colonel and Mrs Chapman were chattering with the Bullett-Finches.

'Leakham has a fine record as a judge,' Colonel Chapman was saying. 'I think we can rely on him to see our point of view.'

By the time he had finished his lunch Lord Leakham was incapable of seeing anyone's point of view but his own. What prawns tabasco and Poule au Pot had begun, the Chambertin '64 and its successor, a refined vinegar that Sir Giles chose to imagine was a Chablis, had completed. That and the Pêche Maud with which Lord Leakham had attempted to soothe the spasms of his peptic ulcer. The tinned peaches had been all right but the ice cream had been larded with a mixture of cloves and nutmeg, and as for the coffee ...

As he hobbled down the steps of the Four Feathers in the vain hope of finding his car waiting for him – it had been moved on by a traffic warden – as he limped up Ferret Lane and across Abbey Close accompanied by his loathsome host, Lord Leakham's internal organs sounded the death knell of what little restraint he had shown before lunch. By the time he reached the Old Courthouse to be booed by a large crowd of farmers and their wives he was less a retired judge than an active incendiary device.

'Have those damned oafs moved on,' he snarled at Sir Giles. 'I will not be subject to hooliganism.'

Sir Giles phoned the police station and asked them to send some men over to the Courthouse. As he took his seat beside Lady Maud it was clear that things were not proceeding as he had expected. Lord Leakham's complexion was horribly mottled and his hand shook as he rapped the gavel on the bench.

'The hearing will resume,' he said huskily. 'Silence in court.' The courtroom was crowded and the Judge had to use his gavel a second time before the talking stopped. 'Next witness.'

Lady Maud rose to her feet. 'I wish to make a statement,' she said. Lord Leakham looked at her reluctantly. Lady Maud was not a sight for sore stomachs. She was large and her manner suggested something indigestible.

'We are here to take evidence,' said the Judge, 'not to listen to statements of opinion.'

Mr Turnbull stood up. 'My lord,' he said deferentially. 'my client's opinion is evidence before this Inquiry.'

'Opinion is not evidence,' said Lord Leakham. 'Your client whoever she may be ...'

'Lady Maud Lynchwood of Handyman Hall, my lord,' Mr Turnbull informed him.

'... is entitled to hold what opinions she may choose,' Lord Leakham continued, staring at the author of Poule au Pot Edward the Fourth with undisguised loathing, 'but she may not express them in this court and expect them to be accepted as evidence. You should know the rules of evidence, sir.'

Mr Turnbull adjusted his glasses defiantly. 'The rules of evidence do not, with due deference to your lordship's opinion, apply in the present circumstances. My client is not under oath and—'

'Silence in court,' snarled the Judge, addressing himself to a drunken farmer from Guildstead Carbonell who was discussing swine fever with his neighbour. With a pathetic look at Lady Maud Mr Turnbull sat down.

'Next witness,' said Lord Leakham.

Lady Maud stood her ground. 'I wish to protest,' she said with a ring of authority that brought a hush to the courtroom. 'This Inquiry is a travesty ...'

'Silence in court,' shouted the Judge.

'I will not be silenced,' Lady Maud shouted back. 'This is not a courtroom—'

'It most certainly is,' snarled the Judge.

Lady Maud hesitated. The courtroom was obviously a courtroom. There was no denying the fact.

'What I meant to say ...' she began.

'Silence in court,' screamed Lord Leakham whose peptic ulcer was in the throes of a new crisis.

Lady Maud echoed the Judge's private thoughts. 'You are not fit to conduct this Inquiry,' she shouted, and was supported by several members of the public. 'You are a senile old fool. I have a right to be heard.'

In his chair Lord Leakham's mottled head turned a plum colour and his hand reached for the gavel. 'I hold you in contempt of court,' he shouted banging the gavel. Lady Maud lurched towards him menacingly. 'Officer, arrest this woman.'

'My lord,' Mr Turnbull said, 'I beg you to ...' but it was too late. As Lady Maud advanced two constables, evidently acting on the assumption that an ex-judge of the High Court knew his law better than they did, seized her arms. It was a terrible mistake. Even Sir Giles could see that. Beside him Mr Turnbull was shouting that this was an unlawful act, and behind him pandemonium had broken out as members of the public rose in their seats and surged forward. As his wife was frogmarched, still shouting abuse, from the courtroom, as Lord Leakham bellowed in vain for the court to be cleared, as fighting broke out and windows were broken, Sir Giles sat slumped in his seat and contemplated the ruin of his plans.

Downstairs the TV cameramen, alerted by the shouts and the fragments of broken glass raining on their heads from the windows above, aimed their cameras on the courtroom door as Lady Maud emerged dishevelled and suddenly surprisingly demure between two large policemen. Somewhere between the courtroom and the cameras her twinset had been quite obscenely disarranged, a shoe had been discarded, her skirt was torn suggestively and she appeared to have lost two front teeth. With a brave attempt at a smile she collapsed on the pavement, and was filmed being dragged across the market square to the police station. 'Help,' she screamed as the crowd parted. 'Please help.' And help was forthcoming. A small dark figure hurtled out of the Courthouse and on to the larger of the two policemen. Inspired by Blott's example several stallholders threw themselves into the fray. Hidden by the crowd from the cameras Lady Maud reasserted her authority. 'Blott,' she said sternly, 'let go of the constable's ears.' Blott dropped to the ground and the stallholders fell back obediently. 'Constables, do your duty,' said Lady Maud and led the way to the police station.

Behind her the crowd turned its attention to Lord Leakham's Rolls-Royce. Apples and tomatoes rained on the Old Courthouse. To roars of approval from the onlookers Blott attempted single-handed to turn the car over and was immediately joined by several dozen farmers. When Lord Leakham, escorted by a posse of policemen, emerged from the Courthouse it was to find his Rolls on its side. It took several baton charges to clear a way through the crowd and all the time the cameras recorded faithfully the public response to the proposed motorway through the Cleene Gorge. In Ferret Lane shop windows were broken. Outside the Goat and Goblet Lord Leakham was drenched with a pail of cold water. In the Abbey Close he was concussed by a portion of broken tombstone, and when he finally reached the Four Feathers the Fire Brigade had to be called to use their hoses to disperse the crowd that besieged the hotel. By that time the Rolls-Royce was on fire and groups of drunken youths roamed the streets demonstrating their loyalty to the Handyman family by smashing street lamps.

In her cell in the police station Lady Maud removed her dentures from her pocket and smiled at the sounds of revelry. If the price of justice was eternal publicity she was assured of a fair trial. She had done what she had set out to do.

CHAPTER SIX

In London the Cabinet, meeting to cope with yet another turn for the worse in the balance of payments crisis, greeted the news of the disturbances in Worford less enthusiastically. The evening papers had headlined the arrest of an MP's wife but it was left to the television news to convey to millions of homes the impression that Lady Maud was the victim of quite outrageous police brutality.

'Oh my God,' said the Prime Minister as he watched her on the screen. 'What the hell do they think they've been doing?'

'It rather looks as if she's lost a couple of teeth,' said the Secretary of State for Foreign Affairs. 'Is that a teat hanging out there?'

Lady Maud smiled bravely and collapsed on to the pavement.

'I shall institute a full investigation at once,' said the Home Secretary.

'Who the hell appointed Leakham in the first place?' snarled the Prime Minister.

'It seemed a suitably impartial appointment at the time,' murmured the Minister of the Environment. 'As I remember it was thought that an Inquiry would satisfy local opinion.'

'Satisfy . . .?' began the Prime Minister, only to be interrupted by a phone call from the Lord Chancellor who complained that the rule of law was breaking down and even after it was explained to him that Lord Leakham was a retired judge muttered mysteriously that the law was indivisible.

The Prime Minister put the phone down and turned on the Minister of the Environment. 'This is your pigeon. You got us into this mess. You get us out. Anyone would think we had an absolute majority.'

'I'll see what I can do,' said the Minister.

'You'll do better than that,' said the Prime Minister grimly. On the screen Lord Leakham's Rolls-Royce was burning brilliantly.

The Minister of the Environment hurried from the room and phoned the home number of his Under-Secretary. 'I want a troubleshooter sent to Worford to sort this mess out,' he said.

'A troubleshooter?' Mr Rees, who was in bed with flu and whose temperature was 102, was in no state to deal with Ministerial requests for troubleshooters.

'Someone with a flair for public relations.'

'Public relations?' said Mr Rees, searching his mind for a subordinate who knew anything about public relations. 'Can I let you know by Wednesday?'

'No,' said the Minister, 'I need to be able to tell the Prime Minister that we have the situation in hand. I want someone despatched tomorrow morning by the latest. We need to have someone up there who will take charge of negotiations. I look to you to pick someone with initiative. None of your run-of-the-mill old fogies. Someone different.'

Mr Rees put the phone down with a sigh. 'Someone different indeed,' he muttered. 'Troubleshooters.' He felt aggrieved. He disliked being phoned at home, he disliked being ordered to make rapid decisions, he disliked the Minister and he particularly disliked the suggestion that his department consisted of run-of-the-mill old fogies.

He took another spoonful of cough mixture and considered a suitable candidate to send to Worford. Harrison was on leave. Beard was engaged on the Tanker Terminal at Scunthorpe. Then there was Dundridge. Dundridge was clearly unsuitable. But the Minister had specified someone different and Dundridge was decidedly different. There was no denying that. Mr Rees lay back in his bed, his head fuzzy with flu and recalled some of Dundridge's initiatives. There had been the one-way system for

Central London, of an inflexibility that would have made it impossible to drive from Hyde Park Corner to Piccadilly except by way of Tower Bridge and Fleet Street. Then there was his pilot project for installing solid-state traffic lights in Clapham, a scheme so aptly named that it had isolated that suburb from the rest of London for almost a week. In practical terms Dundridge was clearly a disaster. On the other hand he did have a flair for public relations. His schemes sounded good and year by year Dundridge had been promoted, carried upward by an ineluctable wave of inefficiency and the need to save the public the practical consequences of his latest idea until he had reached that rarefied zone of administration where, thanks to the inertia of his subordinates, his projects could never be implemented.

Mr Rees, semi-delirious and drugged with cough medicine, decided on Dundridge. He went downstairs and dictated his instructions by phone to the tape recorder on his secretary's desk at the Ministry. Then he poured himself a large whisky and drank to the thought of Dundridge in Worford. 'Troubleshooter,' he said and went back to bed.

Dundridge travelled to work by tube. It was in his opinion the rational way to travel and one that avoided the harsh confusion of reality. Seated in the train he was able to concentrate on essentials and to find some sense of order in the world above by studying the diagram of the Northern Line on the wall opposite. Far above him there was chaos. Streets, houses, shops, blocks of flats, bridges, cars, people, a welter of disparate and perverse phenomena which defied easy categorization. By looking at the diagram he could forget that confusion. Chalk Farm followed Belsize Park and was itself followed by Camden Town in a perfectly logical sequence so that he knew exactly where he was and where he was going. Then again, the diagram showed all the stations as equidistant from their neighbours and while he knew that in fact they weren't, the schematic arrangement suggested that they should be. If Dundridge had had anything to do with it they would have been. His life had been spent in pursuit of order, and abstract order that would have supplanted the perplexities of experience. As far as he was concerned variety was not the spice of life but gave it a very bitter flavour. In Dundridge's philosophy everything conformed to a norm. On one side there was chance, nature red in tooth and claw and everything haphazard; on the other science, logic and numeration.

Dundridge particularly favoured numeration and his flat in Hendon conformed to his ideal. Everything he possessed was numbered and marked on a chart above his bed. His socks for instance were 01/7, the

01 referring to Dundridge himself and the 7 to the socks and were to be found in the top drawer left (1) of his chest of drawers 23 against the wall 4 of his bedroom 3. By referring to the chart and looking for 01/7/1/23/4/3 he could locate them almost immediately. Outside his flat things were less amenable and his attempts to introduce a similar system into his office at the Ministry had met with considerable – grade 10 on the Dundridge scale – resistance and contributed to his frequent transfers from one department to another.

He was therefore not in the least surprised to find that Mr Joynson wanted to see him in his office at 9.15. Dundridge arrived at 9.25.

'I got held up in the tube,' he explained bitterly. 'It's really most irritating. I should have got here by 9.10 but the train didn't arrive on time. It never does.'

'So I've noticed,' said Mr Joynson.

'It's the irregularity of the stops that does it,' said Dundridge. 'Sometimes it stops for half a minute and at other times for a minute and a half. Really, you know, I do think it's time we gave serious consideration to a system of continuous flow underground transportation.'

'I don't suppose it would make any difference,' said Mr Joynson wearily. 'Why don't you just catch an earlier train?'

'I'd be early.'

'It would make a change. Anyway I didn't ask you here to discuss the deficiencies of the Underground system.' He paused and studied Mr Rees' instructions. Quite apart from the incredible choice of Dundridge to handle a situation which demanded intelligence, flexibility and persuasiveness, there was an unusually garbled quality about the syntax that surprised him. Still, there was a lot to be said for getting Dundridge out of London for a while and he couldn't be held personally responsible for his appointment.

'I have here,' he said finally, 'details of your new job. Mr Rees wants you ...'

'My new job?' said Dundridge. 'But I'm with Leisure Activities.'

'And very appropriate too,' said Mr Joynson. 'And now you are with Motorways Midlands. Next month I daresay we'll be able to find you a niche in Parks and Gardens.'

'I must say I find all this moving around very disturbing. I don't see how I can be expected to get anything constructive done when I'm being shifted from one Department to another all the time.'

'There is that to be said for it,' Mr Joynson agreed. 'However, in this case there is nothing constructive for you to do. You will merely be required to exercise a moderating influence.'

'A moderating influence?' Dundridge perked up.

Mr Joynson nodded. 'A moderating influence,' he said and consulted his instructions again. 'You have been appointed the Minister's trouble-shooter in Worford.'

'What?' said Dundridge, now thoroughly alarmed. 'But there's just been a riot in Worford.'

Mr Joynson smiled. He was beginning to enjoy himself. 'So there has,' he said. 'Well now, your job is to see that there are no more riots in Worford. I'm told it is a charming little town.'

'It didn't look very charming on the news last night,' said Dundridge.

'Oh well, we mustn't go by appearances now, must we? Here is your letter of appointment. As you can see it gives you full powers to conduct negotiations—'

'But I thought Lord Leakham was heading the Inquiry,' said Dundridge.

'Well, yes he is. But I understand he's a little indisposed just at the moment and in any case he appears to be under some misapprehension as to his role.'

'You mean he is in hospital, don't you?' said Dundridge.

Mr Joynson ignored the question. He turned to a map on the wall behind him. 'The issue you will have to consider is really quite simple,' he said. 'The M101, as you can see here, has two possible routes. One through the Cleene Gorge here, the other through Ottertown. The Ottertown route is out of the question for a number of reasons. You will see to it that Leakham decides on the Cleene Gorge route.'

'Surely it's up to him to decide,' said Dundridge.

Mr Joynson sighed. 'My dear Dundridge, when you have been in public service as long as I have you will know that Inquiries, Royal Commissions and Boards of Arbitration are only set up to make recommendations that concur with decisions already taken by the experts. Your job is to see that Lord Leakham arrives at the correct decision.'

'What happens if he doesn't?'

'God alone knows. I suppose in the present climate of opinion we'll have to go ahead and build the bloody thing through Ottertown, and then there would be hell to pay. It is up to you to see it doesn't. You have full powers to negotiate with the parties involved and I daresay Leakham will cooperate.'

'I don't see how I can negotiate when I've got nothing to negotiate with,' Dundridge pointed out plaintively. 'And in any case what does it mean by troubleshooter?'

'Presumably whatever you choose to make it,' said Mr Joynson.

Dundridge took the file on the M101 back to his office.

'I'm the Minister's troubleshooter in the Midlands division,' he told his secretary grandly and phoned the transport pool for a car. Then he read his letter of authority once again. It was quite clear that his abilities had been recognized in high places. Dundridge had power, and he was determined to use it.

At Handyman Hall Lady Maud congratulated herself on her skill in disrupting the Inquiry. Released from custody against her own better judgement at the express command of the Chief Constable, she returned to the Hall to be deluged by messages of support. General Burnett called to offer his congratulations. Mrs Bullett-Finch phoned to see if there was anything she needed after the ordeal of her confinement, a term Lady Maud found almost as offensive as Colonel Chapman's comment that she was full of spunk. Even Mrs Thomas wrote to thank her on behalf, as she modestly put it, of the common people. Lady Maud accepted these tributes abruptly. They were she felt quite unnecessary. She had only been doing her duty after all. As she put it to the reporter from the *Observer*, 'Local interests can only be looked after by local authorities,' a sufficiently ambiguous expression to satisfy the correspondent while stating very precisely Lady Maud's own view of her role in South Worfordshire.

'And do you intend to sue the police for unlawful arrest?' the reporter asked.

'Certainly not. I have the greatest respect for the police. They do a magnificent job. I hold Lord Leakham entirely responsible. I am taking legal counsel as to what action I should take against him.'

In the Worford Cottage Hospital Lord Leakham greeted the news that she was considering legal proceedings against him with a show of indifference. He had more immediate problems, the state of his digestive system for one thing, six stitches in his scalp for another, and besides he was suffering from concussion. In his lucid moments he prayed for death and in his delirium shouted obscenities.

But if Lord Leakham was too preoccupied with his own problems to think at all clearly about the disruption of the Inquiry, Sir Giles could think of little else.

'The whole situation is extremely awkward,' he told Hoskins when they conferred at the latter's office the next morning. 'That bloody woman has put the cat among the pigeons and no mistake. She's turned the whole thing into an issue of national interest. I've been inundated with calls from conservationists from all over the country, all supporting our stand. It's bloody infuriating. Why can't they mind their own confounded business?'

Hoskins lit his pipe moodily. 'That's not all,' he said, 'they're sending some bigwig up from the Ministry to take charge of the negotiations.'

'That's all we need, some damned bureaucrat to come poking his nose into our affairs.'

'Quite,' said Hoskins, 'so from now on no more phone calls to me here. I can't afford to be connected with you.'

'Do you think he's going to choose the Ottertown route?'

Hoskins shrugged. 'I've no idea. All I do know is that if I were in his shoes I'm damned if I'd recommend the Gorge.'

'Let me know what the blighter suggests,' said Sir Giles and went out to his car.

CHAPTER SEVEN

To Dundridge, travelling up the M1, the underlying complexities of the situation in South Worfordshire were quite unknown. For the first time in his life he was armed with authority and he intended to put it to good use. He would make a name for himself. The years of frustration were over. He would return to London with his reputation for swift, decisive action firmly established.

At Warwick he stopped for lunch, and while he ate he studied the file on the motorway. There was a map of the district, the outline of the alternative routes, and a list of those people through whose property the motorway would run and the sums they would receive as compensation. Dundridge concentrated his attention on the latter. A single glance was enough to explain the urgency of his appointment and the difficulty of his mission. The list read like a roll-call of the upper class in the county. Sir Giles Lynchwood, General Burnett, Colonel Chapman, Mr Bullett-Finch, Miss Percival. Dundridge peered uncomfortably at the names and incredulously at the sums they were being offered. A quarter of a million pounds for Sir Giles. One hundred and fifty thousand to General Burnett. One hundred and twenty thousand to Colonel Chapman. Even Miss Percival whose occupation was listed as schoolteacher was offered fifty-five thousand. Dundridge compared these sums with his own income and felt a surge of envy. There was no justice in the world and Dundridge (whose socialism was embodied in the maxim 'To each according to his abilities, from each according to his needs', the 'his' in both cases referring to Dundridge himself) found his thoughts wandering in the direction of money. It had been Dundridge's mother who had instilled in him the saying 'Don't marry money, go where money is' and since this had been easier said than done, Dundridge's sex life had been largely confined to his imagination. There, safe from the disagreeable complexities of real life, he had indulged his various passions. In his imagination Dundridge was rich, Dundridge was powerful and Dundridge was the possessor of an entourage of immaculate women – or to be precise of one woman, a composite creature made up of bits and pieces of real woman who had once partially attracted him but without any of their concomitant disadvantages. Now for the first time he was going where money was. It was an alluring prospect. He finished his lunch and drove on.

And as he drove he became increasingly aware that the countryside had changed. He had left the motorway and was on a minor road that twisted and turned. The hedgerows grew taller and more rank. Hills rose up and fell away into empty valleys and woods took on a rougher, less domesticated air. Even the houses had lost the comfortable homogeneous look of the North London suburbs. They were either large and isolated, standing in their own grounds, or stone-built farmhouses surrounded by dark corrugated iron sheds and barns. Every now and again he passed through villages, strange conglomerations of cottages and shops, buildings that loomed misshapenly over the road or retreated behind hedges with an eccentricity of ornaments he found disturbing. And finally there were churches. Dundridge disliked churches most of all. They reminded him of death and burial, guilt and sin and the hereafter. Archaic reminders of a superstitious past. And since Dundridge lived if not for the present at least the immediate future, these memento mori held no attractions for him. They cast horrid doubts on the rational nature of existence. Not that Dundridge believed in reason. He placed his faith in science and numeration.

Now as he drove northwards he had to admit that he was entering a world far removed from his ideal. Even the sky had changed with the landscape and the shadows of large clouds slid erratically across the fields and hills. By the time he reached South Worfordshire he was distinctly perturbed. If Worford was anything like the surrounding countryside it must be a horrid place filled with violent, irrational creatures swayed by strange emotions. It was. As he drove over the bridge that spanned the Cleene he seemed to have moved out of the twentieth century into an earlier age. The houses below the town gate were huddled together higgledy-piggledy and only their scrubbed doorsteps redeemed their squalid lack of uniformity. The gate, a great stuccoed tower with a dark narrow entrance, loomed up before him. He drove nervously through and emerged into a street lined with eighteenth-century houses. Here he felt temporarily more at home but his relief evaporated when he reached the town centre. Dark narrow alleyways, half-timbered medieval houses jutting over the pavement, cobbled streets, and shopfronts which retained the format of an earlier age. Pots and pans, spades and sickles hung outside an ironmongers. Duffel coats, corduroy trousers and breeches were displayed outside an outfitters. A mackerel gleamed on a fishmonger's marble slab while a saddler's was adorned with bits and bridles and leather belts. Worford was in short a perfectly normal market town but to Dundridge, accustomed to the soothing anonymity of supermarkets, there was a disturbing, archaic quality about it. He drove into the Market Square and asked the car-park attendant for the Regional Planning Office. The attendant didn't know or if he did, Dundridge was none the wiser. The accents of Wales and England met in South Worfordshire, met and mingled incomprehensibly. Dundridge parked his car and went into a telephone kiosk. He looked in the Directory and found the Planning Office in Knacker's Yard.

'Where's Knacker's Yard?' he asked the car-park attendant.

'Down Giblet Walk.'

'Very informative,' said Dundridge with a shudder. 'And where's Giblet Walk?'

'Well now, let's see, you can go down past the Goat and Goblet or you can take a short cut through the Shambles,' said the old man and spat into the gutter.

Dundridge considered this unenticing alternative. 'Where are the Shambles?' he asked finally.

'Behind you,' said the attendant.

Dundridge turned round and looked into the shadow of a narrow alley. It was cobbled and led down the hill and out of sight. He walked down it uncomfortably. Several of the houses were boarded up and one or two had actually fallen down and the alleyway had a peculiar smell that he associated with footpaths and tunnels under railway lines. Dundridge held his breath and hurried on and came out into Knacker's Yard where a sign in front of a large red-brick building said Regional Planning Board. He opened an iron gate and went down a path to the door.

'Planning Board's on the second floor,' said a dentist's assistant who emerged from a room holding a metal bowl in which a pair of false teeth rested pinkly. 'You'll be lucky if you find it open though. You looking for anyone in particular?'

'Mr Hoskins,' said Dundridge.

'Try the Club,' said the woman. 'He's usually there this time of day. It's on the first floor.'

'Thank you,' said Dundridge and went upstairs. On the first landing there was a door marked Worford and District Gladstone Club. Dundridge looked at it doubtfully and went on up. As the woman had said, the Regional Planning Board was shut. Dundridge went downstairs and stood uncertainly on the landing. Then, reminding himself that he was the Minister's plenipotentiary and troubleshooter, he opened the door and looked inside.

'You looking for someone?' asked the large red-faced man who was standing beside a billiard table.

'I'm looking for Mr Hoskins, the Planning Officer,' said Dundridge. The red-faced man put down his cue and stepped forward.

'Then you've come to the right place,' he said. 'Bob, there's a bloke wants to see you.'

Another large red-faced man who was sitting at the bar in the corner turned round and stared at Dundridge. 'What can I do for you?' he asked.

'I'm from the Ministry of the Environment,' said Dundridge.

'Christ,' said Mr Hoskins and got down from his bar stool. 'You're early aren't you? Wasn't expecting you till tomorrow.'

'The Minister is most anxious that I should get down to work as rapidly as possible.'

'Quite right,' said Mr Hoskins more cheerfully now that he could see that Dundridge wasn't sixty, didn't wear gold rimmed glasses and didn't carry an air of authority about him. 'What will you have?'

Dundridge hesitated. It wasn't his habit to drink in the middle of the afternoon. 'A half of bitter,' he said finally.

'Make it two pints,' Hoskins told the barman. They took their glasses across to a small table in the corner and sat down. At the billiard table the men resumed their game.

'Awkward business this,' said Mr Hoskins, 'I don't envy you your job. Local feeling's none too good.'

'So I've noticed,' said Dundridge sipping his beer. It tasted, as he had anticipated, both strong and unpleasantly organic. On the wall opposite a portrait of Mr Gladstone glared relentlessly down on this dereliction of the licensing laws. Spurred on by his example, Dundridge attempted to explain his mission. 'The Minister is particularly anxious that the negotiations should be handled tactfully. He has sent me to see that the outcome of these negotiations has the backing of all the parties involved.'

'Has he?' said Mr Hoskins. 'Well, all I can say is that you'll have your work cut out.'

'Now as I see it, the best approach would be to propose an alternative route,' Dundridge continued.

'We've done that already. Through Ottertown.'

'Out of the question,' said Dundridge.

'I couldn't agree more,' said Mr Hoskins. 'Which leaves the Cleene Gorge.'

'Or the hills to the south?' suggested Dundridge hopefully.

Mr Hoskins shook his head. 'Cleene Forest is an area of natural beauty, a designated area. Not a hope in hell.'

'Well that doesn't leave us with many alternatives, does it?'

'It doesn't leave us with any,' said Mr Hoskins.

Dundridge drank some more beer. The mood of optimism with which he had started the day had quite left him. It was all very well to talk about negotiating but there didn't seem any negotiations to conduct. He was faced with the unenviable task of enforcing a thoroughly unpopular decision on a group of extremely influential and hostile landowners. It was not a prospect he relished. 'I don't suppose there is any chance of persuading Sir Giles Lynchwood and General Burnett to drop their opposition,' he said without much hope.

'Not a hope in hell,' Hoskins told him, 'and anyway if they did it wouldn't make the slightest difference. It's Lady Maud you've got to worry about. And she isn't going to budge.'

'I must say you make it all sound extremely difficult,' said Dundridge and finished his beer. By the time he left the Gladstone Club he had a clear picture of the situation. The stumbling block was Handyman Hall and Lady Maud. He would explore the possibilities of that more fully in the morning. He walked back up the Shambles and Giblet Walk to the Market Square and booked in at the Handyman Arms.

At the Hall Sir Giles spent the day sequestered in his study. This seclusion was only partly to be explained by the presence in the house and grounds of half a dozen guard dogs who seemed to feel that he was an intruder in his own home. More to the point was the fact that Lady Maud had expressed herself very forcibly on the matter of his lunch with Lord Leakham. If the Judge regretted that lunch, and from the reports of the doctors at the Cottage Hospital he had cause to, so did Sir Giles.

'I was only trying to help,' he had explained. 'I thought if I gave him a good lunch he might be more prepared to see our side of the case.'

'Our side of the case?' Lady Maud snorted. 'If it comes to that we didn't have a case at all. It was perfectly obvious he was going to recommend the route through the Gorge.'

'There is the Ottertown alternative,' Sir Giles pointed out.

'Alternative my foot,' said Lady Maud. 'If you can't see a red herring when it's thrust under your nose, you're a bigger fool than I take you for.'

Sir Giles had retreated to his study cursing his wife for her perspicacity. There had been a very nasty look in her eye at the mention of Ottertown, and one or two unpleasant cracks about property speculators and their ways over breakfast had made him wonder if she had heard anything about Hoskins' new house. And now there was this damned official from Whitehall to poke his nose into the affair. Finally and most disturbing of all there had been the voices. Or rather one voice: his own. While putting the car away before lunch he had distinctly heard himself assuring nobody in particular that they could look to him to see that nothing was done that would in any way jeopardize ... Sir Giles had stared round the yard with a wild surmise. For a moment he had supposed that he had been talking to himself but the presence in his mouth of a cigar had ended that explanation. Besides the voice had been quite distinct. It had been a most disturbing experience and one for which there was no rational explanation. It had taken two stiff whiskies to convince him that he had imagined the whole thing. Now to take his mind off the occurrence he sat at his desk and concentrated on the motorway.

'Red herring indeed,' he muttered to himself. 'I wonder what she would have said if Leakham had decided in favour of Ottertown.' It was an idle thought and quite out of the question. They would never build a motorway through Ottertown. Old Francis Puckerington would have another heart attack. Old Francis Puckerington ... Sir Giles stopped in his tracks, amazed at his own intuitive brilliance. Francis Puckerington, the Member for Ottertown, was a dying man. What had the doctors said? That he'd be lucky to live to the next general election. There had been rumours that he was going to resign his seat. And his majority at the last election had been a negligible one, somewhere in the region of fifty. If Leakham had decided on the Ottertown route it would have killed old Francis. And then there would have to be a bye-election. Sir Giles' devious mind catalogued the consequences. A bye-election fought on the issue of the motorway and the demolition of seventy-five council houses with a previous majority of fifty. It wasn't to be thought of. The Chief Whip would go berserk. Leakham's decision would be reversed. The motorway would come through the Cleene Gorge after all. And best of all not a shred of suspicion would rest on Sir Giles. It was a brilliant stratagem. It would put him in the clear. He was about to reach for the phone to call Hoskins when it occurred to him that he had better wait to hear what the man from the Ministry had to say. There was no point in rushing things now. He would go and see Hoskins in the morning. Imbued with a new spirit of defiance he left the study and selecting a large walking-stick from the rack in the hall he went out into the garden for a stroll.

It was a glorious afternoon. The sun shone down out of a cloudless sky. Birds sang. The flowering cherries by the kitchen garden flowered and Sir Giles himself blossomed with smug self-satisfaction. He paused for a moment to admire the goldfish in the ornamental pond and was just considering the possibility of pushing up the compensation to three hundred thousand when for the second time that day he heard himself speaking. 'I'm damned if I'm going to allow the countryside to be desecrated by a motorway. I shall take the earliest opportunity of raising the matter in the House.' Sir Giles stared round the garden panic-stricken, but there was no one in sight. He turned and looked at the Hall but the windows were all shut. To his right was the wall of the kitchen garden. Sir Giles hurried across the lawn to the door in the wall and peered inside. Blott was busy in a cucumber frame.

'Did you say anything?' Sir Giles asked.

'Me?' said Blott. 'I didn't say anything. Did you?'

Sir Giles hurried back to the house. It was no longer a glorious afternoon. It was a quite horrible afternoon. He went into his study and shut the door.

CHAPTER EIGHT

Dundridge spent a perfectly foul night at the Handyman Arms. His room there had a sloping floor, a yellowed ceiling, an ochre chest of drawers and a wardrobe whose door opened of its own accord ten minutes after he had shut it. It did so with a hideous wheeze and would then creak softly until he got out of bed and shut it again. He spent half the night trying to devise some method of keeping it closed and the other half listening to the noises coming from the next room. These were of a most disturbing sort and suggested an incompatibility of size and temperament that played havoc with his imagination. At two o'clock he managed to get to sleep, only to be woken at three by a sudden eruption in the drainpipe of his washbasin which appeared to be most unhygienically connected to the one next door. At half past three a dawn breeze rattled the signboard outside his window. At four the man next door asked if someone wanted it again. 'For God's sake,' Dundridge muttered and buried his head under the pillow to shut out this evidence of sexual excess. At ten past four the wardrobe door, responding to the seismic tremors from the next room, opened again and creaked softly. Dundridge let it creak and turned for relief to his composite woman. With her assistance he managed to get back to sleep to be woken at seven by a repulsive-looking girl with a tea-tray.

'Is there anything else you wanted?' she asked coyly.

'Certainly not,' said Dundridge wondering what there was about him that led only the most revolting females to offer him their venereal services. He got up and went along to the bathroom and wrestled with the intricacies of a gas-fired geyser which had evidently set its mind on asphyxiating him or blowing him up. In the end he had a cold wash.

By the time he had finished breakfast he was in a thoroughly bad mood. He had been unable to formulate any coherent strategy and had no idea what to do next. Hoskins had advised him to have a word with Sir Giles Lynchwood and Dundridge decided he would do that later. To begin with he would pay a call on Lord Leakham at the Cottage Hospital.

After wandering down narrow lanes and up a flight of steps behind the Worford Museum he found the hospital, a grey gaunt stone building that looked as though it had once been a workhouse. It fronted on to the Abbey and in the small front garden a number of geriatric patients were sitting around in dressing-gowns. Stifling his disgust, Dundridge went inside and asked for Lord Leakham.

'Visiting hours are two to three,' said the nurse at Admissions.

'I'm here on Government business,' said Dundridge feeling that it was about time someone understood he was not to be trifled with.

'I'll have to ask Matron,' said the nurse. Dundridge went outside into the sunshine to wait. He didn't like hospitals. They were not, he felt, his forte, particularly hospitals which overlooked graveyards, stank of disinfectant and had the gall to call themselves Cottage Hospitals when they were situated in the middle of towns. He was just considering the awful prospect of being treated for a serious complaint in such a dead-and-alive hole when the Matron appeared. She was gaunt, grey-haired and grim.

'I understand you want to see Lord Leakham,' she said.

'On Government business,' said Dundridge pompously.

'You can have five minutes,' said the Matron and led the way down the passage to a private room. 'He's still suffering from concussion and shock.' She opened the door and Dundridge went inside. 'Now nothing controversial,' said the Matron. 'We don't want to have a relapse, do we?'

On the bed, ashen-faced and with his head swathed in bandages, Lord Leakham regarded her venomously. 'There's nothing the matter with me apart from food poisoning,' he said. Dundridge sat down beside his bed.

'My name is Dundridge,' he said. 'The Minister of the Environment has asked me to come up to see if I can do something to ... er ... well to negotiate some sort of settlement in regard to the motorway.'

Lord Leakham looked at him vindictively over the top of his glasses. 'Has he indeed? Well let me tell you what I intend to do about the motorway first and then you can inform him,' he said. He raised himself on his pillows and leant towards Dundridge. 'I was appointed to head the Inquiry into the motorway and I do not intend to relinquish my responsibility.'

'Oh quite,' said Dundridge.

'Furthermore,' said the Judge, 'I have no intention whatsoever of allowing myself to be influenced by hooliganism and riot from doing my duty as I see it.'

'Oh definitely,' said Dundridge.

'As soon as these damnfool doctors get it into their thick heads that there is nothing wrong with me except a peptic ulcer, I shall re-open the Inquiry and announce my decision.' Dundridge nodded.

'Quite right too,' he said. 'And what will your decision be? Or is it too early to ask that?'

'It most certainly isn't,' shouted Lord Leakham. 'I intend to recommend that the motorway goes through the Cleene Gorge, plumb through it, you understand. I intend to see that that damned woman's home is levelled to the ground, brick by brick. I intend ...' He sank back on to the bed exhausted by his outburst.

'I see,' said Dundridge, wondering what possible use there was in trying to negotiate a compromise between an irresistible force and an immovable object.

'Oh no you don't,' said Lord Leakham. 'That woman deliberately sent her husband to poison me. She interrupted the proceedings. She insulted me in my own court. She incited to riot. She made a mockery of the legal process and she shall rue the day. The law shall not be mocked, sir.'

'Oh quite,' said Dundridge.

'So you go and negotiate all you want but just remember the decision to go through the Gorge is mine and I do not for one moment intend to forgo the pleasure of making it.'

Dundridge went out into the passage and conferred with the Matron.

'He seems to think someone tried to poison him,' he said carefully skirting the law of libel. The Matron smiled gently.

'That's the concussion,' she said. 'He'll get over that in a day or two.'

Dundridge went out into the Abbey Close past the geriatric patients and wandered disconsolately down the steps and out into Market Street. It didn't seem likely to him that Lord Leakham would get over his conviction that Lady Maud had tried to poison him and he had a shrewd suspicion that the Judge had in some perverse way enjoyed the contretemps in court and was looking forward to pursuing his vendetta as soon as he was up and about. He was just considering what to do next when he caught sight of his reflection in a shop window. It was not that of a man of authority. There was a sort of dispirited look about it, a hangdog look quite out of keeping with his role as the Minister's troubleshooter. It was time to take the bull by the horns. He straightened his back, marched across the road to the Post Office and telephoned Handyman Hall. He got Lady Maud and explained that he would like to see Sir Giles.

'I'm afraid Sir Giles is out just at present,' she said modulating her tone to suggest a secretary. 'He'll be back shortly. Would eleven o'clock be convenient?'

Dundridge said it would. He left the Post Office and threaded his way through the market stalls to the car park to collect his car.

At Handyman Hall Lady Maud congratulated herself on her performance. She was rather looking forward to a private chat with the man from the Ministry. Dundridge, he had said his name was. From the Ministry. Sir Giles had mentioned the fact that someone had been sent up from London on a factfinding mission. And since Giles had said he would be out until late in the afternoon this seemed an ideal opportunity to provide this Mr Dundridge with facts that would suit her book. She went upstairs to change, and to consider her tactics. She had spiked Lord Leakham's guns by frontal assault but Dundridge on the phone had sounded far less self-assured than she had expected. It might be better to try persuasion, perhaps even a little charm. It would confuse the issue. Lady Maud selected a cotton frock and dabbed a little Lavender Water behind her ears. Mr Dundridge would get the meek treatment, the helpless little girl approach. If that didn't work she could always revert to sterner methods.

In the greenhouse Blott put down the earphones and went back to the broad beans. So an official was coming to see Sir Giles, was he? An official. Blott felt strongly about officials. They had made his early life a misery and he had no time for them. Still, Lady Maud had invited this one to the Hall so presumably she knew what she was doing. It was a pity. Blott would have liked to have been ordered to give this Dundridge the reception he deserved and he was just considering what sort of reception he would have organized for him when Lady Maud came into the garden. Blott straightened up and stared at her. She was wearing a cotton frock and to Blott at least she looked quite beautiful. It was not a notion anyone else would have shared but Blott's standards of beauty were not determined by fashion. Large breasts, enormous thighs and hips were attributes of a good or at least ample mother, and since Blott had never had a good, ample or even *any* mother in a post-natal sense he placed great emphasis on these outward signs of potential maternity. Now, standing among the broad beans, he was filled with a sudden sense of desire. Lady Maud in a cotton frock dappled with a floral pattern combined botany with biology. Blott goggled.

'Blott,' said Lady Maud, oblivious of the effect she was having, 'there's a man from the Ministry of the Environment coming to lunch. I want some flowers in the house. I want to make a good impression on him.'

Blott went into the greenhouse and looked for something suitable while Lady Maud bent low to select a lettuce for lunch. As she did so Blott glanced out of the greenhouse door. It was the turning point in his life. The silent devotion to the Handyman family which had been the passive mainspring of his existence for so long was gone, to be replaced by an active urgency of feeling.

Blott was in love.

CHAPTER NINE

Dundridge left Worford by the town gate, crossed the river and took the Ottertown road. On his left the Cleene wandered through meadows and on his right the Cleene Hills rose steeply to a wooded crest. He drove for three miles and turned up a side road that was signposted Guildstead Carbonell and found himself in evidently hostile territory. Every barn had the slogan 'Save the Gorge' whitewashed on it and there were similar sentiments painted on the road itself. At one point an avenue of beeches had been daubed with letters that spelt out 'No to the Motorway' so that as he drove down it Dundridge was left in no doubt that local feeling was against the scheme.

Even without the slogans Dundridge would have been alarmed. The Cleene Forest was nature undomesticated. There was none of that neatness that he found so reassuring in Middlesex. The hedges were rank, the few farmhouses he passed looked medieval, and the forest itself dense with large trees, humped and gnarled with bracken growing thickly underneath. He was relieved when the road ran into an open valley with hedges and little fields. The respite was brief. At the top of the next hill he came to a crossroads marked by nothing more informative than a decayed gibbet.

Dundridge stopped the car and consulted his map. According to his calculations Guildstead Carbonell lay to the left while in front was the Gorge and Handyman Hall. Dundridge wished it wasn't. Below him the forest lay thicker than before and the road less metalled, with moss and grass growing down the middle. He drove on for a mile and was beginning to wonder if the map had misled him when the trees thinned and he found himself looking down into the Gorge itself.

He stopped the car and got out. Below him the Cleene tumbled between cliffs overgrown with brambles, ivy and creepers. Ahead lay Handyman Hall. It stood, an amalgam in stone and brick, timber and tile and turret, a monument to all that was most eclectic and least attractive in English architecture. To Dundridge, himself a devotee of function, for whom simplicity was all, it was a nightmare. Ruskin and Morris, Gilbert Scott, Vanbrugh, Inigo Jones and Wren to name but a few had all lent their influence to a building that combined the utility of a water-tower with the homeliness of Wormwood Scrubs. Around it lay a few acres of parkland, a wall, and beyond the wall a circle of hills, heavily wooded. Over the whole scene there lay a sense of isolation. Somewhere to the west there were presumably towns and houses, shops and buses, but to Dundridge it seemed that he was standing on the very edge of civilization if not actually beyond it. With the sinking feeling that he was committing himself to the unknown he got back into the car and drove on, down the hill into the Gorge. Presently he came to a small iron suspension bridge across the river which rattled as he drove over. On the far side something large and strange loomed through the trees. It was the Lodge. Dundridge stopped the car and gaped at the building through the windshield.

Constructed in 1904 to mark the occasion of the visit of Edward the Seventh, the Lodge, in deference to the King's Francophilia, had been modelled on the Arc de Triomphe. There were differences. The Lodge was slightly smaller, its frieze did not depict scenes of battle, but for all that the resemblance was remarkable and to Dundridge its existence in the heart of Worfordshire came as final proof that whoever had built Handyman Hall had been an architectural kleptomaniac. Above all the Lodge bespoke a lofty arrogance which, coming so shortly after Lord Leakham's outburst, made a tactful approach all the more necessary. As he stood looking up at it Dundridge was recalled to his task. Some sort of compromise was clearly necessary to avoid his becoming embroiled in an extremely nasty situation. If the Ottertown route was out of the question and he had it on the highest authority that it was, and if the Gorge ... There was no if about the Gorge, Dundridge had seen enough to convince him of that, then a third route was imperative. But there was no third route. Dundridge got back into his car and drove thoughtfully through the great arch and as he did so a vision of the third route dawned upon him. A tunnel. A tunnel under the Cleene Hills. A tunnel had all the merits of simplicity, of straightness and, best of all, of leaving undisturbed the hideous landscape that so many irate and influential people inexplicably admired. There would be no more wrangles about property rights, no compensation, no trouble. Dundridge had discovered the ideal solution.

In the entrance hall Lady Maud, radiant in Tootal, lurked among the ferns. High above her head the stained-glass rooflight cast a reddish glow upon the marble staircase and lent a fresh air of apoplexy to the ruddy faces of her ancestors glowering down from the walls. Lady Maud patted her hair in readiness. She had laid her plans. Mr Dundridge would get the gracious treatment at least to begin with. After that she would see how he responded. As his car crunched on the gravel outside she adjusted her step-in and gave a practice smile to a vase of snapdragons. Then she stepped forward and opened the door.

'Nincompoop? Nincompoop? Did you say nincompoop?' said Sir Giles. In his constituency office situated conveniently close to Hoskins' Regional Planning Board the word had a reassuring ring to it.

'A perfect nincompoop,' said Hoskins.

'Are you sure?'

'Positive. A first rate, Grade A nincompoop.'

'It sounds too good to be true,' said Sir Giles doubtfully. 'You can't always go by appearances. I've known some very slippery customers in my time who looked like idiots.'

'I'm not going by appearances,' Hoskins said. 'He doesn't look an idiot. He is one. Wouldn't know one end of a motorway from the other.'

Sir Giles considered the statement. 'I'm not sure I would come to that,' he said.

'You know what I mean,' said Hoskins. 'He's no more an expert on motorways than I am.'

Sir Giles pursed his lips. 'If he's such a dimwit why did the Minister send him up? He's given him full authority to negotiate.'

'Don't look a gift horse in the mouth, is what I say.'

'I daresay there's something in that,' said Sir Giles. 'So you don't think there's anything to worry about?'

Hoskins smiled. 'Not a thing in the world. He'll nosey around a bit and then he will do just what we want. I tell you this bloke takes the biscuit. Butter wouldn't melt in his mouth.'

Sir Giles considered this mixture of metaphors and found it to his taste. 'I hear Lord Leakham's still foaming at the mouth.'

'He can't wait to re-open the Inquiry. Says he's going to put the motorway through the Gorge if it's the last thing he does.'

'It probably will be if Maud has anything to do with it,' said Sir Giles. 'She's in a very nasty frame of mind.'

'There's nothing much she can do about it once the decision is taken,' said Hoskins.

'I wouldn't be too sure about that.'

Sir Giles got up and stared out of the window and considered his alternative plan. 'You don't think this fellow Dundridge will advise against the Gorge?' he asked finally.

'Lord Leakham wouldn't listen to him if he did. He's got it into his head you tried to poison him,' said Hoskins and went back to his office leaving Sir Giles to ponder on the best-laid plans of mice and men. It was all very well for Hoskins to talk confidently about nincompoops from the Ministry. He had nothing to lose. Sir Giles had. His seat in Parliament for one thing. Well, if the worst came to the worst and Maud carried out her threat he could always get another. It was worth the risk. Reassured by the thought that Lord Leakham had made up his mind to route the motorway through the Gorge Sir Giles went out to lunch.

At Handyman Hall Lady Maud's gracious approach had worked wonders. Like some delicate plant in need of water, Dundridge had blossomed out. He had come expecting to meet Sir Giles but, after the first shock of finding himself alone in a large house with a large woman had worn off, Dundridge began to enjoy himself. For the first time since he had arrived in Worfordshire he was being taken seriously. Lady Maud treated him as a person of consequence.

'It is so good to know that you have come to take over from Lord Leakham,' Lady Maud said as she led him down a corridor to the drawing-room.

Dundridge said he hadn't actually come to take over. 'I'm simply here in an advisory capacity,' he said modestly.

Lady Maud smiled knowingly. 'Oh quite, and we all know what that means, don't we?' she murmured, drawing Dundridge into a warm complicity he found quite delightful.

Dundridge relaxed on the sofa. 'The Minister is most anxious that the proposed motorway should fit in with the needs of local residents as much as possible.'

Maud smothered a snarl with another smile. The notion that she was a local resident made her blood boil, but she had set out to humour this snivelling civil servant and humour him she would. 'And there is the landscape to consider too,' she said. 'The Cleene Forest is one of the few remaining examples of virgin woodland left in England. It would be a terrible shame to spoil it with a motorway, don't you think?'

Dundridge didn't think anything of the sort but he knew better than to say so, and besides this seemed as good an opportunity as any to test out his theory of a tunnel. 'I think I've found a solution to the problem,' he said. 'Of course it's only an idea, you understand, and it has no official standing, but it should be possible to build a tunnel under the Cleene Hills.' He stopped. Lady Maud was staring at him intently. 'Of course, as I say, it's only an idea ...'

Lady Maud had risen and for one terrible moment Dundridge thought she was about to assault him. She lurched forward and took his hand. 'Oh how wonderful,' she said. 'How absolutely brilliant. You dear, dear man,' and she sat down beside him on the sofa and gazed into his face ecstatically. Dundridge blushed and looked down at his shoes. He was quite unused to married women taking his hand, gazing into his face ecstatically and calling him their dear, dear man. 'It's nothing. Only an idea.'

'A splendid idea,' said Lady Maud, engulfing him in a blast of Lavender Water. Out of the corner of his eye Dundridge could see her bosom quivering beneath a nosegay of marigolds. He shrank into the sofa.

'Of course, there would have to be a feasibility study ...' he began but Lady Maud brushed his remark aside.

'Of course there would, but that would take time wouldn't it?'

'Months,' said Dundridge.

'Months!'

'Six months at least.'

'Six months!' Lady Maud relinquished his hand with a sigh and contemplated a respite of six months. In six months so much could happen and if she had anything to do with it a great deal would. Giles would throw his weight behind the tunnel or she would know the reason why. She would drum up support from conservationists across the country. In six months she would do wonders. And she owed it all to this insubstantial little man with plastic shoes. Now that she came to look at him she realized she had misjudged him. There was something almost appealing about his vulnerability. 'You'll stay to lunch,' she said.

'Well ... er ... I really ...'

'Of course you will,' said Lady Maud. 'I insist. And you can tell Giles all about the tunnel when he gets back this afternoon.' She rose and, leaving Dundridge to wonder how it was that Sir Giles who had been coming back at eleven had delayed his return until the afternoon, Lady Maud swept from the room. Left to himself, Dundridge sat stunned by the enthusiasm his suggestion had unleashed. If Sir Giles' reaction was as favourable as that of his wife he would have made some influential friends. And rich ones. He ran his fingers appreciatively over the moulding of a rosewood table. So this was how the other half lived, he thought, before realizing that the cliché was inappropriate. The other two per cent. Useful people to know.

Sir Giles returned from Worford at four to find Lady Maud in a remarkably good mood.

'I had a visit from such a strange young man,' she told him when he inquired what the matter was.

'Oh really?'

'He was called Dundridge. He was from the Ministry of the—'

'Dundridge? Did you say Dundridge?'

'Yes. Such a very interesting man ...'

'Interesting? I understood he was a nincom ... oh never mind. What did he have to say for himself?'

'Oh, this and that,' said Lady Maud, gratified by her husband's agitation.

'What do you mean "this and that"?'

'We talked about the absurdity of putting a motorway through the Gorge,' said Lady Maud.

'I suppose he's in favour of the Ottertown route.'

Lady Maud shook her head, 'As a matter of fact he isn't.'

'He isn't?' said Sir Giles, now thoroughly alarmed. 'What the hell is he in favour of then?'

Lady Maud savoured his concern. 'He has in mind a third route,' she said. 'One that avoids both Ottertown and the Gorge.'

Sir Giles turned pale. 'A third route? But there isn't a third route. There can't be. He's not thinking of going through the Forest, is he? It's an area of designated public beauty.'

'Not through it. Under it,' said Lady Maud triumphantly.

'Under it?'

'A tunnel. A tunnel under the Cleene Hills. Don't you think that's a marvellous idea.'

Sir Giles sat down heavily. He was looking quite ill.

'I said "Don't you think that's a marvellous idea",' said Lady Maud.

Sir Giles pulled himself together. 'Er ... What ... oh yes ... splendid,' he muttered. 'Quite splendid.'

'You don't sound very enthusiastic,' said Lady Maud.

'It's just that I wouldn't have thought it was financially viable,' Sir Giles said. 'The cost would be enormous. I can't see the Ministry taking to the idea at all readily.'

'I can,' said Lady Maud, 'with a little prodding.' She went out through the french windows on to the terrace and looked lovingly across the park. With Dundridge's help she had solved one problem. The house had been saved. There remained the question of an heir and it had just occurred to her that here again Dundridge might prove invaluable. Over lunch he had waxed quite eloquent about his work. Once or twice he had mentioned cementation. The word had struck a chord in her. Now as she leant over the balustrade and stared into the depths of the pinetum it returned to her insistently. 'Sementation,' she murmured, 'sementation.' It was a new word to her and strangely technical for such an intimate act, but Lady Maud was in no mood to quibble.

Sir Giles was. He waddled off to the study and phoned Hoskins. 'What's all this about that bastard Dundridge being a nincompoop?' he snarled. 'Do you know what he's come up with now? A tunnel. You heard me. A bloody tunnel under the Cleene Hills.'

'A tunnel?' said Hoskins. 'That's out of the question. They can't put a tunnel under the Forest.'

'Why not? They're putting one under the blasted Channel. They can put tunnels wherever they bloody well want to these days.'

'I know that, but it would be cost-prohibitive,' said Hoskins.

'Cost-prohibitive my arse. If this sod goes round bleating about tunnels he'll whip up support from every environmental crank in the country. He's got to be stopped.'

'I'll do my best,' said Hoskins doubtfully.

'You'll do better than that,' Sir Giles snarled. 'You get him on to the idea of Ottertown.'

'But what about the seventy-five council houses—'

'Bugger the seventy-five council houses. Just get him off the bloody tunnel.' Sir Giles put down the phone and stared out of the window vindictively. If he didn't do something drastic he would be saddled with Handyman Hall. And with Lady Maud to boot. He got up and kicked the wastepaper basket into the corner.

CHAPTER TEN

Dundridge drove back to Worford with no thought for the landscape. His encounter with Lady Maud had left him stunned and with his sense of self-importance greatly inflated. Lunch had been most enjoyable and Dundridge with two large gins inside him had found Lady Maud a most appreciative audience. She had listened to his exposition of the theory of non-interruptive constant-flow transportation with an evident fervour usually quite absent in his audience and Dundridge had found her enthusiasm extraordinarily refreshing. Moreover she exuded confidence, a supreme self-confidence which was contagious and which exerted an enormous fascination over him. In spite of her lack of symmetry, of beauty, in spite of the manifest discrepancy between her physique and that of the ideal woman of his imagination, he had to admit that she held charms for him. After lunch she had shown him over the house and garden and Dundridge had followed her from room to room with a quite inexplicable sense of weak-kneed excitement. Once when he had stumbled in the rockery Lady Maud had taken his arm and Dundridge had felt limp with pleasure. Again when he had squeezed past her in the doorway of the bathroom he had been conscious of a delicious passivity. By the time he left the house he felt quite childishly happy. He was appreciated. It made all the difference.

He got back to the Handyman Arms to find Hoskins waiting for him in the lounge.

'Just thought I'd drop in to see how you were getting on.'

'Fine. Fine. Just fine,' said Dundridge.

'Got on all right with Leakham?'

The warm glow in Dundridge cooled. 'I can't say I like his attitude,' he said. 'He seems determined to go ahead with the Gorge route. He has evidently developed a quite irrational hatred for Lady Maud. I must say I find his attitude inexplicable. She seems a perfectly charming woman to me.'

Hoskins stared at him incredulously. 'She does?'

'Delightful,' said Dundridge, the warm glow returning gently.

'Delightful?'

'Charming,' said Dundridge dreamily.

'Good God,' said Hoskins unable to contain his astonishment any longer. The notion that anyone could find Lady Maud charming and delightful was quite beyond him. He looked at Dundridge with a new interest. 'She's a bit large, don't you think?' he suggested.

'Comely,' said Dundridge benevolently. 'Just comely.'

Hoskins shuddered and changed the subject. 'About this tunnel,' he began. Dundridge looked at him in surprise.

'How did you hear about that?'

'News travels fast in these parts.'

'It must,' said Dundridge, 'I only mentioned it this morning.'

'You're not seriously proposing to recommend the construction of a tunnel under the Cleene Hills, are you?'

'I don't see why not,' said Dundridge, 'it seems a sensible compromise.'

'A bloody expensive one,' said Hoskins, 'it would cost millions and take years to put through.'

'At least it would avoid another riot. I came up here to try to find a solution that would be acceptable to all parties. It seems to me that a tunnel would be a very sensible alternative. In any case the plan is still in the formative stage.'

'Yes, but ...' Hoskins began but Dundridge had risen and with an airy remark about the need for vision had gone up to his room. Hoskins went back to the Regional Planning Board in a pensive mood. He had been wrong about Dundridge. The man wasn't such a nincompoop after all. On the other hand he had found Lady Maud charming and delightful. 'Bloody pervert,' Hoskins muttered as he picked up the phone. Sir Giles wasn't going to like this.

Nor was Blott. He had had a relatively phone-free day in the kitchen garden. There had been Dundridge's call in the morning but for the most part he had been left in peace. At half past four he had heard Sir Giles call Hoskins and tell him about the tunnel. At half past five he was watering the tomatoes when Hoskins called back to say that Dundridge was serious about the tunnel.

'He can't be,' Sir Giles snarled. 'It's an outrageous idea. A gross waste of taxpayers' money.'

Blott shook his head. The tunnel sounded a very good idea to him.

'You try telling him that,' said Hoskins.

'What about Leakham?' Sir Giles asked. 'He's not going to buy it, is he?'

'I wouldn't like to say. Depends what sort of weight this fellow Dundridge carries in London. The Ministry may bring pressure to bear on Leakham.'

There was a silence while Sir Giles considered this. In the greenhouse Blott wrestled with the intricacies of the English language. Why should Lord Leakham buy the tunnel? How could Dundridge carry weight in London? And in any case why should Sir Giles dislike the idea of a tunnel? It was all very odd.

'I've got another bit of news for you,' Hoskins said finally. 'He's keen on your missus.'

There was a strangled sound from Sir Giles. 'He's what?' he shouted.

'He has taken a fancy to Maud,' Hoskins told him. 'He said he found her charming and delightful.'

'Charming and delightful?' said Sir Giles. 'Maud?'

'And comely.'

'Good God. No wonder she's looking like the cat that's swallowed the canary,' said Sir Giles.

'I just thought you ought to know,' said Hoskins. 'It might give us some sort of lever.'

'Kinky?'

'Could be,' said Hoskins.

'Meet me at the Club at nine,' said Sir Giles, suddenly making up his mind. 'This needs thinking about.' He rang off.

In the greenhouse Blott stared lividly into the geraniums. If Sir Giles had been surprised, Blott's reaction was stronger still. The sudden discovery that he was in love with Lady Maud had coloured his day. The thought of Dundridge sharing his feelings for her infuriated him. Sir Giles he discounted. It was quite clear that Lady Maud despised her husband and from what she had said Blott had gathered that there was another woman in London. Dundridge was another matter. Blott left the greenhouse, tidied up and went home.

Home for Blott was the Lodge. The architect of the arch had managed to combine monumentality with utility and at one time the Lodge had housed several families of estate workers in rather cramped and insanitary conditions. Blott had the place to himself and found it quite adequate. The arch had its little inconveniences; the windows were extremely small and hidden among the decorations on the exterior; there was only one door so that to get from one side of the arch to the other one had to climb the staircase to the top and then cross over, but Blott had made himself very comfortable in a large room that spanned the arch. Through a circular window on one side he could keep an eye on the Hall and through another he could inspect visitors crossing the bridge. He had converted one small room into a bathroom and another into a kitchen, while he stored apples in some of the others so that the whole place had a pleasant smell to it. And finally there was Blott's library filled with books that he had picked up on the market stalls in Worford or in the second-hand bookshop in Ferret Lane. There were no novels in Blott's library, no light reading, only books on English history. In its way it was a scholar's library born of an intense curiosity about the country of his adoption. If the secret of being an Englishman was to be found anywhere it was to be found, Blott thought, in the past. Through the long winter evenings he would sit in front of his fire absorbed in the romance of England. Certain figures loomed large in his imagination, Henry VIII, Drake, Cromwell, Edward I, and he intended to identify if not himself at least other people with the heroes and villains of history. Lady Maud, in spite of her marriage, he saw as the Virgin Queen, while Sir Giles seemed to have the less savoury aspects of Sir Robert Walpole.

But that was for winter. During the summer he was out and about. Twice a week he cycled over to Guildstead Carbonell to the Royal George and sat in the bar until it was time for bed, the bed in question belonging to Mrs Wynn who ran the pub and whose husband had obligingly left her a widow as a result of enemy action on D-Day. Mrs Wynn was the last of Blott's wartime customers and the affair had lingered on owing more to habit than to affection. Mrs Wynn found Blott useful, he dried glasses and carried bottles, and Blott found Mrs Wynn comfortable, undemanding and accommodating in the matter of beer. He had a weakness for Handyman Brown.

But now as he washed his neck – it was Friday night and Mrs Wynn was expecting him – he was conscious that he no longer felt the same way about her. Not that he had ever felt very much, but that little had been swept aside by his sudden surge of feeling for Maud. He was sensible enough not to entertain any expectations of being able to do anything about it. It just didn't seem right to go off to Mrs Wynn any more. In any case it was all most peculiar. He had always had a soft spot for Lady Maud but this was different and it occurred to him that he might be sickening for something. He stuck out his tongue and studied it in the bathroom mirror but it looked all right. It might be the weather. He had once heard someone say something about spring and young men's fancies but Blott wasn't a young man. He was fifty. Fifty and in love. Daft.

He went downstairs and got on his bicycle and cycled off across the bridge towards Guildstead Carbonell. He had just reached the crossroads when he heard a car coming up fast behind him. He got off the bike to let it go by. It was Sir Giles in the Bentley. 'Going to the Golf Club to see Hoskins,' he thought, and looked after the car suspiciously. 'He's up to something.' He got back on to his bike and freewheeled reluctantly down the hill towards the Royal George and Mrs Wynn. Perhaps he ought to tell Maud what he had heard. It didn't seem a good idea and in any case he wasn't going to let her know that Dundridge fancied her. 'He can sow his own row,' he said to himself and was pleased at his command of the idiom.

In the Worford Golf Club, Sir Giles and Hoskins discussed tactics.

'He's got to have a weakness,' said Sir Giles. 'Every man has his price.'

'Maud?' said Hoskins.

'Be your age,' said Sir Giles. 'She isn't going to fartarse around with some tinpot civil servant with that reversionary clause in the contract at stake. Besides, I don't believe it.'

'I distinctly heard him say he found her charming. And comely.'

'All right, so he likes fat women. What else does he like? Money?'

Hoskins shrugged. 'Hard to tell. You need time to find that out.'

'Time is what we haven't got. He's only got to start blabbing about that bleeding tunnel and the fat's in the fire. No, we've got to act fast.'

Hoskins looked at him suspiciously. 'What's all this "We" business?' he asked. 'It's your problem, not mine.'

Sir Giles gnawed a fingernail thoughtfully. 'How much?'

'Five thousand.'

'For what?'

'Whatever you decide.'

'Make it five per cent of the compensation. When it's paid.'

Hoskins did a quick calculation and made it twelve and half thousand. 'Cash on the nail,' he said.

'You're a hard man, Hoskins, a hard man,' Sir Giles said sorrowfully.

'Anyway what do you want me to do? Sound him out?'

Sir Giles shook his head. His little eyes glittered. 'Kinky,' he said. 'Kinky. What made you say that?'

'I don't know. Just wondered,' said Hoskins.

'Boys, do you think?'

'Difficult to know,' said Hoskins. 'These things take time to find out.'

'Drink, drugs, boys, women, money. There's got to be some damned thing he's itching for.'

'Of course, we *could* frame him,' said Hoskins. 'It's been done before.'

Sir Giles nodded. 'The unsolicited gift. The anonymous donor. It's been done before all right. But it's too risky. What if he goes to the police?'

'Nothing ventured nothing gained,' said Hoskins. 'In any case there would be no indication where it came from. My bet is he'd take the bait.'

'If he didn't we would have lost him. No, it's got to be something foolproof.'

They sat in silence and considered a suitably compromising future for Dundridge.

'Ambitious would you say?' Sir Giles asked finally. Hoskins nodded.

'Very.'

'Know any queers?'

'In Worford? You've got to be joking,' said Hoskins.

'Anywhere.'

Hoskins shook his head. 'If you're thinking what I'm thinking ...'

'I am.'

'Photos?'

'Photos?' Sir Giles agreed. 'Nice compromising photos.'

Hoskins gave the matter some thought. 'There's Bessie Williams,' he said. 'Used to be a model, if you know what I mean. Married a photographer in Bridgeminster. She'd do it if the money was right.' He smiled reminiscently. 'I can have a word with her.'

'You do that,' said Sir Giles. 'I'll pay up to five hundred for a decent set of photos.'

'Leave it to me,' Hoskins told him. 'Now then, about the cash.'

By the time Sir Giles left the Golf Club the matter was fixed. He drove home in a haze of whisky. 'The stick first and then the carrot,' he muttered. Tomorrow he would go to London and visit Mrs Forthby. It was just as well to be out of the way when things happened.

CHAPTER ELEVEN

Dundridge spent the following morning at the regional Planning Board with Hoskins poring over maps and discussing the tunnel. He was rather surprised to find that Hoskins had undergone a change of heart about the project and seemed to favour it. 'It's a brilliant idea. Pity we didn't think of it before. Would have saved no end of trouble,' he said, and while Dundridge was flattered he wasn't so sure. He had begun to have doubts about the feasibility of a tunnel. The Ministry wouldn't exactly like the cost, the delay would be considerable and there was still Lord Leakham to be persuaded. 'You don't think we could find an alternative route,' he asked but Hoskins shook his head.

'It's either the Cleene Gorge or Ottertown or your tunnel.' Dundridge, studying the maps, had to concede that there wasn't any other route. The Cleene Hills stretched unbroken save for the Gorge from Worford to Ottertown.

'Ridiculous fuss people make about a bit of forest,' Dundridge complained. 'Just trees. What's so special about trees?'

They had lunch at a restaurant in River Street. At the next table a couple in their thirties seemed to find Dundridge quite fascinating and more than once Dundridge looked up to find the woman looking at him with a quiet smile. She was rather attractive, with almond eyes.

In the afternoon Hoskins took him on a tour of the proposed route through Ottertown. They drove over and inspected the council houses and returned through Guildstead Carbonell, Hoskins stopping the car every now and again and insisting that they climb to the top of some hill to get a better view of the proposed route. By the time they got back to Worford Dundridge was exhausted. He was also rather drunk. They had stopped at several pubs along the way and, thanks to Hoskins' insistence that pints were for men and that only boys drank halves – he put rather a nasty inflection on boys – Dundridge had consumed rather more Handyman Triple XXX than he was used to.

'We're having a little celebration party at the Golf Club tonight,' Hoskins said as they drove through the town gate. 'If you'd care to come over . . .'

'I think I'll get an early night,' said Dundridge.

'Pity,' Hoskins said. 'You'd meet a number of influential local people. Doesn't do to give the locals the idea you're hoity-toity.'

'Oh all right,' said Dundridge grudgingly. 'I'll have a bath and something to eat and see how I feel.'

'See you later, old boy,' said Hoskins as Dundridge got out of the car and went up to his room in the Handyman Arms. A bath and a meal and he'd probably feel all right. He fetched a towel and went down the passage to the bathroom. When he returned having immersed himself briefly in a lukewarm bath – the geyser still refused to operate at all efficiently – he was feeling better. He had dinner and decided that Hoskins was probably right. It might be useful to meet some of the more influential local people. Dundridge went out to his car and drove over to the Golf Club.

'Delighted you could make it,' said Hoskins when Dundridge made his way through the crush to him. 'What's your poison?'

Dundridge said he'd have a gin and tonic. He'd had enough beer for one day. Around him large men shouted about doglegs on the third and water hazards on the fifth. Dundridge felt out of it. Hoskins brought him his drink and introduced him to a Mr Snell. 'Glad to meet you, squire,' said Mr Snell heartily from behind a large moustache. 'What's your handicap?' Suppressing his immediate reaction to tell him to mind his own damned business, Dundridge said that as far as he knew he didn't have one. 'A Beginner, eh? Well, never mind. Give it time. We've all got to start somewhere.' He drifted away and Dundridge wandered in the opposite direction. Looking round the room at the veined faces of men and hennaed hair of the women Dundridge cursed himself for coming. If this was Hoskins' idea of local influence he could keep it. Presently he went out on to the terrace and stared resentfully down the eighteenth. He'd finish his drink and then go home. He drained his glass and was about to go inside when a voice at his elbow said, 'If you're going to the bar, you could get me another one.' It was a soft seductive voice. Dundridge turned and looked into a pair of almond eyes. Dundridge changed his mind about leaving. He went through to the bar and got two more drinks.

'These affairs are such a bore,' said the girl. 'Are you a great golfer?'

Dundridge said he wasn't a golfer at all.

'Nor am I. Such a boring game.' She sat down and crossed her legs. They were really very nice legs. 'And anyway I don't like sporty types. I prefer intellectuals.' She smiled at Dundridge. 'My name is Sally Boles. What's yours?'

'Dundridge,' said Dundridge and sat down where he could see more of her legs. Ten minutes later he got another two drinks. Twenty minutes later two more. He was enjoying himself at last.

Miss Boles, he learnt, was visiting her uncle. She came from London too. She worked for a firm of beauty consultants. Dundridge said he could well believe it. She found the country so boring. Dundridge said he did too. He waxed lyrical about the joys of living in London and all the time Miss Boles' almond eyes smiled seductively at him and her legs crossed and recrossed in the gathering dusk. When Dundridge suggested another drink Miss Boles insisted on getting it.

'It's my turn,' she said, 'and besides I want to powder my nose.' She left Dundridge sitting alone on the terrace in a happy stupor. When she returned with the drinks she was looking thoughtful.

'My uncle's gone without me,' she said, 'I suppose he thought I had gone home already. Would it be too much for you to give me a lift?'

'Of course not. I'd be delighted,' said Dundridge and sipped his drink. It tasted extraordinarily bitter.

'I'm so sorry, I got Campari,' Miss Boles said by way of explanation. Dundridge said it was quite all right. He finished his drink and they wandered off the terrace towards the car park. 'It's been such a lovely evening,' Miss Boles said as she climbed into Dundridge's car. 'You must look me up in London.'

'I'd like to,' said Dundridge. 'I'd like to see a lot more of you.'

'That's a promise,' said Miss Boles.

'You really mean that?'

'Call me Sally,' said Miss Boles and leant against him.

'Oh Sally . . .' Dundridge began, and suddenly felt quite extraordinarily tired, '. . . I do want to see so much more of you.'

'You will, my pet, you will,' said Miss Boles and took the car keys out of his inert fingers. Dundridge had passed out.

In London Sir Giles lay back supine on the bed while Mrs Forthby tightened the straps. Occasionally he struggled briefly for the look of the thing and whimpered hoarsely but Mrs Forthby was, at least superficially, implacable. The scenario of Sir Giles' fantasy called for a brutal implacability and Mrs Forthby did her best. She wasn't very good, being a kindhearted soul and not given to tying people up and whipping them, and as a matter of fact she disapproved of corporal punishment on principle. It was largely because she was so progressive that she was prepared to indulge Sir Giles in the first place. 'If it gives the poor man pleasure who am I to say him nay,' she told herself. Cetainly she had to say nay a great many times to Sir Giles in the throes of his ritual. But if Mrs Forthby wasn't naturally brutal, with the lights down low it was possible to imagine that she was and she had the merit of being strong and wearing her constume – there were several – most convincingly. Tonight she was Cat Woman, Miss Dracula, the Cruel Mistress Experimenting On Her Helpless Victim.

'No, no,' whimpered Sir Giles.

'Yes, yes,' insisted Mrs Forthby.

'No, no.'

'Yes, Yes.'

Mrs Forthby's fingers forced his mouth open and inserted the gag. 'No ...' it was too late. Mrs Forthby inflated the gag and smiled maliciously down at him. Her breasts loomed above him, heavy with menace. Her gloved hands ...

Mrs Forthby went into the kitchen and made a pot of tea. While she waited for the kettle to boil she nibbled a digestive biscuit thoughtfully. There were times when she tired of Sir Giles' desultory attachment and longed for a more permanent arrangement. She would have to speak to him about it. She warmed the teapot, put in two teabags and then a third for the pot and poured the boiling water in. After all she was getting on and she rather fancied the idea of being Lady Lynchwood. She looked round the kitchen. Now where had she put the lid of the teapot?

On the bed Sir Giles struggled with his bonds and was still. He lay back happily exhausted and waited for his cruel mistress. He had to wait a long time. In between spasms of excitement his mind went back to Dundridge. He hoped Hoskins hadn't made a bloody mess of things. That was the trouble with subordinates, you couldn't trust them. Sir Giles preferred to attend to matters himself but he had too much to lose to be closely involved in the actual details of this particular operation. First the stick and then the carrot. He wondered how much the carrot would have to be. Two, three, four thousand pounds? Expensive. Add Hoskins' five thousand. Still, it was worth it. A profit of £150,000 was worth it. So was the prospect of Maud's fury when she realized that the motorway was coming through the Gorge. Teach the stupid bitch. But where was Mrs Forthby? Why didn't she come back?

Mrs Forthby finished her cup of tea and poured another. She was getting rather hot in her tight costume. Perhaps she would go and have a bath. She got up and went into the bathroom and turned on the tap before remembering that there was something she still had to do. 'Silly old me: talk about forgetful,' she said to herself and picked up the thin cane. The Cruel Mistress, Miss Dracula, went through to the bedroom and closed the door.

In the library in the Lodge Blott sat reading Sir Arthur Bryant, but his mind wasn't on the Age of Elegance. It kept slipping away to Maud, Mrs Wynn, Dundridge, Sir Giles. Besides, he didn't much care for the Prince Regent. Nasty piece of goods in Blott's opinion. But then Blott had no time for any of the Georges. His sympathies were all with the Jacobites. The lost cause and Bonnie Prince Charlie. In his present mood of romantic devotion he felt a longing to kneel before Lady Maud and confess his love. It was an absurd notion. She would be furious with him. Worse still, she might laugh. The thought of her contemptuous laughter made him put the book down and go downstairs. It was a lovely evening. The sun had set over the hills to the west but the sky was still bright. Blott felt like a beer. He wasn't going over to Guildstead Carbonell for one. Mrs Wynn would expect him to spend the night and Blott didn't feel like another night with her. He had spent the previous evening wrestling with his conscience and trying to make up his mind to tell her it was all over between them. In the end his sense of realism had prevailed. Lady Maud wasn't for the likes of Blott. He would just have to dream about her. He had done so while making love to Mrs Wynn, who had been amazed at his renewed fervour. 'Just like the old days,' she had said wistfully as Blott got dressed to cycle back to the Lodge. No, he definitely didn't feel like another night at the Royal George. He would go for a walk. There were some rabbits over by the pinetum. Blott fetched his shotgun and set off across the Park. Beside him the river murmured gently and there was a smell of summer in the air. A blackbird called from a bush. Blott ignored his surroundings. He was dreaming of changed circumstances, of Lady Maud in peril, an act of heroism on his part that would reveal his true feelings for her and bring them together in love and happiness. By the time he reached the pinetum it was too dark to see any rabbits. But Blott wasn't interested in rabbits any more. A light had come on in Lady Maud's bedroom. Blott crept across the lawn and stood looking up at it until it went out. Then he walked home and went to bed.

CHAPTER TWELVE

Dundridge woke in a lay-by on the London road. He had a splitting headache, he was extremely cold and the gear lever was sticking into his ribs. He sat up, untangled his legs from under the steering wheel and wondered where the hell he was, how he had got there and what the devil had happened. He had an extremely clear memory of the party at the Golf Club. He could remember talking to Miss Boles on the terrace. He could even recall walking back to his car with her. After that nothing.

He got out of the car to try to get the circulation moving in his legs and discovered that his trousers were undone. He did them up hurriedly and reached up automatically to tighten the knot of his tie to hide his embarrassment only to find that he wasn't wearing a tie. He felt his open shirt collar and the vest underneath. It was on back to front. He pulled the vest out a bit and looked down at the label. St Michael Combed Cotton it said. It was definitely on back to front. Now he came to think of it, his Y-fronts felt peculiar too. He took a step forward and tripped over a shoelace. His shoes were untied. Dundridge staggered against the car, seriously alarmed. He was in the middle of nowhere at . . . He looked at his watch. At six a.m. with his shoes untied, his vest and pants on back to front, and his trousers undone, and all he could remember was getting into the car with a girl with almond eyes and lovely legs.

And suddenly Dundridge had a horrid picture of the night's events. Perhaps he had raped the girl. A sudden brainstorm. That would explain the headache. The years of self-indulgence with his composite woman had come home to roost. He had gone mad and raped Miss Boles, possibly killed her. He looked down at his hands. At least there wasn't any blood on them. He could have strangled her. There was always that possibility. There were any number of awful possibilities. Dundridge bent over painfully and did up his shoes and then, having looked in the ditch to make sure that there was no body there, he got back into the car and wondered what to do. There was obviously no point in sitting in the lay-by. Dundridge started the car and drove on until he came to a signpost which told him he was going towards London. He turned the car round and drove back to Worford, parked in the yard of the Handyman Arms and went quietly up to his room. He was in bed when the girl brought him tea.

'What time is it?' he asked sleepily. The girl looked at him with a nasty smile.

'You ought to know,' she said, 'you've only just come in. I saw you sneaking up the stairs. Been having a night on the tiles, have you?'

She put the tray down and went out, leaving Dundridge cursing himself for a fool. He drank some tea and felt worse. There was no point in doing anything until he felt better. He turned on his side and went to sleep. When he awoke it was midday. He washed and shaved, studying his face in the mirror for some sign of the sexual mania he suspected. The face that stared back at him was a perfectly ordinary face but Dundridge was not reassured. Murderers tended to have perfectly ordinary faces. Perhaps he had simply had a blackout or amnesia. But that wouldn't explain his vest being on back to front, nor his Y-fronts. At some time during the night he had undressed. Worse still, he had dressed in such a hurry that he hadn't noticed what he was doing. That suggested panic or at least an extraordinary urgency. He went downstairs and had lunch. After lunch he would get hold of a telephone directory and look up Boles. Of course her uncle might not be called Boles but it was worth a try. If that didn't work he would try Hoskins or the Golf Club. On second thoughts, that might not be such a good idea. There was no point in drawing attention to the fact that he had taken Miss Boles home. Or hadn't.

In the event there was no need to look in the telephone directory. As he passed the hotel desk, the clerk handed him a large envelope. It was addressed to Mr Dundridge and marked Private and Confidential. Dundridge took it up to his room before opening it and was extremely thankful that he hadn't opened it in the foyer. Dundridge knew now how he had spent the night.

He dropped the photographs on to the bed and slumped into a chair. A moment later he was up and locking the door. Then he turned back and stared at the pictures. They were 10 by 8 glossies and quite revolting. Taken with a flash, they were extremely clear and portrayed Dundridge with an unmistakable clarity, naked and all too evidently unashamed, engaged in a series of monstrous activities beyond his wildest imaginings with Miss Boles. At least he supposed it was Miss Boles. The fact that she seemed ... Not seemed, *was* wearing a mask, a sort of hood, made identification impossible. He thumbed through the pictures and came to the hooded man. Dundridge hurriedly put them back in the envelope and sat sweating on the edge of the bed. He'd been framed. The word seemed wholly inappropriate. Nothing on God's earth would get him to frame these pictures. Someone was trying to blackmail him.

Trying? They had bloody well succeeded, but Dundridge had no money. He couldn't pay anything. Dundridge opened the envelope again and stared at the evidence of his depravity. Miss Boles? Miss Boles? It obviously wasn't her real name. Sally Boles. He had heard that name before somewhere. Of course, Sally Bowles in *I am a Camera*. Dundridge didn't need telling. He'd been had in many more ways than one. In many more ways if the photos were anything to go by.

He was just wondering what to do next when the telephone rang. Dundridge grabbed it. 'Yes,' he said.

'Mr Dundridge?' said a woman's voice.

'Speaking,' said Dundridge shakily.

'I hope you like the proofs.'

'Proofs, you bitch?' Dundridge snarled.

'Call me Sally,' said the voice. 'There's no need to be formal with me now.'

'What do you want?'

'A thousand pounds . . . to be going on with.'

'A thousand pounds? I haven't got a thousand pounds.'

'Then you had better get it, hadn't you sweetie?'

'I'll tell you what I'm going to get,' shouted Dundridge, 'I'm going to get the police.'

'You do that,' said a man's voice roughly, 'and you'll end up with your face cut to ribbons. You're not playing with small fry, mate. We're bigtime, understand.'

Dundridge understood all too well. The woman's voice came back on the line. 'If you do go to the police remember we've had one or two customers there. We'll know. You just start looking for your thousand pounds.'

'I can't—'

'Don't call us. We'll call you,' said Miss Boles, and put the phone down. Dundridge replaced his receiver more slowly. Then he leant forward and held his head in his hands.

Sir Giles returned from London in excellent spirits. Mrs Forthby had excelled herself and he was still tingling with satisfaction. Best of all had been Hoskins' cryptic message over the phone. 'The fish is hooked,' he had said. All that was required now was to provide a net in which Mr Dundridge could flounder. Sir Giles parked his car and went up to his constituency office and sent for Hoskins.

'Here they are. As nice a set of prints as you could wish for,' Hoskins said, laying the photographs out on the desk.

Sir Giles studied them with an appreciative eye. 'Very nice,' he said finally. 'Very nice indeed. And what does lover-boy have to say for himself now?'

'They've asked him for a thousand pounds. He says he hasn't got it.'

'He'll have it, never fear,' said Sir Giles. 'He'll have his thousand pounds and we'll have him. There won't be any more talk about tunnels in future. From now on it's going to be Ottertown.'

'Ottertown?' said Hoskins, thoroughly puzzled. 'But I thought you wanted it through the Gorge. I thought—'

'The trouble with you, Hoskins,' said Sir Giles, putting the photographs back into the envelope and the envelope into his briefcase, 'is that you can't see further than the end of your nose. You don't really think I want to lose my lovely house and my beautiful wife, do you? You don't think I haven't got the interests of my constituents like General Burnett and Mr Bullett-Bloody-Finch at heart, do you? Of course I have. I'm honest Sir Giles the poor man's friend,' and leaving Hoskins completely confused by this strange change of tack, he went downstairs.

There was nothing like throwing people off the scent. Killing two birds with one stone, he thought as he got into the Bentley. The decision to go through Ottertown would kill Puckerington for sure. Sir Giles looked forward to his demise with relish. Puckerington was no friend of his. Snobby bastard. Well, he was bird number one. Then the bye-election in Ottertown and they would have to change the route to the Gorge and Handyman Hall would go. Bird number two. By that time he would be able to claim even more compensation and no one, least of all Maud, could say he hadn't done his damnedest. There was only one snag. That old fool Leakham might still insist on the Gorge route. It was hardly a snag. Maud would create a bit more. He might lose his seat in Parliament but he would be £150,000 richer and Mrs Forthby was waiting. Swings or roundabouts, Sir Giles couldn't lose. The main thing was to see that the tunnel scheme was scotched. Sir Giles parked outside the Handyman Arms, went inside and sent a message up to Dundridge's room to say that Sir Giles Lynchwood was looking forward to his company in the lounge.

Dundridge went downstairs gloomily. The last person he wanted to see was the local MP. He could hardly consult him about blackmail. Sir Giles greeted him with a heartiness Dundridge no longer felt that his position warranted. 'My dear fellow, I'm delighted to see you,' he said shaking Dundridge's limp hand vigorously. 'Been meaning to look you up and have a chat about this motorway nonsense. Had to go to London unfortunately. Looking after you all right here? It's one of our houses, you know. Any complaints, just let me know and I'll see to it. We'll have tea in the private lounge.' He led the way up some steps into a small lounge with a TV set in the corner. Sir Giles plumped into a chair and took out a cigar. 'Smoke?'

Dundridge shook his head.

'Very wise of you. Still they do say cigars don't do one any harm and a fellow's entitled to one or two little vices, eh, what?' said Sir Giles and pierced the end of the cigar with a silver cutter. Dundridge winced. The cigar reminded him of something that had figured rather too largely in his activities with Miss Boles, and as for vices ...

'Now then, about this business of the motorway,' said Sir Giles, 'I think it's as well to put our cards on the table. I'm a man who doesn't beat about the bush I can tell you. Call a spade a bloody shovel. I don't let the grass grow under my feet. Wouldn't be where I was if I did.' He paused briefly to allow Dundridge to savour this wealth of metaphors and the bluff dishonesty of his approach. 'And I don't mind telling you that I don't like this idea of your building a motorway through my damned land one little bit.'

'It was hardly my idea,' said Dundridge.

'Not yours personally,' said Sir Giles, 'but you fellows at the Ministry have made up your mind to slap the bloody thing smack through the Gorge. Don't tell me you haven't.'

'Well, as a matter of fact ...' Dundridge began.

'There you are. What did I tell you? Told you so. Can't pull the wool over my eyes.'

'As a matter of fact I'm against the Gorge route,' Dundridge said when he got the opportunity. Sir Giles looked at him dubiously.

'You are?' he said. 'Damned glad to hear it. I suppose you favour Ottertown. Can't say I blame you. Best route by far.'

'No,' said Dundridge. 'Not through Ottertown. A tunnel under the Cleene Hills ...'

Sir Giles feigned astonishment. 'Now wait a minute,' he said, 'the Cleene Forest is an area of designated public beauty. You can't start mucking around with that.' His accent, as variable as a weathercock, had veered round to Huddersfield.

'There's no question of mucking about ...' Dundridge began but Sir Giles was leaning across the table towards him with a very nasty look on his face.

'You can say that again,' he said poking his forefinger into Dundridge's shirt front. 'Now you just listen to me, young man. You can forget all about tunnels and suchlike. I want a quick decision one way or t'other. I don't like to be kept hanging about while lads like you dither about talking a lot of airy twaddle about tunnels. That's all right for my missus, she being a gullible woman, but it won't wash with me. I want a straight answer. Yes or No. Yes to Ottertown and No to the Gorge.' He sat back and puffed his cigar.

'In that case,' said Dundridge stiffly, 'you had better have a word with Lord Leakham. He's the one who makes the final decision.'

'Leakham? Leakham? Makes the final decision?' said Sir Giles. 'Don't try to have me on, lad. The Minister didn't send you up so that that dry old stick could make decisions. He sent you up to tell him what to say. You can't fool me. I know an expert when I see one. He'll do what you tell him.'

Dundridge felt better. This was the recognition he had been waiting for. 'Well I suppose I do have some influence,' he conceded.

Sir Giles beamed. 'What did I say? Top men don't grow on trees and I've got a nose for talent. Well, you won't find me ungenerous. You pop round and see me when you've had your little chat with Lord Leakham. I'll see you right.'

Dundridge goggled at him. 'You don't mean—'

'Name your own charity,' said Sir Giles with a prodigious wink. 'Mind you, I always say "Charity begins at home". Eh? I'm not a mean man. I pays for what I gets.' He drew on his cigar and watched Dundridge through a cloud of smoke. This was the moment of truth. Dundridge swallowed nervously.

'That's very kind of you ...' he began.

'Say no more,' said Sir Giles. 'Say no more. Any time you want me I'll be in my constituency office or out at the Hall. Best time to catch me is in the morning at the office.'

'But what am I going to say to Lord Leakham?' Dundridge said. 'He's adamant about the Gorge route.'

'You tell him from me that my good lady wife intends to take him to the cleaners about that unlawful arrest unless he decides for Ottertown. You tell him that.'

'I don't think Lord Leakham would appreciate that very much,' said Dundridge nervously. He didn't much like the idea of uttering threats against the old judge.

'You'll tell him I'll sue him for every brass farthing he's got. And I've got witnesses, remember. Influential witnesses who'll stand up in court and swear that he was drunk and disorderly at that Inquiry, and abusive too. You tell him he won't have a reputation and he won't have a penny by the time we've finished with him. I'll see to that.'

'I doubt if he'll like it,' said Dundridge, who certainly didn't.

'Don't suppose he will,' said Sir Giles, 'I'm not a man to run up against.'

Dundridge could see that. By the time Sir Giles left Dundridge had no doubts on that score at all. As Sir Giles drove away Dundridge went up to his room and looked at the photographs again. Spurred on by their obscenity he took an aspirin and went slowly round to the Cottage Hospital. He'd make Lord Leakham change his mind about the Gorge. Sir Giles had said he would pay for what he got and Dundridge intended to see that he got something to pay for. He didn't have any choice any longer. It was either that or ruin.

On the way back to Handyman Hall, Sir Giles stopped and unlocked his briefcase and took out the photographs. They were really very interesting. Mrs Williams was an imaginative woman. No doubt about it. And attractive. Most attractive. He might look her up one of these days. He put the photographs away and drove back to the Hall.

CHAPTER THIRTEEN

At the Cottage Hospital Dundridge had some difficulty in finding Lord Leakham. He wasn't in his room. 'It's very naughty of him to wander about like this,' said the Matron. 'You'll probably find him in the Abbey. He's taken to going over there when he shouldn't. Says he likes looking at the tombstones. Morbid, I call it.'

'You don't think his mind has been affected, do you?' Dundridge asked hopefully.

'Not so's you'd notice. All lords are potty in my experience,' the Matron told him.

In the end Dundridge found him in the garden discussing the merits of the cat o'nine tails with a retired vet who had the good fortune to be deaf.

'Well what do you want now?' Lord Leakham asked irritably when Dundridge interrupted.

'Just a word with you,' said Dundridge.

'Well, what is it?' said Lord Leakham.

'It's about the motorway,' Dundridge explained.

'What about it? I'm re-opening the Inquiry on Monday. Can't it wait till then?'

'I'm afraid not,' said Dundridge. 'The thing is that as a result of an in-depth on-the-spot investigative study of the socio-environmental and geognostic ancillary factors ...'

'Good God,' said Lord Leakham, 'I thought you said you wanted a word ...'

'It is our considered conclusion,' continued Dundridge, manfully devising a jargon to suit the occasion, 'that given the—'

'Which is it to be? Ottertown or the Cleene Gorge? Spit it out, man.'

'Ottertown,' said Dundridge.

'Over my dead body,' said Lord Leakham.

'I trust not,' said Dundridge, disguising his true feelings. 'There's just one other thing I think you ought to know. As you are probably aware the Government is most anxious to avoid any further adverse publicity about the motorway . . .'

'You can't expect to demolish seventy-five brand-new council houses without attracting adverse publicity,' Lord Leakham pointed out.

'And,' continued Dundridge, 'the civil action for damages which Lady Lynchwood intends to institute against you is bound—'

'Against *me*?' shouted the Judge. 'She intends to—'

'For unlawful arrest,' said Dundridge.

'That's a police matter. If she has any complaints let her sue those responsible. In any case no sane judge would find for her.'

'I understand she intends to call some rather eminent people as witnesses,' said Dundridge. 'Their testimony will be that you were drunk.'

Lord Leakham began to swell.

'And personally abusive,' said Dundridge gritting his teeth. 'And disorderly. In fact that you were not in a fit state . . .'

'WHAT?' yelled the Judge, with a violence that sent several elderly patients scurrying for cover and a number of pigeons fluttering off the hospital roof.

'In short,' said Dundridge as the echo died away across the Abbey Close, 'she intends to impugn your reputation. Naturally the Minister has to take all these things into account, you do see that?'

But it was doubtful if Lord Leakham could see anything. He had slumped on to a bench and was staring lividly at his bedroom slippers.

'Naturally too,' continued Dundridge, pursuing his advantage, 'there is a fairly widespread feeling that you might be biased against her in the matter of the Gorge.'

'Biased?' Lord Leakham snuffled. 'The Gorge is the logical route.'

'On the grounds of the civil action she intends to take. Now if you were to decide on Ottertown . . .' Dundridge left the consequences hanging in the air.

'You think she might reconsider her decision?'

'I feel sure she would,' said Dundridge. 'In fact I'm positive she would.'

Dundridge walked back to the Handyman Arms rather pleased with his performance. Desperation had lent him a fluency he had never known before. In the morning he would go and see Sir Giles about a thousand pounds. He had an early dinner and went up to his room, locked the door and examined the photographs again. Then he turned out the light and considered several things he hadn't done to Miss Sally Boles but which on reflection he wished he had. Strangled the bitch for one thing.

At Handyman Hall Sir Giles and Lady Maud dined alone. Their

conversation seldom sparkled and was usually limited to an exchange of acrimonious opinions but for once they were both in a good mood at the same time. Dundridge was the cause of their good humour.

'Such a sensible young man,' Lady Maud said helping herself to asparagus. 'I'm sure that tunnel is the right answer.'

Sir Giles rather doubted it. 'My bet is he'll go for Ottertown,' he said.

Lady Maud said she hoped not. 'It seems such a shame to turn those poor people out of their homes. I'm sure they would feel just as strongly as I do about the Hall.'

'They build them new houses,' said Sir Giles. 'It's not as if they turn them out into the street. Anyway, people who live on council estates deserve what they get. Sponging off public money.'

Lady Maud said some people couldn't help being poor. They were just built that way like Blott. 'Dear Blott,' she said. 'You know he did such a strange thing this morning, he brought me a present, a little figure he had carved out of wood.'

But Sir Giles wasn't listening. He was still thinking about people who lived in council houses. 'What the man in the street doesn't seem able to get into his thick head is that the world doesn't owe him a living.'

'I thought it was rather sweet of him,' said Lady Maud.

Sir Giles helped himself to cheese soufflé. 'What people don't understand is that we're just animals,' he said. 'The world is a bloody jungle. It's dog eat dog in this life and no mistake.'

'Dog?' said Lady Maud, roused from her reverie by the word. 'That reminds me. I suppose I'll have to send all those Alsatians back now. Just when I was getting fond of them. You're quite sure Mr Dundridge is going to advise Ottertown?'

'Positive,' said Sir Giles, 'I'd stake my life on it.'

'Really,' said Lady Maud wistfully, 'I don't see how you can be so certain. Have you spoken to him?'

Sir Giles hesitated. 'I have it on the best authority,' he said.

'Hoskins,' said Lady Maud, 'that horrid man. I wouldn't trust him any further than I could throw him. He'd say anything.'

'He also says that this fellow Dundridge has taken a fancy to you,' Sir Giles said. 'It seems you had a considerable effect on him.'

Lady Maud considered the remark and found it intriguing. 'I'm sure that can't be true. Hoskins is making things up.'

'It might explain why he is in favour of the Ottertown route,' Sir Giles said. 'You bowled him over with your charm.'

'Very funny,' said Lady Maud.

But afterwards as she washed up in the kitchen she found herself thinking about Dundridge, if not fondly, at least with a renewed interest. There was something rather appealing about the little man, a vulnerability that she found preferable to Sir Giles' disgusting self-sufficiency ... and Dundridge had taken a fancy to her. It was useful to know these things. She would have to cultivate him. She smiled to herself. If Sir Giles could have his little affairs in London, there was no reason why she shouldn't avail herself of his absence for her own purposes. But above all there was an anonymity about Dundridge that appealed to her. 'He'll do,' she said to herself and dried her hands.

Next morning Dundridge went round to Sir Giles' constituency office at eleven. 'I've had a word with Lord Leakham and I think he'll be amenable,' he said.

'Splendid, my dear fellow, splendid. Delighted to hear it. I knew you could do it. A great weight off my mind, I can tell you. Now then is there anything I can do for you?' Sir Giles leant back in his chair expansively. 'After all, one good turn deserves another.'

Dundridge braced himself for the request. 'As a matter of fact, there is,' he said, and hesitated before going on.

'I'll tell you what I'll do,' said Sir Giles coming to his rescue. 'I don't know if you're a betting man but I am. I'll bet you a thousand pounds to a penny that old Leakham says the motorway has to go through Ottertown. How about that? Couldn't ask for anything fairer, eh?'

'A thousand pounds to a penny?' said Dundridge, hardly able to believe his ears.

'That's right. A thousand pounds to a penny. Take it or leave it.'

'I'll take it,' said Dundridge.

'Good man. I thought you would,' said Sir Giles, 'and just to show my good faith I'll put the stake up now.' He reached down to a drawer in the desk and took out an envelope. 'You can count it at your leisure.' He put the envelope on the desk. 'No need for a receipt. Just don't spend it until Leakham gives his decision.'

'Of course not,' said Dundridge. He put the envelope in his pocket.

'Nice meeting you,' said Sir Giles. Dundridge went out and down the stairs. He had accepted a bare-faced bribe. It was the first time in his life. Behind him Sir Giles switched off the tape recorder. It was just as well to have a receipt. Once the Inquiry was over he would burn the tape but in the meantime better safe than sorry.

CHAPTER FOURTEEN

Lord Leakham's announcement that he was recommending the Ottertown route provoked mixed reactions. In Worford there was open rejoicing and the Handyman pubs dispensed free beer. In Ottertown the Member of Parliament, Francis Puckerington, was inundated with telephone calls and protest letters and suffered a relapse as a result. In London the Prime Minister, relieved that there hadn't been another riot in Worford, congratulated the Minister of the Environment on the adroit way his department had handled the matter, and the Minister congratulated Mr Rees on his choice of a troubleshooter. No one in the Ministry shared his enthusiasm.

'That bloody idiot Dundridge has dropped us in it this time,' said Mr Joynson. 'I knew it was a mistake to send him up there. The Ottertown route is going to cost an extra ten million.'

'In for a penny in for a pound,' said Rees. 'At least we've got rid of him.'

'Got rid of him? He'll be back tomorrow crowing about his success as a negotiator.'

'He won't you know,' Rees told him. 'He got us into this mess, he can damned well get us out. The Minister had approved his appointment as Controller Motorways Midlands.'

'Controller Motorways Midlands? I didn't know there was such a post.'

'There wasn't. It's been specially created for him. Don't ask me why. All I know is that Dundridge has found favour with one or two influential people in South Worfordshire. Wheels within wheels,' said Mr Rees.

In Worford Dundridge greeted the news of his appointment with consternation. He had spent an anxious weekend confined to his room at the Handyman Arms partly because he was afraid of missing the telephone call from Miss Boles and partly because he had no intention of leaving the money he had received from Sir Giles in his suitcase or of carrying it around on his person. But there had been no phone call. To add to his troubles, there was the knowledge that he had accepted a bribe. He tried to persuade himself that he had merely taken a bet on, but it was no use.

'I could get three years for this,' he said to himself, and seriously considered handing the money back. He was deterred by the photographs.

He couldn't imagine how many years he could get for doing what they suggested he had done.

By the time the Inquiry re-opened on Monday, Dundridge's nerves were frayed to breaking point. He had taken his seat inconspicuously at the back of the courtroom and had hardly listened to the evidence. The presence of a large number of policemen, brought in to ensure that there was no further outbreak of violence, had done nothing to reassure him. Dundridge had misconstrued their role and had finally left the courtroom before Lord Leakham announced his decision. He was standing in the hall downstairs when a burst of cheering indicated that the Inquiry was over.

Sir Giles and Lady Maud were the first to congratulate him. They issued from the courtroom and down the stairs followed by General Burnett and Mr and Mrs Bullet-Finch.

'Splendid news,' said Sir Giles. Lady Maud seized Dundridge's hand.

'I feel we owe you a great debt of gratitude,' she said staring into his face significantly.

'It was nothing,' murmured Dundridge modestly.

'Nonsense,' said Lady Maud, 'you have made me very happy. You must come and see us before you leave.'

Sir Giles had winked prodigiously – Dundridge had come to loathe that wink – and had whispered something about a bet being a bet and Hoskins had insisted on their going to have a drink together to celebrate. Dundridge couldn't see anything to celebrate about.

'You've got friends at court,' Hoskins explained.

'Friends at court?' said Dundridge. 'What on earth do you mean?'

'A little bird has told me that someone has put in a good word for you. You wait and see.'

Dundridge had waited in the hope (though that was hardly the right word) that Miss Boles would call but instead of a demand for a thousand pounds he had received a letter of appointment. 'Controller Motorways Midlands with responsibility for co-ordinating ... Good God!' he muttered. He made a number of frantic phone calls to the Ministry threatening to resign unless he was brought back to London, but the enthusiasm with which Mr Rees endorsed his decision was enough to make him retract it.

Even Hoskins, who might have been expected to resent Dundridge's appointment as his superior, seemed relieved. 'What did I tell you, old boy,' he said when Dundridge told him the news. 'Friends at court. Friends at court.'

'But I don't know anything about motorway construction. I'm an administrator not an engineer.'

'All you have to do is see that the contractors keep to schedule,' Hoskins explained. 'Nothing to it. You leave all the rest of it to me. Basically yours is a public-relations role.'

'But I'm responsible for coordinating construction work. It says so here,' Dundridge protested, waving his letter of appointment, '"and in particular problems relating to environmental factors and human ecology". I suppose that means dealing with the tenants of those council houses in Ottertown.'

'That sort of thing,' said Hoskins. 'I shouldn't worry about that too much. Cross your bridges when you come to them is my motto.'

'Oh well, I suppose I'll just have to get used to the idea.'

'I'll fix you up an office here. You'd better set about finding somewhere to live.'

Dundridge had spent two days looking at flats in Worford before settling on an apartment overlooking Worford Castle. It wasn't a prospect he found particularly pleasing, but the flat had the merit of being comparatively modern and was certainly better than some of the squalid rooms he had looked at elsewhere. And besides it had a telephone and was partly furnished. Dundridge placed particular emphasis upon the telephone. He didn't want Miss Boles to get the false idea that he wasn't prepared to pay a thousand pounds for the photographs and negatives. But as the days passed and there was still no demand from her he began to relax. Perhaps the whole thing had been some sort of filthy practical joke. He even asked Hoskins if he knew anything about the girl at the party but Hoskins said he couldn't remember much about the evening and hadn't known half the people who were there.

'My mind's a blank on the whole evening, old chap,' he said. 'Had a good time, though. I do remember that. Why? Are you thinking of looking her up again?'

'Just wondered who she was,' said Dundridge and went back to his office to draw up plans for the opening ceremony to mark the start of the construction of the motorway. It was going to be a grand affair, he had decided.

So had Lady Maud, though the affair she had in mind was of quite a different sort. She waited until Sir Giles said he was going to spend a fortnight in London before inviting Dundridge to dinner. She sent a formal invitation.

Dundridge hired a dinner-jacket and expected to find a number of other guests. He was extremely nervous and had fortified himself in advance with two stiff gins. In the event he need not have bothered. He arrived to find Lady Maud dressed, if not to kill, at least to seriously endanger anyone who came near her.

'I'm so glad you could come,' she said taking his arm almost as soon as he had entered the front door. 'I'm afraid my husband has had to go to London on business. I hope you don't mind having to put up with me.'

'Not at all,' said Dundridge, conscious once again of that weakness in his legs that Lady Maud's presence seemed to induce in him. They went into the drawing-room and Lady Maud mixed drinks. 'I did think of inviting General Burnett and the Bullett-Finches but the General does tend to monopolize the conversation and Ivy Bullett-Finch is a bit of a wet blanket.'

Dundridge sipped his drink and wondered what the hell she had put into it. It looked innocuous, but clearly wasn't. Lady Maud's dress, on the other hand, practised no such deception. A thing of silk designed to emphasize the curvature of the female form, it had evidently been created with someone more lissom in mind. It bulged where it should have hung and wheezed when it should have rustled. Above all it was so clearly breathtaking in its constriction that Dundridge found himself almost panting in empathy. Besides Lady Maud's voice had undergone a strange alteration. It was curiously husky.

'How do you like your new flat?' she asked, sitting down beside him with a squeak of pre-stressed silk.

'Flat?' said Dundridge momentarily unable to make the transition between adjective and noun. 'Oh flat. Yes. Very pleasant.'

'You must let me come up and see it some time,' said Lady Maud. 'Unless you feel I might be compromising you.' She sighed, and her great bosom heaved like an approaching breaker.

'Compromising?' said Dundridge, who couldn't imagine that he was likely to be compromised by being alone in his flat with her any more than he was already by those beastly photographs. 'I'd be delighted to have you.'

Lady Maud tittered coyly. 'I'm afraid you're going to miss the excitement of life in London,' she murmured. 'We must do what we can to see that you don't get bored.'

It seemed a remote prospect to Dundridge. He sat rigid on the sofa and tried to keep his eyes averted from the incomprehensible fascinations of her body.

'Let me get you another drink,' she breathed softly, and once again he was conscious of a feeling of being overcome. It was partly the drink, partly the waft of perfume, but it was mostly the strength of her self-assurance that held him fascinated. In spite of her size, in spite of her assertiveness, in spite of everything about her that conflicted with his idea of a beautiful woman, Lady Maud was wholly confident. And Dundridge, who wasn't (or at best only partially and whose completeness, depending on achievement and money, lay in the future) was intoxicated by her presence. If the past could confer such assurance there was more to be said for it than Dundridge had previously admitted. Dundridge sipped his drink and smiled at her. Lady Maud smiled back.

By the time they went in to dinner, Dundridge was incongruously gay. He opened the door for her; he held her arm; he pulled back her chair and nudged it forward against her thighs meaningfully; he opened the champagne with a nonchalance that suggested he seldom drank anything else and laughed debonairly as the cork tinkled among the glass lustres of the chandelier. And through the meal, oysters followed by cold duck, Dundridge no longer cared what the world might think of him. Lady Maud's appreciative smile, half yawn and half abyss, beckoned him on to be himself. And Dundridge was. For the first time in his life he lived up to his own expectations, up to and far beyond. The champagne cork flew a second time into the upper reaches of the room, the duck disappeared to be followed by strawberries and cream, and Dundridge lost the last vestiges of inhibition or even the apprehension that there was anything at all unusual about dining alone with a married woman whose husband was away on business. All such considerations vanished in the bubble of his gaiety and in the light of Lady Maud's approval. Under the table her knee confirmed the implications of her smile; on top her hand lay heavily on his and traced the contours of his fingers; and when, their coffee finished, she took his arm and suggested that they dance Dundridge heard himself say he would be delighted to. Arm-in-arm they went down the passage to the ballroom with the sprung floor. Only then, with the chandeliers lighting the great room brilliantly and a record on the turntable, did he realize what he had let himself in for. Dundridge had never danced in his life.

Blott walked down the hill from Wilfrid's Castle. For a week he had been avoiding the Royal George in Guildstead Carbonell and Mrs Wynn's favours. He had taken to going over to a small pub on the lane leading from the church to the Ottertown Road. It wasn't up to the standard of the Royal George, merely a room with benches round the walls and a barrel of Handyman beer in one corner, but its dismal atmosphere suited

Blott's mood. By the time he had silently consumed eight pints he was ready for bed. He wobbled up the hill past the church and stood gazing down at the Hall in amazement. The great ballroom lights were on. Blott couldn't remember when he had last seen them on, certainly not since Lady Maud's marriage. They cast yellow rectangles on to the lawn, and the conservatory which opened out of the ballroom glowed green with ferns and palms. He stumbled down the path and across the bridge into the pinetum. Here it was pitch-dark but Blott knew his way instinctively. He came out at the gate and crossed the lawn to the terrace. Music, old-fashioned music, floated out towards him. Blott went round the corner and peered through the window.

Inside Lady Maud was dancing. Or learning to dance. Or teaching someone to dance. Blott found difficulty in making up his mind. Under the great chandeliers she moved with a tender gracelessness that took his breath away. Up and down, round and about, in great sweeps and double turns she went, the floor moving visibly beneath her, and in her arms she held a small thin man with an expression of intense concentration on his face. Blott recognized him. He was the man from the Ministry who had stayed to lunch the previous week. Blott hadn't liked the look of him then and he liked it even less now. And Sir Giles was away. Sick with disgust Blott blundered off the flower bed and away from the window. He had half a mind to go in and say what he thought. It wouldn't do any good. He walked unsteadily round the front of the house. There was a car standing there. He peered at it. The man's car. Serve him right if he had to walk home, the bastard. Blott knelt by the front tyre and undid the valve. Then he went round to the boot and let the air out of the spare tyre. That would teach the swine to come messing about with other people's wives. Blott staggered off down the drive to the Lodge and climbed into bed. Through the circular window he could see the lights of the Hall. They were still on when he fell asleep and through the night air there came the faint sound of trombones.

CHAPTER FIFTEEN

What drinks, dinner and Lady Maud's assiduous coquetry had done for Dundridge, dancing had undone. In particular her interpretation of the hesitation waltz – Dundridge considered the probability of a slipped disc – while her tango had threatened hernia. All his attempts to get her to do something a little less complicated had been ignored.

'You're doing splendidly,' she said treading on his toes. 'All you need is a little practice.'

'What about something modern?' said Dundridge.

'Modern dancing is so unromantic,' said Maud, changing the record to a quickstep. 'There's no intimacy in it.'

Intimacy was not what Dundridge had in mind. 'I think I'll sit this one out,' he said limping to a chair. But Lady Maud wouldn't hear of it. She whirled him on to the floor and strode off through a series of half-turns clasping him to her bosom with a grip that brooked no argument. When the record stopped Dundridge put his foot down politely.

'I really think it is time I was off,' he said.

'What? So early? Just one more teeny weeny glass of champers,' said Lady Maud, relapsing rather prematurely into the language of the nursery.

'Oh all right,' said Dundridge choosing the devil of drink to the deep blue sea of the dance floor. They took their glasses through to the conservatory and stood for a moment among the ferns.

'What a wonderful night. Let's go out on the terrace,' said Lady Maud and took his arm. They leant on the stone balustrade and looked into the darkness of the pinetum.

'All we need now is a lover's moon,' Lady Maud murmured and turned to face him. Dundridge looked up into the night sky. It was long past his bedtime and besides not even the champagne could disguise the fact that he was in an ambiguous situation. He had had enough of ambiguous situations lately to last him a lifetime and he certainly didn't relish the thought of Sir Giles returning home unexpectedly to find him on the terrace drinking champagne with his wife at one o'clock in the morning.

'It looks as if it's going to rain,' he said to change the topic from lovers' moons.

'Silly boy,' cooed Lady Maud. 'It's a lovely starlit night.'

'Yes. Well, I really do think I must be getting along,' Dundridge insisted. 'It's been a lovely evening.'

'Oh well if you must go . . .' They went indoors again.

'Just one more glass . . .?' Lady Maud said but Dundridge shook his head and limped on down the passage.

'You must look me up again,' said Lady Maud as he climbed into his car. 'The sooner the better. It's been ages since I had so much fun.' She waved goodbye and Dundridge drove off down the drive. He didn't get very far. There was something dreadfully wrong with the steering. The car seemed to veer to the left all the time and there was a thumping sound. Dundridge stopped and got out and went round to the front.

'Damn,' said Dundridge feeling the flat tyre. He went to the boot and got the jack out. By the time he had jacked the car up and taken the left front wheel off, the lights in the Hall had gone out. He fetched the spare wheel from the boot and bolted it into place. He let the jack down and stowed it away. Then he got back into the car and started the engine and drove off. There was a thumping noise and the car pulled to the left. Dundridge stopped with a curse.

'I must have put the flat tyre on again,' he muttered and got out the jack.

In the Hall Lady Maud switched off the ballroom lights sadly. She had enjoyed the evening and was sorry it has ended so tamely. There had been a moment earlier in the evening when she had thought Dundridge was going to prove amenable to her few charms.

'Men,' she said contemptuously as she undressed and stood looking at herself dispassionately in the mirror. She was not, and she was the first to admit it, a beautiful woman by contemporary standards of beauty but then she didn't pay much heed to contemporary standards of any sort. The world she lived for had admired substantial things, large women, heavy furniture, healthy appetites and strong feelings. She had no time for the present with its talk of sex, its girlish men and boyish women, and its reducing diets. She longed to be swept off her feet by a strong man who knew the value of bed, board and babies. She wasn't going to find him in Dundridge.

'Silly little goose doesn't know what he's missing,' she said and climbed into bed.

Outside the silly little goose knew only too well what he was missing. An inflated tyre. He had changed the wheel again and let down the jack only to find that his spare tyre had been flat after all. He got back into the car and tried to think what to do. Nearby something moved heavily through the grass and a night bird called. Dundridge shut the door. He couldn't sit there all night. He got out of the car and trudged back up the drive to the house and rang the doorbell.

Upstairs Lady Maud climbed out of bed and turned on the light. So the silly little goose had come back after all. He had caught her unprepared. She grabbed a lipstick and daubed her lips hastily, powdered her face and put a dollop of Chanel behind each ear. Finally she changed out of her pyjamas and slid into a see-through nightdress and went downstairs and opened the door.

'I'm sorry to bother you like this but I'm afraid I've had a puncture,' said Dundridge nervously. Lady Maud smiled knowingly.

'A puncture?'

'Yes, two as a matter of fact.'

'Two punctures?'

'Yes. Two,' said Dundridge conscious that there was something rather improbable about having two punctures at the same time.

'You had better come in,' said Lady Maud eagerly. Dundridge hesitated.

'If I could just use the phone to call a garage ...'

But Lady Maud wouldn't hear of it. 'Of course you can't,' she said, 'it's far too late for anyone to come out now.' She took his arm and led him into the house and closed the door.

'I'm terribly sorry to be such a nuisance,' said Dundridge but Lady Maud shushed him.

'What a silly boy you are,' she cooed. 'Now come upstairs and we'll see about a bed.'

'Oh really ...' Dundridge began but it was no good. She turned and led the way, a perfumed spinnaker, up the marble staircase. Dundridge followed miserably.

'You can have this room,' she said as they stood on the landing and she switched on the light. 'Now you go down to the bathroom and have a wash and I'll make the bed up.'

'The bathroom?' said Dundridge gazing at her astonished. In the dim light of the hall Lady Maud had been a mere if substantial shape but now he could see the full extent of her abundant charms. Her face was extraordinary too. Lady Maud smiled, a crimson gash with teeth. And the perfume!

'It's down the corridor on the left.'

Dundridge stumbled down the corridor and tried several doors before he found the bathroom. He went inside and locked the door. When he came out he found the corridor in darkness. He groped his way back to the landing and tried to remember which room she had given him. Finally he found one that was open. It was dark inside. Dundridge felt for the switch but it wasn't where he had expected.

'Is there anyone there?' he whispered but there was no reply. 'This must be the room,' he muttered and closed the door. He edged across the room and felt the end of the bed. A faint light came from the window. Dundridge undressed and noticed that Lady Maud's perfune still lingered heavily on the air. He went across to the window and opened it and then, moving carefully so as not to stub his toes, he went back and got into bed. As he did so he knew there was something terribly wrong. A blast of Chanel No. 5 issued from the bedclothes overpoweringly. So did Lady Maud. Her arms closed round him and with a husky, 'Oh you wicked boy,' her mouth descended on his. The next moment Dundridge was engulfed. Things seemed to fold round him, huge hot terrible things, legs, arms, breasts, lips, noses, thighs, bearing him up, entwining him, and bearing him down again in a frenzy of importunate flesh. He floundered frantically while the waves of Lady Maud's mistaken response broke over him. Only his mind remained untrammelled, his mind and his inhibitions. As he writhed in her arms his thoughts raced to a number of ghastly conclusions. He had chosen the wrong room; she was in love with him; he was in bed with a nymphomaniac; she was providing her husband with grounds for divorce; she was seducing him. There was no question about the last. She was seducing him. Her hands left him in no doubt about that, particularly her left hand. And Dundridge, accustomed to the wholly abstract stimulus of his composite woman, found the inexperience of a real woman – and Lady Maud was both real and inexperienced – hard to put up with.

'There's been a terr—' he managed to squeak as Lady Maud surfaced for air, but a moment later her mouth closed over his, silencing his protest while threatening him with suffocation. It was this last that gave him the desperation he needed. With a truly Herculean revulsion Dundridge hurled himself and Lady Maud, still clinging limpetlike to him, out of the bed. With a crash the bedside table fell to the floor as Dundridge broke free and leapt to his feet. The next moment he was through the door and running down the corridor. Behind him Lady Maud staggered to the bed and pulled the light cord. Stunned by the vigour of his rejection and by the bedside table which had caught her on the side of the head, she lumbered into the corridor and turned on the light but there was no sign of Dundridge.

'There's no need to be shy,' she called but there was no reply. She went into the next room and switched on the light. No Dundridge. The next room was empty too. She went from room to room switching on lights and calling his name, but Dundridge had vanished. Even the bathroom was unlocked and empty and she was just wondering where to look next when a sound from the landing drew her attention. She went back and switched on the hall light and caught him in the act of tiptoeing down the stairs. For an instant he stood there, a petrified satyr, and turned pathetic eyes towards her and then he was off down the stairs and across the marble floor, his slender legs and pale feet twinkling among the squares. Lady Maud leant over the balustrade and laughed.

She was still laughing as she went down the staircase, laughing and holding on to the banister to keep herself from falling. Her laughter echoed in the emptiness of the hall and filtered down the corridors.

In the darkness by the kitchen Dundridge listened to it and shuddered. He had no idea where he was and there was a demented quality about that laughter that appalled him. He was just wondering what to do when, silhouetted against the hall light at the end of the passage he saw her bulky outline. She had stopped laughing and was peering into the gloom.

'It's all right, you can come out now,' she called, but Dundridge knew better. He understood now why his car had two flat tyres, why he had been invited to the Hall when Sir Giles was away. Lady Maud was a raving nymphomaniac. He was alone in a huge house in the middle of the back of beyond with no clothes on, a disabled car and an enormously powerful and naked female lunatic. Nothing on God's earth would induce him to come out now. As Lady Maud lumbered down the passage Dundridge turned and fled, collided with a table, lurched into some iron banisters and was off up the servants' stairs. Behind him a light went on. As he reached the landing he glanced back and saw Lady Maud's face staring up at him. One glance was enough to confirm his fears. The smudged lipstick, the patches of rouge, the disordered hair ... mad as a hatter. Dundridge scampered down another corridor and behind him came the final proof of her madness.

'Tally ho,' shouted Lady Maud. 'Gone away.' Dundridge went away as fast as he could.

In the Lodge, Blott woke up and stared out through the circular window. Dimly below the rim of the hills he could see the dark shape of the Hall and he was about to turn over and go back to sleep when a light came on in an upstairs room to be followed almost immediately by another and then a third. Blott sat up in bed and watched as one room after another lit up. He glanced at his clock and saw it was ten past two. He looked back towards the house and saw the stained glass roof-light above the hall glowing. He got up and opened the window and stared out and as he did so there came the faint sound of hysterical laughter. Or crying. Lady Maud. Blott pulled on a pair of trousers, put on his slippers, took his twelve-bore and ran downstairs. There was something terribly wrong up at the house. He ran up the drive, almost colliding in the darkness with Dundridge's car. The bastard was still around. Probably chasing her from room to room. That would explain the lights going on and the hysterical laughter. He'd soon put a stop to that. Clutching his shotgun he went through the stable yard and in the kitchen door. The lights were on. Blott went across to the passage and listened. There was no sound now. He went down the passage to the hall and stood there. Must be upstairs. He was halfway up when Lady Maud emerged from a corridor on to the landing breathlessly. She ran across the landing to the top of the stairs and stood looking down at Blott naked as the day she was born. Blott gaped up at her open mouthed. There above him was the woman he loved. Clothed she had been splendid. Naked she was perfection. Her great breasts, her stomach, her magnificent thighs, she was everything Blott had ever dreamed of and, to make matters even better, she was clearly in distress. Tear-stains ran down her daubed cheeks. His moment of heroism on her behalf had arrived.

'Blott,' said Lady Maud, 'what on earth are you doing here? And what are you doing with that gun?'

'I am here at your service,' said Blott gallantly assuming the language of history.

'At my service?' said Lady Maud, oblivious of the fact that she wasn't exactly dressed for discussions about service with her gardener. 'What do you mean by my service? You're here to look after the garden, not to wander about the house in the middle of the night in your bedroom slippers armed with a shotgun.'

On the staircase Blott bowed before the storm. 'I came to protect your honour,' he murmured.

'My honour? You came to protect my honour? With a shotgun? Are you out of your mind?'

Blott was beginning to wonder. He had come up expecting to find her lying raped and murdered, or at least pleading for mercy, and here she was standing naked at the top of the stairs dressing him down. It didn't seem right. It didn't seem exactly right to Lady Maud now that she came to think of it. She turned and went into her bedroom and put on a dressing-gown.

'Now then,' she said with a renewed sense of authority, 'what's all this nonsense about my honour?'

'I thought I heard you call for help,' Blott mumbled.

'Call for help indeed,' she snorted. 'You heard nothing of the sort. You've been drinking. I've spoken to you about drinking before and I don't want to mention it again. And what's more when I need any help protecting my so-called honour, which God knows I most certainly don't, I won't ask you to come up here with a twelve-bore. Now then go back to the Lodge and go to bed. I don't want to hear any more about this nonsense, do you understand?'

Blott nodded and slunk down the staircase.

'And you can turn the lights off down there as you go.'

'Yes, ma'am,' said Blott and went down the passage to the kitchen filled with a new and terrible sense of injustice. He turned the kitchen light off and went back to the ballroom and switched off the chandeliers. Then he made his way through the conservatory to the terrace and was about to shut the door when he glimpsed a figure cowering among the ferns. It was the man from the Ministry, and like Lady Maud he was naked. Blott slammed the door and went off down the terrace steps, his mind seething with dreams of revenge. He had come up to the house with the best of intentions to protect his beloved mistress from the sexual depravity of that beastly little man and instead he had been blamed and abused and told he was drunk. It was all so unfair. In the middle of the park he paused and aimed the shotgun into the air and fired both barrels. That was what he thought of the bloody world. That was all that the bloody world understood. Force. He stamped off across the field to the Lodge and went upstairs to his room.

To Dundridge, still cowering in the conservatory, the sound of the shotgun came as final proof that Lady Maud's intentions towards him were homicidal. He had been lured to the Hall, his tyres had been punctured, he had suffered attempted rape, he had been chased naked around the house by a laughing and demented woman and now he was being hunted by a man with a gun. And finally he was in danger of freezing to death. He stayed in the conservatory for twenty minutes anxiously listening for any sounds that might indicate pursuit, but the house was silent. He crept out from his hiding-place and went through the door to the terrace and peered outside. There was no sign of the man with the gun. He would have to take a chance. There was a light look about the eastern sky which suggested the coming of dawn and he had to get away while it was still dark. He ran across the terrace and scampered down the steps towards his car.

Two minutes later he was in the driver's seat and had started the engine. He drove off as fast as the flat tyre would allow, crouching low and waiting for the blast of the shotgun. But nothing came and he passed under the Lodge and into the darkness of the wood. He switched on the headlights, negotiated the suspension bridge and headed up the hill, his flat tyre thumping on the road and the steering pulling violently to the left. Around him the Cleene Forest closed in, his headlights picked out monstrous shapes and weird shadows but Dundridge had lost his terror of the wild landscape. Anything was preferable to the human horrors he had left behind and even when two miles further on the tyre finally came away from the rim and he had to jack the car up and change it for the other flat spare he did so with hesitation. After that he drove more slowly and reached Worford as dawn broke. He parked his car on the double yellow line outside his flat, made sure there was nobody about and flitted across the pavement and down the alley to the outside stairs that led up to his apartment. Even here he was baulked. The key to his flat was in the pocket of his dinner-jacket.

Dundridge stood on the landing outside his door, naked, shivering and livid. Deprived of dignity, pretensions, authority and reason, Dundridge was almost human. For a moment he hesitated and then with a sudden ferocity he hurled himself against the door. At the second attempt the lock gave. He went inside slamming it to behind him. He had made up his mind. Come hell or high water he would do his damnedest to see that the route of the motorway was changed. They could bribe him and blackmail him for all they were worth but he'd get his own back. By the time he had finished that fat insane bitch would laugh on the other side of her filthy face.

CHAPTER SIXTEEN

His opportunity came sooner than he had expected and from an unforeseen quarter. Overwhelmed by the volume of complaints arriving at his office from the tenants of the seventy-five council houses due for demolition, harried by the Ottertown Town Council, infuriated by the refusal of the Minister of the Environment to re-open the Inquiry, and warned by his doctors that unless he curtailed most of his activities his heart would end them all, Francis Puckerington resigned his seat in Parliament. Sir Giles was the first to congratulate him on the wisdom of his withdrawal from public life. 'Wish I could do the same myself,' he said, 'but you know how things are.'

Mr Puckerington didn't but he had a shrewd idea that lurking behind Sir Giles' benevolent concern there was financial advantage. Lady Maud shared his suspicion. Ever since the Inquiry there had been something strange about Giles' manner, an air of expectation and suppressed excitement about him which she found disturbing. Several times she had noticed him looking at her with a smile on his face and when Sir Giles smiled it usually meant that something unpleasant was about to happen. What it was she couldn't imagine and since she took no interest in politics the likely consequences of Mr Puckerington's resignation escaped her. Hoskins was understandably more informed. He realized at once why Sir Giles had agreed so readily to the Ottertown route. 'Brilliant,' he told him when he saw him at the Golf Club. Sir Giles looked mystified.

'I don't know what you're talking about. I had no idea the poor fellow was so ill. A great loss to the party.'

'My eye and Betty Martin,' said Hoskins.

'I'd rather have your Bessie Williams myself,' Sir Giles said, relaxing a little. 'I trust she is keeping well?'

'Very well. She and her husband took a holiday in Majorca I believe.'

'Sensible of them,' Sir Giles said. 'So our young friend Dundridge must be a little puzzled by now. No harm in keeping him hanging in the wind, as someone once put it.'

'He's probably blown that money you gave him.'

'I gave him?' said Sir Giles who preferred not to let his right hand know what his left hand was doing.

'Say no more,' said Hoskins. 'I'll tell you one thing though. He's lost all interest in your wife.'

Sir Giles sighed. 'Such a pity,' he said. 'There was a time when I entertained the hope that he would ... One can't expect miracles. Still, it was a nice thought.'

'He's got it in for her now, anyway. Hates her guts.'

'I wonder why,' said Sir Giles thoughtfully. 'Ah well, it happens to us all in the end. Still, it couldn't have come at a better time.'

'That's what I thought,' said Hoskins. 'He's already sent three memoranda to the Ministry asking for the motorway to be re-routed through the Gorge.'

'Quite the little weathercock isn't he? I trust you tried to dissuade him.'

'Every time. Every time.'

'But not too hard, eh?'

Hoskins smiled. 'I try to keep an open mind on the matter.'

'Very wise of you,' said Sir Giles. 'No point in getting yourself involved. Well, things seem to be moving.'

Things certainly were. In London Francis Puckerington's resignation had immediate repercussions.

'Seventy-five council houses due for demolition in a constituency with a bye-election pending?' said the Prime Minister. 'And what did you say his last majority was?'

'Forty-five,' said the Chief Whip. 'A marginal seat.'

'Marginal be damned. It's lost.'

'It does rather look that way,' the Chief Whip agreed. 'Of course if the motorway could be re-routed ...'

The Prime Minister reached for the phone.

Ten minutes later Mr Rees sent for Mr Joynson.

'Done it,' he said beaming delightedly.

'Done what?'

'Pulled the fat out of the fire. The Ottertown scheme is dead and buried. The M101 is going ahead through the Cleene Gorge.'

'Oh, that is good news,' said Mr Joynson. 'How on earth did you do it?'

'Just a question of patience and gentle persuasion. Ministers may come and Ministers may go but in the end they do tend to see the errors of their ways.'

'I suppose this means you'll be recalling Dundridge,' said Mr Joynson, who was inclined to look on the dark side of things.

'Not on your Nelly,' said Mr Rees, 'Dundridge is coping very well. I look forward to his perpetual absence.'

Dundridge received the news with mixed emotions. On the one hand here was his golden opportunity to teach that bitch Lady Maud a lesson. On the other the knowledge that he had accepted a bribe from Sir Giles bothered him. He looked forward to Lady Maud's misery when she learnt that Handyman Hall was going to be demolished after all but he didn't relish the thought of her husband's reaction. He need not have worried. Sir Giles, anxious to be out of the way when the storm broke, had taken the precaution of being tied up in London in advance of the announcement. In any case Hoskins was reassuring.

'You don't have to worry about Giles,' he told Dundridge. 'It's Maud who'll be out for blood.'

Dundridge knew exactly what he meant, 'If she calls I'm not in,' he told the girl on the switchboard. 'Remember that. I am never in to Lady Maud.'

While Hoskins concentrated on the actual details of the new route and arranged for the posting of advance notices of compulsory purchase, Dundridge spent much of his time on field work, which meant in fact sitting in his flat and not answering the telephone. To occupy his mind and to lend some sort of credence to his title of Controller Motorways Midlands, he set about devising a strategy for dealing with the campaign to stop construction which he was convinced Lady Maud would initiate.

'Surprise is of the essence,' he explained to Hoskins.

'She's had that already,' Hoskins pointed out. He had in his time supervised the eviction of too many obstinate householders to be daunted by the threat of Lady Maud, and besides he was relying on Sir Giles to undermine her efforts. 'She's not going to give us any trouble. You'll see. When it comes to the push she'll go. They all do. It's the law.' Dundridge wasn't convinced. From his personal experience he knew how little the law meant to Lady Maud.

'The thing is to move quickly,' he explained.

'Move quickly?' said Hoskins. 'You can't move quickly when you're building a motorway. It's a slow process.'

Dundridge waved his objections aside. 'We must hit at key objectives. Seize the commanding heights. Maintain the initiative,' he said grandly.

Hoskins looked at him doubtfully. He wasn't used to this sort of military language. 'Look, old boy, I know how you feel and all that but ...'

'You don't,' said Dundridge vehemently.

'But what I was going to say was that there's no need to go in for anything complicated. Just let things take their natural course and you'll find people will get used to the idea. It's amazing how adaptable people are.'

'That's precisely what's worrying me,' said Dundridge. 'Now then the essence of my plan is to make random sorties.'

'Random sorties?' said Hoskins. 'What on earth with?'

'Bulldozers,' said Dundridge and spread out a map of the district.

'Bulldozers? You can't have bulldozers roaming the countryside making random sorties,' said Hoskins, now thoroughly alarmed. 'What the hell are they going to randomly sort?'

'Vital areas of control,' said Dundridge, 'lines of communication. Bridgeheads.'

'Bridgeheads? But—'

'As I see it,' Dundridge continued implacably, 'the main centre of resistance is going to be here.' He pointed to the Cleene Gorge. 'Strategically this is the vital area. Seize that and we've won.'

'Seize it? You can't suddenly go in and seize the Cleene Gorge!' shouted Hoskins. 'The motorway has to proceed by deliberate stages. Contractors work according to a schedule and we have to keep to that.'

'That is precisely the mistake you're making,' said Dundridge. 'Our tactics must be to alter the schedule just when the enemy least expects it.'

'But that's impossible,' Hoskins insisted. 'You can't go about knocking people's houses down without giving them fair warning.'

'Who said anything about knocking houses down?' said Dundridge indignantly. 'I certainly didn't. What I have in mind is something entirely different. Now then what we'll do is this.'

For the next half hour he outlined his grand strategy while Hoskins listened. When he had finished Hoskins was impressed in spite of himself. He had been quite wrong to call Dundridge a nincompoop. In his own peculiar way the man had flair.

'All the same I just hope it doesn't have to come to that,' he said finally.

'You'll see,' said Dundridge. 'That bitch isn't going to sit back and let us put a motorway through her wretched house without putting up a struggle. She's going to fight to the bitter end.'

Hoskins went back to his office thoughtfully. There was nothing illegal about Dundridge's plan in spite of the military jargon. In a way it was extremely shrewd.

The Committee for the Preservation of the Cleene Gorge met under the Presidency of General Burnett at Handyman Hall. Lady Maud was the first speaker.

'I intend to fight this project to the bitter end,' she said, fulfilling Dundridge's prediction. 'I have no intention of being driven from my own home simply because a lot of bureaucratic dunderheads in London take it into their thick skulls to ignore the recommendations of a properly constituted Inquiry. It's outrageous.'

'It's so unfair,' said Mrs Bullett-Finch, 'particularly after what Lord Leakham said about preserving the wildlife of the area. What I can't understand is why they changed their minds so suddenly.'

'As I see it,' said General Burnett, 'the change is a direct consequence of Puckerington's resignation. I have it on the hightest authority that the Government felt that the new candidate was bound to lose the bye-election if they went ahead with the route through Ottertown.'

'Why did Puckerington resign?' asked Miss Percival.

'Ill-health,' said Colonel Chapman. 'He's got a dicky heart.'

Lady Maud said nothing. What she had just heard explained a great many things and suggested more. She knew now why Sir Giles had smiled so secretively at her and why he had had that air of expectation. Everything suddenly fell into place in her mind. She understood why he had been so alarmed about the possibility of a tunnel, why he had insisted on Ottertown, why he had been so pleased at Lord Leakham's decision. Above all, she realized for the first time the full enormity of his betrayal. Colonel Chapman put her thoughts into numbers.

'I suppose there is this to be said for it. I've heard a rumour that we are going to get increased compensation,' he said. 'The figure mentioned was twenty per cent. That makes your sum, Lady Maud, something in the region of three hundred thousand pounds.'

Lady Maud sat rigid in her chair. Three hundred thousand pounds. It was not her share. Sir Giles owned the Hall. Owned it and had put it up for sale in the only way legally available to him. Faced with such treachery there was nothing left for her to say. She shook her head wearily and while the discussion continued round her she stared out of the window to where Blott was mowing the lawn.

The meeting broke up without any decision being taken on the next move.

'Poor old Maud seems quite broken up about this dreadful business,' General Burnett said to Mrs Bullett-Finch as they walked across the drive to their cars. 'It's knocked all the spirit out of her. Bad business.'

'One does feel so terribly sorry for her,' Mrs Bullett-Finch agreed.

Lady Maud watched them leave and then went back into the house to think. Committees would achieve nothing now. They would talk and pass resolutions but when the time for taking action came they would still be talking. Colonel Chapman had given the game away by talking about money. They would settle.

She went down the passage to the study and stood there looking round the room. It was here that Giles had thought the whole thing out, in this sanctum, at this desk where her father and grandfather had sat, and it was here that she would sit and think until she had planned some way of stopping the motorway and of destroying him. In her mind the two things were inextricably linked. Giles had conceived the idea of the motorway, he would be broken by it. There was no compunction left in her. She had been outwitted and betrayed by a man she had always despised. She had sold herself to him to preserve the house and the family and the knowledge of her own guilt added force to her determination. If need be she would sell herself to the devil to stop him now. Lady Maud sat down behind the desk and stared at the filigree of her grandfather's silver inkstand for inspiration. It was shaped like a lion's head. An hour later she had found the solution she was looking for. She reached for the phone and was about to pick it up when it rang. It was Sir Giles calling from London.

'I just thought I had better let you know I shan't be back this weekend,' he said. 'I know it is a damned inconvenient time for me to be away with all this motorway business going on, but I really can't get away.'

'That's all right,' said Lady Maud, feigning her usual degree of indifference, 'I daresay I'll be able to cope without you.'

'How are things going?'

'We've just had a committee meeting to discuss the next move. We are thinking of organizing protest meetings round the county.'

'That's the sort of thing we need,' said Sir Giles. 'I'm doing my damnedest down here to get the Ministry to reconsider. Keep up the good work at your end.' He rang off. Lady Maud smiled grimly. She would keep up the good work all right. And he could go on doing his damnedest. She picked up the phone and dialled. In the next two hours she spoke to her bank manager, the Head Keeper at Whipsnade Zoo, the Game Warden at Woburn Wildlife Park, the managers of five small private Zoos and a firm of fencing experts in Birmingham. Finally she went outside to look for Blott.

Ever since the night of Dundridge's visit she had been worried by Blott's attitude. It hadn't been like him to behave like that and she had been alarmed by the sound of the shotgun going off outside. She rather regretted what she had said about his drinking too. It certainly hadn't had any good effect. If anything he had taken to going off to the Royal George more often and late one night she had heard him singing in the pinetum. 'Typically Italian,' she thought, confusing 'Wir Fahren Gegen England' with *La Traviata*. 'Probably pining for Naples.' But Blott stumbling through the park was merely drunk and if he was pining for anything it was for her innocence which Dundridge's visit had destroyed.

She found him, as she had expected, in the kitchen garden. 'Blott,' she said, 'I want you to do something for me.'

Blott grunted morosely. 'What?'

'You know the wall safe in the study?' Blott nodded. 'I want you to open it for me.'

Blott shook his head and went on weeding the onion bed. 'Not possible without the combination,' he said.

'If I had the combination I wouldn't have to ask you to open it,' Lady Maud said tartly. Blott shrugged. 'If I don't know the combination,' he said, 'how do I open it?'

'You blow it open,' said Lady Maud. Blott straightened up and looked at her.

'Blow it open?'

'With explosive. Use a ... what are those things with flames ... oxy ...'

'Acetylene torch,' said Blott. 'It wouldn't work.'

'I don't mind how you do it. You can pull it out of the wall and drop it from the roof for all I care but I want that safe opened. I've got to know what is inside it.'

Blott pushed back his hat and scratched his head. This was a new Lady Maud speaking. 'Why don't you ask him for the combination?' he said.

'Him?' said Lady Maud with a new contempt. 'Because I don't want him to know. That's why.'

'He'll know it if we blow it open,' Blott pointed out.

Lady Maud thought for a moment. 'We can always say it was burglars,' she said finally.

Blott considered the implications of this remark and found them to his liking. 'Yes, we could do that. Let's go and have a look at it.'

They went into the house and stood in the study examining the safe which was set into the wall behind some books.

'Difficult,' said Blott. He went into the dining-room next door and looked at the wall on that side. 'It's going to do a lot of damage,' he said when he came back.

'Do whatever damage you have to. The house is coming down if we don't do something. What does it matter if we do some damage to it now? It can always be repaired.'

'Ah,' said Blott, who had begun to understand. 'Then I'll use a sledgehammer.' He went round to the workshop in the yard and returned with a sledgehammer, a metal wedge and a crowbar.

'You're quite sure?' he asked. Lady Maud nodded. Blott swung the sledgehammer against the dining-room wall. Half an hour later the safe was out of the wall. Together they carried it outside and laid it on the drive. It was quite small. Blott twiddled the knob idly and tried to think what next to do.

'What we need is some high-explosive,' he said. 'Dynamite would do it.'

'We haven't got any dynamite,' Lady Maud pointed out. 'And you can't go into a shop and buy it. You couldn't bore a hole in it and hoik things out with a wire?'

'Too thick and the steel is too hard,' said Blott. 'It's like armour-plate on a tank.' He stopped. Like a tank. Somewhere among the armoury of weapons he had collected during the war there was a rocket-launcher. It was in a long wooden box and labelled PIAT. Projectile Infantry Anti-Tank. Now where had he buried it?

CHAPTER SEVENTEEN

As dusk fell over the Cleene Gorge Blott left the Lodge with a spade. He had had his supper, sausages and mashed potatoes, and was comfortably full. Above all he was happy. As he followed the park wall round to the west and found the exact spot where he had climbed over as a prisoner of war he was boyishly excited. There had been a piece of iron fencing which he had propped against the wall to give himself a leg-up. It was still there, rusting in a patch of stinging nettles. Blott dragged it out and leant it against the wall and climbed up. The barbed-wire had gone but as he straddled the top of the wall and dropped down on the other side he had the same feeling of freedon he had experienced night after night over thirty years before. Not that he had disliked life in the camp. He had felt freer then than at any time before. To sneak out at night and roam the woods on his own was to escape from the orphanage in Dresden and all the petty restrictions of his dreadful childhood. It had been to cock a snook at authority and to be himself.

And so it was now as he pushed through the bracken and began to climb through the trees. He was doing the forbidden thing again and he exulted in it. Half a mile up the hillside he came to a clearing. You turned left here. Blott turned left, following the old instinct as surely as if there had been a path there, and came out into the setting sunlight behind a mound of stones that had once been a cottage. Here he turned up the hill again until he found the tree he was looking for. It was a large old oak. Blott went round the trunk and found the slash he had made in the bark. He walked away from the tree, counting his paces. Then he took off his jacket and began to dig. It took him an hour to get down to the cache but it was there exactly where he had recalled. He pulled out a box and prised the lid open with a hammer. Inside caked in grease and wrapped in oilskin was a two-inch mortar. He dragged out another box. Mortar bombs. Finally he found what he was looking for. The long box and the four cases of armour-piercing rockets. He sat down on the box and wondered what to do next. Now that he came to think about it, all he needed were the rockets. All he had to do was to tie a piece of string to the fin and drop it from a height on to the safe. That would do the trick just as well as firing the rocket at the safe.

Still, he had come so far, he might as well take the PIAT home with him and clean it up. It would make an interesting souvenir. Blott put the mortar back with the cases of bombs, and covered them with earth. Then he went back down the hill with the long box. It was very heavy and he had to stop fairly frequently to rest. By the time he got back to the Lodge it was dark. He humped the box up to his room and went back for the rockets. He didn't take those up to his room but left them in the grass outside. He didn't feel like sleeping beside some rockets that were thirty years old.

In the morning he was up early and busy in the Gorge. He fetched the safe down on a wheelbarrow and stood it upright at the bottom of the cliff. Then he took a long piece of twine and tied it to the knob of the combination lock before going back up the cliff with it and attaching it to an overhanging branch so that it ran in a straight line some fifty feet down to the safe. Finally he fetched two of the finned projectiles and tied a short length of string to the fin of the first. At the other end of the string he tied a small ring, undid the twine and fitted the ring over it and tied it back on to the branch. Then he lay down at the top of the cliff and removed the cap from the detonator on the nose of the rocket. Blott peered over the edge. There was the safe directly below. He held the PIAT bomb out and let go and watched as it plummeted down the twine. The next moment there was a flash and a roar. Blott shut his eyes and pulled his head back and as he did so something hurtled past him into the air above. He looked up. The fin of the rocket reached its peak, curved over and fell into the road behind him. Blott got up and went down to the safe. The bomb had missed the combination lock but it had done its job. A small hole the size of a pencil was blown in the front of the safe and the door was loose.

Lady Maud was having breakfast when the blast came. For a moment she thought Blott was out shooting rabbits but there had been a concussion and an echo about the explosion that had suggested something more powerful than a shotgun. She went outside and saw Blott coming down the cliff path on the other side of the river. Of course, the safe. He had sworn he would blow it open and that's what he had done. She ran across the lawn and through the pinetum and over the footbridge.

Blott was bending over the safe when she came up.

'Have you done it?' she asked.

'Yes, it's open,' said Blott, 'but there's nothing much in it.' Lady Maud could see that. The safe was much smaller inside than she had expected and it appeared to be filled with burnt, charred and torn fragments of paper. She reached in and picked one out. It was a portion of what had once been a photograph. She held it up and looked at it. It appeared to be the legs of a naked man. She reached in and took out another piece, this time an arm, a bare arm and what looked like a woman's breast. She peered into the safe again but apart from the shreds of photographs there was nothing inside.

'I'll go and get an envelope,' Lady Maud said. 'Don't touch anything until I get back.' She walked off thoughtfully towards the Hall while Blott went back to the top of the cliff and collected the unused PIAT bomb. At least he knew now that they worked. 'Might come in handy,' he said to himself and took it back to the Lodge.

An hour later the safe was buried under some bushes at the base of the cliff and Blott had gone back to the kitchen garden. In the study Lady Maud sat at the desk and examined the fragments of photographs, trying to sort out which portion of anatomy fitted the next. It was a difficult task and an unedifying one. The photographs were too charred and torn to be reassembled properly and besides the force of the explosion had decapitated the participants in what even on this slender evidence appeared to be a series of extremely unnatural acts. And slender was the word. Certainly in the case of the man. That ruled out Sir Giles. It was a pity. She could have done with some photographic proof of his obscene habits. She picked up another fragment and was about to look for the appropriate place in the jigsaw puzzle where it would fit when she suddenly realized where she had seen those slender legs and pale feet. Of course. Twinkling across the marble floor of the hall. She looked again at the portion of leg, at the arm. She was certain now. Dundridge. Dundridge engaged in ... It was unthinkable. She was just trying to work out what this extraordinary idea implied when the front doorbell rang. She went out and opened the door. It was the manager of the high-security fencing company.

'Ah, good,' said Lady Maud. 'Now then, to business. I'll show you exactly what I want.' They went inside to the billiard room and Lady Maud unrolled a map of the estate. 'I am opening a wildlife park,' she explained. 'I want a fence extending the entire perimeter of the park. It must be absolutely secure and proof against any sort of animal.'

'But I understood ...' the manager began.

'Never mind what you understood,' said Lady Maud. 'Just understand that I am opening a wildlife park in three weeks' time.'

'In three weeks? That's out of the question.'

Lady Maud rolled up the map. 'In that case I shall employ someone else,' she said. 'Some enterprising firm that can erect a suitable fence ...'

'You won't get any firm to do it in three weeks,' said the manager. 'Not unless you pay a fortune.'

'I am prepared to pay a fortune,' said Lady Maud.

The manager looked at her and rubbed his jaw. 'Three weeks?' he said.

'Three weeks,' said Lady Maud.

The manager took out a notebook and made some calculations. 'This is simply a rough estimate,' he said finally, 'but I would say somewhere in the region of twenty-five thousand pounds.'

'Say thirty and be done with it,' said Lady Maud. 'Thirty thousand pounds for the fence to be completed in three weeks from today with a bonus of one thousand a day for every day under three weeks and a penalty clause of two thousand pounds for every day after three weeks.'

The manager gaped at her. 'I suppose you know what you're doing,' he muttered.

'I know precisely what I'm doing, thank you very much,' said Lady Maud. 'What is more you will work day and night. You will bring your materials in at night. I don't want any lorries coming here during the day and you will house your men here. I will provide accommodation. You will see to their bedding and their food. This whole operation must be done in the strictest secrecy.'

'If you don't mind,' said the manager and sat down in a chair. Lady Maud sat down opposite him.

'Well?'

'I don't know,' said the manager. 'It *can* be done ...'

'It will be,' Lady Maud assured him. 'Either by you or someone else.'

'You realize that if we were to finish the job in a fortnight the cost would have risen to thirty-seven thousand pounds.'

'And I should be delighted. And if you can finish in a week I shall be happy to pay forty-two thousand pounds,' she said. 'Are we agreed?' The manager nodded. 'Right, in that case I shall make out a cheque to you for ten thousand now and two post-dated cheques for the same amount. I trust that will be a sufficient earnest of my good faith.' She went through to the study and wrote the cheques. 'I shall expect the arrival of materials tonight and work to begin at once. You can bring the contract tomorrow for me to sign.'

The manager went out and got into his car in a state of shock. 'Mad as a March bloody hare,' he muttered as he drove down the drive.

Behind him Lady Maud went back to the study and sat down. It was costing more than she had anticipated but it was worth every penny. And then there was the price of the animals. Lions didn't come cheap. Nor did a rhinoceros. And finally there was the puzzle of the photographs. What were obscene pictures of Mr Dundridge doing in Giles' safe? She got up and went out into the garden and walked up and down the path by the wall of the kitchen garden. And suddenly it dawned on her. It explained everything and in particular why Dundridge had changed his mind about the tunnel. The wretched little man had been blackmailed. Well, two could play at that game. By God they could. She went through the door into the kitchen garden.

'Has my husband ever put through a call to a woman in London?' she asked Blott.

'His secretary,' said Blott. Lady Maud shook her head. Sir Giles' secretary wasn't the sort of woman who would take kindly to the suggestion that she should tie her employer to a bed and beat him and in any case she was happily married.

'Anyone else?'

'No.'

'Has he ever mentioned a woman in any of his conversations on the phone?'

Blott tried to remember. 'No, I don't think so.'

'In that case, Blott,' she said, 'you and I are going to London tomorrow.'

Blott gazed at her in astonishment. 'To London?' He had never been to London.

'To London. We shall be away for a few days.'

'But what shall I wear?' said Blott.

'A suit of course.'

'I haven't got one,' said Blott.

'Well then,' said Lady Maud, 'we had better go into Worford and get you one. And while we're about it we'll get a camera as well. I'll pick you up in ten minutes.'

She went back into the house and put the photographs into an envelope and hid it behind a set of Jorrocks on the bookshelf. It might be worth paying Mr Dundridge a visit while she was in Worford.

CHAPTER EIGHTEEN

But Dundridge was not to be found in Worford. 'He's out,' said the girl at the Regional Planning Board.

'Where?' said Lady Maud.

'Inspecting the site,' said the girl.

'Well, kindly tell him when he comes back that I have some sights I would like him to inspect.'

The girl looked at her. 'I'm sure I don't know what you mean,' she said nastily. Lady Maud suppressed the reaction to tell the little hussy exactly what she did mean.

'Tell Mr Dundridge that I have a number of photographs in which I feel sure he will take a particular interest. You had better write it down before you forget it. Tell him that. He knows where he can find me.'

She went back to the outfitters where Blott was trying on a salmon-pink suit of Harris Tweed. 'If you think I'm going to be seen with you in London in that revolting article of menswear, you've got another think coming,' she snorted. She ran an eye over a number of less conspicuous suits and finally selected a dark grey pinstripe. 'That'll do.' By the time they left the shop Blott was fitted out with shirts, socks, underwear and ties. They called at a shoe shop and bought a pair of black shoes.

'And now all we need is a camera,' said Lady Maud as they stowed Blott's new clothes in the back of the Land-Rover. They went into a camera shop.

'I want a camera with an excellent lens,' she told the assistant, 'one that can be operated by a complete idiot.'

'You need an automatic camera,' said the man.

'No, she doesn't,' said Blott who resented being called a complete idiot in front of strangers. 'She means a Leica.'

'A Leica?' said the man. 'But that's not a camera for a novice. That's a ...'

'Blott,' said Lady Maud, taking him out on to the pavement, 'do you mean to say that you know how to take photographs?'

'In the Luft ... before the war I was trained in photography. I was ...'

Lady Maud beamed at him. 'Oh Blott,' she said, 'you're a godsend. An absolute godsend. Go and buy whatever you need to take good clear photographs.'

'What of?' asked Blott. Lady Maud hesitated. Oh well, he would have to know sooner or later. She took the plunge. 'Him in bed with another woman.'

'Him?'

'Yes.'

It was Blott's turn to beam now. 'We'll need flash and a wide-angle lens.' They went back into the shop and came out with a second-hand Leica, an enlarger, a developing tank, an electronic flash, and everything they needed. As they drove back to Handyman Hall Blott was in his seventh heaven.

*

Dundridge, on the other hand, was in the other place. The girl at the switchboard had phoned him as soon as Lady Maud had left.

'Lady Maud's been,' she told him. 'She's left a message for you.'

'Oh yes,' said Dundridge. 'I hope you didn't tell her where I was.'

'No, I didn't,' said the girl. 'She's a horrid old bag isn't she? I wouldn't wish her on my worst enemy.'

'You can say that again,' Dundridge agreed. 'What was the message?'

'She said "Tell Mr Dundridge that I have a number of photographs in which I feel sure he will take a particular interest". She made me write it down. Hullo, are you still there? Mr Dundridge. Hullo. Hullo. Mr Dundridge, are you there?' But there was no reply. She put the phone down.

In his flat Dundridge sat in a state of shock. He still clutched the phone but he was no longer listening. His thoughts were concentrated on one terrible fact, Lady Maud had those ghastly photographs. She could destroy him. There was nothing he could do about it. She would use them if the motorway went ahead and there was absolutely no way he could stop it now. The fucking bitch had arranged the whole thing. First the photographs, then the bribe, and finally the attempt to murder him. The woman was insane. There could be no doubt about it now. Dundridge put down the phone and tried desperately to think what to do. He couldn't even go to the police. In the first place they would never believe him. Lady Maud was a Justice of the Peace, a respected figure in the community and what had that Miss Boles told him? 'We'll know if you tell the police. We've had customers in the police.' And in any case he had no proof that she was involved. Only the word of the girl at the Planning Board and Lady Maud would claim she had been talking about photographs of the Hall or something like that. He needed proof but above all he needed legal advice. A good lawyer.

He picked up the telephone directory and looked in the yellow pages under Solicitors. 'Ganglion, Turnbull and Shrine.' Dundridge dialled and asked to speak to Mr Ganglion. Mr Ganglion would see him in the morning at ten o'clock. Dundridge spent the evening and most of the night pacing his room in an agony of doubt and suspense. Several times he picked up the phone to call Lady Maud only to put it down again. There was nothing he could say to her that would have the slightest effect and he dreaded what she would have to say to him. Towards dawn he fell into a restless sleep and awoke exhausted at seven.

At Handyman Hall Lady Maud and Blott slept fitfully too; Blott because he was kept awake by the rumble of lorries through the arch; Lady Maud because she was superintending the whole operation and explaining where she wanted things put.

'Your men can sleep in the servants' quarters,' she told the manager. 'I shall be away for a week. Here is the key to the back door.'

When she finally got to bed in the early hours Handyman Hall had assumed the aspect of a construction camp. Concrete mixers, posts, lorries, fencing wire, bags of cement and gravel were arranged in the park and work had already begun by the light of lamps and a portable generator.

She lay in bed listening to the voices and the rumble of the machines and was well satisfied. When money was no object you could still get things done quickly even in England. 'Money no object,' she thought and smiled to herself at the oddity of the phrase. She would have to do something about money before very long. She would think about it in the morning.

At seven she was up and had breakfasted. Through the window of the kitchen she was pleased to note that several concrete posts had already been installed and that a strange machine that looked like a giant corkscrew was boring holes for some more. She went along to the study and spent an hour going through Sir Giles' filing-cabinets. She paid particular attention to a file marked Investments and took down the details of his shareholdings and the correspondence with his stockbroker. Then she went carefully through his personal correspondence, but there was no indication to be found there of any mistress with a penchant for whips and handcuffs.

At nine she signed the contract and went up to her room to pack and at ten she and Blott, now dressed in his pinstripe suit and wearing a blue polka-dot tie, drove off in the Land-Rover for Hereford and the train to London. Behind them in the study the phone was off the stand. There would be no phone calls to Handyman Hall from Sir Giles.

Dundridge arrived promptly at the offices of Ganglion, Turnbull and Shrine and was kept waiting for ten minutes. He sat in an outer office clutching his briefcase and looking miserably at the sporting prints on the walls. They didn't suggest the sophisticated modern approach to life that he felt an understanding of his particular case required. Nor did Mr Ganglion, who finally deigned to see him. He was an elderly man with gold-rimmed glasses over which he looked at Dundridge critically. Dundridge sat down in front of his desk and tried to think how to begin.

'And what did you wish to consult me about, Mr Dundridge?' Mr Ganglion inquired. 'I think you should know in advance that if this has anything to do with the motorway we are not prepared to handle it.'

Dundridge shook his head. 'It hasn't got anything to do with the motorway, well not exactly,' he said. 'The thing is that I'm being blackmailed.'

Mr Ganglion put the tips of his fingers together and tapped them. 'Blackmailed? Indeed. An unusual crime in this part of the world. I can't remember when we last had a case of blackmail. Still it does make a change, I must say. Yes, blackmail. You interest me, Mr Dundridge. Do go on.'

Dundridge swallowed nervously. He hadn't come to interest Mr Ganglion or at least not in the way his smile suggested. 'It's like this,' he said. 'I went to a party at the Golf Club and I met this girl ...'

'A girl, eh?' said Mr Ganglion and drew his chair up to the desk. 'An attractive girl I daresay.'

'Yes,' said Dundridge.

'And you went home with her, I suppose,' said Mr Ganglion, his eyes alight with a very genuine interest now.

'No,' said Dundridge. 'At least I don't think so.'

'You don't think so?' said Mr Ganglion. 'Surely you know what you did?'

'That's the whole point,' Dundridge said, 'I don't know what I did.' He stopped. He did know what he had done. The photographs proclaimed his actions all too clearly. 'Well actually ... I know what I did and all that ...'

'Yes,' Mr Ganglion said encouragingly.

'The thing is I don't know where I did it.'

'In a field perhaps?'

Dundridge shook his head. 'Not in a field.'

'In the back of a car?'

'No,' said Dundridge. 'The thing is that I was unconscious.'

'Were you really? Extraordinary. Unconscious?'

'You see, I had a Campari before we left. It tasted bitter but then Campari does, doesn't it?'

'I have no idea,' said Mr Ganglion, 'what Campari tastes like but I'll take your word for it.'

'Very bitter,' said Dundridge, 'and we got into the car and that's the last thing I remember.'

'How very unfortunate,' said Mr Ganglion, clearly disappointed that he wasn't going to hear the more intimate details of the encounter.

'The next thing I knew I was sitting in my car in a lay-by.'

'A lay-by. Very appropriate. And what happened next?'

Dundridge shifted nervously in his chair. This was the part he had been dreading. 'I got some photographs.'

Mr Ganglion's flagging interest revived immediately. 'Did you really? Splendid. Photographs indeed.'

'And a demand for a thousand pounds.'

'A thousand pounds? Did you pay it?'

'No,' said Dundridge. 'No I didn't.'

'You mean they weren't worth it?'

Dundridge chewed his lip. 'I don't know what they're worth,' he muttered bitterly.

'Then you've still got them,' said Mr Ganglion. 'Good. Good. Well I'll soon tell you what I think of them.'

'I'd rather ...' Dundridge began but Mr Ganglion insisted.

'The evidence,' he said, 'let's have a look at the evidence of blackmail. Most important.'

'They're pretty awful,' said Dundridge.

'Bound to be,' said Mr Ganglion. 'For a thousand pounds they must be quite revolting.'

'They are,' said Dundridge. Encouraged by Mr Ganglion's broad-mindedness, he opened his briefcase and took out the envelope. 'The thing is you've got to remember I was unconscious at the time.'

Mr Ganglion nodded understandingly. 'Of course, my dear fellow, of course.' He reached out and took the envelope and opened it. 'Good God,' he muttered as he looked at the first one. Dundridge squirmed in his chair and stared at the ceiling, and listened while Mr Ganglion thumbed through the photographs, grunting in an ecstasy of disgust and astonishment.

'Well?' he asked when Mr Ganglion sat back exhausted in his chair. The solicitor was staring at him incredulously.

'A thousand pounds? Is that really all they asked?' he said. Dundridge nodded. 'Well, all I can say is that you got off damned lightly.'

'But I didn't pay,' Dundridge reminded him. Mr Ganglion goggled at him.

'You didn't? You mean to tell me you baulked at a mere thousand pounds after having ...' he stopped at a loss for words while his finger wavered over a particularly revolting photograph.

'I couldn't,' said Dundridge feeling hard done by.

'Couldn't?'

'They never called me back. I had one phone call and I've been waiting for another.'

'I see,' said Mr Ganglion. He looked back at the photograph. 'And you've no idea who this remarkable woman is?'

'None at all. I only met her the once.

'Once is enough by the look of things,' Mr Ganglion said. 'And no more phone calls? No letters?'

'Not until last night,' said Dundridge, 'and then I got a message from the girl at the desk at the Regional Planning Board.'

'The girl at the desk at the Regional Planning Board,' said Mr Ganglion, eagerly reaching for a pencil. 'And what's her name?'

'She's got nothing to do with it,' Dundridge said, 'she was simply phoning to give me the message. It said Lady Maud Lynchwood had called and wanted me to know that she had some photographs of particular interest to me ...' He stopped. Mr Ganglion had half risen from his seat and was glaring at him furiously.

'Lady Maud?' he yelled. 'You come in here with this set of the most revolting photographs I've ever set eyes on and have the audacity to tell me that Lady Maud Lynchwood has something to do with them. My God, sir, I've half a mind to horse-whip you. Lady Maud Lynchwood is one of our most respected clients, a dear sweet lady, a woman of the highest virtues, a member of one of the best families ...' He fell back into his chair, speechless.

'But—' Dundridge began.

'But me no buts,' said Mr Ganglion, trembling with rage. 'Get out of my office. If I have one more word out of you, sir, I shall institute proceedings for slander immediately. Do you hear me? One more word here or anywhere else. One breath of rumour from you and I won't hesitate, do you hear me?'

Dundridge could still hear him fulminating as he dashed downstairs and into the street clutching his briefcase. It was only when he got back to his apartment that he realized he had left his photographs on Mr Ganglion's desk. They could stay there for all he cared. He wasn't going back for the beastly things.

Behind him Mr Ganglion simmered down. On the desk in front of him Dundridge and the masked woman lay frozen in two-dimensional contortions. Mr Ganglion adjusted his bifocals and studied them with interest. Then he put the photographs into the envelope and the envelope into his safe. The good name of the Handymans was safe with him. Mind you, come to think of it, he wouldn't put anything past her. Remarkable woman, Maud, quite remarkable.

By the time they reached London Lady Maud had explained Blott's new duties to him.

'You will hire a taxi and wait outside his flat until he comes out and then you will follow him wherever he goes. Particularly in the evening. I want to know where he spends his nights. If he goes into a block of flats, go in after him and make a note of the floor the lift stops at. Do you understand?'

Blott said he did.

'And on no account let him catch sight of you.' She studied him critically. In his dark grey suit Blott was practically unrecognizable anyway. Still, it was best to be careful. She would buy him a bowler at Harrods. 'If you see him with a woman follow them wherever they go and if they separate follow the woman. We have got to find out who she is and where she is and where she lives.'

'And then we break in and take the photographs of them?' said Blott eagerly.

'Certainly not,' said Lady Maud. 'When we find out who the woman is we'll decide what we're going to do.'

They took a taxi to an hotel in Kensington, stopping on the way to buy Blott's bowler, and at five o'clock Blott was sitting in a taxi outside Sir Giles' flat in Victoria.

'I suppose you know what you're doing,' said the driver when they had been sitting there for an hour with the meter running. 'This is costing you a packet.' Blott, with a hundred pounds in his pocket, said he knew what he was doing. He was enjoying himself watching the traffic go by and studying the pedestrians. He was in London, the capital of Great Britain, the heart of what had been the world's greatest Empire, the seat of those great Kings and Queens he had read so much about and all the romance in Blott's nature thrilled at the thought. What was even better he was tracking down him – Blott had never deigned to call him anything else – him and his mistress. He was doing Lady Maud a service after all.

At seven Sir Giles came out and drove to his Club for dinner. Behind him Blott's taxi followed relentlessly. At eight he came out and drove across to St John's Wood, Blott's taxi still behind. He parked in Elm Road and went into a house while Blott stared out of the taxi and noticed that he pressed the second bell. As soon as Sir Giles had gone inside, Blott got out and walked across the road and took a note of the name on the doorbell. It read Mrs Forthby. Blott went back to the taxi.

'Mrs Forthby, Mrs Forthby,' said Lady Maud when Blott reported to her. 'Elm Road.' She looked Mrs Forthby up in the telephone directory. 'That's very clever of you, Blott. Very clever indeed. And you say he didn't come out?'

'No. But the taxi-driver wouldn't wait any longer. He said it was time for his supper.'

'Never mind. You've done very well. Now the only thing to do is to find out what sort of woman she is. I would like to get to know Mrs Forthby a little better. I wonder how I can do that.'

'I can follow her,' said Blott.

'I don't see what good that would do,' said Lady Maud. 'And in any case how would you know her to follow?'

'She's the only woman living in the house,' Blott said. 'There's a Mr Sykes on the top floor and a Mr Billington on the ground floor.'

'Excellent,' said Lady Maud. 'You are an observant man. Now then how can I get to know her? There must be some way of arranging a meeting.'

'I could,' said Blott, adopting the voice of Sir Giles, 'ring her up and pretend I was him and ask her to meet me somewhere ...' he said.

Lady Maud gazed at him. 'Of course. Oh Blott what would I do without you?' Blott blushed. 'But no, that wouldn't do,' Lady Maud continued. 'She would tell him. I'll have to think of something else.'

Blott went up to his room and went to bed. He was tired and very hungry but these little inconveniences counted for nothing beside the knowledge that Lady Maud was pleased with him. Blott fell asleep blissfully happy.

So did Lady Maud, though her happiness was more practical and centred on the solution to a problem that had been worrying her. Money. The fence for the Wildlife Park was going to cost at least thirty thousand pounds and the animals she had ordered came to another twenty. Fifty thousand pounds was a lot of money to pay to save the Hall and besides there was no guarantee that it would work. If anybody should be paying it was Giles, who was responsible for the whole wretched business. And she had found a way of making him pay. She would ruin him yet.

Next morning at eight o'clock she and Blott were sitting in a taxi at the end of Elm Road. At nine they saw Sir Giles leave. Lady Maud paid the taxi-driver and with Blott at her heels strode down to number six.

'Now remember what to say,' Lady Maud told Blott as she pressed the bell. There was a buzz.

'Who is it?' Mrs Forthby asked.

'It's me. I've left my car keys,' said Blott in the accents of Sir Giles.

'And I thought I was the forgetful one,' said Mrs Forthby.

The door opened. Blott and Lady Maud went upstairs. Mrs Forthby opened the door of her flat. She was dressed in a housecoat and was holding a yellow duster.

'Good morning,' said Lady Maud and walked past her into the flat.

'But I thought ...' Mrs Forthby began.

'Do let me introduce myself,' said Lady Maud. 'I am Lady Maud Lynchwood and you must be Mrs Forthby.' She took Mrs Forthby's hand. 'I've been looking forward to meeting you. Giles has told me so much about you.'

'Oh dear,' said Mrs Forthby. 'How frightfully embarrassing.' Behind her Blott closed the door. Lady Maud took stock of the furniture, including Mrs Forthby in the process, and then sat down in an armchair.

'Quite the little love nest,' she said finally. Mrs Forthby stood plumply in front of her wringing the duster.

'Oh this is awful,' she said, 'simply awful.'

'Nonsense. It's nothing of the sort. And do stop twisting that duster. You make me nervous.'

'I'm so sorry,' said Mrs Forthby. 'It's just that I feel ... well ... just that I owe you an apology.'

'An apology? What on earth for?' said Lady Maud.

'Well ... you know ...' Mrs Forthby shook her head helplessly.

'If you imagine for one moment that I have anything against you, you're mightily mistaken. As far as I am concerned you have been a positive godsend.'

'A godsend?' Mrs Forthby mumbled and sat down on the sofa.

'Of course,' said Lady Maud. 'I have always found my husband a positively disgusting man with the very vilest of personal habits. The fact that you appear to be prepared, presumably out of the goodness of your heart, to satisfy his obscene requirements leaves me very much in your debt.'

'It does?' said Mrs Forthby, her world being stood on its head by this extraordinary woman who sat in her armchair and addressed her in her own flat as if she were a servant.

'Very much so,' Lady Maud continued. 'And where do these absurdities take place? In the bedroom I suppose.' Mrs Forthby nodded. 'Blott, have a look in the bedroom.'

'Yes, ma'am,' said Blott and went through first one door and then another. Mrs Forthby sat and stared at Lady Maud, hypnotized.

'Now then, you and I are going to have a little chat,' Lady Maud continued. 'You seem to be a sensible sort of woman with a head on your shoulders. I'm sure we can come to some mutually advantageous arrangement.'

'Arrangement?'

'Yes,' said Lady Maud, 'arrangement. Tell me, have you ever been a co-respondent in a divorce case?'

'No, never,' said Mrs Forthby.

'Well my dear,' Lady Maud went on, 'unless you are prepared to do exactly what I tell you down to the finest detail I'm afraid you are going to find yourself involved in quite the most sordid divorce case this country has seen for a very long time.'

'Oh dear,' Mrs Forthby whimpered, 'how simply awful. What would Cedric think of me?'

'Cedric?'

'My first husband. My late husband I should say. The poor dear would be absolutely furious. He'd never speak to me again. He was very particular, you know. Doctors have to be.'

'Well, we wouldn't want to upset Cedric, would we?' said Lady Maud. 'And there will be absolutely no need to if you do what I say. First of all I want you to tell me what Giles likes you to do.'

'Well ...' Mrs Forthby began only to be interrupted by Blott who emerged from the bedroom with the Miss Dracula, the Cruel Mistress, costume.

'I found this,' he announced.

'Oh dear, how frightfully embarrassing,' said Mrs Forthby.

'Not half as embarrassing, my dear, as it will be when we produce that in court as an exhibit. Now then, the details.'

Mrs Forthby got up. 'It's all written down,' she said. 'He writes it all down for me. You see I'm terribly forgetful and I do tend to get things wrong. I'll get you the game plan.' She went through to the bedroom and returned with a notebook. 'It's all there.'

Lady Maud took the book and studied a page. 'And what were you last night?' she asked finally. 'Miss Catheter, the Wicked Nurse, or Sister Florinda, the Nymphomaniac Nun?'

Mrs Forthby blushed. 'Doris, the Schoolgirl Sexpot,' she tittered.

Lady Maud looked at her doubtfully. 'My husband must have a truly remarkable imagination,' she said, 'but I find his literary style rather limited. And what are you going to be tonight?'

'Oh he doesn't come tonight. He's had to go to Plymouth for a business conference. He's coming again the day after tomorrow. That's Nanny Whip's night.'

Lady Maud put the book down. 'Now then, this is the arrangement,' she said. 'In return for your co-operation I will settle for a divorce on the grounds of incompatibility. There will be no mention of you at all and Sir Giles need know nothing about the help you have given me. All I want you to do is to go out for a little while on Thursday night so that I can have a little chat with him.'

Mrs Forthby hesitated. 'He'll be awfully cross,' she said.

'With me,' Lady Maud assured her. 'I don't think he'll worry about you by the time I've had my say. He'll have other things on his mind.'

'You won't do anything nasty to him, will you?' said Mrs Forthby. 'I wouldn't want him to be hurt or anything. I know he's not very nice but I'm really quite fond of him.'

'I won't touch him,' Lady Maud said. 'I give you my word of honour I won't so much as lift a little finger to him. And let me say I think your feelings do you great credit.'

Mrs Forthby began to weep. 'You're very kind,' she said.

Lady Maud stood up. 'Not at all,' she said truthfully. 'And now if you'll be so good as to give me the key of the flat I'll send Blott to get a duplicate cut.'

By the time they left the flat Mrs Forthby was feeling better. 'It's been so nice meeting you and getting things straightened out,' she said. 'It's taken a great weight off my mind. I do hate deception so.'

'Quite,' said Lady Maud. 'Unfortunately men seem to live in a fantasy world and as the weaker sex we have to follow suit.'

'That's what I keep telling myself,' Mrs Forthby said. 'Felicia, I say, you may find it peculiar but if it makes him happy you can't afford to be choosey.'

'My sentiments exactly,' said Lady Maud. She and Blott went downstairs. They took a taxi across London to Sir Giles' flat in Victoria. On the way Lady Maud coached Blott in his new role.

CHAPTER NINETEEN

In Worford Dundridge asserted himself. Now that he came to think about it, he could see that he had been wise to visit Mr Ganglion. The old man's reaction might have been violent but at least it had been genuine and served to indicate that the solicitor was far too respectable to be a party to a blackmail attempt by one of his clients no matter how influential she might be. And Mr Ganglion could do one of two things: he could let Lady Maud know that Dundridge had visited him and had accused her of blackmail, or, more likely, since it was unprofessional to disclose one client's business to another, he could keep silent. In either case Dundridge was in a fairly strong position. If Ganglion spoke to Lady Maud she would not dare to repeat her threat. If he kept silent ... Dundridge considered the most likely consequence. There would be another message from her. Dundridge got up and went out and bought himself a tape recorder. The next time he visited Mr Ganglion he would tape evidence, solid evidence that Lady Maud was involved. That was the thing to do.

Having arrived at that conclusion he felt better. He had spiked the bitch's guns. Operation Overland could proceed. He went round to the Regional Planning Board and sent for Hoskins.

'We are going ahead,' he told him.

'Of course we are,' said Hoskins. 'Work has already started at Bunnington.'

'Never mind that,' said Dundridge, 'I want a task force to begin work in the Gorge.'

Hoskins consulted his schedule. 'We're not due there until October.'

'I know that but all the same I want work to begin there at once. Just a token force, you understand.'

'At Handyman Hall? A token force?'

'Not at the Hall. In the Gorge itself,' said Dundridge.

'But we haven't even served a compulsory purchase order on the Lynchwoods yet,' Hoskins protested.

'In that case it is about time we did. I want orders out to Miss Percival, General Burnett, and the Lynchwoods at once. We've got to bring pressure to bear on them as quickly as possible. Do you understand?'

'Well, I understand that,' said Hoskins who was beginning to resent Dundridge's authoritarian manner, 'but quite frankly I can't see what all the hurry is about.'

'You wouldn't,' said Dundridge, 'but I'm telling you to do it so get it done. In any case we don't need a compulsory purchase order for the entrance to the Gorge. It's common land. Move men in there tomorrow.'

'And what the hell do you expect them to do? Storm the bloody Hall under cover of darkness?'

'Hoskins,' said Dundridge, 'I'm getting a little tired of your sarcasm. You seem to forget that I am Controller Motorways Midlands and what I say goes.'

'Oh all right,' said Hoskins. 'Just remember that if anything goes wrong you'll have to take the can back. What do you want the task force to do?'

Dundridge looked at the plans for construction. 'It says here that the cliffs have to be cleared and the Gorge widened. They can start work on that.'

'That means dynamiting,' Hoskins pointed out.

'Excellent,' said Dundridge, 'that ought to serve notice on the old bag that we mean business.'

'It will do that all right,' said Hoskins. 'She'll probably be round here like a flash.'

'And I shall be only too glad to see her,' Dundridge said. Hoskins went back to his office puzzled. The more he saw of the Controller Motorways Midlands the odder he found him.

'I never thought he would stand up to Lady Maud like this,' he muttered. 'Well, better him than me.'

In his office Dundridge smiled to himself. Dynamite. That was just the thing to bring Lady Maud rushing into the trap he had set. He took the tape recorder out of his briefcase and tested it. The thing worked perfectly.

In Sir Giles' flat in Victoria, Lady Maud and Blott sat down by the desk. In front of her were the details of Sir Giles' shareholdings. In front of Blott the telephone and the script of his part.

'Ready?' said Lady Maud.

'Ready,' said Blott and dialled.

'Schaeffer, Blodger and Vaizey,' said the girl at the stockbrokers.

'Mr Blodger please,' said Blott.

'Sir Giles Lynchwood on the line for you, Mr Blodger,' he heard the girl say.

'Ah Lynchwood,' said Blodger, 'good morning.'

'Good morning Blodger,' said Blott. 'Now then, I want to sell the following at best. Four thousand President Rand. One thousand five hundred ICM. Ten thousand Rio Pinto. All my Zinc and Copper ...'

At the other end of the line there was a choking sound. Mr Blodger was evidently having some difficulty coming to terms with Sir Giles' orders. 'I say, Lynchwood,' he muttered, 'are you all right?'

'All right? What the devil do you mean? Of course I'm all right,' snarled Blott.

'It's just that ... well ... I mean the market's rock bottom just at the moment. Wouldn't it be better to wait ...'

'Listen Blodger,' said Blott, 'I know what I'm doing and when I say sell I mean sell. And if you'll take my advice you'll get out now too.'

'You really think ...' Mr Blodger began.

'Think?' said Blott. 'I know. Now then see what you can get and call me back. I'll be here at the flat for the next twenty minutes.'

'Well if you say so,' said Mr Blodger.

Blott put the phone down.

'Brilliant, Blott, absolutely brilliant. For a moment even I thought it was Giles talking,' said Lady Maud. 'Well that should put the cat among the pigeons. Or the bulls among the bears. Now, when he calls back give him the second list.'

At the offices of Schaeffer, Blodger and Vaizey there was consternation. Blodger consulted Schaeffer and together they sent for Vaizey.

'Either he's gone out of his mind or he knows something,' shouted Blodger. 'He's dropping eighty thousand on the President Rand.'

'What about Rio Pinto?' Schaeffer yelled. 'He bought in at twenty-five and he's selling at ten.'

'He's usually right,' said Vaizey. 'In all the years we've handled his account he hasn't put a foot wrong.'

'A foot! He's putting his whole damned body wrong if you ask me.'

'Unless he knows something,' said Vaizey.

They looked at one another. 'He must know something,' said Schaeffer.

'Do you want to speak to him?' asked Blodger.

Schaeffer shook his head. 'My nerves couldn't stand it,' he muttered.

Blodger picked up the phone. 'Get me Sir Giles Lynchwood,' he told the girl on the switchboard. 'No, come to think of it, don't. I'll use the outside line.' He dialled Sir Giles' number.

Ten minutes later he staggered through to Schaeffer's office whitefaced.

'He wants out,' he said and slumped into a chair.

'Out?'

'Everything. The whole damned lot. And today. He knows something all right.'

'Well,' said Lady Maud, 'that's taken care of that. We had better spend another hour or two here in case they phone back. It's a great pity we can't do the same thing with some of his property. Still, there's no point in overdoing things.'

At two o'clock Blodger phoned again to say that Sir Giles' instructions had been carried out.

'Good,' said Blott. 'Send the transfers round tomorrow. I'm going to Paris overnight. And by the way, I want the money transferred to my current account at Westlands in Worford.'

Sir Giles returned from Plymouth the following afternoon by car. He was in a good humour. The conference had gone well and he was looking forward to an evening with Nanny Whip. He went to his flat, had a bath, dined in a restaurant and drove round to Elm Road to find Mrs Forthby already dressed for the part.

'Now then you naughty boy,' she said with just that touch of benign menace he found most affecting, 'off with your clothes.'

'No, no,' said Sir Giles.

'Yes, yes,' said Nanny Whip.

'No, no.'

'Yes, yes.'

Sir Giles succumbed to the allure of her apron. It smelt of childhood. Nanny Whip's breath, on the other hand, suggested something more mature but Sir Giles was too intoxicated with her insistence that he behave himself while she fixed his nappy that he took no notice. It was only when he was finally strapped down and was having his bonnet adjusted that he caught a full whiff. It was brandy.

'You've been drinking,' he spluttered.

'Yes, yes,' said Mrs Forthby and stuffed a dummy into his mouth. Sir Giles stared up at her incredulously. Mrs Forthby never drank. The bloody woman was a teetotaller. It was one of the things he liked about her. She didn't cost much to entertain. She might be absent-minded but she was . . . My God, if she was absent-minded sober what the hell was she going to be like drunk? Sir Giles writhed on the bed and realized that he was tied down rather more firmly than he had expected. Nanny Whip had excelled herself. He could hardly move.

'I'm just going to pop downstairs for some fish fingers,' she said, 'I won't be a moment.'

Sir Giles stared lividly at her while she took off her cap and put on a coat over her costume. What in God's name did the bloody woman want with fish fingers at this time of night? A moment? Sir Giles knew her moments. He was liable to be left strapped up in baby clothes and with a dummy in his mouth until the small hours while she went to some fucking concert. Sir Giles gnawed frantically at the dummy but the damned thing was tied on too tightly.

'Now you be a good boy while I'm away,' said Nanny Whip, 'and don't do anything I wouldn't do. Ta, ta.'

She went out and shut the door. Sir Giles subsided. There was no point in worrying now. He might as well enjoy his impotence while he could. There would probably be plenty of time later on for genuine concern. With the necessarily silent prayer that she hadn't been given tickets for the Ring Cycle he settled down to be Naughty Boy and he was just beginning to get into the role when the front doorbell rang. Sir Giles assumed an even greater rigidity. A moment later he was petrified.

'Is anyone at home?' a voice called. Sir Giles knew that voice. It was the voice of hell itself. It was Lady Maud.

'Oh well, the key's in the door,' he heard her say, 'so we might as well go in and wait.'

On the bed Sir Giles had palpitations. The thought of being discovered in this ghastly position by Lady Maud was bad enough but the fact that she had somebody with her was utterly appalling. He could hear them moving about the next room. If only they would stay there. And what the hell was Lady Maud doing there anyway? How on earth had she discovered about Mrs Forthby? And just at that moment the door opened and Lady Maud stood framed in it.

'Ah there you are,' she said cheerfully, 'I had an idea we'd find you here. How very convenient.'

From under his frilled bonnet Sir Giles peered up at her venomously, his face the colour of the sheet on which he was lying and his legs jerking convulsively in the air. Convenient! Convenient! The fucking woman was out of her mind. The next moment he was certain of it.

'You can come in, Blott,' she said, 'Giles won't mind.' Blott came into the room. He was carrying a camera and a flash gun.

'And now,' said Lady Maud, 'we're going to have a little chat.'

'What about the pictures?' said Blott. 'Shouldn't we take them first?'

'Do you think he would prefer the pictures first?' she asked. Blott nodded his head vigorously while Sir Giles shook his. For the next five minutes Blott went round the room taking photographs from every conceivable angle. Then he changed the film and took some close-ups. 'That will do for now,' he announced finally. 'We should have enough.'

'I'm sure we have,' said Lady Maud and drew up a chair beside the bed. 'Now then we are going to have our little chat about your future, my dear.' She bent over and took out the comforter.

'Don't touch me,' squealed Sir Giles.

'I have no intention of touching you,' said Lady Maud with evident disgust. 'It has been one of the few compensations for our wholly unsatisfactory marriage that I don't have to. I am simply here to arrange terms.'

'Terms? What terms?' squawked Sir Giles. Lady Maud rummaged in her handbag.

'The terms of our divorce,' she said and produced a document. 'You will simply append your signature here.'

Sir Giles stared up at it blankly. 'I need my reading-glasses,' he muttered.

Lady Maud perched them on his nose. Sir Giles read the document. 'You expect me to sign that?' he yelled. 'You really think I'm going to—'

Lady Maud replaced the dummy. 'You unspeakable creature,' she snarled, 'you'll sign this document if it's the last thing you do. And this.' She waved another piece of paper in front of him. 'And this.' Another. 'And this.'

On the bed Sir Giles struggled with the straps convulsively. Nothing on God's earth would make him sign a document that was an open confession that he had made a habit of deceiving his lawful wife, had denied her her conjugal rights, had committed adultery on countless occasions and had subjected her for six years to mental and physical cruelty. Lady Maud read his thoughts.

'In return for your signature I will not distribute copies of the photographs we have just taken to the Prime Minister, the Chief Whip, the members of your constituency party or the press. You will sign that document, Giles, and you will see that the motorway is stopped within a month. A month, do you hear me? Those are my terms. What do you say to that?' She removed the dummy.

'You filthy bitch.'

'Quite,' said Lady Maud, 'so you agree to sign?'

'I do not,' screamed Sir Giles and was promptly silenced.

'I don't know if you know your Shakespeare,' she said, 'but in *Edward the Second* . . .'

Sir Giles didn't know his Marlowe either but he did know about Edward the Second.

'Blott,' said Lady Maud, 'go into the kitchen and see if you can find—'

But already Sir Giles was nodding his head. He would sign anything now.

While Blott untied his right hand Lady Maud took a fountain pen out of her handbag. 'Here,' she said pointing to a dotted line. Sir Giles signed. 'Here,' and 'Here.' Sir Giles signed and signed. When he had finished Blott witnessed his signatures. Then he was tied down again.

'Good,' said Lady Maud, 'I will institute proceedings for divorce at once and you will stop the motorway or face the consequences. And don't you dare to set foot on my property again. I will have your things sent down to you.' She took out the dummy. 'Have you anything to say?'

'If I do manage to stop the motorway will you guarantee to let me have the photographs and negatives back?'

'Of course,' said Lady Maud, 'we Handymans may have our faults, but breaking our promises isn't one of them.' She stuffed the dummy back into his mouth and tied it behind his head. Then, having removed his glasses, she adjusted his bonnet and left the room.

On the staircase they met Mrs Forthby in a dither. 'You didn't do anything horrid, did you?' she asked.

'Of course not,' Lady Maud assured her, 'just got him to sign a document consenting to divorce.'

'Oh dear, I do hope he isn't too cross. He gets into such terrible tantrums.'

'Come, come, Nanny Whip, be your true self,' said Lady Maud. 'You must be firm.'

'Yes, you're quite right,' said Mrs Forthby. 'But it's very difficult. It's not in my nature to be unkind.'

'And before I forget, here's a little honorarium for your assistance.' Lady Maud produced a cheque from her bag but Mrs Forthby shook her head.

'I may be a silly woman and not very nice but I do have my standards,' she said. 'And besides I'd probably forget to cash it.' She went upstairs a little wistfully.

'That woman,' said Lady Maud as they drove to Paddington to catch the train to Worford, 'is far too good for Giles. She deserves something better.' On the way they stopped to post the share transfers to Messrs Schaeffer, Blodger and Vaizey.

CHAPTER TWENTY

By the time they reached Handyman Hall it was two o'clock in the morning but the park was well lit. Under the floodlights men were busily engaged in erecting the fencing posts and already one side of the park was fenced in. Lady Maud drove round to have a look and congratulated Mr Firkin, the manager, on the progress.

'I'm afraid you're going to have to pay the bonus,' he told her. 'At this rate we'll be finished in ten days.'

'Make it a week,' said Lady Maud. 'Money's no problem.' She went into the house and up to bed well content. Money was no object now.

In the morning she would withdraw every penny from their joint account at Westland Bank in Worford and deposit it in her own private account at the Northern. Sir Giles would scream blue murder but there was nothing he could do. He had signed the share transfer certificates if not of his own free will at least in circumstances which made it impossible for him to argue otherwise. And besides she still held one card up her sleeve, the photographs of Dundridge. She would call on the little goose and force him to admit that he had been blackmailed by Giles. Once she had proof of that there would be no question of the motorway continuing. She wouldn't even have to bother with her own awful photographs. Giles would be in jail, his seat in Parliament empty, a bye-election, and the whole wretched business finished.

Whatever happened now she was safe and so was the Hall. 'Fight fire with fire,' she thought and lay in bed considering the strange set of circumstances that had turned her from a plain, simple home-loving woman, a Justice of the Peace and a respectable member of the community, into a blackmailer dealing in obscene photographs and extorting signatures under threat of torture. Evidently the blood of her ancestors who had held the Gorge (by fair means and foul) against all comers still ran in her veins.

'You can't make omelettes without breaking eggs,' she murmured, and fell asleep.

In Mrs Forthby's flat one of the eggs in question lay in his frilly bonnet desperately trying to think of some way out of both his predicaments and promising himself that he would murder Nanny Fucking Whip as soon as he got free. Not that there seemed much chance of that before morning. Nanny Whip was snoring loudly on the sofa in the sitting-room. One look at Sir Giles' suffused face had been enough to persuade her that Naughty Boy's naughtiness had not diminished during her absence. A policy of continued restraint seemed called for. Nanny Whip went into the kitchen and hit the bottle of cooking brandy. 'A drop will give me some Dutch courage,' she thought and poured herself a large glass. By the time she had finished it she had forgotten what she had been taking it for. 'A little of what you fancy does you good,' she murmured, and collapsed on to the sofa.

A little of what Sir Giles fancied wasn't doing him any good at all. Besides, eight hours wasn't a little. As the clock on the mantelpiece chimed the hours Sir Giles' thoughts turned from murder to the more lurid forms of slow torture and in between he tried to think what the hell to do about Maud. There didn't seem anything he could do short of applying for the Chiltern Hundreds, resigning from all his clubs, realizing his assets and taking a quick trip to Brazil where the extradition laws didn't apply. And even then he wasn't sure he had any assets to realize. At about four in the morning it dawned on him that some of those pieces of paper he had signed had looked remarkably like share transfer certificates. At the time he hadn't been in any shape to consider them at all carefully. Not that he was in any better shape now but at least the threat of following Edward the Second to an agonizing death had been removed. Finally exhausted by his ordeal he fell into a semi-coma, waking every now and then to consider new and more awful fates for that absent-minded old sot in the next room.

Mrs Forthby woke with a hangover. She staggered off the sofa and ran a bath and it was only when she was drying herself that she remembered Sir Giles.

'Oh dear, he will be cross,' she thought, and went through to the kitchen to make a pot of tea. She carried the tray through to the bedroom and put it down on the bedside table. 'Wakey, wakey, rise and shine,' she said cheerfully and untied the straps. Sir Giles spat the dummy out of his mouth. This was the moment he had been waiting twelve hours for but there was no rising and shining for Sir Giles. He slithered sideways off the bed and crawled towards Mrs Forthby like a crab with rheumatoid arthritis.

'No, no, you naughty boy,' said Mrs Forthby horrified at his colour. She rushed out of the room and locked herself in the bathroom. There was no need to hurry. Behind her Sir Giles was stuck in the bedroom door and one of his legs had attached itself inextricably to a standard lamp.

In his office at the Regional Planning Board the Controller Motorways Midlands was having second thoughts about his plan for proving that Lady Maud was a blackmailer. The wretched woman had phoned the switchboard to say that she was coming in to Worford and wanted a word in private with him. Dundridge could well understand her desire for privacy but he did not share it. He had seen more than enough of Lady Maud in private and he had no intention of seeing any more. On the other hand she was hardly likely to threaten him with blackmail in front of a large audience. Dundridge paced up and down his office trying to find some way out of the quandary. In the end he decided to use Hoskins as a bodyguard. He sent for him.

'We've flushed the old cow out with that dynamiting,' he said.

'We've done what?' said Hoskins.

'She's coming to see me this morning. I want you to be present.'

Hoskins had his doubts. 'I don't know about that,' he muttered. 'And anyway, we haven't started dynamiting yet.'

'But the task force has moved in, hasn't it?'

'Yes, though I do wish you wouldn't call it a task force. All this military jargon is getting on my nerves.'

'Never mind that,' said Dundridge. 'The point is that she's coming. I want you to conceal yourself somewhere where you can hear what she has to say and make an appearance if she turns nasty.'

'*Turns* nasty?' said Hoskins. 'The bloody woman *is* nasty. She doesn't have to turn it.'

'I mean if she becomes violent,' Dundridge explained. 'Now then, we've got to find somewhere for you to hide. He looked hopefully at a filing cabinet but Hoskins was adamant.

'Why can't I just sit in the corner?' he asked.

'Because she wants to see me in private.'

'Well then see her in private for God's sake,' said Hoskins. 'She isn't likely to assault you.

'That's what you think,' said Dundridge. 'And in any case I want you as a witness. I have reason to believe that she is going to make an attempt to blackmail me.'

'Blackmail you?' said Hoskins turning pale. He didn't like that 'reason to believe'. It smacked of a policeman giving evidence.

'With photographs,' said Dundridge.

'With photographs?' echoed Hoskins, now thoroughly alarmed.

'Obscene photographs,' said Dundridge, with a deal more confidence than Hoskins happened to know was called for.

'What are you going to do?' he asked.

'I'm going to tell her to go jump in a lake,' said Dundridge.

Hoskins looked at him incredulously. To think that he had once described this extraordinary man as a nincompoop. The bastard was as tough as nails.

'I'll tell you what I'll do,' he said finally, 'I'll stand outside the door and listen to what she says. Will that do?'

Dundridge said it would have to and Hoskins hurried back to his office and phoned Mrs Williams.

'Sally,' he said, 'this is you-know-who.'

'I don't, you know,' said Mrs Williams, who had had a hard night.

'It's me. Horsey, horsey catkins,' snarled Hoskins desperately searching for a pseudonym that would deceive anyone listening in on the switchboard.

'Horsey horsey catkins?'

'Hoskins, for God's sake,' whispered Hoskins.

'Oh, Hoskins, why didn't you say so in the first place?'

Hoskins controlled his frayed temper. 'Listen carefully,' he said, 'the gaff's blown. The gaff. Gee for Gifuckingraffe. A for Animal. F for Freddie.'

'What's it mean?' interrupted Mrs Williams.

'The fuzz,' said Hoskins. 'It means the balloon's going to go up. Burn the lot, you understand. Negatives, prints, the tootee. You've never heard of me and I've never heard of you. Get it. No names, no pack drill. And you've never been near the Golf Club.'

By the time he had put the phone down Mrs Williams had got the message. So had Hoskins. If Mrs Williams was going to be nabbed, he could be sure that he would be standing in the dock beside her. She had left him in no doubt about that.

He went back to Dundridge's office and was there to open the door for Lady Maud when she arrived. Then he stationed himself outside and listened.

Inside Dundridge nerved himself for the ordeal. At least with Hoskins outside the door he could always call for help and in any case Lady Maud seemed to be rather better disposed towards him than he had expected.

'Mr Dundridge,' she said, taking a seat in front of his desk, 'I would like to make it quite clear that I have come here this morning in no spirit of animosity. I know we've had our little contretemps in the past but as far as I am concerned all is forgiven and forgotten.'

Dundridge looked at her balefully and said nothing. As far as he was concerned nothing was ever likely to be forgotten and certainly he wasn't in a forgiving mood.

'No, I have come here to ask for your co-operation,' she went on, 'and I want to assure you that what I am about to say will go no further.'

Dundridge glanced at the door and said he was glad to hear it.

'Yes, I rather thought you might,' said Lady Maud. 'You see I have reason to believe that you have been the subject of a blackmail attempt.'

Dundridge stared at her. She knew damned well he had been subject to blackmail.

'What makes you think that?'

'These photographs,' said Lady Maud and, producing an envelope from her handbag, she spread the torn and charred fragments of the photographs out on the desk. Dundridge studied them carefully. Why the hell were they torn and charred? He sorted through them looking for his face. It wasn't there. If she thought she was going to blackmail him with this lot she was very much mistaken.

'What about them?' he asked.

'You know nothing about them?'

'Certainly not,' said Dundridge, thoroughly confident now. He knew what had happened. He had left these photographs on Mr Ganglion's desk. Ganglion had torn them up and thrown them in the fire and had then changed his mind. He had taken them out and had visited Lady Maud and explained that he, Dundridge, had accused her of blackmail. And here she was trying to wriggle out of it. Her next remark confirmed this theory.

'Then my husband has never tried to influence you in any of your decisions by using these photographs,' she said.

'Your husband? Your husband?' said Dundridge indignantly. 'Are you suggesting that your husband has attempted to blackmail me with these ... obscene photographs?'

'Yes,' said Lady Maud, 'that is exactly what I am suggesting.'

'Then all I can say is that you are mistaken. Sir Giles has always treated me with the greatest consideration and courtesy, which is,' he glanced at the door before continuing courageously, 'more than I can say for you.'

Lady Maud looked at him, mystified. 'Is that all you have to say?'

'Yes,' said Dundridge, 'except this. Why don't you take those photographs to the police?'

Lady Maud hesitated. She hadn't bargained on this attitude from Dundridge. 'I don't think that would be very sensible, do you?'

'Yes,' said Dundridge, 'as a matter of fact I do. Now then I am a busy man and you are wasting my time. You know your way out.'

Lady Maud rose from her chair wrathfully. 'How dare you speak to me like that?' she shouted.

Dundridge leapt out of his chair and opened the door. 'Hoskins,' he said, 'show Lady Maud Lynchwood out.'

'I will find my own way,' said Lady Maud, and stormed past them and down the corridor. Dundridge went back into his office and collapsed into his chair. He had called her bluff. He had shown her the door. Nobody could say the Controller Motorways Midlands wasn't master in his own house. He was astonished at his own performance.

So was Hoskins. He stared at Dundridge for a moment and staggered back to his own office shaken by what he had just heard. She had confronted Dundridge with those awful photographs and he had had the nerve to tell her to take them to the police. My God, a man who could do that was capable of doing anything. The fat was really in the fire now. On the other hand she had said it wouldn't be sensible. Hoskins agreed with her wholeheartedly. 'She must be protecting Sir Giles,' he thought and wondered how the hell she had got hold of the photographs in the first place. For a moment he thought of phoning Sir Giles but decided against it. The best thing to do was to sit tight and keep his mouth shut and hope that things would blow over.

He had just reached this comforting conclusion when the bell rang. It was Dundridge again. Hoskins went back down the corridor and found the Controller in a jubilant mood.

'Well that's put paid to that little scheme,' he said. 'You heard her threatening me with filthy photographs. She thought she was going to get me to use my influence to change the route of the motorway. I told her.'

'You most certainly did,' said Hoskins deferentially.

'Right,' said Dundridge turning to a map he had pinned on the wall, 'we must strike while the iron is hot. Operation Overland will proceed immediately. Have the compulsory purchase orders been served?'

'Yes,' said Hoskins.

'And the task force has begun demolition work in the Gorge?'

'Demolition work?'

'Dynamiting.'

'Not yet. They've only just moved in.'

'They must start at once,' said Dundridge. 'We must keep the initiative and maintain the pressure. I intend to establish a mobile HQ here.' He pointed to a spot on the map two miles east of Guildstead Carbonell.

'A mobile HQ?' said Hoskins.

'Arrange for a caravan to be set up there. I intend to supervise this operation personally. You and I will move our offices out there.'

'That's going to be frightfully inconvenient,' Hoskins pointed out.

'Damn the inconvenience,' said Dundridge, 'I mean to have that bitch out of Handyman Hall before Christmas come hell or high water. She's on the run now and by God I mean to see she stays there.'

'Oh all right,' said Hoskins gloomily. He knew better than to argue with Dundridge now.

Lady Maud drove back to the Hall pensively. She could have sworn that the thin legs in the photographs were the legs she had seen twinkling across the marble floor but evidently she had been wrong. Dundridge's self-righteous indignation had been wholly convincing. She had expected the wretched little man to blush and stammer and make excuses but instead he had stood up to her and ordered her out of his office. He had even suggested she should take the photographs to the police and, considering his pusillanimity in other less threatening circumstances, it was impossible to suppose he had been bluffing. No, she had been wrong. It was a pity. She would have liked to have seen Sir Giles in court, but it hardly mattered. She had enough to be going on with. Sir Giles would move heaven and earth to see that the motorway was stopped now and if he failed she would force him to resign his seat. There would have to be another bye-election and what had worked in the case of Ottertown would work again in the case of the Gorge. The Government would cancel the motorway. And finally if that too failed there was always the Wildlife Park. It was one thing to demolish half a dozen houses and evict the families that lived there, but it was quite a different kettle of fish to deprive ten lions, four giraffes, a rhinoceros and a dozen ostriches of their livelihood. The British public would never stand for cruelty to animals. She arrived at the Hall to find Blott busy washing his films in the kitchen.

'I've turned the boiler-room into a darkroom,' he explained, and held up a film for her to look at. Lady Maud studied it inexpertly.

'Have they come out all right?' she asked.

'Very nicely,' said Blott. 'Quite lovely.'

'I doubt if Giles would share your opinion,' said Lady Maud and went out into the garden to pick a lettuce for lunch. Blott finished washing his films in the sink and took them down to the boiler-room and hung them up to dry. When he came back lunch was ready on the kitchen table.

'You'll eat in here with me,' said Lady Maud. 'I'm very pleased with you, Blott, and besides, it's nice to have a man about the house.'

Blott hesitated. It seemed an illogical remark. There appeared to be a great many men about the house, tramping up and down the servants' stairs to their bedrooms and working day and night on the fencing. Still, if Lady Maud wanted him to eat with her, he was not going to argue. Things were looking up. She was going to get a divorce from her husband. He was in love and while he had no hope of ever being able to do anything about it, he was happy just to sit and eat with her. And then there was the fence. Blott was delighted by the fence. It brought back memories of the war and his happiness as a prisoner. It would shut out the world and he and Maud would live singly but happily ever after.

They had just finished lunch and were washing-up when there was a dull boom in the distance and the windows rattled.

'I wonder what that was,' said Lady Maud.

'Sounds like blasting,' said Blott.

'Blasting?'

'In a quarry.'

'But there aren't any quarries round here,' said Lady Maud. They went out on to the lawn and stood looking at a cloud of dust rising slowly into the sky a mile or two to the east.

Operation Overland had begun.

CHAPTER TWENTY-ONE

And Operation Overland continued. Day after day the silence of the Gorge was broken by the rumbling of bulldozers and the dull thump of explosions as the cliffs were blasted and the rocks cleared. Day after day the contractors complained to Hoskins that the way to build a motorway was to start at the beginning and go on to the end, or at least to stick to some sort of predetermined schedule and not go jumping all over the place digging up a field here and rooting out a wood there, starting a bridge and then abandoning construction to begin a flyover. And day after day Hoskins took their complaints and some of his own to Dundridge, and was overruled.

'The essential feature of Operation Overland lies in the random nature of our movements,' Dundridge explained. 'The enemy never knows where we are going to be next.'

'Nor do I, come to that,' said Hoskins bitterly. 'I had a job finding this place this morning. You might have warned me you were going to move it before I went home last night.'

Dundridge looked round the Mobile Headquarters. 'That's odd,' he said, 'I thought *you* had it moved.'

'Me? Why should I do that?'

'I don't know. To be nearer the front line I suppose.'

'Nearer the front line?' said Hoskins. 'All I want is to be back in my bloody office, not traipsing round the countryside in a fucking caravan.'

'Well anyway, whoever had it moved had a good idea,' said Dundridge. 'We are nearer the scene of action.'

Hoskins looked out of the window as a giant dumper rumbled past.

'Nearer?' he shouted above the din. 'We're bloody well in it if you ask me.' As if to confirm his words there was a deafening roar and two hundred yards away a portion of cliff collapsed. As the dust settled Dundridge surveyed the scene with satisfaction. This was nature as man, and in particular Dundridge, intended. Nature conquered, nature subdued, nature disciplined. This was progress, slow progress but inexorable. Behind them cuttings and embankments, concrete and steel, ahead the Gorge and Handyman Hall.

'By the way,' said Hoskins when he could hear himself speak, 'we've had a complaint from General Burnett. He says one of our trucks damaged his garden wall.'

'So what?' said Dundridge. 'He won't have a garden or a wall in two months' time. What's he complaining about?'

'And Mr Bullett-Finch phoned to say—'

But Dundridge wasn't interested. 'File all complaints,' he said dismissively, 'I haven't got time for details.'

In London Sir Giles didn't share his opinion. He was obsessed with details, particularly those concerned with the sale of his shares and what Lady Maud was going to do with those damned photographs.

'I lost half a million on those shares,' he yelled at Blodger. 'Half a bleeding million.'

Blodger commiserated. 'I said at the time I thought you were being a little hasty,' he said.

'You thought? You didn't think at all,' Sir Giles screamed. 'If you'd thought you would have known that wasn't me on the phone.'

'But it sounded like you. And you asked me to call you back at your flat.'

'I did nothing of the sort. You don't seriously imagine I would sell four thousand President Rand when the market was at rock bottom. I'm not fucking insane you know.'

Blodger looked at him appraisingly. The thought had crossed his mind. It was Schaeffer who brought the altercation to an end.

'If you must swear,' he said, 'I can only suggest that you would do so more profitably before a Commissioner of Oaths.'

'And what would I want with a Commissioner of Fucking Oaths?'

'A sworn statement that the signatures on the share transfer certificates were forgeries,' said Schaeffer coldly.

Sir Giles picked up his hat. 'Don't think this is the end of the fucking matter,' he snarled. 'You'll be hearing from me again.'

Schaeffer opened the door for him. 'I can only hope fucking not,' he said.

But if his stockbrokers were not sympathetic, Mrs Forthby was.

'It's all my fault,' she wailed squinting at him through the two black eyes he had given her for her pains. 'If only I hadn't gone out for those fish fingers this would never have happened.'

'Fish fucking ...' he began and pulled himself up. He had to keep a grip on his sanity and Mrs Forthby's self-denunciations didn't help. 'Never mind about that. I've got to think what to do. That bloody wife of mine isn't going to get away with this if I can help it.'

'Well, if all she wants is a divorce ...'

'A divorce? A divorce? If you think that's all she wants ...' He stopped again. Mrs Forthby mustn't hear anything about those photographs. Nobody must hear about them. The moment that information got out he would be a ruined man and he had just three weeks to do something about them. He went back to his flat and sat there trying to think of some way of stopping the motorway. There wasn't much he could do in London. His request to discuss the matter with the Minister of the Environment had been turned down, his demand for a further Inquiry denied. And his private source in the Ministry had been adamant that it was too late to do anything now.

'The thing is under construction already. Barring accidents nothing can stop it.'

Sir Giles put down the phone and thought about accidents, nasty accidents, like Maud falling downstairs and breaking her neck or having a fatal car crash. It didn't seem very likely somehow. Finally he thought about Dundridge. If Maud had something on him, he had something on the Controller Motorways Midlands. He telephoned Hoskins at the Regional Planning Board.

'He's out at SHMOCON,' said the girl on the switchboard.

'Shmocon?' said Sir Giles desperately trying to think of a village by that name in South Worfordshire.

'Supreme Headquarters Motorway Construction,' said the girl. 'He's Deputy Field Commander.'

'What?' said Sir Giles. 'What the hell's going on up there?'

'Don't ask me,' said the girl, 'I'm only a field telegraphist. Shall I put you through?'

'Yes,' said Sir Giles. 'It sounds batty to me.'

'It is,' said the girl. 'It's a wonder I don't have to use morse code.'

Certainly Hoskins sounded peculiar when Sir Giles finally got through to him. 'Deputy Field—' he began but Sir Giles interrupted.

'Don't give me that crap, Hoskins,' he shouted. 'What the hell do you think you're playing at? Some sort of war game?'

'Yes,' said Hoskins looking nervously out of the window. There was a deafening roar as a charge of dynamite went off.

'What the hell was that?' yelled Sir Giles.

'Just a near miss,' said Hoskins as small fragments of rock rattled on the roof of the caravan.

'You can cut the wisecracks,' said Sir Giles, 'I didn't call you to talk nonsense. There's been a change of plan. The motorway has got to be stopped. I've decided ...'

'Stopped?' Hoskins interrupted him. 'You haven't a celluloid rat's hope in hell of stopping this little lot now. We're advancing into the Gorge at the rate of a hundred yards a day.'

'Into the Gorge?'

'You heard me,' said Hoskins.

'Good God,' said Sir Giles. 'What the hell's been going on? Has Dundridge gone off his head or something?'

'You could put it like that,' said Hoskins hesitantly. The Controller Motorways Midlands had just come into the caravan covered in dust and was taking off his helmet.

'Well, stop him,' shouted Sir Giles.

'I'm afraid that is impossible, sir,' said Hoskins modulating his tone to indicate that he was no longer alone. 'I will make a note of your complaint, and forward it to the appropriate authorities.'

'You'll do more than that,' bawled Sir Giles, 'you'll use those photographs. You will—'

'I understand the police deal with these matters, sir,' said Hoskins. 'As far as we are concerned I can only suggest that you use an incinerator.'

'An *incinerator*? What the hell do I want with an incinerator?'

'I have found that the best method is to burn that sort of rubbish. The answer is in the negative.'

'In the negative?'

'Quite, sir,' said Hoskins. 'I have found that it avoids the health risk to incinerate inflammable material. And now if you'll excuse me, I have someone with me.' Hoskins rang off and Sir Giles sat back and deciphered his message.

'Incinerators. Police. Negative. Health risks.' These were the words Hoskins had emphasized and it dawned on Sir Giles that all hope of influencing Dundridge had gone up in flames. He was particularly alarmed by the mention of the police. 'Good God, that little bastard Dundridge has been to the cops,' he muttered, and suddenly recalled that his safe at Handyman Hall contained evidence that hadn't been incinerated. Maud was sitting on a safe containing photographs that could send him to prison. 'Inflammable material. That bitch can get me five years,' he thought. 'I'd like to incinerate her.' Incinerate her? Sir

Giles stared into space. He had suddenly seen a way out of all his problems.

He picked up a pencil and detailed the advantages. Number One, he would destroy the evidence of his attempt to blackmail Dundridge. Number Two, he would get rid of those photographs Blott had taken of him in Mrs Forthby's flat. Number Three, by acting before Maud could divorce him he would still be the owner of the ashes of Handyman Hall and liable for the insurance money and possibly the compensation from the motorway. Number Four, if Maud were to die ... Number Four was a particularly attractive prospect and just the sort of accident he had been hoping for.

He picked up the sheet of paper and carried it across to the fireplace and lit a match. As the paper flared up Sir Giles watched it with immense satisfaction. There was nothing like a good fire for cleansing the past. All he needed now was a perfect alibi.

At Handyman Hall Lady Maud surveyed her handiwork with equal satisfaction. The fence had been finished in ten days, the lions, giraffes, and the rhinoceros had been installed and the ostriches were accommodated in the old tennis court. It was really very pleasant to wander round the house and watch the lions padding across the park or lying under the trees.

'It gives one a certain sense of security,' she told Blott, whose movements had been restricted to the kitchen garden and who complained that the rhinoceros was mucking up the lawn.

'It may give you a sense of security,' said Blott, 'but the postman has other ideas. He won't come further than the Lodge and the milkman won't either.'

'What nonsense,' said Lady Maud. 'The way to deal with lions is to put a bold front on and look them squarely in the eyes.'

'That's as maybe,' said Blott, 'but that rhino needs spectacles.'

'The thing with rhinos,' said Lady Maud, 'is to move at right angles to their line of approach.'

'That didn't work with the butcher's van. You've no idea what it did to his back mudguard.'

'I have a very precise idea. Sixty pounds worth of damage but it didn't charge the van.'

'No,' said Blott, 'it just leant up again it and scratched its backside.'

'Well at least the giraffes are behaving themselves,' said Lady Maud.

'What's left of them,' said Blott.

'What do you mean "What's left of them"?'

'Well, there's only two left.'

'Two? But there were four. Where have the other two got to?'

'You had better ask the lions about that,' Blott told her. 'I have an idea they rather like giraffes for dinner.'

'In that case we had better order another hundredweight of meat from the butchers. We can't have them eating one another.'

She strode off across the lawn imperiously, stopping to prod the rhinoceros with her shooting stick. 'I won't have you in the rockery,' she told it. Outside the kitchen door a lion was snoozing in the sun. 'Be off with you, you lazy beast.' The lion got up and slunk away.

Blott watched with admiration and then shut the door of the kitchen garden. 'What a woman,' he murmured and went back to the tomatoes. He was interrupted five minutes later by a dull thump from the Gorge. Blott looked up. They were getting nearer. It was about time he did something about that business. So far his efforts had been confined to moving Dundridge's mobile headquarters about the countryside at night and altering the position of the pegs that marked the route so that had the motorway proceeded as the contractors desired it would have been several degrees off course. Unfortunately Dundridge's insistence on random construction had defeated Blott's efforts. His only success had been the felling of all the trees in Colonel Chapman's orchard which was a quarter of a mile away from the supposed route of the motorway. Blott was rather proud of that. The Colonel had raised Cain with the authorities and had been promised additional compensation. A few more miscalculations like that and there would be a public outcry. Blott applied his mind to the problem.

That night Blott visited the Royal George at Guildstead Carbonell for the first time in several weeks.

Mrs Wynn greeted him enthusiastically. 'I'm so glad you've come,' she said, 'I thought you'd given me up for good.'

Blott said he had been busy. 'Busy?' said Mrs Wynn. 'You're one to talk. I've been rushed off my feet with all the men from the motorway. They come in here at lunch and they're back at night. I tell you, I can't remember anything like it.'

Blott looked round the bar and could see what she meant. The pub was filled with construction workers. He helped himself to a pint of Handyman Brown and went to a table in the corner. An hour later he was deep in conversation with the driver of a bulldozer.

'Must be interesting work knocking things down,' said Blott.

'The pay's good,' said the driver.

'I imagine you've got to be a real expert to demolish a big building like Handyman Hall.'

'I don't know. The bigger they is the harder they falls is what I say,' said the driver, flattered by Blott's interest.

'Let me get you another pint,' said Blott.

Three pints later the driver was explaining the niceties of demolition to a fascinated Blott.

'It's a question of hitting the corner stone,' he said. 'Find that, swing the ball back and let it go and Bob's your uncle, the whole house is down like a pack of cards. I tell you I've done that more times than you've had hot dinners.'

Blott said he could well believe it. By closing time he knew a great deal about demolition work and the driver said he looked forward to meeting him again. Blott helped Mrs Wynn with washing the glasses and then did his duty by her but his heart wasn't in it. Mrs Wynn noticed it.

'You're not your usual self tonight,' she said when they had finished. Blott grunted. 'Mind you I can't say I'm any great shakes myself. My legs are killing me. What I need is a holiday.'

'Why don't you take a day off?' said Blott.

'How can I? Who would look after the customers?'

'I would,' said Blott.

At five he was up and cycling down the main street of Guildstead Carbonell towards Handyman Hall. At seven he had fed the lions and when Lady Maud came down to breakfast Blott was waiting for her.

'I'm taking the day off,' he announced.

'You're what?' said Lady Maud. Blott didn't take days off.

'Taking the day off. And I'll need the Land-Rover.'

'What for?' said Lady Maud who wasn't used to being told by her gardener that he needed her Land-Rover.

'Never you mind,' said Blott. 'No names, no pack drill.'

'No names, no pack drill? Are you feeling all right?'

'And a note for Mr Wilkes at the Brewery to say he's to give me Very Special Brew.'

Lady Maud sat down at the kitchen table and looked at him doubtfully. 'I don't like the sound of this, Blott. You're up to something.'

'And I don't like the sound of that,' said Blott as a dull thump came from the Gorge. Lady Maud nodded. She didn't like the sound of it either.

'Has it got anything to do with that?' she asked. Blott nodded. 'In that case you can have what you want but I don't want you getting into any trouble on my account, you understand.'

She went through to the study and wrote a note to Mr Wilkes, the manager of the Handyman Brewery in Worford, telling him to give Blott whatever he asked for.

At ten Blott was in the manager's office.

'Very Special?' said Mr Wilkes. 'But Very Special is for special occasions. Coronations and suchlike.'

'This is a special occasion,' said Blott.

Mr Wilkes looked at the letter again. 'If Lady Maud says so, I suppose I must, but it's strictly against the law to sell Very Special. It's twenty per cent proof.'

'And ten bottles of vodka,' said Blott. They went down to the cellar and loaded the Land-Rover.

'Forget you've seen me,' Blott said when they had finished.

'I'll do my best,' said the manager, 'this is all bloody irregular.'

Blott drove to the Royal George and saw Mrs Wynn on to the bus. Then he went back into the pub and set to work. By lunchtime he had emptied one barrel of Handyman Bitter down the drain and had refilled it with bottles of Very Special and five bottles of vodka. He tried it out on a couple of customers and was delighted with the result. During the afternoon he had a nap and then took a stroll through the village and up past the Bullett-Finches' house. It was a large house in mock Tudor set back from the road and with a very fine garden. Outside the gates a sign announced that Finch Grove was For Sale. The Bullett-Finches didn't fancy living within a hundred yards of a motorway. Blott didn't blame them. Then he walked back through the village and looked at Miss Percival's cottage. That wasn't for sale. It was due for demolition and Miss Percival had already vacated it. A large crane with a steel ball on the end of its arm stood nearby. Blott climbed into the driver's seat and played with the controls. Then he walked back to the pub and sat behind the bar, waiting for opening time.

CHAPTER TWENTY-TWO

Sir Giles busied himself in Mrs Forthby's flat. He altered the date on the clock on the mantelpiece. He turned the pages of the *Radio Times* to the following day and hid the newspaper. Several times he asserted that today was Wednesday.

'That just goes to show what a muddlehead I am,' said Mrs Forthby, who was busy making supper in the kitchen, 'I could have sworn it was Tuesday.'

'Tomorrow's Thursday,' said Sir Giles.

'If you say so, dear,' said Mrs Forthby. 'I'm sure I don't know what day of the week it is. My memory is simply shocking.'

Sir Giles nodded approvingly. It was on Mrs Forthby's appalling memory that his alibi depended, that and sleeping pills. 'Silly old bitch won't miss a day in her life,' he thought as he crunched six tablets up in the bottom of a glass with the handle of a toothbrush before adding a large tot of whisky. According to his doctor the lethal dose was twelve. 'Six would probably put you out for twenty-four hours,' the doctor had told him and twenty-four hours was all Sir Giles needed. He went through to the kitchen and had supper.

'What about a nightcap?' he said when they had finished.

'You know I never drink,' said Mrs Forthby.

'You did the other night. You finished half a bottle of cooking brandy.'

'That was different. I wasn't feeling myself.'

It was on the tip of Sir Giles' tongue to tell her that she wouldn't feel anything let alone herself by the time she had finished that little lot but he restrained himself. 'Cheers,' he said, and finished his glass.

'Cheers,' said Mrs Forthby doubtfully and sipped her whisky.

Sir Giles poured himself another glass. 'Down the hatch,' he said.

Mrs Forthby took another sip. 'You know I could have sworn today was Tuesday,' she said.

Sir Giles could have sworn, period. 'Today is Wednesday.'

'But I've got a hair appointment on Wednesday. If today is Wednesday I must have missed it.'

'You have,' said Sir Giles truthfully. Whatever happened, Mrs Forthby had missed her hair appointment. He raised his glass. 'Mud in your eye.'

'Mud in your eye,' said Mrs Forthby and sipped again. 'If today is

Wednesday, tomorrow must be Thursday in which case I've got a pottery class in the afternoon.'

Sir Giles poured himself another whisky hurriedly. It was on just such insignificant details that the best plans floundered. 'I was thinking of going down to Brighton for the weekend,' he improvised. 'I thought you would like that.'

'With me?' said Mrs Forthby, her eyes shining.

'Just us two together,' said Sir Giles.

'Oh, you are thoughtful.'

'A votre santé,' said Sir Giles.

Mrs Forthby finished her drink and got to her feet. 'It's Nurse Catheter tonight, isn't it?' she said moving unsteadily towards him.

'Forget it,' said Sir Giles, 'I'm not in the mood.' Nor was Mrs Forthby. He carried her through to the bedroom and put her to bed. When he left the flat five minutes later she was snoring soundly. By the time she woke up he would be back and in bed beside her. He got into his car and began the drive north.

At the Royal George in Guildstead Carbonell Blott's experiment in induced narcosis proceeded more slowly but with gayer results. By nine o'clock the pub was filled with singing dumper drivers, two fights had erupted and died down before they could get well under way, a darts match had had to be cancelled when a non-participant had been pinned by his ear to last year's calendar, and two consenting adults had been ejected from the Gents by Blott and Mrs Wynn's Alsatian. By ten o'clock Blott's promise that the Very Special was needed for a special occasion had been fulfilled to the letter. Two more fights, this time between locals and the men from the motorway, had started and had not died down but had spread to the Saloon Bar where the operator of a piledriver was attempting to demonstrate his craft to the fiancée of the secretary of the Young Conservatives, the darts match had been resumed using a portrait of Sir Winston Churchill as a dartboard, and half a dozen bulldozer drivers were giving an exhibition of clog dancing on the bar-billiards table. In between whiles Blott had coaxed Mr Edwards, who claimed to have knocked down more houses than Blott had had hot dinners, into a nicely belligerent mood.

'I can knock any damned house you like to show me down with one bloody blow,' he shouted.

Blott raised an eyebrow. 'Tell me another one.'

'I tell you I can,' Mr Edwards asserted. 'One knock in the right place and Bob's your uncle.'

'I'll believe it when I see it,' said Blott and poured him another pint of Very Special.

'I'll show you. I'll bloody show you,' said Mr Edwards and took a swig.

By closing time Very Special had cast if not a healing balm at least a soporific one on the whole proceedings. As the motorway men stumbled off to their cars and the Young Conservatives drove off nursing their wounds, Blott shut up shop and helped Mr Edwards to his feet.

'I tell you I can,' he mumbled.

'Never,' said Blott.

Together they staggered off down the street towards Miss Percival's cottage, Blott clutching a bottle of vodka and Mr Edwards' arm.

'I'll show you,' said Mr Edwards as they crossed the field to the cottage. 'I'll fucking show you.'

He climbed into the crane and started it up. Blott stood behind him and watched.

'Oh what a pity she's only one titty to bang against the wall,' Mr Edwards sang as the crane jerked forward through the hedge and into the garden. Behind them the iron ball wobbled and swung. Mr Edwards stopped the crane and adjusted the controls. The arm of the crane swung round and the ball followed. It went wide.

'I thought you said you could do it in one,' said Blott.

'That,' said Mr Edwards, 'was just a practice swing.' He lowered the crane and a sundial disintegrated. Mr Edwards raised it again.

'Never been laid, never been made, Queen of all the Fairies,' he bawled. The crane swung round and Blott darted out of the way as the iron ball lolloped past him. The next moment it hurtled into the side of the cottage. There was a roar of falling bricks, tiles, breaking glass and a great cloud of dust momentarily obscured what had once been Miss Percival's attractive home. When the dust finally cleared what remained of the cottage held few attractions. On the other hand it was not entirely demolished. A chimney still stood and the roof while hanging at a disreputable angle was still recognizably the roof. Blott regarded the result sceptically.

'I don't think much of that,' he said superciliously. 'Still I suppose there's always a first time.'

'Whadja mean always a first time?' said Mr Edwards. 'I knocked it down, didn't I?'

'No,' said Blott, 'not with one blow.'

Mr Edwards consoled himself with vodka. ''sonly a fucking cottage. Can't expect much with a cottage. Got no bulk to it. Gotta have bulk, got to have weight. Show me a house, a proper house, a big bulky house and I'll . . .' He slumped over the controls. Blott climbed up into the cab and shook him.

'Wake up,' he shouted. Mr Edwards woke up.

'Show me a proper house . . .'

'All right, I will,' said Blott. 'Show me how to drive this thing and I'll show you a proper house.'

Mr Edwards did his best to show him. 'You pull that lever and you press that 'celerator.' Five minutes later Guildstead Carbonell, already disturbed by the eruption of violence at the Royal George, was convulsed a second time as Blott with Mr Edwards' assistance attempted to negotiate the High Street at something over the statutory speed limit. As the mobile crane hurtled into the first of several corners at forty miles per hour Blott struggled to keep it on the road. He wasn't helped by Mr Edwards' inertia nor by that of the iron ball which, swinging behind, tended to demonstrate the attractions of centrifugal force. On the first corner it gave a glancing blow to the plate-glass window of a newly opened mini-market, bounced off the roof of a parked car, entered the front parlour of Mrs Tate's house and came out through Mr and Mrs Williams' sitting-room, decapitated the War Memorial and took a telegraph pole and fifty yards of wire in tow. On the second it took a short cut through the forecourt of Mr Dugdale's garage neatly severing the stanchions that had formerly supported the roof and demolishing four petrol pumps and a sign advertising free tumblers. By the time they had traversed the rest of the High Street, the ball had left its imprint on seven more cars and the façades of twelve splendid examples of eighteenth-century domestic architecture while the telegraph pole, not to be left out of things, had vaulted through every third window before disentangling itself from the crane and coming to rest in the vestry of the Primitive Methodist Chapel taking with it a large sign announcing the Coming of the Lord. As they left the village, the iron ball made its last contribution to the peace and tranquillity of the place by nudging an electricity transformer which exploded with a galaxy of blue sparks and plunged the entire district into darkness. At this point Mr Edwards woke up.

'Where are we?' he mumbled.

'Almost there,' said Blott, managing to slow the crane down. Mr Edwards took another swig of vodka.

'Show me the way to go home,' he sang, 'I'm tired and I want to go to bed.'

'Not yet,' said Blott and turned the crane up the drive towards the Bullett-Finches' house.

*

It was one of Mrs Bullett-Finch's pleasanter qualities from her husband's point of view that she went to bed early. 'It's the early bird that catches the worm,' she would say at nine o'clock every night and take herself upstairs, leaving Mr Bullett-Finch to sit up by himself and read about lawns in peace and quiet. And lawns interested him. They held a charm for him that Ivy Bullett-Finch had long since relinquished. Lawns improved with age, which was more than could be said for wives and what Mr Bullett-Finch didn't know about browntop and chewing fescue and velvet bent was not worth knowing. And the lawns around Finch Grove were in his opinion among the finest in the country. They stretched immaculately in front of the house down to the stream at the bottom of the garden. Not a dandelion scarred their surface, not a plantain, not a daisy. For six years Mr Bullett-Finch had nurtured his lawns, sanding, mowing, spiking, fertilizing, weedkilling, even going so far as to prohibit visitors with high heels from walking on them. And when Ivy wanted to go down to the orchard she had to wear her bedroom slippers. It may have been this insistence on his part that the front garden was sacrosanct that had contributed to her nervous disposition and sense of guilt. What the garden was to her husband, the house was to Ivy, a source of obsessive concern in which everything had its place, was dusted twice a day and polished three times a week so that she went to bed early less out of indolence than from sheer exhaustion and lay there wondering if she had turned everything off.

On this particular night Mr Bullett-Finch was deep in a chapter on hormone weedkillers when the lights went out. He got up and stumbled through to the fusebox only to find that the fuses were intact.

'Must be a power failure,' he thought and went up to bed in the dark. He had just undressed and was putting on his pyjamas when he became aware that something extremely large and powered by an enormous diesel engine appeared to be making its way up his drive. He rushed to the window and peered out into two powerful headlights. Temporarily blinded, he groped for his dressing-gown and slippers, found them and put them on and looked out of the window again. What looked like a gigantic crane had stopped on the gravel forecourt and was backing on to his lawn. With a scream of rage Mr Bullett-Finch told it to stop but it was too late. A moment later there was a winching noise and the crane began to swing. Mr Bullett-Finch pulled his head in the window and raced for the stairs. He was halfway down them when all concern for his precious lawn disappeared, to be replaced by the absolute conviction that Finch Grove was at the very centre of some gigantic earthquake. As the house disintegrated around him – Mr Edwards' claim to be a demolition expert entirely vindicated – Mr Bullett-Finch clung to the banisters and peered through a dust-storm of plaster and powdered brick while the furnishings of which his wife had been so rightly proud hurtled past him from the upstairs rooms. Among them came Mrs Bullett-Finch herself, screaming and hysterically proclaiming her innocence, which had until then never been in doubt, and he was just debating why she should assume responsibility for what was obviously a natural cataclysm when he was saved the trouble by the roof collapsing on top of him and the staircase collapsing underneath. Mr Bullett-Finch descended into the cellar and lay unconscious, surrounded by his small stock of claret. Mrs Bullett-Finch, still clinging to her mattress and the conviction that she had left the gas on, had meanwhile been catapulted into the herb-garden where she sobbed convulsively among the thyme.

From the cab of his crane Mr Edwards regarded his handiwork with pride.

'Told you I could do it,' he said and seized the bottle of vodka from Blott who had been steadying his nerves with it. Blott let him finish it. Then dragged him down from the cab and climbed back to wipe any fingerprints from the controls. Finally, hoisting Mr Edwards over his shoulder, he set off down the drive.

By the time he reached the Royal George Mrs Wynn was back from Worford, and washing glasses by candlelight.

'Look at all this mess,' she said irately, 'I leave you to look after the place for one day and what do I find when I get back. Anyone would think there had been an orgy here. And what's been going on in the village, I'd like to know? The place looks like it's been bombed.'

Blott helped with the glasses and then went out to the Land-Rover. Mr Edwards was still sleeping soundly in the back. He drove slowly out of the yard and turned towards Ottertown. It was a longer way round but Blott didn't want to be seen in the High Street. He stopped at the caravan site where the motorway workers lived and deposited Mr Edwards on the grass. Then he drove on towards the Gorge and Handyman Hall. At two o'clock he was in bed in the Lodge. All in all it had been a good day's work.

In Dundridge's flat the phone rang. He groped for it sleepily and switched on the light. It was Hoskins. 'What the hell do you want? Do you realize what time it is?'

'Yes,' said Hoskins, 'as a matter of fact I do. I just wanted to tell you that you've gone too far this time.'

'Gone too far?' said Dundridge. 'I haven't gone anywhere.'

'Don't give me that,' said Hoskins. 'You and your random sorties and your task forces and assault groups. Well you've certainly landed us in it this time. There were people living in that fucking house, you know, and it wasn't even scheduled for demolition in the first place and as for what you've done to Guildstead Carbonell ... I hope you realize that the motorway wasn't supposed to go within a mile of that village. It's a historical monument, Guildstead Carbonell is ... was. It's a fucking ruin now, a disaster area.'

'A disaster area?' said Dundridge. 'What do you mean a disaster area?'

'You know very well what I mean,' shouted Hoskins hysterically. 'I always thought you were mad but now I know it.' He slammed the phone down, leaving Dundridge mystified. He sat on the edge of his bed and wondered what to do. Clearly something had gone wrong with Operation Overland. He was just about to call Hoskins back when the phone rang again. This time it was the police.

'Is that Mr Dundridge?'

'Yes, speaking.'

'This is the Chief Constable. I wonder if I could have a word with you. It's about this business at Guildstead Carbonell ...'

Dundridge got dressed.

Sir Giles parked his car outside Wilfrid's Castle Church. It was an unfrequented spot and nobody was likely to be out and about at two o'clock in the morning. It was one of the great advantages of a Bentley that it was not a noisy car. For the last five miles Sir Giles had driven without lights, coasting past farmhouses and keeping to back roads. He had seen no other vehicles and, so far as he could tell, had been seen by nobody. So far so good. Leaving the car he made his way down the footpath to the bridge. It was dark down there under the trees and he had some difficulty in finding his way. On the far side of the bridge he came to a wire-mesh gate. Using his torch briefly he unlatched it and went through into the pinetum. The gate puzzled Sir Giles. It was a long time since he had been over the bridge, not since the day of his wedding in fact, but he felt sure there had been no gate there then. Still he hadn't time to worry about little things like that. He had to move quickly. It wasn't easy. The pinetum was dark enough by daylight. At night it was pitch black. Sir Giles shone his torch on the ground and moved forward cautiously grateful to the carpet of pine needles that deadened his footsteps. He was halfway through the wood when he became conscious that he was not alone. Something was breathing nearby.

He switched off his torch and listened. Above him the pine trees sighed in a light breeze and for a moment Sir Giles hoped he had been mistaken. The next moment he knew he hadn't. An extraordinary whistling, wheezing noise issued from the wood. 'Must be a cow with asthma,' he thought though how an asthmatic cow had got into the pinetum he couldn't imagine. A moment later he was disabused of the notion of a cow. With a horrible snort whatever it was got to its feet, a process that involved breaking a number of branches, large branches by the sound of things, and lumbered off with a singlemindedness of purpose that seemed to bring it into contact with a great many trees. Sir Giles stood and quaked, partly from fear and partly because the ground beneath his feet was also quaking, and when finally the creature smashed through the iron fence at the edge of the wood with as little regard for property as for its own health and welfare he was in two minds about going on. In the end he forced himself to continue, though more cautiously. After all, whatever he had disturbed, it *had* run away.

Sir Giles came to the gate and stared at the house. The place was in darkness. He walked quickly across the lawn and round to the front door. Then taking off his shoes he unlocked the door and stepped inside. Silence. He went down the corridor to his study and shut the door. Then he switched on his torch and shone it on the safe – or rather on the hole in the wall where the safe had been. Sir Giles stared at it in horror. No wonder Hoskins had talked so insistently about incinerators and inflammable material and health risks. It hadn't been Dundridge who had been threatening to go to the police. It was Maud. But had she been already? There was no way of telling. He switched off the torch and stood in the darkness thinking. There was certainly one way of ensuring that if she hadn't been already she wasn't going to in future. Any doubts he had had, and they were few, about the wisdom of disposing of Handyman Hall and Maud disappeared. He would make certain of the bitch. He opened the door of the study and listened for a moment before tiptoeing down the passage towards the kitchen. Kitchens were the logical place for fires to start of their own accord and besides there were the oil tanks that fed the Aga cooker. On the way he stopped to put on his Wellington boots in the cloakroom under the stairs.

The twang of the iron fence woke Lady Maud. She sat up in bed and wondered what it portended. Iron fences didn't twang of their own accord and rhinoceroses didn't go charging across rockeries in the small hours of the morning without good reason. She switched on the bedside lamp to see what time it was but thanks to the power failure at Guildstead Carbonell the light didn't come on. Peculiar. She got out of bed and went to the window and was just in time to see a shadow slip across the lawn and disappear round the side of the house. It was a distinctly furtive shadow and it came from the pinetum. For a moment she supposed it to be Blott, but there was no reason for Blott to be running furtively about the park at ... she looked at her watch ... half past two in the morning. Anyway she could always check. She picked up the phone and dialled the Lodge.

'Blott,' she whispered, 'are you there?'

'Yes,' said Blott.

'Are the gates locked?'

'Yes,' said Blott, 'why?'

'I just wanted to make sure.' She put the phone down gently and got dressed. Then she went downstairs quietly and tried the front door. It was unlocked. Lady Maud looked around. A pair of shoes on the doorstep. She picked them up and sniffed. Giles. Unmistakably Giles. Then she put the shoes down again and shutting the front door behind her went round to the workshop. So the little beast had come back. She could imagine what for. Well, come back he might but he wouldn't get away so easily. A moment later she was running, remarkably swiftly for so large a woman and so dark a night, across the lawn towards the pinetum. Even there in the pitch darkness her pace did not slacken. A life-time's familiarity with the path gave her an unerring sense of when to twist or turn through the trees. Five minutes later she was at the gate to the footbridge. She reached into her pocket and took out a large lock, fitted it to the bolt and closed the hasp. Then, having tested it to see that it was firmly fastened, she turned and made her way back towards the Hall.

In the kitchen Sir Giles took his time. The essence of successful arson lay in simplicity, and murder was best when it looked like natural death. The Aga cooker was self-igniting. It came on automatically at intervals during the night. Sir Giles shone his torch on the time switch and saw that it was set for four o'clock. Plenty of time. He took an adjustable spanner out of his pocket and undid the nut that secured the feedpipe from the oil tanks to the stove. Oil began to pour out over the floor. Sir Giles sat down on a chair and listened to it. It slurped out steadily and spread under the table. Presently it would begin to run down the passage into the hall. There were a thousand gallons of heating oil in those tanks and as Sir Giles knew they had recently been filled. He would wait until they were empty and then replace the feedpipe but not tightly. To the police and the insurance investigators it would look as though there had been a simple leak. Yes, a thousand gallons of heating oil would certainly do the trick. Handyman Hall would turn into a raging furnace in seconds. The fire brigade would take at least half an hour to come from Worford and by that time the place would be in ashes. So would Maud. Sir Giles knew her too well to suppose that she would be sensible enough to jump from her bedroom window even if she had time. She might not even wake before the flames reached the first floor and if she did her first thought would be to rush out on to the landing and try to save her precious family home. It would be Blott in the Lodge who would raise the alarm. It was a pity about Blott. Sir Giles would have liked him to be cremated too.

Outside in the garden Lady Maud stood looking at the house. Giles had come back to look for the negatives of the pictures they had taken of him. Well, he was hardly likely to find them. Blott had cut them into strips of six and had taken them back to the Lodge with him. Or perhaps he had come to get those photographs from his safe. He was going to be disappointed there too. Whichever way she looked at it he was going to be in for a nasty surprise. She went round to the front door and picked up his shoes. It might not be a bad idea to remove those while she was about it. She took them round to the garage and put them in an empty bucket and she was just coming out again when it struck her that there might be a more sinister purpose in Giles' visit. Six years of cohabitation with the brute had taught her that he was as ruthless as he was devious. It would pay her to be careful.

'I had better watch my step,' she thought, and went round to the kitchen door. She was just about to unlock it when she stepped in something slippery. She steadied herself and reached down. Oil. It was seeping out from under the kitchen door and down the steps into the yard. A moment later she understood the purpose of his visit. He was going to burn the Hall. By God, he wasn't. With a howl of rage Lady Maud hurled herself at the door, unlocked it and charged into the kitchen. For a moment she remained upright, the next she was flat on her back and sliding across the floor. So was Sir Giles though in a different direction. As Lady Maud's great bulk swept under him carrying his chair with her, Sir Giles catapulted through the air, landed on his face and slid irresistibly down the corridor and across the marble floor of the great hall. As he floundered about trying to get to his feet in a sea of oil he could hear Maud ricocheting about the kitchen. By the sound of things she had been joined by the entire complement of pots, pans, and kitchen utensils. Sir Giles slithered to the front door and managed to get to his feet on the mat. He grasped the handle and tried to turn it. The fucking thing wouldn't turn. He groped in his pocket for a handkerchief and wiped his hands and the doorknob and an instant later he was outside and reaching for his shoes. The bloody things weren't there.

There wasn't time to look for them. Behind him Maud had finally overcome the combined forces of grease and gravity and was coming down the passage promising to strangle him with her own bare hands. Sir Giles waited no longer. He galumphed off in his gumboots down the drive and across the lawn towards the pinetum. Behind him Lady Maud slithered into the downstairs lavatory and emerged with a shotgun. She went to the front door and opened it. Sir Giles was still visible across the lawn. Lady Maud raised the gun and fired. He was out of range but at least she had the satisfaction of knowing that he wouldn't come near the house again in a hurry. She put the gun back and began to clean up the mess.

CHAPTER TWENTY-THREE

In the Lodge Blott heard the shot and leapt out of bed. Lady Maud's telephone call had disturbed him. Why should she want to know if the gates were locked? And why had she whispered? Something was up. And with the sound of the shotgun Blott was certain. He dressed and went downstairs with his twelve-bore to the Land-Rover which he had parked just inside the archway. Before getting in he checked the lock on the gate. It was quite secure. Then he drove off up to the Hall and parked outside the front door and went inside.

'It's me, Blott,' he called into the darkness. 'Are you all right?'

From the kitchen there came the sound of someone sliding about and a muffled curse.

'Don't move,' Lady Maud shouted. 'There's oil everywhere.'

'Oil?' said Blott. Now that he came to think of it there was a stench of oil in the house.

'He's tried to burn the house down.'

Blott stared into the darkness and promised that if he got the chance he would kill him. 'The bastard,' he muttered. Lady Maud slithered down the passage with a squeegee.

'Now listen carefully, Blott,' she said. 'I want you to do something for me.'

'Anything,' said Blott gallantly.

'He came in through the pinetum. I've locked the gate there so he can't get out but his car must be up at Wilfrid's Castle. I want you to drive round there and remove the dis . . . the thing that goes round.'

'The rotor arm,' said Blott.

'Right,' said Lady Maud. 'And while you are about it you might as well put extra locks on both the gates. We must make quite sure that innocent people don't get into the park. Do you understand?'

Blott smiled in the darkness. He understood.

'I'll take the rotor arm off the Land-Rover too,' he said.

'A wise precaution,' Lady Maud agreed. 'And when you have finished come back here. I don't think he'll return tonight but it might be as well to take precautions.'

Blott turned to the door.

'There's just one other thing,' said Lady Maud. 'I don't think we'll feed the lions in the morning. They'll just have to fend for themselves for a day or two.'

'I didn't intend to,' said Blott and went outside.

Lady Maud sighed happily. It was so nice to have a real man about the house.

At Finch Grove Ivy Bullett-Finch's feelings were quite the reverse. What was left of the house seemed to be about the man and in any case what was left of Mr Bullett-Finch was real only in a material sense. He had died, as he had lived, concerned for the welfare of his lawn. Dundridge arrived with the Chief Constable in time to pay his last respects. As firemen carried her husband's remains out of the cellar, Mrs Bullett-Finch, relieved of the burden of guilt about the oven, vented her feelings on the Controller Motorways Midlands.

'You murderer,' she screamed, 'you killed him. You killed him with your awful ball.' She was led away by a policewoman. Dundridge looked balefully at the ball and crane.

'Nonsense,' he said, 'I had nothing to do with it.'

'We have been led to understand by your deputy, Mr Hoskins, that you gave orders for random sorties to be made by task forces of demolition experts,' said the Chief Constable. 'It would rather appear that they've carried out your instructions to the letter.'

'My instructions?' said Dundridge. 'I gave no instructions for this house to be demolished. Why should I?'

'We were rather hoping you would be able to tell us,' said the Chief Constable.

'But it's not even scheduled for demolition.'

'Quite. Nor to the best of my knowledge was the High Street. But since your equipment was used in both cases—'

'It's not my equipment,' shouted Dundridge, 'it belongs to the contractors. If anyone is fucking responsible—'

'I'd be glad if you didn't use offensive language,' said the Chief Constable. 'The situation is unpleasant enough as it is. Local feeling is running high. I think it would be best if you accompanied us to the station.'

'The station? Do you mean the police station?' said Dundridge.

'It's just for your own protection,' said the Chief Constable. 'We don't want any more accidents tonight, now do we?'

'This is monstrous,' said Dundridge.

'Quite so,' said the Chief Constable. 'And now if you'll just step this way.'

As the police car wound its way slowly through the rubble that littered the High Street, Dundridge could see that Hoskins had been telling the truth when he called Guildstead Carbonell a disaster area. The transformer still smouldered in the grey dawn, the Primitive Methodist Chapel lived up to at least part of its name, while the horribly mis-shapen relics of a dozen cars crouched beside the glass-strewn pavement. What the iron ball hadn't done with the aid of the telegraph pole to end Guildstead Carbonell's reputation for old-world charm, the conflagration at Mr Dugdale's garage had. Ignited by some unidentifiable public-spirited person who had brought out a paraffin lamp to warn passers-by to watch out for the debris, the blast from the petrol storage tanks had blown in what few windows remained unbroken after Blott's passing and had set fire to the thatched roofs of several delightful cottages. The fire had spread to a row of almshouses. The simultaneous arrival of fire engines from Worford and Ottertown had added to the chaos. Working with high-pressure hoses in total darkness they had swept a number of inadequately clothed old-age pensioners who had escaped from the almshouses down the street before turning their attention to the Public Library which they had filled with foam. To Dundridge, staring miserably out of the window of the police car, the knowledge that he was held responsible for the catastrophe was intolerable. He wished now that he had never set eyes on South Worfordshire.

'I must have been mad to have come up here,' he thought.

The same thought had already occurred to Sir Giles though in his case the madness he had in mind was in no way metaphorical. As dawn broke over the Park, Sir Giles wrestled with the lock on the gate to the footbridge and tried to imagine how it had got there. It had not been on the gate when he arrived. He wouldn't have been able to enter if it had. But if the existence of the lock was bad enough, that of the fence was worse and it certainly hadn't been there when he had last been at the Hall. It was an extremely high fence with large metal brackets at the top and four strands of heavy barbed-wire overhanging the Park so that it was evidently designed to stop people getting out rather than trespassers getting in.

It was at this point that Sir Giles gave up the struggle with the lock and decided to look for some other way out. He followed the fence along the edge of the pinetum and was about to clamber over the iron railings when the sense of unreality that had come over him with the sudden appearance of a large lock where no lock had previously been took a decided turn for the worse. Against the grey dawn sky he saw a head, a small head with a long nose and knobs on it. Below the head there was a neck, a long neck, a very long neck indeed. Sir Giles shut his eyes and hoped to hell that when he opened them he wouldn't see what he thought he had seen. He opened them but the giraffe was still there. 'Oh my God,' he murmured and was about to move away when his eye caught sight of something even more terrifying. In the long grass fifty yards behind the giraffe there was another face, a large face with a mane and whiskers.

Sir Giles gave up all thought of looking for a way out in that direction. He turned and stumbled back into the pinetum. Either he had gone mad or he was in the middle of some fucking zoo. Giraffes? Lions? And what the hell was it that he had almost stumbled across during the night? An elephant? He got back to the gate and looked at the lock hopefully. But instead of one lock there were now two and the second was even larger than the first. He was just trying to think what this meant when he heard a noise on the path across the river. Sir Giles looked up. Blott was standing there with a shotgun, smiling down at him. It was a horrible smile, a smile of quiet satisfaction. Sir Giles turned and ran into the pinetum. He knew death when he saw it.

By the time Blott got back to the Hall Lady Maud was down and making breakfast in the kitchen.

'What took you so long?' she asked.

'I moved the Bentley,' Blott told her. 'I brought it round and put it in the garage. I thought it would look more natural.'

Lady Maud nodded. 'You are probably right,' she said. 'People might have started asking questions if they found it left up by the church. Besides if he did get out he might have telephoned the AA for assistance.'

'He isn't going to get out,' said Blott, 'I saw him. He's in the pinetum.'

'Well it's his own fault. He came up here to burn the house down and whatever happens now he has only himself to blame.' She handed Blott a plate of cereal. 'I'm afraid I can't give you a cooked breakfast. The electricity has been cut off. I telephoned the electricity office in Worford but they say there has been a power failure.'

Blott ate his cereal in silence. There didn't seem much point in telling her about his part in the power failure and besides she seemed in a talkative mood herself.

'The trouble with Giles was,' she said using the past tense in a way that Blott found most agreeable, 'that he liked to think of himself as a self-made man. I have always thought it an extremely presumptuous phrase and in his case particularly inappropriate. I suppose he had some right to call himself a man, though from my experience of him I wouldn't have said virility was his strong point, but as for being self-made, he was nothing of the kind. He made his money, and of course that's what he meant by self, by speculating in property, by evicting people from their homes and by obtaining planning permission to put up office blocks. At least my family made its money selling beer, and very good beer at that. And it took them generations to do it. There's nothing so splendid about that but at least they were honest men.' She was still talking and doing the washing-up when Blott left to go out to the kitchen garden.

'Is there anything else you want done about him?' he asked as he left.

Lady Maud shook her head. 'I think we can just leave nature to take its course,' she told him. 'He was a great believer in the law of the jungle.'

In Worford Police Station Dundridge was having difficulty with the law of the land. Hoskins had been no great help.

'According to him,' said the Superintendent in charge of the case, 'you gave specific orders for random sorties to be made by bulldozers on various properties. Now you say you didn't.'

'I was speaking figuratively,' Dundridge explained. 'I certainly didn't give any instructions that could lead anyone but a complete idiot to suppose that I wanted the late Mr Bullett-Finch's house demolished.'

'Nevertheless it was demolished.'

'By some lunatic. You don't seriously imagine I went out there and smashed the house up myself?'

'If you'll just keep calm, sir,' said the Superintendent, 'all I am trying to do is to establish the chain of circumstances that led up to this murder.'

'Murder?' mumbled Dundridge.

'You're not claiming it was an accident, are you? A person or persons unknown deliberately take a large crane and use it to pulverize a house in which two innocent people are sleeping. You can call that all sorts of things but not an accident. No sir, we are treating this as a case of murder.'

Dundridge thought for a moment. 'If that's the case there must have been a motive. Have you given any thought to that?'

'I'm glad you mentioned motive, sir,' said the Superintendent. 'Now I understand that Mr Bullett-Finch was an active member of the Save the Gorge Committee. Would you say that your relations with him were marked by an unusual degree of animosity?'

'Relations?' shouted Dundridge. 'I didn't have any relations with him. I never met the man in my life.'

'But you did speak to him over the telephone on a number of occasions.'

'I may have done,' said Dundridge. 'I seem to remember his phoning once to complain about something or other.'

'Would that have been the occasion on which you told him that quote "If you don't stop pestering me I'll see to it that you'll lose a bloody-sight more than a quarter of an acre of your bleeding garden" unquote?'

'Who told you that?' snarled Dundridge.

'The identity of our informant is irrelevant, sir. The question is did you or did you not say that.'

'I may have done,' Dundridge admitted, promising himself that he would make Hoskins' life difficult for him in future.

'And wouldn't you agree that the late Mr Bullett-Finch has in fact lost more than a quarter of an acre of his bleeding garden?'

Dundridge had to admit that he had.

As the morning wore on the Controller Motorways Midlands had the definite impression that a trap was closing in around him.

In Sir Giles' case there was the absolute conviction. His attempts to scale the wire fence had failed miserably. Oily gum-boots were not ideal for the purpose and Sir Giles' physical activities had been of too passive a nature to prepare him at all adequately for scrambling up wire mesh or coping with barbed-wire overhangs. What he needed was a ladder, but his only attempt to leave the pinetum to look for one had been foiled by the sight of a rhinoceros browsing in the rockery and of a lion sunning itself outside the kitchen door. Sir Giles stuck to the pinetum and waited for an opportunity. He waited a long time.

By three o'clock in the afternoon he was exceedingly hungry. So were the lions. From the lower branches of a tree over-looking the park Sir Giles watched as four lionesses stalked a giraffe, one moving upwind while the other three lay in the grass downwind. The giraffe moved off and a moment later was thrashing around in its death throes. From his eyrie Sir Giles watched in horror as the lionesses finished it off and were presently joined by the lions. Stifling his disgust and fear Sir Giles climbed down from the branch. This was his opportunity. Ignoring the rhinoceros which had its back to him he raced across the lawn towards the house as fast as his gumboots would allow. He reached the terrace and hurried round past the conservatory where Lady Maud was watering a castor-oil plant. As he ran past she looked up and for a moment he had an impulse to stop and beg her to let him in but the look on her face was enough to tell him he would be wasting his time. It expressed an indifference to his fate, almost an ignorance of his existence, which was in its way even more frightening than Blott's terrible smile. As far as Maud was concerned he simply wasn't there. She had married him to save the Hall and preserve the family. And now she was prepared to murder him by proxy for the same purpose. Sir Giles had no doubt about that. He ran on into the yard and opened the garage door. Inside stood the Bentley. He could get away at last. He pushed the doors back and got into the car. The keys were still in the ignition. He turned them and the starter whirred. He tried again but the car wouldn't start.

In the kitchen garden Blott listened to the engine turning over. He was wasting his time. He could go on till Doomsday and the car wouldn't start. Blott had no sympathy for him. 'Nature must take its course,' Lady Maud had said and Blott agreed. Sir Giles meant nothing to him. He was like the pests in the garden, the slugs or the greenfly. No that wasn't true. He was worse. He was a traitor to the England that Blott revered, the old England, the upstanding England, the England that had carved an Empire by foolhardiness and accident, the England that had built this garden and planted the great oaks and elms not for its own immediate satisfaction but for the future. What had Sir Giles done for the future? Nothing. He had desecrated the past and betrayed the future. He deserved to die. Blott took his shotgun and went round to the garage.

Lady Maud in the conservatory was having second thoughts. The look on Sir Giles' face as he hesitated outside had awakened a slight feeling of pity in her. The man was afraid, desperately afraid, and Lady Maud had no time for cruelty. It was one thing to talk in the abstract about the law of the jungle, but it was another to participate in it.

'He's learnt his lesson by now,' she thought, 'I had better let him go.' And she was about to go out and look for him when the phone rang. It was General Burnett.

'It's about this business of poor old Bertie,' said the General. 'The committee would like to come over and have a chat with you.'

'Bertie?' said Lady Maud. 'Bertie Bullett-Finch?'

'You know he's dead, of course,' said the General.

'Dead?' said Lady Maud. 'I had no idea. When did this happen?'

'Last night. House was knocked down by the motorway swine. Bertie was inside at the time.'

Lady Maud sat down, stunned by the news. 'How absolutely dreadful. Do they know who did it?'

'They've taken that fellow Dundridge in for questioning,' said the General. Lady Maud could think of nothing to say. 'Knocked half Guildstead down too. The Colonel and I thought we ought to come over and have a talk to you about it. Puts a very different complexion on the whole business of the motorway, don't you know.'

'Of course,' said Lady Maud. 'Come over at once.' She put the phone down and tried to imagine what had happened. Dundridge taken in for questioning. Mr Bullett-Finch dead. Finch Grove demolished. Guildstead Carbonell ... It was such astonishing news that it drove all thoughts of Giles from her mind.

'I must phone poor dear Ivy,' she muttered and dialled Finch Grove. Not surprisingly, she got no reply.

In the garage Sir Giles was doing his best to persuade Blott to stop pointing the twelve-bore at his chest.

'Five thousand pounds,' he said. 'Five thousand pounds. All you've got to do is open the gates.'

'You get out of here,' said Blott.

'What do you think I want to do? Stay here?'

'Out of the garage,' said Blott.

'Ten thousand. Twenty thousand. Anything you ask ...'

'I'll count to ten,' said Blott. 'One.'

'Fifty thousand pounds.'

'Two,' said Blott.

'A hundred thousand. You can't ask better than that.'

'Three,' said Blott.

'I'll make it—'

'Four,' said Blott.

Sir Giles turned and ran. There was no mistaking the look on Blott's face. Sir Giles stumbled round the house and across the lawn to the pinetum. He scrambled over the iron railings and climbed back into his tree. The lions had finished the giraffe and were licking their paws and wiping their whiskers. Sir Giles wiped the sweat off his face with an oily handkerchief and tried to think what to do next.

Dundridge was saved that trouble by the discovery of an empty vodka bottle in the cab of the crane and by eye-witnesses who testified that one of the two men seen driving the crane up the High Street had been singing bawdy songs and was very clearly intoxicated.

'There seems to have been some mistake,' the Superintendent told him apologetically. 'You're free to go.'

'But you told me you were treating the case as one of murder,' shouted Dundridge indignantly. 'Now you turn round and say it was simply drunken driving.'

'Murder in my view implies premeditation,' explained the Superintendent. 'Now, two blokes go out and have one too many. They get a bit merry and pinch a crane and knock a few houses down, well you can't feel the same about it, can you? There's no premeditation there. Just a bit of fun, that's all. Now I'm not saying I approve. Don't get me wrong. I'm as hard on vandalism and drunkenness as the next man, but there are mitigating circumstances to be taken into account.'

Dundridge left the police station unconvinced, and as far as Hoskins' behaviour was concerned he could find no mitigating circumstances whatsoever.

'You deliberately led the police to believe that I had given orders for the Bullett-Finches' house to be demolished,' he shouted at him in the Mobile HQ. 'You gave them to understand that I set out to murder Mr Bullett-Finch.'

'I only told them that you had had a row with him on the phone. I'd have said the same thing about Lady Maud if they had asked me,' Hoskins protested.

'Lady Maud doesn't happen to have been murdered,' yelled Dundridge. 'Nor does General Burnett or the Colonel and I've had rows with them too. I suppose if any of them get run over by a bus or die of food poisoning you'll tell the police I'm responsible.'

Hoskins said he didn't think that was being fair.

'Fair,' yelled Dundridge, 'fair? Now you just listen to what I've had to put up with since I've been up here. I've been threatened. I've been given doctored drinks. I've been ... Well never mind about that. I've been shot at. I've been subject to abuse. I've had my car tyres slashed.

I've been accused of murder and you have the fucking gall to stand there and talk to me about fairness. My God, I've fought clean up to now but not any longer. From now on anything goes and the first thing to go is you. Get out of here and don't come back.'

'There's just one thing I think you ought to know,' said Hoskins edging towards the door. 'You've got a new problem on your hands. Lady Maud Lynchwood is opening a Wildlife Park at Handyman Hall on Sunday.'

Dundridge sat down slowly and stared at him.

'She is what?'

Hoskins edged back into the office. 'Opening a Wildlife Park. She's had the whole place wired in and she's got lions and rhinoceroses and . . .'

'But she can't do that. She's had a compulsory purchase order served on her,' said Dundridge stunned by this latest example of opposition.

'She's done it all the same,' said Hoskins. 'There are signs up along the Ottertown Road and there was an advertisement in last night's *Worford Advertiser*. I've got a copy here.' He went through to his office and returned with a full-page advertisement announcing Open Day at Handyman Hall Wildlife Park. 'What are you going to do about that?'

Dundridge reached for the phone. 'I'm going to get on to the legal department and tell them to apply for an injunction to stop her,' he said. 'In the meantime you can see that work resumes in the Gorge immediately.'

'Don't you think we should hold off for a day or two,' said Hoskins, 'and wait for this fuss over the Bullett-Finches' house and Guildstead Carbonell to die down a bit.'

'Certainly not,' said Dundridge. 'If the police choose to regard the whole thing as a trivial matter, I see no reason why we shouldn't. Work will proceed as before. If anything, faster.'

CHAPTER TWENTY-FOUR

At Handyman Hall what was left of the Save the Gorge Committee met in the sitting-room lamenting the passing of Mr Bullett-Finch and seeking to take advantage from his sacrifice.

'The whole thing is an outrage against humanity,' said Colonel Chapman. 'A more inoffensive fellow than poor old Bertie you couldn't imagine. Never a harsh word from him.'

Lady Maud could remember several harsh words from Mr Bullett-Finch when she had taken the liberty of walking across his lawn, but she kept her thoughts to herself. Whatever his faults in life, Mr Bullett-Finch dead had been canonized. General Burnett put her thoughts into words.

'Terrible way to go,' he said, 'having a dashed great iron ball smash you to smithereens like that. Rather like a gigantic cannonball.'

'He probably didn't feel a thing,' said Colonel Chapman. 'It was late at night and he was in bed ...'

'He wasn't you know. They found him in his dressing-gown. Must have heard it coming.'

'In the midst of life we are ...' Miss Percival began but Lady Maud interrupted her.

'There is no point in dwelling on the past,' she said. 'We must concentrate our mind on the future. I have invited Ivy to come and stay here.'

'I rather doubt if she will accept,' said Colonel Chapman looking nervously out of the window. 'Her nerves were never up to much and this latest shock hasn't done them any good and those lions ...'

'Nonsense,' said Lady Maud briskly. 'Perfectly harmless creatures provided you know how to handle them. The main thing is to show you're not afraid of them. The moment they smell fear they become dangerous.'

'I'm sure I'd be no good at all,' said Miss Percival. General Burnett nodded.

'I remember once in the Punjab ...' he began.

'I think we should keep to the matter in hand,' said Lady Maud. 'Much as I regret what has happened to poor Mr Bullett-Finch and indeed to Guildstead Carbonell, there is this to be said for it, it does put us all in a much stronger position vis-à-vis the Ministry of the Environment and this infernal motorway. I think you said, General, that the police were questioning that man Dundridge.'

General Burnett shook his head. 'The Chief Constable has been keeping me abreast of events,' he said. 'I'm afraid they've dropped that line of inquiry. It appears that there was some sort of shindig at the Royal George last night. Seems they're working on the theory that a couple of navvies had a bit too much beer and ...'

'Beer?' said Lady Maud with a strange look on her face. 'Did I hear you say "Beer"?'

'My dear lady,' said the General apologetically, 'I only mentioned beer because I believe that is what these fellows drink. I wasn't for one moment imputing ...'

'As a matter of fact I believe it was vodka,' said Colonel Chapman tactfully. 'In fact I'm sure it was. They found a bottle.'

But the damage had already been done. Lady Maud was looking quite distraught.

In the pinetum Sir Giles was desperately trying to make up his mind. From his tree he had watched General Burnett and Colonel Chapman and Miss Percival arrive. They had come in one car – Miss Percival had left her car outside the main gates and had joined the General in his – and their coming seemed to offer Sir Giles an opportunity to escape if only he could reach the house. Maud could hardly shoot him down in cold blood in front of her neighbours. There might be a nasty scene. She might accuse him of arson, of blackmail and bribery. She might expose him to ridicule but he was prepared to run these risks to get out of the Park alive. On the other hand he wasn't sure that he was prepared to run the gauntlet of the lions who had sauntered away from their last meal and were lying about on the lawn in front of the terrace. Then again he was now extremely hungry and the lions on the contrary weren't. They had just eaten their fill of giraffe.

At least Sir Giles hoped they had. It was a risk he had to take. If he stayed in the tree he would starve to death and sooner or later he would have to come down. Better sooner, he thought, than later. Sir Giles climbed down and got over the railings. Perhaps if he walked confidently ... He didn't feel confident. He hesitated and then moved cautiously forward. If only he could reach the terrace. And as he moved across the grass he was conscious that he was increasing the distance between himself and the safety of the tree while decreasing that between himself and the lions. He reached the point of no return.

In the sitting-room General Burnett was lamenting Sir Giles' absence. 'I've tried ringing his flat in London and his office but nobody seems to know where he's got to,' he said. 'If only we could get in touch with him, I'm convinced we could bring pressure to bear on the Minister to call a halt to the motorway. I'm the last one to complain, but it's at a time like this that a constituency needs its MP.'

'I'm afraid my husband tends to let his business interests get in the way of his Parliamentary duties,' Lady Maud agreed.

'Of course, of course,' said Colonel Chapman. 'He's bound to have a lot of irons in the fire. Wouldn't have got where he has if he hadn't.'

'I think ...' said Miss Percival nervously staring out of the window.

'All I'm saying is that it's about time he made his presence felt,' said the General.

'I really do think you ought to ...' Miss Percival began.

'It's at times like this he ought to raise his voice ... Good God! What the hell was that?'

There was a ghastly scream from the garden.

'I think it was Sir Giles raising his voice,' said Miss Percival, and fainted. The General and Colonel Chapman turned and looked out of the window in horror. Sir Giles was visible for a moment and then he disappeared beneath a lion. Lady Maud seized a poker and opened the french windows.

'How dare you?' she shouted charging across the terrace. 'Shoo, Shoo.'

But it was too late. The General and Colonel Chapman rushed out and dragged her back still waving the poker and shooing.

'Damned plucky little woman,' said the General as they drove home. Colonel Chapman said nothing. He was trying to rid his mind of the memory of those gumboots, and besides, he found the General's description of Lady Maud a little inappropriate even in these distressing circumstances. His left ear was still ringing from the blow she had given him for telling her she mustn't blame herself for what had happened.

'Mind you, I'm afraid it's put an end to the Wildlife Park,' continued the General. 'Pity really.'

'It's also put an end to Sir Giles,' said Colonel Chapman, who felt that General Burnett was taking the whole affair too calmly.

'There is that to be said for it,' said the General. 'Never could stomach the fellow.'

In the back seat Miss Percival fainted for the sixth time.

At Handyman Hall the Superintendent explained to Lady Maud as tactfully as possible that there would have to be a coroner's inquest.

'An inquest? But it's perfectly obvious what happened. General Burnett and Colonel Chapman were here.'

'Just a formality, I assure you,' said the Superintendent. 'And now I'll be getting along.'

He went out to his car with the gumboots and drove off. In the Park the lions were licking their paws and wiping their whiskers. Lady Maud stared out of the window at them. They would have to go of course. Sir Giles might not have been a nice man but Lady Maud's sense of social propriety wouldn't allow her to keep animals that couldn't be trusted not to eat people. And then there was Blott. Blott and the events of the previous evening in Guildstead Carbonell. It was all too obvious what he had wanted Very Special for and it was all her fault. And to think she had invited Ivy Bullett-Finch to come and stay. Well, at least she had a good excuse for cancelling the invitation now. She went through the kitchen and was about to go out when it occurred to her that having tasted human flesh once the lions might not succumb quite so readily to her fearlessness. She ought really to carry some sort of weapon. Lady Maud hesitated and then went on regardless. She owed it to her conscience to take some risks. She went down the path and into the kitchen garden.

'Blott,' she said, 'I want a word with you. Do you realize what you have done?'

Blott shrugged. 'He got what was coming to him,' he said.

'I'm not talking about him,' said Lady Maud, 'I'm talking about Mr Bullett-Finch.'

'What about him?'

'He's dead. He was killed last night when his house was demolished.'

Blott took off his hat and scratched his head. 'That's a pity,' he said thoughtfully.

'A pity? Is that all you've got to say?' said Lady Maud sternly.

'I don't know what else I can say. I didn't know he was in the house any more than you knew he was going to go and get eaten by those lions.' He picked a caterpillar off a cabbage and squashed it absent-mindedly.

'I must say if I had known what you were going to do I would never have given you the day off,' said Lady Maud and went back into the house.

Blott went on with his weeding. Women were odd things, he thought. You did what they wanted and all the thanks you got for it was a telling off. A telling off. That was an odd expression too, come to think of it. But then the world was full of mysteries.

In London Mrs Forthby woke with a vague sense that something was missing. She rolled over in bed, switched on the light and looked at the clock. It said eleven forty-eight and since it was dark it must be nearly midnight. On the other hand it didn't feel like midnight. She felt as though she had been asleep a lot longer than four hours, and where was Giles? She got out of bed and looked in the kitchen, the bathroom, but he wasn't in the flat. Oh well, he had probably gone out. She went back to the kitchen and made herself some tea. She was feeling very hungry too. That was strange because she had had a big dinner. She made some toast and boiled an egg. And all the time she had the nagging feeling that something was wrong. She had gone to bed at eight o'clock and here she was at midnight wide awake and famished. To while away the time she picked up a book but she didn't feel like reading. She turned on the radio and caught the news headlines. '... Lynchwood, Member of Parliament for South Worfordshire, who was killed at his home Handyman Hall near Worford by a lion. In Arizona a freak whirlwind destroyed ...' Mrs Forthby switched off the radio and poured herself another cup of tea before remembering what the announcer had just said. 'Oh dear,' she said, 'this afternoon? But ...' She went through to the sitting-room and looked at the date on the clock. It read Friday the 20th. But yesterday was Wednesday. Giles had said so. She had said it was Tuesday and he had said Wednesday. And now it was Friday morning and Giles had been killed by a lion. What was a lion doing at Handyman Hall? What was Sir Giles doing there, come to that? They had been going to Brighton together for the weekend. It was all too awfully perplexing and horrible. It couldn't be true. Mrs Forthby dialled the nice lady who told the time. 'At the third stroke it will be twelve ten and twenty seconds.'

'But what's the date? What day is it?' Mrs Forthby asked.

'At the third stroke it will be twelve ten and thirty seconds.'

'Oh dear, you really aren't being very helpful,' said Mrs Forthby, and began to cry. Giles hadn't been a very nice man but she had been fond of him and it was all her fault.

'If I hadn't been so forgetful and had remembered to wake up he would still be alive,' she murmured.

At his Mobile HQ Dundridge greeted the news next morning jubilantly.

'That'll teach the stupid bitch to build a bloody Wildlife Park,' he told Hoskins.

'I don't see how you can say that,' said Hoskins. 'All it's done is to create another vacancy in Parliament. There will have to be a bye-election and you know what happened last time.'

'All the more reason for pressing ahead as quickly as possible.'

'What? With Maud Lynchwood in mourning? The poor woman has just lost her husband under the most tragic circumstances and you –'

'Don't give me that bull,' said Dundridge. 'If you ask me she's probably delighted. Wouldn't surprise me to learn she'd arranged the whole thing just to stop us.'

'That's bloody libel, that is,' said Hoskins. 'She may be a bit of a tartar but ...'

'Listen,' said Dundridge, 'she didn't give a tuppenny damn about her husband, I know.'

'You know?'

'Yes I do know as a matter of fact. I'll tell you something. That old cow tried to seduce me one night and when I wouldn't play ball she took a potshot at me with a twelve-bore. So don't come that crap about a sorrowing widow. We're going ahead, and fast.'

'Well all I can say is that you're flying in the face of public opinion,' said Hoskins, stunned by Dundridge's story of his attempted seduction. 'There's Bullett-Finch dead and now Sir Giles. There's bound to be a public outcry. I should have thought now was the time to lie doggo.'

'Now is the time to establish ourselves at the Park itself,' said Dundridge. 'I'm going to move two bulldozers and a base camp up by that arch of hers. If she wants to squawk let her squawk.'

But Lady Maud didn't squawk. She had been more shocked by Sir Giles' death than she would have expected and she felt personally responsible for what had happened to Mr Bullett-Finch. She went about her duties automatically but with an abstracted air, occupied with the moral dilemma in which she found herself. On the one hand she was faced with the destruction of everything she loved, the Hall, the Gorge, the wild landscape, the garden, the world her ancestors had fought for and created. All this would go, to be replaced by a motorway which would be a useless, obsolescent eyesore in fifty years when fossil fuel ran out. It wasn't as if the motorway was needed. It had been concocted by Giles to make himself a paltry sum of money, a mean, cruel gesture to hurt her. Well Giles had got his comeuppance but the legacy of the motorway remained and the methods she had had to use had degraded her. She had fought fire with fire and other people had been burnt, Bertie Bullett-Finch and – quite literally – the poor man who had put the paraffin lamp in front of Mr Dugdale's garage.

It was in this mood of self-recrimination that she attended the coroner's inquest which returned a verdict of accidental death on Sir Giles Lynchwood and commended his widow on her bravery while pointing out the unforeseen dangers of keeping undomesticated animals on domestic premises. It was in the same mood that she superintended the removal of the lions, the last giraffe and the ostriches, before going off to a Memorial Service at Worford Abbey. All this time she avoided Blott, who stuck to the kitchen garden in low dudgeon. It was only when, on her return from the Abbey, she saw the bulldozers parked near the iron suspension bridge opposite the Lodge that she felt a pang of remorse for the way she had upbraided him. She found him sulking among the blackcurrants.

'Blott, I'm sorry,' she said. 'I feel I owe you an apology. We all make mistakes from time to time and I've come to say how grateful I am to you for all the sacrifices you've made on my behalf.'

Blott blushed under his tanned complexion. 'It was nothing,' he mumbled.

'That's just not true,' said Lady Maud graciously, 'I don't know how I would have managed without you.'

'You don't have to thank me,' said Blott.

'I just wanted you to know that I appreciate it,' said Lady Maud. 'By the way as I came in I noticed the bulldozers by the Lodge ...'

'You want them stopped, I suppose?'

'Well, now that you come to mention it ...' Lady Maud began.

'Leave it to me,' said Blott, 'I'll stop them.'

Lady Maud hesitated. This was the moment of decision. She chose her words carefully.

'I wouldn't like to think that you were going to do anything violent.'

'Violent? Me?' said Blott sounding almost convincingly aggrieved at the suggestion.

'Yes, you,' said Lady Maud. 'Now, I don't mind spending money if it's needed. You can have what you want but I won't have anyone else getting hurt. There's been quite enough of that already.'

'Your forefathers fought for ...'

'I think I'm a rather better authority on what my ancestors did than you are,' said Lady Maud. 'I don't need telling. That was quite different. For one thing they were agents of the Crown and acting within the law and for another the only people to get hurt were the Welsh and they were savages. Besides, I'm a Justice of the Peace and I can't condone anything illegal. Whatever you do must be lawful.'

'But ...' began Blott.

Lady Maud interrupted him. 'I don't want to hear any more. What you do is your own affair. I want no part of it.'

She strode away and left Blott to consider her words.

'No violence,' he muttered. It was going to make things a little difficult but he would think of something. Women, even the best of them, were illogical creatures. He walked out of the garden and down the drive to the Lodge. On the far side of the suspension bridge two bulldozers, symbols of Dundridge's task force, stood under the trees. It would have been so easy to disable them with the PIAT or even to put sugar in their fuel tanks but if Maud said he must stay within the law ... Stay within the law? That was another strange expression. As if the law was some sort of fortress. Blott looked up at the great arch towering above him.

He had just had an idea.

CHAPTER TWENTY-FIVE

In spite of his intention to act swiftly the Controller Motorways Midlands found it difficult to act at all. Work on the motorway came to a virtual standstill while the various authorities responsible for the preservation of Guildstead Carbonell and law and order on the one hand wrangled with those responsible for the construction of the motorway and the destruction of the village on the other. To make matters worse there was a walk-out by dumper drivers who claimed they were being victimized by being barred from the Royal George for the damage done to the bar-billiards table by the clog-dancing of the bulldozer men, and a work-to-rule by the demolition experts who asserted that the arrest of Mr Edwards constituted a threat to their basic rights as Trade Unionists. To end the dispute Dundridge paid for the bar-billiards table out of incidental expenses and interceded with the police to release Mr Edwards on bail pending a psychiatrist's report. In the middle of the confusion he was summoned to London to explain remarks he had made in a television interview filmed in front of the ruins of Finch Grove.

'Couldn't you have thought of something better than "That is the way the cookie crumbles"?' Mr Rees demanded. 'And what in God's name did you mean by "There's many a slip twixt cup and lip"?'

'All I meant was that accidents do happen,' Dundridge explained. 'I was being bombarded with –'

'Bombarded? What do you think we've been since then? How many letters have we had?'

Mr Joynson consulted his list. 'Three thousand four hundred and eighty-two to date, not including postcards.'

'And what about "We all have to make sacrifices"? What sort of impression do you think that makes on three million viewers?' shouted Mr Rees. 'A man living peacefully in a quiet corner of rural England minding his own business is battered to death in the middle of the night by some fucking idiot with an iron ball weighing two tons and you talk about making sacrifices!'

'As a matter of fact he wasn't minding his own business,' Dundridge protested, 'he was continually ringing up to –'

'And I suppose you think that justifies . . . I give up.'

'I think we have to look at it from the point of view of the potential housebuyer,' said Mr Joynson tactfully. 'It's difficult enough for the average wage-earner to get a mortgage these days. We don't want to give people the idea that they run the risk of having their houses demolished without the slightest warning.'

'But the house wasn't even scheduled for demolition,' Mr Rees pointed out.

'Quite,' said Mr Joynson. 'The point I'm trying to make is that Dundridge here must adopt a more tactful approach. He should use persuasion.'

But Dundridge had had enough. 'Persuasion?' he snarled. 'You don't seem to understand what I'm up against. You seem to think all I've got to do is serve a compulsory purchase order and people simply get out of their houses and everything is hunky-dory. Well let me tell you it isn't that simple. I'm supposed to be in charge of building a motorway through a house and park belonging to a woman whose idea of persuasion is to take potshots at me with a twelve-bore.'

'And evidently missing,' sighed Mr Rees.

'Why didn't you inform the police?' Mr Joynson asked more practically.

'The police? She *is* the police,' said Dundridge. 'They eat out of her hand.'

'Like those lions I suppose,' said Mr Rees.

'And what do you think she built that Wildlife Park for?' Dundridge asked.

'I suppose you're going to tell us next that she wanted to find a way of disposing of her husband,' Mr Rees said wearily.

'To stop the motorway. She intended to whip up public support, gain sympathy and generally cause as much confusion as possible.'

'I should have thought she could have safely left that to you,' said Mr Rees.

Dundridge looked at him balefully. It was obvious that he did not enjoy the confidence of his superiors.

'If that's the way you feel I can only resign my position as Controller Motorways Midlands and return to London,' he said. Mr Rees looked at Mr Joynson. This was the ultimatum they had feared. Mr Joynson shook his head.

'My dear Dundridge, there is absolutely no need for you to do that,' said Mr Rees with forced affability. 'All we ask is that you try to avoid any more unfavourable publicity.'

'In that case I look to you to give me your full support,' said Dundridge. 'I can't be expected to overcome the sort of opposition I'm faced with unless the Ministry is prepared to throw its weight behind my efforts.'

'Anything we can do,' said Mr Rees, 'to help, we will certainly do.'

Dundridge left the office mollified and with the feeling that his authority had been enhanced after all.

'Give the swine enough rope and I daresay he'll hang himself,' said Mr Rees when he had gone. 'And frankly I wish Lady Maud the best of British luck.'

'Must be a terrible thing to lose a husband like that,' said Mr Joynson. 'No wonder the poor woman is upset.'

But it was less the loss of her husband that was upsetting Lady Maud than the bills she was receiving from various shops in Worford.

'One hundred and fifty tins of frankfurters? One thousand candles? Sixty tons of cement? Two hundred yards of barbed-wire? Forty six-foot reinforcing rods?' she muttered as she went through the bills. 'What on earth can Blott be thinking of?' But she paid the bills without question and kept herself to herself. Whatever Blott was up to she wanted to know as little about it as possible. 'Ignorance is bliss,' she thought, demonstrating a lack of understanding of the law which did her little credit as a magistrate.

And Blott was busy. He had spent the lull provided by Dundridge's troubles in preparing his defence. Lady Maud had specified that there must be no violence on his part and as far as he was concerned there would be no necessity for it. The Lodge was practically impregnable to anything short of a full-scale assault by tanks and artillery. He had filled all the rooms on either side of the archway with bits of old iron and cement and had sealed the stairway with concrete. He had covered the roof with sharpened iron rods embedded in concrete and entangled with barbed-wire. To secure an independent water supply he had run a plastic pipe down to the river before the concrete was poured into the rooms below and to ensure that he could withstand a prolonged siege he had laid in enough foodstuffs to last him for two years. If his electricity was cut off he had a thousand candles and several dozen containers of bottled gas and finally, to prevent any attempt to drive him out with tear gas, he had unearthed an old army gas-mask from his cache in the forest. Just in case the mask was no longer proof against the latest gases he had turned his library into an air-tight room to which he could retreat. All in all he had converted the Lodge from a very large ornamental arch into a fortress. The only entrance was through a hatch in the roof under the barbed-wire and spikes, and to enable him to leave when he wanted Blott had constructed a rope ladder which he could let down. Finally and just in case things did get violent he had collected a rifle, a Bren gun, a two-inch mortar, several cases of ammunition and hand-grenades with which to deter boarders. 'Of course, I'll only fire over their heads,' he told himself. But there would be no need. Blott knew the British too well to suppose they would do anything to endanger life. And yet without endangering life, and Blott's life in particular, there was no way of building the motorway on through the Park and Handyman Hall. The Lodge, now Festung Blott, stood directly in the path of the motorway. On either side the cliffs rose steeply. Before anything could be done the Lodge would have to be demolished and since Blott was encased within it, demolishing the arch would mean demolishing him. They couldn't even use dynamite to blast the cliffs on either side without seriously risking his life and threatening the collapse of the arch. Finally to ensure that no one could even drive through the gateway he erected a series of concrete blocks in the middle of the archway. It was this last that forced Lady Maud to ask him what the hell he thought he was doing.

'How do you expect me to do my shopping if I can't drive in and out?' she demanded.

Blott pointed to the Bentley and the Land-Rover parked beside the two bulldozers on the other side of the suspension bridge.

'Good Lord,' said Lady Maud, 'do you mean to say you moved them without my permission?'

'You said you didn't want to know what I was doing so I didn't tell you,' Blott told her. Lady Maud had to admit to the logic of the answer.

'It's going to be very inconvenient,' she said. She looked at the Lodge. Apart from the spikes and the barbed-wire on the roof it looked as it had always looked. 'I just hope you know what you're doing,' she said and made her way through the concrete blocks and across the bridge to her car. She drove into Worford to see Mr Ganglion about Sir Giles' will. From where she had been able to ascertain she had been left a widow of very considerable means, and Lady Maud intended to put those means to good use.

'A fortune, my dear lady,' said Mr Ganglion, 'an absolute fortune even by today's standards. Properly invested, you should be able to live quite royally.' He looked at her appreciatively. Now that he came to think of it she had every right to live royally. There was that business of Edward the Seventh. 'And as a widower myself . . .' He looked at her even more appreciatively. She might not be to every man's taste but then he wasn't up to much himself and he was getting on in years. And ten million pounds in property was an inducement. So too were those photographs of Mr Dundridge.

'I intend to re-marry as soon as possible,' said Lady Maud. 'Sir Giles may have left me well provided for but he did not fulfil his proper functions as a husband.'

'Quite so. Quite so,' said Mr Ganglion, his mind busily considering Dundridge's accusation of blackmail. It might be worth his while to try a little expeditious blackmail himself. He turned to his safe and twiddled the knob.

'Besides, it's not good for you to have to live alone in that great house,' he continued. 'You need company. Someone to look after you.'

'I have already seen to that,' said Lady Maud. 'I have invited Mrs Forthby to come and make it her home.'

'Mrs Forthby? Mrs Forthby? Do I know her?'

'No,' said Lady Maud, 'I don't suppose you do. She was Giles' ... er ... governess in London.'

'Really?' said Mr Ganglion glancing at her over the top of his glasses. 'Now that you come to mention it I did hear something ...'

'Well never mind that,' said Lady Maud, 'there's no point in flogging a dead horse. The thing is that from what I have seen of the will he had made no provision for the poor woman. I intend to make good the deficiency.'

'Very generous of you. Magnanimous,' said Mr Ganglion and took an envelope from the safe. 'And while we're on the subject of human frailties, I wonder if you would mind glancing at these photographs and telling me if you have seen them before.' He opened the envelope and spread them out before her. Lady Maud stared at them intently. It was obvious she had seen them before.

'Where did you get those?' she shouted.

'Ah,' said Mr Ganglion, 'now I'm afraid that would be telling.'

'Of course it would,' snarled Lady Maud, 'what do you think I asked you for?'

'Well,' said Mr Ganglion, putting the photographs back into the envelope, 'a certain person, let us say a prospective client, consulted me ...'

'Dundridge. I knew it. Dundridge,' said Lady Maud.

'Your guess is as good as mine, my dear Lady Maud,' said Mr Ganglion. 'Well this client did suggest that you had been using these ... er ... rather revealing pictures to ... er ... blackmail him.'

'My God,' shouted Lady Maud, 'the filthy little beast!'

'Of course I did my best to assure him that such a thing was out of the question. However he remained unconvinced ...' But Lady Maud had heard enough. She rose to her feet and seized the envelope. 'Now if you feel that we should institute proceedings for slander ...'

'Accused me of blackmail? By God I'll make him regret the day he was born,' Lady Maud snarled and stumped out of the room with the photographs.

Dundridge was in his Mobile HQ drawing up plans for his next move against Handyman Hall when Lady Maud drove up. Now that he was assured that the Ministry would throw their full weight behind his efforts he viewed the future with renewed confidence. He had spoken to the Chief Constable and had demanded full police co-operation should Lady Maud refuse to comply with the order to move out of Handyman Hall and the Chief Constable had reluctantly agreed. He was just giving Hoskins his instructions to move into the Park when Lady Maud stormed through the door.

'You filthy little swine,' she shouted and tossed the photographs on to his desk. 'Take a good look at yourself.' Dundridge did. So did Hoskins.

'Well?' continued Lady Maud. 'And what have you got to say now?'

Dundridge stared up at her and tried to think of words to match his feelings. It was impossible.

'If you think you can get away with this you're mistaken,' bawled Lady Maud.

Dundridge clutched the telephone. The filthy bitch had come back to haunt him with those horrible photographs and this time there was no mistaking who was playing the main role in these obscene contortions and this time too Hoskins was present. The look of horror on Hoskins' face decided him. There was no way of avoiding a scandal. Dundridge dialled the police.

'Don't think you can wriggle out of this by calling a lawyer,' Lady Maud yelled.

'I'm not,' said Dundridge finding his voice at last, 'I am calling the police.'

'The police?' said Lady Maud.

'The police?' whispered Hoskins.

'I intend to have you charged with attempted blackmail,' said Dundridge.

Lady Maud launched herself across the desk at him. 'Why, you filthy little bastard,' she screamed. Dundridge lurched off his chair and ran for the door. Lady Maud turned and raced after him. Behind them Hoskins replaced the telephone and picked up the photographs. He went into the lavatory and shut the door. When he came out Dundridge was cowering behind a bulldozer, Lady Maud was being restrained by six bulldozer drivers and the photographs had been reduced to ashes and flushed down the pan. Hoskins sat down and wiped his face with a handkerchief. It had been a near thing.

'Don't think you're going to get away with this,' Lady Maud shouted as she was escorted back to her car. 'I'll sue you for slander. I'll take every penny you've got.' She drove away and Dundridge staggered back to the caravan.

'You heard her,' he said to Hoskins slumping into his chair. 'You heard her attempt to blackmail me.' He looked around for the photographs.

'I burnt them,' said Hoskins. 'I didn't think you'd want them lying around.'

Dundridge looked at him gratefully. He certainly didn't want them lying around. On the other hand the evidence of an attempted crime had been destroyed. There was no point in calling in the police now.

'Well at least if she does sue me you were a witness,' he said finally.

'Definitely,' said Hoskins. 'But she'll never dare.'

'I wouldn't put anything past that bitch,' said Dundridge recovering his confidence now that both Lady Maud and the photographs were out of the way. 'But I'll tell you one thing. We're going to move into Handyman Hall now. I'll teach her to threaten me.'

'Without the photographs I'm afraid you would have no case,' said Mr Ganglion when Lady Maud returned to his office.

'But he told you that I was blackmailing him. You told me so yourself,' said Lady Maud.

Mr Ganglion shook his head sadly. 'What he said to me, my dear Lady Maud, was by way of being a confidential communication. He was after all consulting me as a solicitor and since I represent you in any case my evidence would never be accepted by a court. Now if we could get Hoskins to testify that he had heard him accuse you of blackmail ...' He phoned the Regional Planning Board and was put through to Hoskins at the Mobile HQ.

'Certainly not. I never heard anything of the sort,' said Hoskins. 'Photographs? I don't know what you're talking about.' The last thing he wanted to do was to appear in court to testify about those bloody photographs.

'Peculiar,' said Mr Ganglion. 'Most peculiar, but there it is. Hoskins won't testify.'

'That just goes to show you can't trust anyone these days,' said Lady Maud.

She drove home in a filthy temper which wasn't improved by having to park the Bentley outside the Lodge and walk up the drive.

CHAPTER TWENTY-SIX

If her temper was bad when she returned to the Hall that afternoon it was ten times worse the next morning. She woke to the sound of lorries driving down the Gorge road and men shouting outside the Lodge. Lady Maud picked up the phone and called Blott.

'What the devil is going on down there?' she asked.

'It's started,' said Blott.

'Started? What's started?'

'They've come to begin work.'

Lady Maud dressed and hurried down the drive to find Dundridge, Hoskins and the Chief Constable and a group of policemen standing looking at the concrete blocks under the archway.

'What's the meaning of this?' she demanded.

'We have come to begin work here,' said Dundridge keeping close to the Chief Constable. 'You are in receipt of a compulsory purchase order served on you on the 25th of June and ...'

'This is private property,' said Lady Maud. 'Kindly leave.'

'My dear Lady Maud,' said the Chief Constable, 'I'm afraid these gentlemen are within their rights ...'

'They are within my property,' said Lady Maud. 'And I want them off it.'

The Chief Constable shook his head sorrowfully. 'I'm sorry to have to say this ...'

'Then don't,' said Lady Maud.

'But they are fully entitled to act in accordance with their instructions and begin work on the motorway through the Park. I am here to see that they are not hindered in any way. Now if you would be so good as to order your gardener to vacate these ... er ... premises.'

'Order him yourself.'

'We have attempted to serve an eviction order on him but he refuses to come down. He appears to have barricaded the door. Now we don't want to have to use force but unless he is prepared to come out I'm afraid we will have to make a forcible entry.'

'Well, I'm not stopping you,' said Lady Maud. 'If that's what you have to do, go ahead and do it.'

She stood to one side while the policemen went round the side of the Lodge and hammered at the door. Lady Maud sat on a concrete block and watched them.

The police battered at the door for ten minutes and finally broke it down only to find themselves confronted by a wall of concrete. Dundridge sent for a sledgehammer but it was quite clear that something more than a sledgehammer would be required to make an entry.

'The bastard has cemented himself in,' said Dundridge.

'I can see that for myself,' said the Chief Constable. 'What are you going to do now?'

Dundridge considered the problem and consulted Hoskins. Together they walked back to the bridge and looked up at the arch. In the circumstances it had assumed a new and quite daunting stature.

'There's no way round it,' said Hoskins, indicating the cliffs. 'We would have to move thousands of tons of rock.'

'Can't we blast a way round?'

Hoskins looked up at the cliffs and shook his head. 'Could do but we'd probably kill the stupid bugger in that arch in the process.'

'So what?' said Dundridge. 'If he won't come down it's his own fault if he gets hurt.' He didn't say it very convincingly. It was quite clear that killing Blott would come under the heading of very unfavourable publicity at the Ministry of the Environment.

'In any case,' Hoskins pointed out, 'the authorized route runs through the Gorge, not round it.'

'What about the blasting we did back at the entrance?'

'We were authorized to widen the Gorge there because of the river and besides that section doesn't come within the area designated as of natural beauty.'

'Fuck,' said Dundridge. 'I knew that old bitch would come up with something like this.'

They went back to the arch where the Chief Constable was arguing with Lady Maud.

'Are you seriously suggesting that I ordered my gardener to cement himself into the Lodge?'

'Yes,' said the Chief Constable.

'In that case, Percival Henry,' said Lady Maud, 'you're a bigger fool than I took you for.'

The Chief Constable winced. 'Listen, Maud,' he said, 'you know as well as I do he wouldn't have done this without your permission.'

'Nonsense,' said Lady Maud, 'I told him he could do what he wanted with the Lodge. He's been living there for thirty years. It's his home. If he chooses to fill the place with cement that's his business. I refuse to accept any responsibility for his actions.'

'In that case I shall have no option but to arrest you,' said the Chief Constable.

'On what grounds?'

'For obstruction.'

'Codswallop,' said Lady Maud. She got down from the block and walked round to the back of the arch and looked up at the window.

'Blott,' she called. Blott's head appeared at the circular window.

'Yes.'

'Blott, come down this instant and let these men get on with their work.'

'Won't,' said Blott.

'Blott,' shouted Lady Maud, 'I am ordering you to come down.'

'No,' said Blott and shut the window.

Lady Maud turned to the Chief Constable. 'There you are. I have told him to come down and he won't. Now then, are you still going to have me arrested for obstruction?'

The Chief Constable shook his head. He knew when he was beaten. Lady Maud strode back up the drive to the Hall. He turned to Dundridge. 'Well, what do you suggest now?'

'There must be something we can do,' said Dundridge.

'If you've got any bright ideas, just let me know,' said the Chief Constable.

'What happens if we just go ahead and demolish the arch with him in it?'

'The question is,' said the Chief Constable, 'what would happen to him if you did that?'

'That's his problem,' said Dundridge. 'We've got a legal right to remove that arch and if he's in it when we do we're not responsible for what happens to him.'

The Chief Constable shook his head. 'You try telling that to the judge when they try you for manslaughter. I should have thought you'd have learnt your lesson from what happened at Guildstead Carbonell.' He got into his car and drove away.

Dundridge walked back across the bridge and spoke to the foreman of the demolition gang.

'Is there any way of taking that arch down without injuring the man inside?' he asked.

The foreman looked at him doubtfully. 'Not if he doesn't want us to.'

As if to give added weight to his argument Blott appeared on the roof. He was carrying a shotgun.

'You see what I mean,' said the foreman.

Blott looked expectantly over their heads, raised his gun and fired. A wood pigeon plummeted out of the sky. Dundridge could see exactly what he meant.

'There's nothing in our contract to say we've got to take unnecessary risks,' said the foreman, 'and a bloke who cements himself into an arch and shoots pigeons on the wing constitutes more than an unnecessary risk. He's a bloody loony, and a crack shot into the bargain.'

Dundridge thought wistfully of Mr Edwards. He turned to Hoskins.

'I think,' said Hoskins, 'that we ought to contact the Ministry in London. 'This thing's too big for us.'

At the Hall Lady Maud heard the shot and picked up a pair of binoculars. Through them she could see Blott on the roof with the shotgun. She telephoned the Lodge.

'They're not shooting at you, are they?' she asked hopefully.

'No,' said Blott, 'I was just shooting a pigeon. They're still talking.'

'Remember what I said about violence,' Lady Maud told him. 'We must keep public sympathy on our side. I am going to get in touch with the BBC and ITV and all the national newspapers. I think we can make a big song and dance about this business.'

Blott put down the phone. Song and dance. The English language was *most* expressive. Song and dance.

At his Mobile HQ Dundridge was on the phone to London.

'Are you seriously trying to tell me that Lady Lynchwood's gardener has cemented himself into an ornamental arch?' said Mr Rees incredulously. 'It doesn't sound possible.'

'The arch in question happens to be eighty feet high,' Dundridge explained. 'It has rooms inside. He's filled all the bottom ones with concrete. There's barbed-wire on the roof and short of blowing the place up there's no way of getting him out.'

'I should try the local fire brigade,' Mr Rees suggested. 'They use them to get cats out of trees.'

'I have tried the fire brigade,' said Dundridge.

'Well, what do they say?'

'They say their business is putting out fires, not storming fortresses.'

Mr Rees considered the problem. 'I imagine he'll have to come out sometime,' he said finally.

'Why?'

'Well, to eat for one thing.'

'Eat?' shouted Dundridge. 'Eat? He doesn't have to come out to eat. I've got a list here of the things he ordered from the local supermarket. Four hundred tins of baked beans, seven hundred cans of corned beef, one hundred and fifty tins of frankfurters. Need I go on?'

'No,' said Mr Rees hastily, 'the fellow must have a constitution like an ox. You would have thought he would have chosen something a little more appetizing.'

'Is that all you've got to say?' said Dundridge.

'Well I must admit that it does sound as if he intends to make a long stay of it,' Mr Rees agreed.

'And what are we going to do? Cancel the motorway for a couple of years while he munches his way through that little lot?'

Mr Rees tried to think. 'Can't you talk him down?' he asked. 'That's what they usually do with people threatening to commit suicide.'

'But he isn't threatening suicide,' Dundridge pointed out.

'It amounts to the same thing,' said Mr Rees. 'A diet of corned beef, baked beans and frankfurters in the quantities you've mentioned would certainly kill me. Still, I see what you mean. A man who can even contemplate living off that muck obviously means business. Have you any ideas on the subject?'

'As a matter of fact I have,' said Dundridge.

'Not another ball and crane job I hope,' said Mr Rees anxiously. 'We can't have another little episode of that sort so shortly after the last one.'

'I was thinking of using the army,' said Dundridge.

'The army? My dear fellow, this is a free country. We can't possibly ask the army to blast a perfectly innocent Englishman out of his own home with tanks and artillery.'

'To be precise,' said Dundridge, 'he doesn't happen to be an Englishman and I wasn't thinking of blasting him out with tanks and artillery.'

'I should think not. The public would never stand for it,' Mr Rees said. 'But if he's not an Englishman what is he?'

'An Italian.'

'An Italian? Are you sure? It doesn't sound like them to go in for this sort of thing,' said Mr Rees.

'He's naturalized,' said Dundridge.

'That explains it,' said Mr Rees. 'In that case I can't see any objection to using the army. They're used to dealing with foreigners. What precisely did you have in mind?'

Dundridge explained his plan.

'Well I'll see what I can do,' said Mr Rees. 'I'll call you back when I've had a word with the Minister.'

In Whitehall the wires buzzed. Mr Rees spoke to the Minister of the Environment and the Minister spoke to Defence. By five o'clock Army Command had agreed to supply a team of commandos trained in rock climbing on the explicit understanding that they were to be used simply in a police support role and would not use firearms. As the Minister of the Environment explained, the essence of the operation was to occupy the Lodge and hold Blott until the police could evict him in a lawful fashion. 'The great thing is that the media haven't got on to the story yet. If we can get him out of there before the newsmen start nosing around we can hush the whole thing up. The essence of the thing must be speed.'

It was a point that Dundridge made to the commandos when they arrived for briefing that night at his Mobile HQ. 'I have here a number of photographs taken this afternoon of the target,' he said handing them round. 'As you can see it is amply provided with handholds and there are two means of access. The two circular windows on either side and the hatch in the roof. I should have thought the best method of attack would be a diversionary move to the rear and a frontal assault –'

'I think you can leave the tactical details of the exercise to us,' said the Major in charge who didn't like being told his business by a civvy.

'I was only trying to help,' said Dundridge.

'Now then,' said the Major. 'We'll rendezvous at the Gibbet at twenty-four hundred hours and proceed on foot ...' Dundridge left them to it and went into the other office.

'Well, for once we're getting things done,' he told Hoskins. 'That old bitch isn't going to know what's hit her.'

Hoskins nodded doubtfully. He had been in the army himself and he didn't have Dundridge's faith in the efficiency of the military machine.

Blott spent the evening reading Sir Arthur Bryant but his mind was not on the past. He was considering the immediate future. They would either act quickly or try to wear him down psychologically by sending a succession of well-meaning people to talk to him. Blott had seen the sort of visitor he could expect on the television. Social workers, psychiatrists, priests and policemen, all of them imbued with an invincible faith in the possibility of compromise. They would argue and cajole (Blott looked the word up in his dictionary to see if it meant what he thought and found he was right) and do their best to make him see the error of his ways and they would fail, fail hopelessly because their assumptions were all wrong. They would assume he was an Italian whereas he wasn't. They would think he was acting on instructions of that he was simply being loyal, whereas he was in love. They would think a compromise was possible ... With a motorway? Blott smiled to himself at the stupidity of the idea. The motorway would either go through the Park and Handyman Hall or it wouldn't. Nothing they could tell him would alter that fact. But above all the people who came to talk to him would be city-dwellers for whom talk was currency and words were coins. An Englishman's word is his bond, Blott thought, but then he had never had much time for stocks and shares. 'Word merchants' old Lord Handyman had called such people, with contempt in his voice, and Blott agreed with him. Well they could talk themselves blue in the face but they wouldn't shift him. Everything that he cared for and loved and was lay there in the Park and the Garden and the Hall. Handyman Hall. And Blott was the handyman. He would die rather than give up the right to be needed. He undressed and climbed into bed and lay listening to the river tumbling by and the wind in the trees. Through his window he could see the light on in Lady Maud's bedroom. Blott watched it until it went out and then he fell asleep.

He was woken at one o'clock by a noise outside. It was a very slight noise but it awoke in him some instinct, an early-warning system that told him that there were people outside. He got out of bed and went to the window and peered into the darkness below. There was someone at the foot of the left-hand column. Blott went across the room to the other window. There was someone in the Park too. They must have climbed the fence to get in. Blott listened and presently he heard someone moving below. They were climbing up the side of the Lodge. Climbing? In the dark? Interesting.

He crossed to a cupboard and took out the Leica and the flash gun and went back to the window and leant out. The next moment the entire side of the Lodge was a brilliant white. There was a cry and a thud. Blott went to the other window and took another photograph. This time whoever it was who was climbing to the side of the arch shut his eyes and clung on. Blott put the camera down. Something stronger was needed. What would make climbing difficult? Something greasy. He went into his kitchen and came out with a gallon can of cooking oil and climbed the ladder in the corner of the room to the hjatch in the roof. Then he crawled to the edge and began pouring the oil down the wall. There was a curse from below, the sound of slithering and another thud followed by a cry. Blott emptied the rest of the can down the back wall and went down the ladder into his room and shone a torch out of the window. There was no one on the side of the arch now. At the foot a number of men in army uniforms stared up at him angrily. They had blackened faces and one of them was lying on the ground.

'Is there anything I can do for you?' Blott asked.

'Wait till we get hold of you, you bastard,' shouted the Major. 'You've broken his leg.'

'Not me,' said Blott, 'I never touched him. He broke it himself. I didn't ask him to climb up my wall in the middle of the night.'

He was interrupted by a sound from the other side of the Lodge. The sods were coming up there too. He went into the kitchen and fetched two cans of cooking oil and repeated the process. By the time he was finished the sides of the Lodge were streaked with oil and two more climbers had fallen.

Down below there was a muttered conference.

'We'll use the grappling irons,' said the Major.

Blott peered out of the window and shone his torch on them. There was an explosion and a three-pronged hook shot past him on to the roof and stuck in the barbed-wire. It was followed by another. Blott raced into the kitchen and grabbed a knife. A moment later he was on the roof and had cut through one rope. He crawled under the wire and cut another. There was another thud and a yell. Blott peered over.

'Anyone else coming up?' he asked. But the army was already in retreat. As they carried their wounded back across the suspension bridge and up the road Blott watched them wistfully. He rather regretted their going. A full-scale battle would have been marvellous publicity. A full-scale battle? Blott went to the cupboard where he kept his armoury. He would have to act quickly. Then he climbed up on the roof and let down the rope ladder. Ten minutes later he was standing on the suspension bridge with the Bren gun.

As the commandos trudged back up the road towards their transport at the Gibbet they were startled to hear the sound of automatic fire behind them. It lasted for several seconds and was repeated again and again. They stood still and listened. It stopped. A few moments later there was a much larger thump and it was followed by a second. Blott had tried out the PIAT and it still worked.

At the Hall Lady Maud sat up in bed and struggled to find the light switch. She was used to the occasional shot in the night but this was something entirely different. A positive bombardment. She reached for the phone and rang the Lodge. There was no reply.

'Oh my God,' she moaned, 'they've killed him.' She got out of bed and dressed hurriedly. The firing had stopped now. She phoned the Lodge again and still there was no reply. She put the phone down and called the Chief Constable.

'They've murdered him,' she shouted, 'they've attacked the Lodge and killed him!'

'Killed who?' asked the Chief Constable.

'Blott,' yelled Lady Maud.

'No?' said the Chief Constable.

'I tell you they have. They've been using machine-guns and something much bigger.'

'Oh my goodness gracious me,' said the Chief Constable. 'Are you sure? I mean couldn't there be some mistake?'

'Percival Henry,' screamed Lady Maud, 'you know me well enough to know that when I say something I mean it. Remember what happened to Bertie Bullett-Finch.'

The Chief Constable remembered all too well. Midnight assassinations were becoming a commonplace occurrence in South Worfordshire and besides Lady Maud's tone had the ring of sincere hysteria about it. And Lady Maud, whatever else she might be was not a woman who got hysterical for nothing.

'I'll get every available patrol car there as soon as possible,' he promised.

'And an ambulance too,' screamed Lady Maud.

Within minutes every police car in South Worfordshire was converging on the Gorge. At the Gibbet twelve men of the 41st Marine Commando, two of them with broken legs, were detained for questioning as they were about to leave in their transport. They were driven to Worford Police Station loudly protesting that they had been acting under the orders of the Area Commander and that the police had no legal authority to hold them.

'We'll see about that in the morning,' said the Inspector as they were herded into their cells.

At the Lodge Blott climbed up his rope ladder and hauled it up behind him. He was delighted with his experiment. All the weapons had worked splendidly and, while it was impossible in the darkness to tell what damage they had done to the Lodge, the sound of splintering stonework had suggested that there was plenty of evidence to show that the army had carried out its assault with undue force and quite unwarranted violence. It was only when he was back in his room that he could see how effective the Projectiles Infantry Anti-Tank had been. They had blown two substantial holes in the frieze and the room was littered with bits of stone. Both windows had been blown out by the blast and there were holes in the ceiling. He was just wondering what to do next when he heard footsteps running down the drive. Blott switched off his torch and went to the window. It was Lady Maud.

'Don't come any nearer,' he shouted, to lend verisimilitude to his recent ordeal and to tell her that he was unhurt. 'Lie down. They may start firing again.'

Lady Maud stopped in her tracks. 'Oh thank Heavens, you're all right, Blott,' she shouted. 'I thought you'd been killed.'

'Me? Killed?' said Blott. 'It would take more than that to kill me.'

'Who was it? Did you get a good look at them?'

'It was the army,' Blott told her. 'I've got photographs to prove it.'

CHAPTER TWENTY-SEVEN

By next morning Blott was famous. The news of the attack came too late to be carried by the early editions but the later ones all bore his name in their headlines. The BBC broadcast news of the atrocity and its legal implications were discussed on the *Today* programme. At one o'clock there were further developments when it was announced that twelve Marine Commandos were helping the police in their inquiries. During the afternoon questions were asked in the House and the Home Secretary promised a full Inquiry. And all day reporters and cameramen swarmed into the Gorge to interview Blott and Lady Maud and to photograph the damage. It was clearly visible and extensive. Bullet holes pockmarked the entire arch, suggesting that the army's fire had been quite extraordinarily wild. The heads of several figures in the frieze were missing and the PIATs had torn gaping holes in the wall. Even hardened correspondents used to the tactics adopted against the urban guerrillas in Belfast were astonished by the extent of the damage.

'I've never seen anything like this,' the BBC correspondent told his audience from the top of a ladder before interviewing Blott at the window. 'This might be Vietnam or the Lebanon but this is a quiet corner of rural England. I can only say that I am horrified that this could happen.

And now Mr Blott, could you tell us first what you know about this attack?'

Blott looked out of the window into the camera.

'It must have been about one o'clock in the morning. I was asleep and I heard a noise outside. I got up and went to the window and looked out. There appeared to be men climbing up the wall. Well I didn't want that so I poured oil down the wall.'

'You poured oil down the wall to stop them?'

'Yes,' said Blott, 'olive oil. They slipped down and then the firing began.'

'The firing?'

'It sounded like machine-gun fire,' said Blott, 'so I ran into the kitchen and lay on the floor. Then a minute or two later there was an explosion and things flew around the room and a few seconds afterwards there came another explosion. After that there was nothing.'

'I see,' said the interviewer. 'Now at any time during the attack did you fire back? I understand you have a shotgun.'

Blott shook his head. 'It all happened too suddenly,' he said. 'I was all shook up.'

'Quite understandably. It must have been a terrifying experience for you. Just one more question. Was the oil you poured down the wall hot?'

'Hot?' said Blott. 'How could it be hot? I poured it out of the can. I hadn't got time to heat it up.'

'Well thank you very much,' said the interviewer and climbed down the ladder. 'I think we'll cut that last remark out,' he told the sound man. 'It made him sound as if he would have liked to have poured hot oil on them.'

'I can't say I blame him after what he's been through,' said the sound man. 'The buggers deserve boiling oil.'

It was an opinion shared by the Chief Constable.

'What do you mean, a police support role?' he shouted at the Colonel from the Commando Base who came up to explain that he had been ordered by the Ministry of Defence to send a team of rock-climbers to assist the police. 'There weren't any of my men within miles of the place. You send your killers in armed with rockets and machine-guns and blow hell out of ...'

'My men were without any weapons,' said the Colonel.

The Chief Constable looked at him incredulously. 'Your men were without weapons? You can stand there and tell me to my face that your men were unarmed when I've seen what they did to that building. You'll be telling me next that they had nothing to do with the incident.'

'That's what they say,' said the Colonel. 'They all swear blue they had left and were on their way back to their transport when the firing occurred.'

'I'm not bloody surprised,' said the Chief Constable. 'If I had just bombarded somebody's private house in the middle of the night I'd say I hadn't been near the place. That doesn't mean anyone with any sense is going to believe them.'

'They weren't carrying weapons when you arrested them.'

'Probably ditched the damned things,' said the Chief Constable. 'And in any case for all I know there were others who got away before my men arrived.'

'I can assure you –' the Colonel began.

'Damn your assurances!' shouted the Chief Constable. 'I don't want assurances. I've got the evidence of the attack itself and I have twelve men trained in the use of the weapons needed for that attack who admit that they attempted to force an entry into the Lodge last night. What more do I need? They'll appear before a magistrate in the morning.'

The Colonel had to admit that the circumstantial evidence ...

'Circumstantial evidence, my foot,' snarled the Chief Constable, 'they're as guilty as hell and you know it.'

'I still think you ought to look into the business of the civil servant who gave them their instructions,' said the Colonel despondently as he left. 'I believe his name is Dundridge.'

'I have already attended to that,' the Chief Constable told him. 'He is in London at the moment but I have sent two officers down to bring him back for questioning.'

But Dundridge had already spent five hours being questioned by Mr Rees and Mr Joynson and finally by the Minister himself.

'All I did was tell them to climb into the arch and hold Blott till the police could come and evict him legally,' he explained over and over again. 'I didn't know they were going to use guns and things.'

Neither Mr Rees nor the Minister was impressed.

'Let us just look at your record,' said the Minister as calmly as he could. 'You were appointed Controller Motorways Midlands with specific instructions to insure that the construction of the M101 went through with the minimum of fuss and bother, that local opinion felt that local interests were being looked after and that the environment was being protected. Now can you honestly say that the terms of reference of your appointment have been fulfilled in any single particular?'

'Well . . .' said Dundridge.

'No you can't,' snarled the Minister. 'Since you went to Worford there have been a series of appalling disasters. A Rotarian has been beaten to a pulp in his own house by a demented demolition expert who claims he was incited . . .'

'I didn't know Mr Bullett-Finch was a Rotarian,' said Dundridge desperately trying to divert the floodwaters of the Minister's mounting fury.

'You didn't know . . .' The Minister counted to ten and took a sip of water. 'Next, an entire village has been wrecked . . .'

'Not an entire village,' said Dundridge. 'It was only the High Street.'

The Minister stared at him maniacally. 'Mr Dundridge,' he said finally, 'you may be able to make these fine distinctions between Rotarians and human beings and entire villages which consist only of High Streets and the High Streets themselves but I am not prepared to. An entire village was wrecked, a pedestrian was incinerated and twenty persons injured, some of them seriously. And this village, mark you, was over a mile away from the route of the proposed motorway. A Member of Parliament has been devoured by lions . . .'

'That had absolutely nothing to do with me,' Dundridge protested. 'I didn't suggest he fill his ruddy garden with lions.'

'I wonder,' said the Minister, 'I wonder. Still, I shall reserve judgement on that question until the full facts have been ascertained. And finally at your instigation the army has been called in to evict an Italian gardener . . . No, don't say it . . . an Italian gardener from his home by bombarding it with machine-guns and anti-tank weapons.'

'But I didn't tell them –'

'Shut up,' roared the Minister. 'You're fired, you're sacked . . .'

'You're under arrest,' said the detective who was waiting outside Mr Rees' office when Dundridge finally staggered out. Dundridge went down in the lift between two police officers.

Mr Rees sat down at his desk with a sigh.

'I told you that stupid bastard would hang himself,' he said with quiet satisfaction.

'What about the motorway?' asked Mr Hoskins.

'What about it?'

'Do you think we can continue with it?'

'God alone knows,' said Mr Rees, 'but frankly I doubt it. You seem to forget there's another bye-election due in South Worfordshire.'

It was not a point that had escaped Lady Maud's attention. While the reporters and cameramen still swarmed about the Lodge, photographing it from all angles and interviewing Blott from the tops of ladders hired for the purpose, she had been applying her mind to the question of a successor to Sir Giles. A meeting of the Save the Gorge Committee was held at General Burnett's house to discuss the next move.

'Stout fellow, Blott,' said the General, 'for an Eyetie. Remarkable, standing up to a bombardment like that. They used to run like rabbits in the desert.'

'I think we all owe him a debt of gratitude for his sense of duty and self-sacrifice,' Colonel Chapman agreed. 'Frankly I think this latest episode has put the kybosh on the motorway. They'll never be able to carry on with it now. I hear there's a proposal for a sit-in of conservationists from all over the country outside the Lodge to see that there's no repetition of this disgraceful action.'

'I must say I was most impressed by Mr Blott's command of the English language on television the other night,' said Miss Percival. 'He handled the interview quite wonderfully. I particularly liked what he had to say about English traditions.'

'That bit about an Englishman's home being his castle. Couldn't agree with him more,' the General said.

'I was thinking rather about what he said about England being the home of freedom and the need for Englishmen to stand up for their traditional values.'

Lady Maud looked at them all contemptuously. 'I must say I think it is a poor show when we have to rely on Italians to look after our interests for us,' she said.

The General shifted in his seat. 'I wouldn't go so far as to say that,' he murmured.

'I would,' said Lady Maud. 'Without him we would have all lost our homes.'

'As it is Miss Percival's lost hers already,' said Colonel Chapman.

'You can hardly blame Blott for that.'

Miss Percival took out a handkerchief and wiped her eyes. 'It was such a pretty cottage,' she sighed.

'The point I am trying to make,' Lady Maud continued, 'is that I think the best way we can demonstrate our gratitude and support for

Blott is by proposing him as the candidate for South Worfordshire in the forthcoming bye-election.'

The Committee stared at her in astonishment.

'An Italian standing for South Worfordshire?' said the General. 'I hardly think ...'

'So I've noticed,' said Lady Maud brusquely. 'And Blott is not an Italian. He is a nationalized Englishman.'

'Surely you mean naturalized,' said Colonel Chapman. 'Nationalized means state-controlled. I would have thought he was the exact opposite.'

'I stand corrected,' said Lady Maud magnanimously. 'Then we are agreed that Blott should represent the party at the bye-election?'

She looked round the table. Miss Percival was the first to agree. 'I second the proposal,' she murmured.

'Motion,' Lady Maud corrected her, 'the motion. The proposal comes later. All those in favour.'

The General and Colonel Chapman raised their hands in surrender, and since the Save the Gorge Committee was the party in South Worfordshire Blott's candidacy was ensured.

Lady Maud announced their decision to the press outside the Lodge. As the newsmen dispersed to their cars she climbed the ladder to the window in the Lodge.

'Blott,' she called through the broken panes, 'I have something to tell you.'

Blott opened the window and leant out. 'Yes,' he said.

'I want you to prepare yourself for a shock,' she told him. Blott looked at her uncertainly. He had been prepared for a shock for some time. The British army didn't use 303 ammunition nowadays and PIATs had been scrapped years ago. It was a point he had overlooked at the time.

'I have decided that you are to succeed Sir Giles,' said Lady Maud gazing into his face.

Blott gaped at her. 'Succeed Sir Giles? Gott in Himmel,' he muttered.

'I very much doubt it,' said Lady Maud.

'You mean ...'

'Yes,' said Lady Maud, 'from now on you will be the master of Handyman Hall. You can come out now.'

'But ...' Blott began.

'If you'll hand me the machine-gun and whatever else it was you used I'll take them down with me and we'll bury them in the pinetum.'

As they walked back up the drive with the PIAT and the Bren gun, Blott's mind was in a state of confusion. 'How did you know?' he asked.

'How did I know? I telephoned you of course as soon as I heard the firing,' said Lady Maud with a smile. 'I'm not as green as I'm cabbage-looking.'

'Meine Liebling,' said Blott and took what he could of her in his arms.

At Worford magistrates court Dundridge was charged with being party to a conspiracy to commit a breach of the peace, attempted murder, malicious damage to property, and obstruction of the police in the course of their duty.

It was the last charge that particularly infuriated him.

'Obstruction?' he shouted at the bench. 'Obstruction? Who's talking about obstruction?'

'Remanded in custody for a week,' said Colonel Chapman. Dundridge was still shouting abuse as he was dragged out to the Black Maria. In the cells he was interviewed by Mr Ganglion, who had been appointed by the court to conduct his defence.

'I should plead guilty to all charges,' he advised him.

'Guilty? I haven't done anything wrong. It's all a pack of lies!' Dundridge shouted.

'I understand how you feel,' Mr Ganglion said, 'but I understand the police are considering additional charges.'

'Additional charges? But they've charged me with everything under the sun already.'

'There's just that little business of blackmail to be attended to. Now I know you wouldn't want those photographs to be produced in court. You could get life for that, you know.'

Dundridge stared at him despairingly. 'For blackmail?' he asked. 'But I was the one being blackmailed.'

'For what you were doing in those photographs.'

Dundridge considered the prospect and shook his head. Life for something that had been done to him. He had been blackmailed, obstructed, shot at and here he was being charged with these offences. If there was any conspiracy it was directed against him.

'I don't know what to say,' he mumbled.

'Just stick to "Guilty",' Mr Ganglion advised. 'It will save a lot of time and the court will appreciate it.'

'Time?' said Dundridge. 'How long do you think I'll get?'

'Difficult to say really. Seven or eight years I should imagine, but you'll probably be out in five.'

He gathered up his papers and left the cell. As he walked back to his chambers he smiled to himself. It was always nice to combine business with pleasure. He found Lady Maud and Blott waiting for him to discuss the marriage settlement.

'My fiancé has decided to change his name,' Lady Maud announced. 'From now on he wants to be known as Handyman. I want you to make the necessary arrangements.'

'I see,' said Mr Ganglion. 'Well there shouldn't be any difficulties. And what Christian name would he like?'

'I think we'll just stick to Blott. I'm used to it and all the men in the family have been Bs.'

'True,' said Mr Ganglion, with the private thought that some of the women had been too. 'And when is the happy day?'

'We are going to wait until after the election. I wouldn't want it to be thought that I was trying to influence the outcome.'

Mr Ganglion went out to lunch with Mr Turnbull.

'Amazing woman, Maud Lynchwood,' he said as they walked across to the Handyman Arms. 'I wouldn't put anything past her. Marrying her damned gardener and putting him up for Parliament.'

They went into the bar.

'What'll you have?' said Mr Turnbull.

'I feel like a large whisky,' said Mr Ganglion. 'I know it's prohibitively expensive but I need it.'

'Have you heard, sir?' said the barman. 'There's fivepence off a tot of whisky and tuppence off a pint of beer. Lady Maud's instructions. Seems she can afford to be generous now.'

'Good Lord,' said Mr Turnbull, 'you don't think it has anything to do with this election, do you?'

But Mr Ganglion wasn't listening. He was thinking how little things had changed since he was a boy. What was it his father had said? Something about Mr Gladstone being swept out of office on a tide of ale. And that was in '74.

CHAPTER TWENTY-EIGHT

It was a white wedding. Lady Maud with her customary frankness had prevailed over the Vicar.

'I can damned well prove it if you insist,' she had told him when he had raised one or two minor objections but the Vicar had surrendered meekly. Wilfrid's Castle Church was packed. Half the county was there as Lady Maud strode through the pinetum with Mrs Forthby as her bridesmaid. Blott, now Blott Handyman, MP, was waiting at the church in top-hat and tails. As the organist broke into 'Rule Britannia', which Blott had chosen, Lady Maud Lynchwood went down the aisle beside General Burnett, emerging half an hour later Lady Maud Handyman. They posed for photographs and then led the way down the path and across the footbridge to the Hall. The place was resplendent. Flags flew from the turrets; there was a striped marquee on the lawn and the conservatory was a blaze of colour. Everything that Sir Giles' fortune afforded had been provided. Champagne, caviar, smoked salmon, jellied eels for those that liked them, cucumber sandwiches, trifle. Mrs Forthby had seen to them all. Only the cake was missing. 'I knew I had forgotten something,' she wept but even that was found eventually in the pantry. It was a perfect replica of the Lodge.

'It seems a pity to spoil it,' said Blott as he and Maud stood poised with Busby Handyman's old sword.

'You should have thought of that before,' Maud whispered in his ear. They cut the cake and the photographs were taken. Even Blott's speech, authentically English in its inarticulacy, went down well. He thanked everyone for coming and Mrs Forthby for her catering and made everyone laugh and Lady Maud blush by saying that it wasn't every man who had either the opportunity or the good fortune to be able to marry his mistress.

'Extraordinary fellow,' General Burnett told Mrs Forthby, who rather appealed to him, 'got a multitude of talents. They say there's talk of him becoming a Whip.'

Mrs Forthby shook her head. 'I do hope not,' she said. 'It's so degrading.'

Mr Ganglion and Mr Turnbull took a bottle of champagne into the garden.

'They say that the occasion produces the man,' said Mr Turnbull philosophically. 'I must admit he's turned out better than I ever expected. Talk about silk purses out of sows' ears.'

'My dear fellow, you've got it quite wrong,' said Mr Ganglion. 'It takes a sow's ear to know a silk purse when she's got one.'

'What on earth do you mean by that?'

Mr Ganglion sat down on a wrought-iron bench. 'I was just considering Sir Giles. Remarkable how conveniently he timed his death. Have you ever thought about that? I have. What do you suppose he was doing in gumboots in August? It hadn't rained for weeks. Driest summer we've had for years and he dies with his gumboots on.'

'You're surely not suggesting ...'

Mr Ganglion chuckled. 'I'm not suggesting anything. Merely cogitating. These old families. They haven't survived by relying on chance. They know their onions.'

'You're just being cynical,' said Mr Turnbull.

'Nonsense, I'm being realistic. They survive, my God, how they survive, and thank Heavens they do. Where would we be without them?' His head nodded. Mr Ganglion fell asleep.

In bed that night the Handymans lay in one another's arms, blissfully happy. Blott was himself at last, the possessor of a new past and a perfect present. There was no railway station waiting-room in Dresden, no orphanage, no youth, no uncertainties or doubts. Above all no motorway. He was an Englishman whose family had lived in the Gorge for five hundred years and if Blott had anything to do with it they would be living there still five hundred years hence. He had said as much in his maiden speech in the House on membership of the Common Market.

'What do we need Europe for?' he had asked. 'Ah, but you say "Europe needs us". And so she does. As an example, as a pole-star, as a haven. I speak from experience ...'

It was a remarkable speech and too reminiscent of Churchill and the younger Pitt and of Burke to give the front bench much comfort.

'We've got to shut him up,' said the Prime Minister and Blott had been offered the Whip.

'You're not going to take it, are you?' Lady Maud had asked anxiously.

'Certainly not,' said Blott. 'There is a tide in the affairs of men ...'

'Oh darling,' said Maud, 'how wonderful you are.'

'Which taken at its flood leads on to families.'

Lady Maud sighed with happiness. It was so good to be married to a man who had his priorities right.

In Ottertown Prison Dundridge began his sentence.

'Behave yourself properly and you'll be transferred to an open prison,' the Governor told him. 'With remission for good behaviour you should be out in nine months.'

'I don't want to go to an open prison,' said Dundridge. 'I like it here.'

And it was true. There was a logic about prison life that appealed to him. Everything was in its place and there were no unforeseen occurrences to upset him. Each day was exactly the same as the day before and each cell identical to its neighbour. Best of all, Dundridge had a number. It was what he had always wanted. He was 58295 and perfectly satisfied with it. Working in the prison library he felt safe. Nature played no part in prison life. Trees, woods, and all the gross aberrations of the landscape lay beyond the prison walls. Dundridge had no time for them. He was too busy cataloguing the prison library. He had discovered a far more numerate system than the Dewey Decimal.

It was called the Dundridge Digit.